MY LAST DOM

DEANNDRA HALL

My Last Dom

Celtic Muse Publishing, LLC
P.O. Box 3372
Paducah, KY 42002-3722

Copyright 2015 Deanndra Hall

Cover design 2015 M.D. Halliman

Formatting by Drue Hoffman at Buoni Amici Press, LLC

FOREWORD

As BDSM and kink have been drawn into the limelight over the last few years, the lifestyle has become more of a curiosity. And if there's some general confusion, allow me to clarify.

A Dominant is not a king; rather, he is a leader and instructor, one who is steady, dependable, and conscientious. A submissive is not a subject, a serf, or a slave; rather, their submission is offered freely and without coercion. Discipline and punishment are not abuse; rather, they are the means by which lessons are learned and reinforced. A proper Dominant's first commitment is always to the welfare of their submissive; with that in mind, there are times when a submissive asks for pain in such a mindset that it becomes a Dominant's responsibility to decline in the submissive's best interest. Both SSC (safe, sane, and consensual) and R.A.C.K. (risk-aware consensual kink) exist to serve as guidelines under negotiation between parties, with trust, communication, honesty, and genuine care and compassion being critical.

That said, if a particular story or book takes on a

sinister bend, know that it's a story—fiction—and nothing more. True submission is a gift given to a trusted Dominant/Dominatrix by a submissive, not something that is required or demanded. The submissive has the power to comply or decline. Anything else is abuse. There has been a proliferation in recent years of so-called "Dominants" who declare themselves such solely for their own pleasure, with no regard for the submissive. These Dominants/Dominatrices give the lifestyle a horrible reputation and the community a black eye, just one more thing kinksters don't need.

Keeping all of this in mind, please enjoy this story of one couple's journey through the minefield of the lifestyle. And as I've said so many times, there is no such thing as a BDSM expert. Every partnership decides what the lifestyle is to them, and in what capacity and to what degree they'll serve. Make the lifestyle your own, make it glorious for you and yours, and accept nothing less.

Brightest blessings.

To Kimberly S.
Thanks for being the kind of friend everyone needs.

CHAPTER ONE

It's a gray day. There are lots of those in my world these days, but this one is particularly gray. It's a weepy, can't-get-out-of-bed kind of day. The wind is blowing like gangbusters, and it's all I can do to keep my bag on my shoulder as old leaves and fast food wrappers skitter around my feet in the barely-out-of-winter bluster. Even though the walk from the car to the building is short, it's all I can do to stay upright in the gusts.

Measure twice, cut once. I keep hearing that in my head, the mantra of my father as he worked around my childhood home. I can still hear the steel tape measure retracting, feel the grain of the wood, and smell the sawdust.

I'm the same way with my work. My customers are paying for quality, and I aim to deliver. I'm careful with the leather, making sure it's stored so that it's supple and soft but doesn't get moldy, which is a real danger. There's no warp or weft in leather, so I can place my patterns wherever I want and don't have to worry about stretching or binding. My scissors are always razor sharp, and they cut through the pliver like butter. In my hands it's velvet, and I can manipulate it to make the most glorious of shapes, but none more glorious than the female form.

Cut, stitch. Cut, stitch. Two more hours and I can clean up this rat hole of a workshop and go. But I'm not sure why I want to go anywhere. There's nothing for me anywhere else. This is as close to having a place in the world as I ever get, and I like this space too. It's in an old high-rise office building, and I can see far out over the city. The walls are old paneling, and they're real wood, not that fake stuff they make nowadays. It's small and cramped, but I still love it.

Every time I move, I have to yank up on my corset. Either the damn thing is getting bigger or I'm getting smaller, and I know which it is. Food doesn't interest me anymore. Once it's in my mouth and I start to chew, it gets more soured and bitter with every passing moment until I can't even swallow it. I quit eating weeks ago. I just don't care anymore.

When the buzzer sounds at the door, I already know who it is. Everything I do is by appointment only, so surprises are rare. Sometimes the maintenance guy comes in to do something, but once he looks around, he high-tails it out of here. I think I scare him. Good. Opening the door reveals exactly who I expected. They both smile, but as quickly as I can, I drop my eyes to the floor respectfully. I know my place. Of course, Michael puts a finger under my chin and tips my head back, then bobs his head back and forth, trying to catch my gaze.

"Kimberly?" His voice is strong but soft. "Kimberly, look at me." I don't want to, but my eyes finally go to his face and I know he can see everything there. "Honey, you aren't eating, are you?"

I just shake my head. "No, sir."

He takes my chin in his hand again. "Quit, Kimmer. I'm not your master. I'm your friend. So is Robyn. And we're concerned about you, honey."

"No need." Managing to escape his grasp, I busy myself shuffling pattern pieces around and generally trying to look too busy to talk. Then I remember and look back to him, my hands pressed against my ribcage. "Could you help me? This thing is so loose."

He turns to the woman with him. "Robyn, please help Kimberly with her corset. Further proof that I'm right," Michael snorts.

"Yes, Sir." Robyn moves behind me and, after untying the corset, pulls hard to make it tighter. She's strong and I gasp. "Any more and you'll just need a new corset."

"I can make one," I giggle.

"I'm sure you can," Robyn replies with a sly little smile.

"Now that the two of you have that little chore taken care of, let's get down to it. I want Robyn to have a new underbust corset. Red. With some fancy stitching. I drew a little picture of what I want." Michael pulls a folded piece of paper from his shirt pocket and places it on the workbench even as he motions for me to join him. "See? I want these little things added to it. Can you do that?"

"Sure. No problem."

I'm still making little notes when I hear his voice from across the room. "There's nothing in this refrigerator." I look over to see Michael staring into the little apartment-sized fridge I keep in the shop. A lot of people would consider that snooping; Michael considers it a wellness check.

"There's water."

"Water's not food. What are you having for lunch?" I just shrug and Michael sighs again. "You're not taking care of yourself. You need to find another Dominant, a decent one. Just because Phil was a prick doesn't mean that—"

"Don't care." I can feel the hot tears collecting in my lower lids.

Michael turns to lean his ass against the workbench, folds his arms across his chest, and glares at me. "Okay. Let's just not talk about this anymore. I've tried to talk to you and I've gotten nowhere. You resist my every attempt to help you. You won't listen to reason. You keep coming to the club and letting yourself be used like a piece of meat. I feel like I'm beating my head against the wall. So let's drop it, okay? But quit starving yourself."

"Yes, sir," I nod but deep down, I know that won't change. I don't care what happens to me anymore.

He harrumphs at the way I've addressed him but says nothing. "Okay then. You need anything from Robyn? For the corset, I mean? Measurements or anything?"

I shake my head. "No. Looks like she hasn't changed in size since the last time I measured her." I start to say something else, but Michael interrupts me.

"Why don't you come to our house on Sunday for dinner? I'm sure Robyn can whip something up, right, honey?"

"Yes, Sir. We'd love to have you, sweetie." With a smile that could light up a mall, Robyn waits to see what I'm going to say.

I take a long look at the two people in front of me. Michael and Robyn have been my only friends. When Phil walked out, they held my hand, brought me food, helped me pack up his things, and have just generally been here for me whenever and however I've needed them. And they seem such an unlikely pair too, her all curvy and delicious with those big icy blue eyes and long blond hair, and him, short and heavy with all that dark, curly hair and the scruff on his jawline. Robyn always looks like a supermodel, and Michael always looks like a reject from the cast of *The Big Lebowski*. But they get along unbelievably well, and when Michael collared Robyn and asked her to marry him, everyone at the club had cheered, slapped him on the back, and hugged her.

I know full well why: Michael is one of those guys who's a caretaker. That's just how he operates, simple and clean. If there's a woman anywhere around, he's watching out for her, keeping an eye on her, making sure she's safe and cared for. Phil had been like that once upon a time ...

Tears sting my eyes as I think about him yet again, and a prickly mess grows in my stomach. I want to hate him, but I still miss him every day. I'd pledged my life to him, as his submissive and as his wife. I'd done whatever he asked, I let him to do anything to me that he wanted, and I never used a safeword in all the years we were together.

I remember that night like it's happening this very instant. My forty-third birthday party. Phil had planned a huge party for me at my favorite restaurant. I thought it was weird that, among the people he invited, he'd included a woman from his office. After all, it was my birthday party, and I barely knew her. But when I caught them in the back hallway up against the wall, arms and legs in a tangle, their tongues down each other's throats, I knew why the woman was there. Two weeks later, I found a slip of paper on the floor and picked it up—a receipt from a florist downtown for a dozen red roses delivered to Phil's office building. It wasn't hard to put two and two together.

And that was just the tip of the iceberg. What followed was a veritable Macy's Thanksgiving Day Parade of younger women, most barely thirty-five. At the end, where Santa Claus always makes his appearance, Phil told me he wasn't interested in me anymore, that he was leaving, and rode away in his brand-new Corvette, red like a sleigh. But that wasn't the worst part.

He told me he'd never loved me.

I haven't gotten over that, and I don't think I ever will. But it was his answer when I asked why he'd stayed with me through the years that laid me low and cut through me like a razor blade.

"Because I didn't think I could do any better."

The idea that I'd sacrificed my body to him, his cane, his whip, his flogger, his hands and mouth and cock, for all those years, and he'd simply settled for me, ripped a hole in my heart that the space shuttle could've flown through. I remember throwing up for hours, drinking until I was almost blind, and wondering how I could kill myself in a way that would make it look as though he'd done it. Bitterness has grown in my soul like cancer, and I can't stop it. There's no cure. There's no drug. There's no hope.

So I spend my evenings at the club as one Dom after another, sometimes more than one, uses me. Yeah, I know what they think of me, but I don't care. It's the only time I feel alive. It's terrifying and exhilarating at the same time, and I've gone back over and over until I've worked my way through the entire membership and then started over. Michael has begged me to stop or, at the very least, let him be the one to administer whatever I think I need, all in the name of safety.

Safety isn't what I want. It's pain, just pain. Pain to make me worthy, to make me wanted, to take the other pain away. And it works ... until the cane or the whip or the flogger stops. And then it comes right back.

A home cooked meal—I guess I could use one of those. "What time would you like for me to come?" I ask, but I never look directly at Michael.

"Oh, I don't know, anytime you want, I guess. Robyn?"

"I can have it ready by one o'clock. Would that be okay?"

I think for a second before I answer. "Sure. That would be fine. Thank you so much for having me, sir."

I hear Michael sigh yet again. "Kimmer, look up at me." Even though I don't want to, I turn my eyes up to his face, and I'm surprised at the misery I see there. Is that what I've done? I never meant to hurt anyone but myself. "I'm glad you're coming. We'll enjoy having you." That's all he says before he tells Robyn, "Let's go, babe. Ice cream on the way home?"

"Ooooo, thank you, Sir!" Robyn's practically dancing. "Bye, Kimmer! See you Sunday if not sooner."

"Sure." I know Robyn means the club. And I'll definitely be there.

❦

The music is a little too loud for my taste, but it covers up the sounds of the submissives crying out during play. Ronnie, the DJ with the chain running from his earlobe to his nose, chose heavy bass beats to work the crowd into the mood, and it's getting the job done. Even outside the play areas, there's already a lot of bumping and grinding going on.

After I've changed into my fetwear, I stroll out into the main room. All the usual suspects are hanging out at the bar, and most of them eye me as I head that way. Angus and Ross are standing there, and I hope one of them has plans for me when they see me. If not, there are plenty of other guys who'll be interested, but those two are long-time members and I know them to be clean and recently-tested, which I prefer when possible. I've intentionally worn my school girl outfit, knowing that if I want to play, it will garner plenty of attention. Sure enough, it doesn't take two minutes for Angus to march up and smile. "Were you planning to scene tonight?" he asks as he leans against the bar. Most of the club members don't like him. They think he's crazy. Yeah—crazy enough to give me what I need.

"Maybe, sir. What did you have in mind?" My eyes never leave the floor as I speak.

"I think you've been a naughty girl. Have you been a naughty girl?"

"Yes, sir. Very naughty."

Angus laughs. "And what did you do that was so naughty?"

I think for a second, then improvise by blurting out, "I did the whole football team."

Ross hears what I say and he starts laughing too. "Well, well, well, that's quite an accomplishment, young lady," Angus chortles. "I think we're going to have to find an appropriate punishment for that." He leads me by the arm to a nearby table and sits down. "Let's negotiate."

I set my lips in a firm line. "No negotiation."

"No negotiation?"

"No." Out of pure nervousness, I lick my lips and finally look up into his eyes. "Whatever you want, however hard, for however long." Then I repeat, "Whatever you want."

"No safeword?"

I shake my head. "No safeword."

He laughs again, a sound that has a menacing edge to it. "You're a sadist's fucking wet dream, girl. Let's do it." Glancing around, he points. "Platform three is open. Let's go."

When we've mounted the platform, Angus looks out into the crowd and pinches the back of my neck in his hand. "This is Ashley. She's been a bad girl. One of the guys told me she did the entire football team last night after the game. Ashley, what do you have to say for yourself?"

Involuntarily, I shudder, wondering what he's setting me up for. "I'm sorry, sir. It was a bad thing to do, but it felt so good. But I know I deserve to be punished."

"Very well. First things first. Turn around and pull up your skirt." When my hands find the hem and I pull it upward, the cool air hits me through the waist-high cotton panties I've put on. "My, my, my, little girl, look at those panties. Those look like panties a virgin would wear."

I decide to make the role play a little more interesting. "They are, sir."

"But I thought you did the entire team last night."

I nod and pretend to be embarrassed. "I did, but I only used my mouth, sir. I didn't do anything else."

"Meaning what?" Angus has a gleam in his eye.

"Meaning, well, you know," I mumble, pretending to be humiliated.

"No. I don't. You need to tell everyone what you did and didn't do," he barks.

"Um, I, uh—"

"Say it, child!" Angus roars.

"I sucked them, sir, but I didn't let them fuck me."

"Very good. We'll take care of that little detail tonight." He looks at my cotton-clad ass again. "You'll get a bare-handed spanking first. Grab your knees and get ready." I'm sure he's drawing his hand back.

When it strikes me, it nearly knocks me over. "Stand still!" Angus yells as he lets loose another one. After four, he announces, "The panties have to come down. Pull them down to your knees."

I yank them downward until they're binding around my knees. As Angus keeps up his relentless spanking, I look down at the white cotton. The entire crotch is wet with my juices, and I smile even as tears sting my eyes. When he's given me twenty swats, he chuckles. "Time for the paddle. Across my knee, girl," he says and points as he sits down. I move to get into position, but he stops me. "Ah, there's a detail I forgot. Turn toward me." When I do, he unbuttons my blouse, pulls it off, and then unsnaps my white cotton bra and throws it on the floor. Once both are gone, he gives my nipples a savage pinch and I squeal. "Nice titties for a school girl. Now, get into position."

"But the people, they can all see my, um, you know," I groan, feigning embarrassment.

"Yes. They can. That's what I want. Now. Get into position. I won't tell you again."

Draped over his legs, I take the paddling and try not to move or cry aloud, but Angus is a strong guy and he can really swing the wood. I know my ass will be bruised the next day, but I don't care. It'll make the pain last longer, and that's all I really want. When he's finished with the licks from the worn board, he helps me up off his lap and pulls up my panties. "You're just not learning your lesson, little slut. Let's see ..." He rummages around in a chest off to the side and comes back with something that makes me start to shake. "These are pretty damn strong. I think they'll do the job."

Binder clamps. I use them around the shop; they're great for holding the leather pieces together without making marks or holes like pins would. Over the years I've tried several times to clip them to my fingers when I'm working, but they're so strong that I can't stand it. There's no doubt where Angus is planning to put them.

And I want it. I brace myself as he holds one up and pinches it open and closed in front of my face. "No safeword?" he whispers with a sneer.

I shake my head. "No safeword."

"You asked for it. Pass out and I'll fuck you while you're unconscious." With that, he places the first one over my nipple and releases it.

The pain blinds me for a few seconds, and a ringing sets up in my ears. Before I can process everything, he clamps the second one on my other nipple and my knees buckle, but Angus grabs me before I can fall and makes sure I'm on my feet before he addresses me again. "Over to the post," he says as he points to a large column at the edge of the play area.

When I've managed to get there, gasping in pain, Angus turns me to face the post. He fastens a cord onto one of the binder clips, then draws it around the post to the other side and fastens it to the other clip. Once both ends are secured, he grabs the cord and pulls.

I shriek—I can't help it. As soon as I do, Angus ties a

knot in the cord so my nipples are stretched with its tension, and all I can do is pant. It's like the pain has paralyzed me, rendering me unable to move or speak except to scream. I can hear him moving behind me, and then, in just a few seconds, I hear him say, "You won't be a virgin in a couple of minutes, little girl. Maybe next time you'll let the team fuck you." Rope encircles my wrists as he binds them tightly, and whatever type it is, it cuts into my flesh mercilessly. He slips my panties down and taps each foot in turn to get me to lift it so he can remove them completely. The next thing I hear is his zipper coming down. Then he growls, "I'm so gonna enjoy this."

In one heart-stopping flash, he grabs the insides of my thighs, forces them forward and up, and lifts me up the pole. The cord from the clamps drags on the pole's surface and I scream again. Up high enough, he drops me down and impales me on his rigid cock, the cord from the clamps dragging down again, and I fight to stay conscious, to soak up the pain, to enjoy it in the way I do. The combination of his thrusting into me and him pulling me up and down the pole leaves me so pain-riddled that I can't speak, can't think, can't even whimper, just scream. Vaguely aware of voices around me, I wonder if all of those people out there, the ones watching me writhe and shriek, are enjoying the show even as my mind tries to rid itself of the sensations. In what feels like an eternity but has to be only minutes, I feel his release through the condom he's wearing and he stops.

Hoping against hope that he's finished, he lets my legs down and I stand, leaning into the post while I wait for him to release me. But instead, I feel his body pressing against my back. When his arms wrap around me, I pray he isn't planning what I think he's planning.

But he is. His hands wrap around my hips and find my hardened clit, and he begins to stroke it with his finger like a man possessed. All I can do is wait for my body to implode, knowing what that will mean. It's all out of my control, and at this point, I really don't care. I just want to fall into the pain like it's a big old feather bed and wallow in it. I will myself to come, hoping to get it over with. As his strokes become more insistent and intense, I feel my body slipping, slipping, slipping into the orgasm, and when I turn loose and convulse, my writhing pulls on the binder clips again, letting the pain make my climax even more intense. He forces it to go on and on, and I start to feel cold all over, like there's an invisible force passing through the room and seeping into my body. It seems as though someone is turning the lights down and I'm not sure if I'll be able to see when a buzzing takes over my brain.

My eyes flutter open and I'm surprised to find that I'm looking straight up at the ceiling. It takes me a minute, but I finally realize I'm in a bed in one of the private rooms. And, true to his promise, Angus is fucking me. Knees pressed to my chest, my legs are wide open and he kneels between them, his large dick piercing me over and over. When he notices me blinking at him, he laughs. "I told you if you passed out I'd fuck you while you were gone! You'll just have to take it now." One of my shoulders is cramping and that tells me that my hands are still tied. Blessedly, the binder clips are gone, but my nipples sport a purple welt to either side, reminders of the bite of the clips. I lie still, letting him take his pleasure, until his fingers find my nub and he begins stroking it again, forcing another orgasm out of me, tweaking my sore nipples with the other hand to listen to me cry out.

When he finally empties himself into me, he falls onto the bed beside me. Damn him—no condom. Yep. That's Angus. "Roll." Without the use of my arms, I can't, so he pushes me until I can and unties my hands. As I rub my wrists to help the circulation, Angus grins at me. "Work you over good enough?"

"Yeah, sure, sir," my lips say, but I already want the pain back. I want another fix. As long as I hurt, I don't think about Phil. I know how sick that is, but I can't help it.

"Get up. Leave the skirt pulled up far enough that everyone can see your pussy lips and my cum dripping out of them. Just like that. Nice. Good. Go on back out there and strut around. And thanks for the fun."

"Sure thing, sir." I feel the warm stickiness of him trickling down one of my legs. There's nothing to be ashamed of—everyone out there witnessed what he'd done to me. A glimmer of pride works its way into my psyche. I want everyone to know that I'm strong. I need the pain, and I can take whatever these Doms dish out.

But when I return to the bar, it's to find Michael glaring at me. I can't figure out what the problem is. I'm a consenting adult. I can practice R.A.C.K. if I want—risk-aware consensual kink. That's my prerogative. "Kimmer, we need to talk."

"Yes, sir." I'm not sure what he's about to say, but I'm fairly certain how it'll go.

Michael's eyes are wide. "How in the world could you take that? I don't even know how you managed to stay conscious as long as you did."

I shrug. "Not as painful as what Phil did."

Michael shakes his head. "I'm convinced you've lost your mind." He turns to Robyn, who stands silently beside him, tears coursing down her face. "Come on, baby. We're going home. If she wants to let some so-called Dom tear her apart, who are we to decide if it's right or wrong?" He spins to look at me again. "We love you. Please stop this. That's all I've got to say. Oh, and for fuck's sake, stay away from Angus. The son of a bitch is crazy." Arms around each other's waists, they move as one toward the door. I watch them leave and think, *Of course they don't understand. They have each other.*

My back to the bar, I lean against it from my stool and just sit there. I watch other couples scene, but it's all boring. I finally get up and wander into the locker room to change. Once I've got everything off, I drag into the shower and turn it on. As I watch the water swirl around and go down the drain, I see everything I ever thought I had going with it, the life I thought I'd have now, and it's all gone. Damn Phil, damn the years, damn wrinkles and gravity and all of that shit. I just want to curl up on the shower stall floor and die.

When my skin is wrinkled and prune-like, I figure that's a sign that I should probably leave. As I wrap myself in the towel and head to the dressing room to dry off and dress, I see the big mirror on the wall and just turn away. I don't want to look. What will greet me there will confirm what Michael says, and I don't want to think about it. In my mind, when I see myself, I see a wisp of smoke that just dissipates into nothing. That's me—nothing.

Scenes are still going on, and several of the guys watch me as I leave. There's every possibility that I could find another one to throw me a bone of agony, but it's getting late, and I decide maybe I've had enough for the night. Then, on the way home, I find myself wishing I had ten more minutes of that pain. If I did, I just might be able to sleep. But I have a feeling it's going to be another sleepless night.

～

"Would it be possible for me to send her by at about three this afternoon?"

I like Mr. Augustino, but sometimes I want to strangle him. He always wants to send his submissive over here by herself, and then he always has a problem with something that could've been alleviated if he'd just come with her in the first place.

His submissive, Candy, is a beautiful girl, with girl being the operative word here. They come to the club a lot, but they never scene in public. I have my own theories on that, but I'll keep those to myself. When she shows up, she's prompt and about ten pounds heavier than the last time she was here. I look her over and try to figure out what's going on with her when she finally blurts out, "I'm pregnant."

I know my eyebrows must be rocketing to the ceiling when I manage to reply, "Um, yeah, I guess you are."

"I know you probably think that's weird."

I shake my head. "None of my business. Not my right to judge."

"Yeah, but he's so old and all, and I'm so ... not old." Now that she's mentioned it, I don't think she's even thirty. And he's maybe sixty-five? So yeah. But again, not my place to judge. I start to say something when she adds, "I hope he keeps me."

What an odd plight to find oneself in, I have to think. That's got to be hard, carrying a child for a man who may or may not want to keep her. "Why wouldn't he want you to stay? You're having his child."

"It's not his." That gets my attention. When I turn from the notepad where I'm writing her measurements to look into her face, she explains. "He shoots blanks. He had me bred by a guy at the club."

Well, I *liked* Mr. Augustino. Now I'm pretty sure I don't anymore. Breeding her? What the hell? Her next sentence throws me for a loop: "My family disowned me when I started my career. I don't know why; it's not like I was a hooker." I have no idea what she means by that. "So he says he wants me to have someone I love who loves me in case he's not around anymore."

Without thinking how it will sound, I ask, "Is he sick or something?"

Candy shrugs. "I'm not sure. But he is in his seventies." That's a shocker. I hadn't pegged him as being quite *that* old. She stops for a second and then leans in as though she's shielding us from others in this room of only two people. "Can I tell you a secret?"

"Sure." I'm well known for my non-gossiping trait. I don't talk about other people because I don't want them talking about me.

"He's been talking to me about getting married."

The look on her face is odd—definitely not the look I'd expect from someone who could be a happy bride—so I have to ask, "Do you not want to marry him?"

Now her eyes just droop to match the corners of her mouth. "I'm not sure. I want to, but not if he's doing it because he's about to die or something. I don't want to be a widow."

I give her what I hope is a reassuring smile. "Who knows? He could have twenty more good years! Maybe you should take a chance—if you love him and he loves you."

"I do and he does." After a few seconds, she grins. "He can fuck forever just like he was twenty years old! He never slows down."

Okay. Information I didn't need. "Really? Okay, let's get you measured." And my attempt at deflection works. Twenty minutes later, I've got what I need and send her out the door.

Old guys. Young women. Good god.

I'm about to leave when my phone rings, and the number is unfamiliar. I almost don't answer it, then decide what the hell, I'll take a chance. My tenuous greeting is rewarded.

A deep, sexy voice floats out of the speaker. "Is this Kimberly Hendricks?"

"Yes, speaking. May I help you?"

"I got your name from Michael O'Malley." I start to relax a little. "My name is Jasper Givens. Do you have a minute?"

"Sure. What can I do to help you, Mr. Givens?"

"I need a new pair of leathers. Michael said you were the best, and that's what I want. Would you have time in your schedule to make a pair for me?"

A new client! That's just what I need. A couple of my old ones have moved away and one left the lifestyle, so I've been close to desperate for a while, not to mention that I'm rather secretive. Being secretive really limits your marketing opportunities, I've found. "Absolutely, Mr. Givens. I'd need to take measurements first. When might you be available?"

"Hold on please and let me look at my calendar." I assume he means on his phone, but I hear the rustle of pages, so I know he's flipping through a hard copy. "Um, looks like I've got next Tuesday afternoon mostly free. Would that be possible?"

I look at the big calendar on my wall and find Tuesday's square blank. "Sure. Name your time. Whenever you'd like."

"Two o'clock?"

"Two's good."

"And what should I wear?"

"Wear something that you're already comfortable in, something that fits nicely. That'll help me tremendously," I tell him, penciling him in on the big square. "Did you say your first name is Jasper?"

"Yes. But my friends call me Jaz."

I ignore that. "Okay, Mr. Givens, I've got you down for two o'clock next Tuesday, the twenty-third. Do you know where my workshop is?" When he says he doesn't, I spend the next three or four minutes explaining to him where it's located and how to get here based on his starting location. Oddly, I find that address familiar. "Is that a convention center or something?" I quiz.

"No. It's Reliable Industries. The company Michael works for. I'm in product development."

"Oh! I thought the area sounded familiar." So *that's* how they know each other—they work for the same company. You can bet I'll ask Michael about him before Tuesday comes. "So I'll see you on Tuesday the twenty-third at two o'clock, Mr. Givens," I repeat, trying desperately to get off the phone.

"Yes, ma'am. I'll be there. And thank you again." With that, the call ends.

I stand and try to catch my breath. God, his voice is hot molten sex; it made me want to rip my clothes off.

And then I laugh because I know he's probably short and broad and has a beer belly. Isn't that always the way?

The drive home is uneventful. As soon as I make it through the door, I send Michael a text: *Could you please call me if possible, sir? I need to ask a question. Thank you.*

In about two minutes, the phone rings. Before I can say anything, he barks, "I've *told* you not to call me sir. It's not necessary. I swear, Kimmer, you are the most hard-headed woman I've ever met."

"Good to hear from you too, sir," I mock back.

"Oh, stuff it. What's up?"

"Jasper Givens."

He starts to laugh. "Oh, I see he called you!"

I snort. "Yes, sir, he did."

Still laughing, he wheezes out, "Well, whenever he's supposed to be there, just make sure you have an ample supply of cold water."

That doesn't make any sense. "Why?"

"Because you'll need it. That's all I'm saying." He sobers, then says, "And listen, he's a genuinely nice guy. I wouldn't have given him your number if he wasn't."

"I know. I trust you, sir."

"Would you quit with that already?" Laughter shoots out of the phone, and then, all of a sudden, he asks in a voice that's almost a whisper, "Are you doing okay?"

"Yes, sir. As well as can be expected."

"Still coming to lunch Sunday?"

"Of course, sir. If I weren't, I'd be sure to let you know."

Michael sighs. "Of course you would. You're just like that, the model of responsibility. You really should cut loose sometime." When I don't respond, he sighs. "Okay,

Kimmer, I'll quit ragging you. Call if you need anything. And we'll see you Sunday."

"Sure. Thank you, sir. See you then." Feeling another lecture coming on, I hang up before he gets the chance.

Sunday dinner and a chance to ask more questions about Jasper Givens.

CHAPTER TWO

For a Saturday night, the club is too quiet. Then I remember: Ballgame. Everyone's somewhere watching it. The club management doesn't allow TVs here. They say people are coming to watch scening, not soap operas. Funny but true.

A look around doesn't give me much hope. I'm about to just give up and order a drink when I notice Alexander on the other side of the room, talking up some girl who's wearing nothing but a smile and a belly chain. To my surprise, he says something to her and I watch her face contort in disgust, which draws a huge frown from him. Casting his eyes around the room, he spots me and makes a beeline. And I'm okay with that.

"Good evening, sub," he says with a nod.

"Good evening, sir." My mind floods with memories of scening with Alexander in the past. Not only is he very good looking, but he's very, very proficient with a single tail, and he's another member in good standing. With my eyes cast downward, I ask, "How are you this evening?"

He takes a seat on the stool next to me and, this time, I

see from my peripheral vision that the corners of his lips turn upward. "Quite well, thank you. You're looking very pretty."

"Why, thank you, sir." He doesn't have to blow smoke up my ass. I'll take him on regardless. The wait is excruciating. Finally, he throws me a bone.

"Would you like to scene this evening?"

I try not to break out in a huge grin. "Yes, sir! I certainly would."

With a nod, he adds, "And as I recall, you're an enormous pain slut."

My head bobs. "Yes, sir. That's correct."

Standing from his seat on the bar stool, he reaches for my hand. "I think I can satisfy that urge. Last time I scened with you, you made it clear that you didn't want a safeword."

"That still holds true, sir."

"Very well. I think I can make you regret that." Tingling starts all over my body, and I can feel my clit swelling. "Green card on file?"

I nod. "Yes, sir. Submitted last Monday. Yours?"

"Yes. Submitted Thursday before last. We both in the clear?" I nod. "Good. Let's go." He leads the way, and I walk a couple of feet behind.

Taking care to sway my hips seductively as I walk to the platform, my arousal is in full swing when we reach the play area, my juices almost rolling down my legs. Nerve endings crackle on the surface of my skin, and I want to grab his hand and force his fingers up my pussy. I wait patiently, or as patiently as I can, squirming the whole time like the wobble of a gelatin shot. "To the cross, submissive. Face in." I head straight over, step up onto the footrests, and let him bind my wrists and ankles to it.

When I'm secured, he leans in and whispers, "Sure you don't want a safeword?"

There's not a hint of trepidation when I answer back, "Yes, sir. I'm sure."

"Okay then. I'm starting with the flogger, then I'll move to the single tail." I hear him behind me, feel the *whoosh* of air as he drags the flogger's falls in a pattern, and then it makes contact.

I almost cry out, not from surprise or pain, but from pure bliss. Every cell in my body is singing, and I can't help but drop into that bottomless pit that is agony-induced relief. And this is nothing compared to what I'll feel when he starts with that whip. My skin is growing warm and tingly, and I think about that vampire movie where their skin is sparkly. I wonder if mine looks like that, and I imagine that it does, that everywhere the light hits it, it looks like it's been sprinkled with diamond dust that shoots out into a tiny cloud in the spotlights.

Just when I'm about to zone out, he stops. I know what's coming even before he says anything. And the only words he speaks are, "I hope you're ready." In my stupor, I don't have time to answer before I hear the whistling of the leather cutting through the air, and then the first strike falls.

I hear my own voice wail as the tip of the single tail makes that *pop* against my skin, and where it connects, I experience ecstasy in the form of red-hot pain. I doubt that a glowing branding iron could hurt any more than this, and yet I want more, need more. As the pops grow more distant in my ears and the silence grows deeper, a million images blow through my mind. Me, walking up the aisle on my wedding day, looking toward the altar. A man stands there, and I know it's Phil, but he has no face—it's blank. In every image—us at our son Jeffrey's graduation, us at the beach in Florida, us at the car lot buying Phil's truck—there's no face on the man there with me. And I love it, the pain erasing his memory, blotting out his likeness, until all I feel is a numbness that smothers me. I feel my consciousness hovering above me, looking down and watching for the perfect time to escape. In a few minutes, it's gone.

In what seems like the next instant, I find myself warm and wrapped up like a mummy. Alexander's just a few feet away, coiling up the whip and putting it into his gig bag, and when I wiggle a tiny bit, I suppose I make a little noise, because he turns to look at me and smiles. All he says is, "Hey!"

"Hey." I'm still groggy and before I can ask anything, he slides back under the covers next to me and pulls me up against him, and I suddenly remember that we haven't even had sex. He doesn't even seem interested in it. One thing I can say for Alexander—regardless of his sadistic streak, he really is a conscientious, caring person. "Kimberly, you have an amazing tolerance for pain. I really don't know what to think."

"Think I'm crazy, because I am. I want more right now. If you asked me to go right back out there and—"

"But I won't." His brow wrinkles and so do the corners of his mouth as he half frowns, half scowls at me. "You've had enough for one night—" he starts, and when I try to interrupt him, he puts a finger to my lips. "And you don't need any more. You need to rest. Just lie here with me and stare at the ceiling. Look at the pinholes in the tiles. I see a dog, and a car, and the Empire State Building." He's smiling gently and pointing, but all I can do is lie there and stare. It's all starting to come back now.

And my brain screams, *Please, take me back out there and beat me.*

～

"Hi! Oh, no, Kimmer, I wasn't expecting you to bring anything with you! You shouldn't have done that!" Robyn greets me at the door and gives me a huge hug. "What is that?"

"It's this slaw that I make. Angel hair shredded cabbage, a tablespoon of minced garlic, and enough balsamic vinaigrette to coat it. It looks horrible, but it tastes divine."

"That's great! I know Master will love it. Sir, Kimmer's here!" she calls to him as she takes the bowl from me.

I hear footsteps on the stairs and Michael strides across the room to hug me. "I'm so glad to see you, babe."

"Thanks, sir. I'm glad to see you too."

"Would you *please* cut it out with the sir? I'm your friend, Kimmer. I swear." He huffs and puffs and grabs a bowl of pretzels. "I'm sitting it out in the den. Call me when it's done, little one." He drops a kiss on Robyn's cheek and heads out of the room.

I should wait, but I just can't. "So, Robyn, who's this Jasper guy?"

She peers over her shoulder at the door to the den, then turns back to me with a naughty gleam in her eye. "Oh, god, Kimmer, he's fucking gorgeous." He must be fucking gorgeous; Robyn never, ever talks like that.

"Gorgeous, huh?"

"Oh, god, yes. Holy shitballs. The guy is unbelievable. And super, super sweet. You'll love him, I promise."

"And he's a Dominant?"

Robyn nods. "Yep. Was a member of some big club out in Hollywood."

I have to ask the obvious. "What the hell's he doing here?"

"Well, the company he worked for closed up shop. He looked for over a year and couldn't find anything. When he found this job, he jumped on it."

I toy with a twist tie while I talk. My hands always need something to do. "So what exactly does he do?" I know Michael's company makes automotive parts. He came from Hollywood to make automotive parts? That sounds pretty odd.

"He goes from plant to plant to see what their production is like, then goes from company to company to figure out how to pair supply with demand."

I nod absentmindedly. "Kind of like a salesman."

"No, not at all, from what Michael says." She's spooning filling into deviled eggs, and it's all I can do to keep from reaching for one. "It's like, well, he goes to a production plant and checks to see which parts they use on the products they're making, then ties them in directly to the plant in the company that makes those parts. It's all computerized. The parts have these codes on them that a scanner can read. So all of their computers have these scanners, and as they use the parts, they scan them to take them out of inventory. Then, when they need a new item, he comes back in, takes the specifications, brings them back to the factory, and helps the engineers translate it into a product they can sell. I guess you'd call him some kind of coordinator."

I shake my head. "That doesn't make sense."

"I know. I don't really understand it either. But what I

do know is that he travels a lot, and I do mean a lot. He's probably got a woman in every damn town."

I lick what's left of the deviled egg filling off my finger as I scoop it out of the bowl. "So have you scened with him?"

"I wish!" She leans in and whispers, "Michael's made it very, very clear that it's never going to happen. I think he's intimidated."

"Michael? Intimidated?" She has to be joking.

"I think so. I think he's afraid I'd fall for the guy. And, in reality, it could happen. You just haven't seen him, Kimmer. Just wait."

Oh, god. Now I don't want to see him. The last thing I need is some self-absorbed player coming into my life. I wish I'd told him I didn't have time for him, but Tuesday's just around the corner. He can't be all that great.

Can he?

~

"Frankly, I've never fitted a pregnant woman before. I'll try, but I don't know what'll happen." I've got Candy's new corset finished, and we're in the studio, working hard to get the desired effect without potentially harming the baby with far-too-tight lacing. "How does that feel?"

"Like I've got on a pair of leather baby doll pajamas." She's wiggling and squirming, and I can tell she's uncomfortable.

I step back to take a look and I see it—too much flare at the hips and not enough at the waist. And then I realize what it needs: Gussets. I've got to put gussets in it. I help her out of it, then fold it carefully. She looks relieved that it's off. "I promise you, when I get it finished, it'll be comfortable."

"I believe you." She smiles gently at me and then, to my surprise, leans over and gives me a peck on the cheek. "Thank you for being kind to me. Most of the women are really nasty to me. They think I'm a gold digger. But I really do love Mr. Augustino."

"Why do you call him Mr. Augustino?" I have to ask.

She giggles. "Because his name is Waldo. And I can't bring myself to call him that."

I laugh out loud at that. Bless his heart. "Ah! I see your predicament!" But I feel my face fall, and I have another question I just have to ask her. "Candy, why the baby?"

"Because I have no one." Her eyes are sad, and I know what she's thinking. Same thing I was thinking, only for her, it'll be devastating.

"What about the actual father?"

"Nope. He signed away everything before he bred me. So that's that."

So cut and dried. I'm wondering if the document would stand up in court, and I remember that Mr. Augustino was a very, very successful trial lawyer before he retired. If he drew up the documents, they're most likely iron-clad and unbreakable. Using a white grease pencil, I write on the corset while she dresses, then lock the door after I've seen her out.

I'm cleaning off the workbench when I find a flyer that was stuck in the door one day from a pizzeria down the street, Rudolfo's. On it is a picture of a calzone, and they're half price for the month. I don't really want to eat, but that's a pretty good deal and it does look really good, or at least the picture does anyway, so I order one. The damn things are probably huge, but I don't have to eat the whole thing—I can eat just a few bites if I want. The bathroom sink gets a quick once-over, and I pour some bowl cleaner in the toilet, then go back out front and putter around in the shop while I wait. The buzzer heralds the arrival of the mighty calzone, so I pick up my wallet and head for the door to pay. But when I yank it open, I get quite the surprise.

The man standing there holding the box isn't one of the teenagers who usually delivers to the building. This man has a strong jaw, full lips, and dark eyes and brows. The headful of shaggy, dark hair matches the scruff on his jaws, and he reeks of sex and possibility. And he's no child either; he has to be at least forty, possibly older, with just the tiniest touch of gray at his temples. Is this their new tack to get more tips for their employees? Because it's damn sure gonna work on me. I'm betting this calzone is going to cost me forty bucks, and I don't even care. All I manage to stammer out is, "Wha-a-a-a-at do I owe you?"

"Nothing. On the house." He reaches outward with the box and I reach toward it but just as my hands touch the box, he snatches it back and laughs. Then he extends his right hand. "Hi. I'm Jasper." At my blank expression, he adds, "Jasper Givens? Your two o'clock?" I'm trying to speak, but no sound is coming out, and I'm feeling more awkward by the minute. Finally, he says, "May I come in?"

Like an idiot, I manage to squeak, "Yeah, um, sure, uh, come on in, sir. So sorry. I'm, um ..."

"Kimberly, I presume?" I nod mutely, like a five year old. "Pleasure meeting you." He strides across the room to put down the box, and I can't help but watch his firm ass in those tailored chinos. Holy shit. And I'm going to ask him to strip down so I can measure him? I'm in deep doo, no doubt about it. "By the way, I paid for the calzone when I saw the kid standing there at the door with it. My treat."

"Th-th-th-thanks, sir." Wow. I sound so fucking intelligent right now. Einstein's daughter. "Um, so, they're so big that there's plenty. I'd be glad to share it with you, sir." Heat washes over my face and I'm sure it's flaming red.

"Nah. Thanks, but I just had lunch. You go ahead. I've got time." He looks around. "Mind if I sit?"

"Oh, god, sorry. So stupid of me. Sure, please, have a seat, sir." I don't want to get too close because I'm sure he could feel the heat of total mortification radiating from my skin. "Would you care for something to drink?"

"That would be great! Got bottled water?"

Ah—a health nut. "Sure. Here." I hand him a bottle out of my little refrigerator, then take one for myself before settling on the other stool at the countertop and opening the box. I have to say, I'm guessing Rudolfo's outdid themselves this time. It's huge and smells amazing. I cut it in half and start on the first portion. It's absolutely packed with gooey melted cheese and pepperoni.

I've gotten about three bites in and realize he's watching me. After my next bite, he says, "Ummmmm, that looks really good. Mind if I change my mind about sharing?"

Sounding way too much like an eighth grader for comfort, I wheeze, "Oh, no, sir! Go right ahead! I'm glad to share." I reach over to my stack of paper plates for one, then plop the other half of the calzone on it.

"I'm not sure I can eat all of this!" he laughs.

"Doesn't matter. Please eat it or it'll be thrown away."

Now I'm wondering if Michael put him up to this, and then I remember: That couldn't be. Michael couldn't possibly have known I'd order food. Hell, even I couldn't imagine that I would.

"You'd better snatch it," he says around a mouthful. "This is delicious. I wouldn't mind having a whole one for myself." He looks at the box. "Rudolfo's. Is that far from here? I'm not familiar with the city yet."

"Right down the block, sir." I'm chewing and trying to talk at the same time, covering my mouth with my hand. "You should get Michael to show you around. He knows it like the back of his hand."

He shakes his head. "I'd rather have a prettier guide." Then he stops and stares off into space. "I don't really have time to wander around anyway. Work takes up most of my time."

"You managed to get here today," I point out.

"True." Then he grins. "Maybe you'll show me around sometime."

Oh, god, I'd love that, my inner slut almost pleads. Then I remember: Client. Don't mix business with pleasure. And oh what pleasure it would be. Visceral doesn't even begin to describe my reaction to his presence. That would best be described as flat-out turned on. Trying to think of something to take my mind off the bulge in the front of his slacks, my mind turns to Alexander and the other night. Nope. That's not working either. Then I remember why he's here in the first place. "So, sir, what did you have in mind? Zippers? Laces?"

He crushes the empty paper plate in half and looks around for the trash, but I take it out of his hands and to the can as he answers with, "Zippers. I'd like a pair in black and a pair in brown. And I want the brown ones to be wider boot cut. I have westerns that I wear from time to time."

"Yes, sir."

"And quit calling me sir."

"Yes, si ... um, okay."

"Why do you keep calling me that?"

I shrug. "Because you're obviously a Dominant. And I'm obviously—"

"Pretty caught up in the lifestyle. I am too, but I don't expect that from every submissive I see. Only from *my* submissive." There's not a hint of a smile on his face with that statement.

"Yes, si ... of course. Yes." I'm not sure what to say now. Then I decide a little fishing's in order. "So do you also need a corset for your submissive? Because I make very nice corsets in all colors and—"

"So I've heard. And no, no corset. I don't have a sub. Not right now anyway. I have had in the past, but, well, it was somewhere between 'absence makes the heart grow fonder' and 'familiarity breeds contempt.' In the end, familiarity won." Does he mean for himself or for her? Since I don't dare ask, it's fortuitous for me that he adds, "Apparently I'm an object of contempt."

"Oh, sir, I don't think you'd ever be—"

He stops me with a raised palm. "You don't know me. Looks can be deceiving." Then he looks me up and down like he's picking out a Christmas tree before he speaks. "I'm guessing if I told you I wanted you to do the measurements and fittings bare-breasted, you'd comply, would you not?"

Oooooo, god, if only. "Well, sir, you *are* a Dominant, and I *am* a submissive, and—"

"And you need to learn who is worthy of your service

and submission and who is not." His eyes bore a hole into me that I'm sure is smoldering like a volcano crater. "I understand from Michael that you spend some time at the club."

"Yes, si ... yes. I do."

"I also understand that you're quite the little pain slut." There's no gleam in his eye, no smile, not even a smirk. His face is just passive.

"Yes. That's correct." He twiddles with a pencil on the counter for a bit while I work up the courage to ask, "So what exactly is your specialty?"

"Me?" Dropping the pencil, he stands and walks to the window, taking in the view of the city from my perch. Before he speaks, he crosses his arms and his biceps flex, to my delight. "High-level restraint and suspension." He turns to look at me over his shoulder. "Some punishment and discipline, but not much. I like to bind a submissive creatively, suspend them just right, and then fuck the hell out of them. But I suppose you wouldn't be interested in anything like that, now would you?"

The throbbing of my clit is like a pump in an oil field, forcing my wetness out to flood my slit. Holy hell. How do I answer that question? Fuck yeah, I'd be interested. Wouldn't I? Would I? Now I'm really confused. I want pain, but right this second I just really want this guy's hands all over me. His cock in me would just be a bonus and, from the looks of things, a big bonus as well. My mind is rolling through all of the possible ways I could answer his question when he says, "Well, okay, down to business. How do you do this?"

"Um, uh, well," I manage to stammer. He grins at me, and I feel that rush of heat across my cheeks and down my neck again. "I usually have the guys slip off their slacks and measure in their underwear."

"Uh-oh. I'm commando." That would absolutely be my undoing right there. I'm screwed. As the wave of panic takes hold, he laughs. "Just kidding! Just kidding, really. No problem." He looks around. "Got a dressing room?"

"Oh, yeah, sure. Right through there. I'll do the measuring back there. I mean, the door's locked and all, but still—"

"Thanks for the consideration of my privacy." Strolling toward the dressing room doorway, he calls back, "I'll call out to you when I'm ready."

"Sure thing." I want to die. I want to hide under the table, change my name, move to a different city, kill off my phone number. Humiliation lives large with me right now. I don't know how I'm going to go in there and measure him so close to his, well, attributes, without coming apart at the seams. Uh-oh. Sewing clichés. I'm coming apart pretty fast.

"Okay. Ready."

I grab my tape measure, pad, and pencil, and head that way. It takes everything I have to say nothing when I step through the doorway and see him standing there. Guarding my facial expressions is more work than I've done in five years. He's left his tee shirt on and he's standing there in his socks and briefs. If that's not a ball bat in his shorts, I don't know what the hell it is. Sure, my brain is exaggerating it—I know that—but it's still lip-smacking impressive. I just place my pad and pencil in the chair, unroll my tape, and kneel down to take the first measurement.

And I'm stopped short when his hands wind into my

hair, but as quickly as they do, they disappear and he gasps. Did I do something wrong? He murmurs, "Oh, my god, I'm so sorry."

"No, it's okay, really," my voice says in reassurance, but it's shaky, and I know he can hear the tremor.

"It's just that when a woman kneels in front of me, I'm accustomed to it being … oh, never mind." Now *he's* blushing.

"No, perfectly all right. Don't worry about it." Can he see my hands trembling? Feel the heat rolling off my skin? He's a Dominant. Can he pick up on how nervous I am? Every ounce of strength I have is called into play to keep me on track as I measure and write, measure and write. And even though I don't want it, I need the feel of his hands in my hair again, crave it.

Neither of us says anything—I didn't know how awkward taking someone's measurements could be until now. I force myself to keep my eyes averted from his crotch, but I want to look so badly that I'm feeling lightheaded. My eyes keep trying to wander there, but I hold them hostage to the tape measure and note pad. The whole time I'm wondering: Is he looking down at me? Staring off into nothing? Thinking about me the way I'm thinking about him? I'm pretty sure the last one is a no. As Phil was so quick to point out at his exit, I'm now a *woman of a certain age*. We're hags; they're distinguished. I got the message loud and clear. It's a sure bet that Jasper Givens is staring at the ceiling, praying for this to be over. And at this very moment, he interrupts my reverie with, "Are you about finished?"

"Yes, si … um, yes, I am." And his next words make my heart skip three beats.

"Good. It's getting harder and harder to keep from touching you."

A shrieking sets itself up in my head, and I want him gone. If he doesn't leave soon, I'm going to do some things I'm going to regret later, things that Michael and Robyn will probably throttle me for, damn it. *Keep it together, Kimberly*, I catch myself reciting in my head, and I'm finally finished. I reach for something to put my hand on to help myself up from crouching, and in a smooth, gasp-worthy move, he takes it and helps me to my feet. Once standing, I find myself looking directly into his eyes.

Not what I'd intended. At all.

But it's like I'm mesmerized, and I can't tear my eyes from his. In my peripheral vision I can see him lick his lips, and then he simply says, "Thank you."

Please, let him lean in and kiss me. Please, let him wrap his arms around my waist and pull me close. I know I shouldn't want that, but I do, damn it, I do. And before I can process my thoughts completely, he drops my hand and smiles.

And the spell is broken. Ever the good sub, my eyes drop to the floor, and I turn and pick up my pencil, paper, and tape, the ones I'd been holding in my hands and dropped when our eyes locked. Apparently the heat and redness are to be permanent fixtures when he's around, my cheeks burning like they've been scalded, and I can't turn away and leave the dressing room fast enough. I'm at the work table, laying things out and organizing the measurements I took, when he comes out, dressed and straightened up as though nothing had happened in there. And in reality, nothing had. It was all in my mind, obviously. "Well, do you need anything else from me?"

I shake my head. "Nope. Oh, yes. Here. Can you fill

this out so I know a little more about what I'm doing?" I hand him the form I have all my clients fill out. It's an innocuous little thing, just contact information and things like that.

"Sure. No problem." He picks up a pen from the countertop and stands there, filling out the form and occasionally glancing my way. I'm trying so hard to pretend I don't notice. When he's finished, he takes the pen that was lying on the countertop and returns it to the pen cup, then stands behind me with the form. "Here you go. If you need anything else, my phone number's on here."

"Thanks." I finally turn to take the form and look up into his face. There's something there that I can't quite define. Mirth? Confusion? Sadness? Annoyance? What the hell is it? I'm not sure what to do or say, so I just force out, "Well, thank you for your business."

"Business." He almost spits the words. "Yeah, business. You're welcome. I can't wait to see what you come up with. So, I guess I'll just let myself out. Bye, Kimberly Hendricks. I'll see you around."

"I doubt that," I throw at his receding back. That's when he spins to look at me.

"Oh, you do, do you?"

"Yes. Why would I see you around?"

"You go to the club, don't you?"

Now I'm starting to tremble. "Y-y-y-y-yes. Why?"

"Because." A sly grin shoots its way across his face. "Because I was just accepted for membership yesterday. So I'm betting I do. See you around, that is."

Oh shit. No. This can't happen. "Um. I don't go very often so ..."

He smirks and I want to slap him. "Whatever.

Thanks again." With that, he opens the door and closes it gently behind him.

Damn it. I'm in deep shit.

~

I've managed to stay away for four days. Four long days. I can't hold out much longer. Last night I had the granddaddy of all nightmares, and I know it's because I'm holding all the pain in. Something's gotta give. So I decide I'll go. I'm sure he doesn't go *every* night. Maybe this'll be the one he doesn't.

But after twenty minutes, those hopes get dashed when I hear another woman three stools down the bar mutter, "Holy fuck. Sex on a stick just walked through the door. Wouldja take a look at that." I don't even have to turn around; I know exactly who she's talking about.

"Um, how about a Sam Cold Snap," I hear him tell the bartender, followed by a, "and hello, ladies." I don't turn and look, but before I can slink away, I get nailed to the wall with, "And hello down there, Kimberly Hendricks!"

Shit.

I turn to see him grinning at me and the other three women sitting there glaring my way. Great. I force out a less-than-clever, "Hello, sir."

"Ah! Now *this* is the place for you to address me that way! Very nice. Very nice indeed." He throws a five down, thanks the bartender, and picks up his beer. And, to my discomfort, he heads directly toward me. "Mind if I sit?" he asks, pointing to the stool next to mine.

"No, sir. Suit yourself."

He takes a sip, followed by a long, "Ahhhhhh." Then

he stares directly into my face. "Kimberly, you look lovely tonight."

"Thank you, sir."

"You're welcome." He waits a few seconds, then says, "Oh, that's usually followed by a, 'And you look amazing yourself, sir.'"

Damn him. I counter with, "Yes, sir, you're looking well."

He chuckles, and it makes me furious. "Tough crowd, I see. Oh, well, the night is young, isn't it? Think I'll go change." Standing from the stool, he grins at me, this mischievous grin that makes my stomach flutter. "Never know where the evening will lead." That statement is followed by a wink as he walks away.

As I watch, half a dozen other guys walk into the locker room as they come in, but he's still in there. They come out one by one, and then the last one comes out, accompanied by Jasper. They're chatting, but that doesn't matter. What matters is Jasper Givens.

He's wearing a pair of skin-tight leathers that disappear down into his knee-high, silver-adorned biker boots. The boots have flip clasps all the way up the sides and they had to have cost a fortune. And the leathers weren't cheap either. They're just about the nicest I've ever seen, a far cry from the simple ones I make, and I'm almost embarrassed. Why would he want any from me if he can afford something like that? But studying all of that is my attempt at avoiding the obvious.

His chest. God have mercy. It's broad and sculpted, with a smattering of smooth, dark hair between his nipples that's headed straight down the center of his torso, down the center of those ripped abs, and disappearing into his leathers. The tips of his "V" are peeking out the waistband of the pants, and I desperately want to see where that covetous letter points. Refusing to stare, I try to watch out the corner of my eye, checking to see where he is and what he's doing.

Before he's been standing there a minute and a half, one of the women down the bar rises and heads straight to him. She walks right up, practically gets in his face, and starts to chat. Of course, she's about ten or more years younger than me, toned, blond, tanned, and has the whitest teeth I've ever seen. I think they're lit from the inside, actually, or coated with some kind of phosphorescent paint. Still watching without watching, I see him change his stance, spread his legs wider apart, lean back into it, fold his arms across his chest, and flex those pecs. She's laughing and nodding and generally coming on strong. And something I never expected happens.

I'm completely overcome by a wave of jealousy the likes of which startles me. What the hell? Well, at least I'm honest with myself about what it is, but really? Jealous? I have no reason to be jealous. And yet I am, horribly so, frighteningly so. Even though I'm fighting it, my head swivels toward them and I find myself straight out watching them both.

To my absolute horror, he turns his head ever so slightly and looks directly at me, his eyes meeting mine. With that action there's that look on his face again, the one I couldn't identify, and I feel my stomach flip and knot. It's a look that's instantaneous and is over as quickly as it happens, his eyes pivoting back to the blond, laughing with her, pecs flexing again. I can feel my face blooming with blood once more, can practically hear the capillaries popping, smell my eyebrows as they're singed right off from the heat. Spinning on my bar stool, I see a sofa on the other side of the room, completely unoccupied and in a corner, and I pick up my drink and head there without ever giving him another glance. When I'm there and settled, I look around, but he's nowhere to be seen. Just when I figure he's gone to a private room with the blond, I see her over there, chatting up Ross. Jasper's nowhere in sight.

My drink is good—a mojito—and I take another sip, but I spit it everywhere when a voice whispers directly into my ear from behind, "I wondered where you'd gone."

"Shit! You scared me to death!" I blurt out just as he steps around from behind the sofa into my line of vision.

"Sorry. Didn't mean to startle you. Well, actually, I did, but not that badly. Are you finished?"

"Finished? With what?"

"Ignoring me."

"Whaaaa ... what are you talking—"

"Kimberly." He points to the sofa. "Mind if I sit?"

Before I can stop myself, I snarl, "Does it make a difference?"

His eyebrows shoot up into his hairline but, instead of snapping back at me, he starts to laugh, which just makes me furious in a hot, sexy kind of way, damn it. "Well, no, I guess not! I'm going to sit regardless," he announces, which he then does. Once he's gotten comfortable, and by that I mean legs crossed, arm stretched across the back of the sofa behind me, and drink in the other hand, he smiles. "Let's cut the bullshit, shall we?"

Now I'm seething. "What bullshit?"

"We both know you're attracted to me."

"And I know you're an arrogant ass," I manage to gasp.

"Who's also attracted to you."

Now I can't think of one damn clever thing to say. He's attracted to me? He's attracted to me. Holy hell. Instead of uttering one feeble word, I just take another sip of my mojito and wish I had a five gallon bucket of the stuff. "You are attracted to me, right?" he asks.

Out of force of habit from dealing with puffed-up Dominants for years, I just roll my eyes. "Well, actually ..." I begin, not knowing exactly how to finish the sentence, when he holds up a hand.

"Never mind. My mistake. I'm sorry. I just thought that there was some kind of," he stammers as he stands, "I don't know, chemistry or something. I guess I misread it. I'm very sorry." I watch in horror as he turns and takes about three steps.

And then I do the thing I know I'm going to do, the thing I know I'll hate myself for doing, that I'm probably going to wish I could take back, when I call out, "Wait!"

He stops, and this time when he turns to me, I can read full well the look on his face. It's sadness. Something in my chest spasms and the pain is almost unbearable. There's this wounded look about him, like someone who's been kicked in the gut one too many times, and it surprises me. The idea that someone like Jasper Givens could ever be broken like that has never crossed my mind prior to this moment. In that instant, I wonder if all that swagger and starch is actually a cover for hurt and loneliness, and that thought makes my insides melt. "Sit back down, sir. Please? I'm sorry, really."

He doesn't move, but instead, he just says, "Are you sure? I didn't mean to intrude. I was just trying to be honest."

"I'm sure." I pat the seat beside me. "Come on back and sit down." *Now what the hell do I do?* I wonder.

He heads back slowly, almost as though he expects a bear trap to snap from somewhere beneath him, and then sits down beside me again on the sofa. He doesn't say anything, and he doesn't settle in like he did before, just kind of slumps there, leaning forward over his lap, left elbow on his knee and right forearm resting on the other thigh, drink still in hand. He hangs his head. I feel terrible, and I'm wondering what to do or say when I hear him mumble, "Ever wish you could erase time and go back, do things differently?"

I snicker. "Boy, do I ever. About twenty-five or thirty years."

He tips his head and looks back at me, a hopeless smile on his face. "I'd take thirty minutes."

I can grant him that wish. "Know what? You've got it." I move my drink into my left hand and stick out my right one. "Hello, sir. My name is Kimberly Hendricks. Nice to make your acquaintance."

The smile he gives me is warm and genuine as he takes my hand, and there's a sizzling sensation on my palm when his connects. "Hello, Kimberly Hendricks. It's nice to meet you. I'm Jasper Givens, but my friends all call me Jaz."

"Hello," I say, and add with hesitation, "Jaz."

The lines on his face soften, and he settles back into the sofa like before, looking straight into my eyes. "Hi. I've only seen you smile about twice since the first time I saw you, and both times I couldn't miss how beautiful you are." I hope he can't see my heart slamming right through my cami, and I'm fumbling for something to say when he quietly says, "Just a simple thank you is plenty."

"Thanks. Sir."

"Can I ask you a question?"

I nod. "Sure."

As he speaks, he turns away from me to his drink. "What are you afraid of?"

I snort, "After what I've been through? Pretty much everything."

That sad look faces me again. "Me too."

"You, sir? You're afraid? Of what? I just watched three women at that bar almost puddle at your feet."

For the second time since I met him, he says, "Ah, looks can be deceiving, Kimberly Hendricks." There's that look again, and I get the distinct impression that he wants to say something, but he doesn't, just turns back to his beer. We sit in companionable silence for a few minutes before he finally says, "Well, enough gloom and doom, huh? Let's talk about something a little more cheerful. Would you like to scene with me sometime?"

Hot damn. I almost blurt out, *Of course!* but then I think, *No, wait; is this a loaded question?* My brain is running ninety miles a minute. Yes, I want to scene with this guy—he's fucking gorgeous. No, I don't want to scene with this guy—I have this feeling he'd be my newest addiction. I don't know what I want. I *do* know that I don't want to fall for someone. "So what exactly did you have in mind?"

His smile is gentle and warm. "I don't have anything in mind. That would be up to you. I don't know you well enough to know what you need. I do know you're supposed to be some kind of enormous pain slut, but I don't know about that. You don't really seem the type."

I counter with, "Looks can be deceiving, sir. How could you know that?"

"You're right. I don't. I'm just saying what I see. And I don't see a pain slut." He finishes his beer and sets the glass on the floor by his feet. "What I see is someone who's trying to forget something. Or should I say someone?"

Now I'm getting pissed again. "What has Michael told you?"

He shakes his head. "Michael hasn't told me shit. I'm just telling you what I see."

I smirk. "Is this one of those 'it takes one to know one' things?"

He's not smiling but he's not being sarcastic when he says, "Probably. But you'll never know if you don't get to know me."

I feel one of my eyebrows creep up. "Did you just issue me some kind of challenge?"

"No challenge." After reaching down to pick up his beer glass, he stands. "I'm not that difficult to get to know. Unlike most people, I'm pretty forthcoming when I'm asked a question." He stands for a few seconds, staring off into space, then seems to come back to himself and sighs. "Think about it and let me know. Good night, Kimberly Hendricks."

I watch his back as he walks away, all the while trying to come up with a way to get him to come back. I'm not sure why I want him to, but I do.

I'm not that difficult to get to know. Unlike most people, I'm pretty forthcoming when I'm asked a question. Well, Jasper Givens, I think I have a few questions.

CHAPTER THREE

For the next several days, that evening plays in my mind. One of the things I see over and over was the moment I left the club and looked back to find him sitting on a sofa with Kylie, a brunette who's about thirty and stacked. The shocking part was that, once he walked away from me, he never looked at me again that night. Never. As he talked to her, I made my way past them to the door, and he never looked away from her toward me, just kept talking to her like she was the only one in the room. Whether or not they scened later, I have no idea. Just thinking about it makes me feel sick to my stomach, and I'm really not sure why.

Mid-morning on Wednesday, my phone rings and I see his name pop up. A dozen greetings run through my mind, but when I answer all I get out is a simple, "Hello?"

"Hello, Kimberly?"

"Yes. Jaz. How are you?"

"I'm fine, thanks. And you?"

"Good."

"Listen, I'm not trying to rush you or anything, but I

was wondering if you had my leathers ready for a fitting. I'm in town today, but I'm going to be gone for the next five days or so. I thought if you did, I mean, before I leave town, if you had—"

"Actually, yes. They're together enough that it would be a good idea to fit them for tailoring. What time did you want to come?"

"What time do you have open?"

I look at my planner. "I don't have anyone else until four o'clock this afternoon. Yours will only take about thirty minutes, so any time until three thirty should be okay."

There's a pause before he answers me. "I'm thinking twelve thirty. How does that sound?"

"Sounds fine."

"Can I pick up something for lunch? Would that be okay?"

Lunch. That actually sounds kind of nice. "Sure. Whatever you want to bring will be fine. I have water here."

"Great. I'll show up at noon with food if that's okay."

"See you then." I hang up and clutch the phone to my chest. Even though I don't want to feel it, the idea of seeing him and eating lunch with him excites me. I keep thinking about him saying that he was forthcoming with information if someone really wanted to get to know him. Did he mean that? I'm about to find out.

When the buzzer sounds at noon on the dot, I open the door to find him standing there with a large bag in his hands. Without saying a word, I stand aside so he can come in. He sets the bag down, then faces me. "Submarine sandwiches from Carlton's Delicatessen. Michael says they're the best."

"Michael would be right." I reach into the fridge and pull out two bottles of water. "Do they have onions on them?"

"No." He takes the two enormous sandwiches out of the sack and sets them down on the counter. "I always order things without onions if I know I'm going to be in close proximity to someone else, like when you'll be measuring and fitting. I wouldn't do that to you."

"Thanks. I hate them anyway."

"Good to know." He pulls out a box. "And these are their homemade pub chips. I don't know what they taste like, but they smell awesome."

"They're good. I've had them before." I pull up the box lid and take in the sight of the chips, all golden and crispy. With my mouth watering, I unwrap the sandwich, then pull out a few of the chips and put them on the paper beside it. Then I decide I'd better throw him a scrap. "This was very kind of you. Thanks so much."

"You're very welcome." He takes a big bite of the sandwich and chews thoughtfully, and I do the same. Once again, we sit in silence, this time eating, and it's oddly comforting. With most people, I find it important to fill the time with chatter, but not with Jasper. We're about halfway through the meal when, out of the blue, he asks, "So, have you given any thought to my question?"

I try to deflect a little. "You mean about scening?"

"Yes." I wait, hoping he'll elaborate, but he doesn't. He leaves the ball rolling about in my court. And in that moment, I decide on honesty.

"Yes. Frankly," I say, deciding to step out on a limb, "I haven't thought about much else since you asked."

I expect him to grin in victory, but he doesn't. "Can I ask you something?"

"Of course."

His question shocks me to the core. "Did it unnerve you that I didn't look at you again after we talked the other night?"

Oh my god, he HAD done that on purpose! It wasn't my imagination. I feel vindicated and ridiculous at the same time. How do I answer that question? Honesty flies out the window in that moment. "You didn't? I didn't notice."

"Kimberly." I don't want to look at him, but he tries again. "Kimberly, look at me." When I finally do manage to look at him, I feel my face overheat, and I'm sure I'm especially tomato-looking. "Uh-huh. That's what I thought." Damn him—he knows. "Finish your lunch and then we need to talk."

"Yes, sir," I manage to choke out.

He nods. "Good. Very good."

And that's when it hits me: He's known all along. That first day, when I opened the door and almost passed out at the sight of him, he knew. That means that either he's as attracted to me as I am to him, or he can read me like a book and I'm in deep shit because he's going to try to manipulate me and use me. Damn. How do these things happen to me? How do I get myself into these situations? I chew slowly, hoping to prolong the agony, when he throws out, "You can only masticate for so long and then you have to swallow it. Don't worry. I'm not going to make you suffer. I'll make it as painless as possible."

Well, fuck me. I hear my inner slut say, *Oh, just swallow it all and get it over with.* I decide that I'll just swallow the food whole, take whatever he thinks he needs to dish out, fit the damn leathers, and get him the hell out of my life. Once they're fitted, I can put them in a box and mail them to him. Who cares that it's just across town? I don't give a shit, as long as I get him out of my hair.

When I'm done with the sandwich, I wad up my paper wrapper, then pick his up and do the same. He's not even done, and when I snatch it up and crumple it, he stops, mouth open and in mid-bite, and just stares at me. I guess he's never seen a woman pissed off about being admired by him before. Now I'm wondering if he thinks he's going to fuck me in the dressing room before he leaves. Fuck that shit. Not happening.

I sit back down, arms folded and resting on the table, and wait. When he's finally finished, he throws away what's left of his mess and sits back down in his seat. The clock ticks and I wait, not looking at him. Apparently he's had enough when he says, "Now, can we talk without all the walls, please?"

I try so hard to come across as ignorant. "What do you mean?"

He sighs. "I mean, can we talk without both of us acting like we're sworn enemies? Like we're sure the other one is going to lay us low? Because I don't mean you any harm. Just the opposite. I think we could be good for each other, but I really don't know where you're coming from because you're so damn prickly."

"Prickly?" My voice rises in timbre. "Prickly? That's a helluva thing to say!"

"Yep. You're getting pricklier by the minute."

The flush I feel on my face this time is pure fury. "You've got a lot of nerve calling me something like that!"

"And that doesn't fit?"

I'm finding it harder and harder to control myself, and now I shriek, "Are you purposely trying to pick a fight with me? Because if you're not, please don't ever try to. One of us will wind up dead if you ever do. And I'm not 'coming from' anywhere. This chat, the scening, all of that, it's all your idea, not mine. And you're acting like it's me who's instigated the whole thing and now trying to back out or something. You asked me, if you'll remember."

His face is still passive when he says, "Could you please quit being so goddamn defensive? I'm not trying to hurt you. I'm just trying to see past that cold, stony exterior you put up for everyone."

If he was trying to knock the wind out of me, he just succeeded. He reads me like a book, and it's so damn unnerving that I don't know which end is up. Up and out of my chair, I stalk over to the window and stand there, my back to him, twitching all over. I'm so fucking rattled now that I'm not sure what to do or say, so I just blurt out, "You know what? I don't need your business badly enough to put up with this. How about we just call it even and you leave? I think that would—" Without warning I'm being spun around to face him, and then I get the surprise of my life.

He kisses me. I try to pull away, but he puts a hand behind my head, just at the base of my skull, and crushes my lips with his. And when his other arm wraps around my waist and pulls me against him, all logic and reason fly out the window. Deep self-loathing sets up as my arms come up, independent of my will, and my hands find their way into his hair, my fingers weaving into its satiny thickness like honeysuckle in a fence row. Every gram of self-control I had seems to have taken an Alaskan cruise, frozen out and set aside while my body superheats. Kissing him back is the last thing on earth I really want to do, and yet I find myself doing it, opening to him, hungering for him, meeting his tongue with mine, and I can't breathe, can't think, can't move, just hang on for dear life.

Pulling back to let us come up for air, he smiles down into my face. "Now that wasn't too bad, was it?"

I mutter, "Just shut up," and drag his face back to mine. He chuckles softly against my lips, then traps my lower lip between his teeth and pulls back just a little.

When he turns loose, I open my eyes to find him gazing into them, his brown ones intent on probing the depths of my hazel ones. Before I have a chance to speak, he murmurs softly, "I'm not going to hurt you, Kimmie. I'd never do that."

"What do you want from me, Jasper?"

"I want you to let go." He tips his head and dives for the side of my neck, and when his teeth nip it, I let loose a hiss. That only spurs him on, and he kisses and nips it until I think I'll go insane. Slowly, sweetly, he kisses on up my neck, up my jaw, and traps my lips again for a few seconds, then releases me again and repeats, "Let go, Kimmie."

An ache sets up in my chest. "I can't."

"Yes you can. Come here." He pulls me across the room to my little desk, pulls out the chair, and sits down, then draws me onto his lap and wraps his arms around my waist. "Tell me: Why can't you let go?"

I try to find a reason, any reason. "Because I don't know you well enough."

He nods. "Okay. We'll fix that. Any other reason?"

"Because I don't know what you want."

"I want to be able to let go with you, and I want you to be able to let go with me. But somebody has to go first."

I shrug. "Why can't it be you?"

He smiles. "I think it already was."

"Oh." Now I just feel foolish.

"I've been very clear with you about how I feel. I'm very attracted to you. I asked if you'd like to scene with me. If I didn't want to scene with you, do you think I would've asked you that?" I shake my head. "Okay. And then there's the fact that I just kissed you. And twice now I've bought you food, which I think is significant."

"Why? What's significant about that?"

"Because it's obvious to me that you don't eat. The very first time I met you, the first thing I noticed is that your clothes looked too big. You haven't been eating. That worries me."

"Worries you?" I'm finding all of this hard to grasp.

"Yeah, worries me. You need to know that the first time I laid eyes on you, right there in that doorway, I felt something I haven't felt in a long time."

Now I'm starting to get really scared. This guy is getting way too close, and that's not what I want. At least I don't think so. I'm not sure. I'm not sure of anything anymore. "If you're trying to tell me it's love at first—"

"No. I'm not. As you said, we don't know each other well enough. But I want to get to know you, little girl. There's something about you that shakes up something in me. So what keeps you from letting go?"

Might as well get it over with; he's going to keep asking until I open up, so I just tell him outright. "I told you—I'm scared of getting hurt."

"Baby, you have no idea what hurt is." I've been sitting here looking at my hands, but when those words leave his lips, I direct my gaze at his face. Something there makes me suck in a breath, like an agony that won't leave.

"I've been looking for someone like you for a good while now."

"Someone like me?"

"Yes. Someone like you. Someone who's not a child, a grown woman who can make up her own mind. Someone who isn't put off by differences or," and I could swear I can feel him shudder, "scars. Someone who cares about another person because of who they are, not because of how they look."

What the hell is he talking about? He's absolutely gorgeous. I've seen his chest, his back, and his legs, and he's perfect. There's not enough real estate under those Fruit of the Looms to make any difference unless that's a pair of socks stuck down in them, and I'm pretty sure that's the real deal based on what I've seen through the fabric. I don't know what to do at this point. I don't understand anything he's talking about, and I don't want to seem insensitive and just question away. Then something crosses my mind. "You do realize I'm older than you, right? Significantly older."

"I'm betting you're not as much older than me as you think."

"I'm fifty-one."

"And I'm forty-eight." He's right—I guess he's not as much younger than me as I thought. Then he says something that surprises me. "By the way, you don't need pain the way you think you do."

I can feel my brow wrinkle. "What do you mean by that?"

"You'll see." He grins. "Now, let's get these leathers fitted and then I have something to tell you."

"Okay." I climb up out of his lap and he stands too, then heads toward the dressing room. In just a couple of minutes I hear him call to me, and I grab my tape, pencil, and note pad, along with one of the pairs of leathers, and head in to find him in his polo and briefs again. I hand him the pants through the doorway. "Put them on wrong side out, just like I've got them."

"Gotcha." Seconds later he says, "Okay. Got 'em."

They look great. I don't have to do much to get them ready for the final seams. When they're all marked and clipped, I have him pull them down to his thighs, then sit while I pull them the rest of the way off, careful not to disturb the clips. He reaches for his slacks and, before he can grab them, I snatch them and hang on. "Kimmie, what are you doing?"

"Don't put them on yet. Please?" I manage to get them out of his hands and toss them to the floor, then spread his knees and crawl between them. Kneeling there on the floor, I reach up and put a hand on each of his cheeks, then draw his face down to mine and kiss him. Once I've got him locked into the kiss, I run my hands on down his neck, down his chest, down his abs, and they're headed toward the promised land when he grabs them and holds them. "What?"

"Not yet. Not for a while. Give me my pants." When I reach for them, he snatches them again, and I won't let go. "Give me my pants, Kimmie. Now." He almost sounds angry, so I let go. What is it with him? I rock back and sit down on my ass to watch him pull them on. When he's finished, he stands and reaches down for my hand. I hesitate until he says, "Don't sit there and pout like a little bitch. There's a reason for everything I do, so know that up front. Now, get up and come out here with me. We need to talk for a second before I go."

I let him help me up and then follow him out to the

door. He's leaving. I knew he would. And he tells me he'll never hurt me, but he's in a hurry to get away. He turns there and looks down into my face. "Listen, I've got to go out of town on business for the next few days. I think I'll be back on Saturday, but I'm not sure. There's something I'd like for you to do while I'm gone."

Finish his leathers? Walk his dog? At this moment, I think I'd do anything he asked. What the hell is wrong with me? "Okay, what is it?"

He clasps my chin in his hand. "I want you to think about everything that's been said between us. I want you to think about scening with me. Think about the fact that I'm a Dominant and you're a submissive, and what that should mean for us. Think about these kisses. And think about the way I stopped you from going too fast." His eyes lock with mine. "Do you want me to call you while I'm gone?"

A little squeaky "Uh-huh" comes from my lips.

"Okay. I will. It'll be late at night because I'm going west, so what's late for you will still be early for me. Maybe we'll have a little phone sex. Maybe we won't. But know this." My heart is thumping wildly while I wait to hear what he's going to say next. "Kimberly Hendricks, as sure as I'm standing here, we were meant to be together. I don't know how I know—I just know. And I think if you're honest with yourself, you know it too. We've got to find a way to meet in the middle and trust each other. Once we do, we're going to be amazing together. Believe it." He wraps both arms around my waist. "Kiss me goodbye?"

I do. It's a kiss I won't soon forget, our tongues stroking each other's, and then he breaks it and gives me that look I still can't decipher. "I'm going home to pack. I'll call you tomorrow night."

"Okay." Before I can stop myself, I blurt out, "But I'm scared."

I'm shocked right out of my shoes when he says, "I'm scared too." Opening the door, he steps out, then looks at me again and smiles. "Bye, baby. I'll talk to you tomorrow night."

"Bye." I watch him close the door and hear the ding of the elevator. Everything inside me is jumbled and confused. Even though I have a client coming later, I sit down right there in the floor and cry my eyes out for fifteen minutes. What's happening to me? Who is this guy? And why do I even care?

But god help me, I do.

The first night, I really don't expect him to call, but he does. It's a fairly benign conversation, mostly a how-are-you and what-did-you-do-today kind of thing. Not much to say. I find it sort of awkward, really. But to my surprise, I also find it comforting to hear his voice. I keep reminding myself that I really don't know this man, but that doesn't seem to matter. He ends the conversation with the exact same thing he said as he walked out the door yesterday: "Bye, baby. I'll talk to you tomorrow night."

But on the second night, something amazing happens. I'm standing at the sink when the phone rings, and I answer, "Hello, sir."

He doesn't say hello back, just says, "Do you want me to be your sir?"

I'm taken completely aback. "Well, I, uh—"

"You don't have to answer right now. Just think about it. Oh, and hello. You doing okay?"

I fumble around verbally, trying to find things to say to fill in the space so I don't have to think about his question. Five minutes in, he says, "Kimmie, just put the phone down and go do it. I'll wait."

"Huh? What? What are you talking about?"

"You know full well what I'm talking about. Just go do it. I'll wait."

"Do what?"

There's an exasperated sigh on the other end. "Sweetie, I can hear it in your voice. Want to call me back?" I'm so glad he can't see me because I'm blushing the color of the Red Delicious apple on the counter. And then he adds, "Or I can stay on the phone and listen if that'll help you get off."

I'm trying to make myself sound incensed, but it's pretty feeble. "What makes you think I'm—"

"I told you. I can hear it in your voice. When was the last time you had an orgasm?"

Oh, shit. I can't believe this. How can he possibly tell? I decide I should probably be truthful because if he can tell how I feel just from my voice, he'll be able to tell if I'm lying. "Um, let's see ... this morning about five o'clock."

"So you're about due."

"About due? Am I some kind of nymphomaniac or something?" I spit back. Who does this guy think he is?

"You haven't told me everything. Something happened today and you're really tense. What happened?"

Now I'm rattled. Is he really that perceptive? I stew for a little bit and finally say, "I, um, I got a bill from the doctor's office. Apparently my insurance didn't cover everything I had done there, and I just don't have the money for it."

"That would make anyone tense. We'll talk about it when I get back, but for now, you need to relieve the tension. Just do it, Kimmie. I'll wait."

I snarl, "Maybe I should put you on speaker."

I hear him snicker. "Maybe so. I'd like that very much."

Well, damn it, he should have to suffer, so that's exactly what I do. "Can you hear me?"

"Yep. Go for it."

I'm too mad now to be embarrassed. I unzip my jeans and push them down around my thighs, then my panties go with them. I lean back against the counter and run my hands down my belly, straight down past my shaved mound, and into my slit to find that I'm soaked and ready. I start to tease and tickle, and I hear him say, "Hard?"

My aroused brain answers, "Um-hmmmm."

"Wet?"

"Um-hmmmm."

"I bet you taste good."

That does it, and I shudder and come, my hips thrusting against my hand. Every effort is made on my part to make not one sound, but I must because I hear him say, "Good girl. Very nice. You have good self-control, Kimmie."

I want to scream, *Not where you're concerned!* but I don't. I just mutter, "Thanks."

"You're welcome. If I were there, would you want me to do that for you?"

"Maybe."

"Fair enough."

"Um, sir?"

"Yes?"

"Did you get off too?"

"Nope." Before I have a chance to feel offended, he adds, "I don't tend to do that. I try to hold off so I'm very, very frustrated. It's a point of self-control for me. Makes everything more intense when I'm actually with someone later."

The question I've been wanting to ask is right there and I can't hold it back anymore. "So when did you last scene with someone?"

I hear him chuckle. "Ah, questions, questions. All in good time, baby girl. Tell me something: Did you eat today?"

I stutter, "Uhhhhh, like a horse."

"Very good. Just make sure it's healthy. And now I guess I'd better go so you can finish fixing your dinner."

I'm shocked. "How did you know that's what I was doing?"

He laughs. "Because you're obviously in your kitchen. The sound echoes more there than any other room in a house. Not as much soft surface to absorb it. What are you making?"

I harummph into the phone, "Tortellini with lemon pesto sauce."

"Sounds excellent. Enjoy it and I'll talk to you tomorrow night, baby."

"Okay." As an afterthought, I add, "Thank you, sir."

"For what?"

"You know."

"You're thanking *me* for *you* masturbating? No. Thank you for trusting me enough to do that with me over the phone. I promise you won't be sorry."

I have no idea what that means, but my entire body zings with that promise. "Good night, sir."

"Good night, Kimmie. Sweet dreams." And the phone goes silent.

I'm very, very confused. This man is invading my every thought, and I barely know him, but for some reason, I trust him completely. Something about him tells me that he'd never hurt me.

Two more nights pass with phone calls that are, like the first night, pretty simple. On the fifth night, however, he doesn't call at the usual time. I start to get fidgety and then downright worried. He's been right on the mark every time until now. Finally, at eleven thirty, I can't stand it anymore and I call his number. He answers with a soft, "Hello?"

"Hi, sir. I'm sorry for calling you."

"Why? I'm glad you did."

"You are?" I was sure he'd pop a blood vessel.

"Yeah, of course. I wanted to call you, but by the time I got up here to the room, I was afraid I'd wake you. You okay?"

I can feel my bottom lip begin to tremble. "Yeah. I was just, it was just that, before tonight ..." I want to ask, but it's none of my business.

"I know. I'm sorry. The manager of the office here wanted to take me to dinner. I kept trying to get away, but god, that guy can talk. Did you have a good day?"

"Yes, sir. It was okay." For reasons I'm not quite sure of, I feel like I'm about to cry. I kind of hiccup a sob, and I hope he doesn't notice.

Fat chance.

"Kimmie, you okay?" When I don't respond, he asks again, "You okay, babe? Something wrong?"

I try to get my quivering voice under control. "No, nothing's wrong, sir. I was just, um, I was worried. That's all." Another little sob escapes.

His voice is warm as honey. "Oh, baby girl, it's okay. I'm fine. I'm sorry I worried you. I never dreamed you'd even notice. Kimmie?"

"Yes, sir?"

"I'll be home tomorrow night, but it'll probably be late. I'll call if I can, but if I can't, please don't be afraid. I'll catch up with you the next morning, okay?"

"Sure, sir. But please, don't worry about it being late. Just let me know you've made it home okay, please? Text me or something?"

"All right. I'll do that. I'll call if it's before eleven and text if it's not. How's that?"

"Perfect. Thank you."

"No. Thank you for caring. I'll talk to you or text you tomorrow night. Get some sleep. It's late."

"Yes, sir. Night, sir."

"Night, little one."

I throw down my phone and sob into my pillow. It's like something foreign is living in my body, making me do things I don't usually do, and it all revolves around him. I go to the bathroom, splash water on my face, then go and lie back down to think.

Yes, he's good looking. Yes, he genuinely seems to care about me; I'm not sure why, but he does. It's so weird, though. We haven't even had sex, and yet I feel closer to him than any man I've been near since Phil. I don't understand it. Has he hypnotized me or something and I'm unaware of it? None of it makes sense, but I am sure of one thing.

Do I want to scene with him? Yes. I absolutely do.

CHAPTER FOUR

I get a big surprise the next day—Phil's sister, Leona, is in town and calls to ask if we can have lunch. I've always liked Leona. She never did anything to me, and there's really no reason why I shouldn't see her. We make arrangements to meet at Amelia's Bakery. They have some of the best craft sandwiches in the world.

"Kimberly! It's so good to see you!" Leona rushes me and hugs me, and I hug her back. I hadn't realize how much I've missed his family until this moment, but I have. It's been three years since I've seen any of them. It's not that they don't care about me. My guess is that they just felt like hanging onto me would keep me from moving forward, so they walked away and gave me space. But it really is good to see her after all the years I was in their family.

"You're looking good, Leona! How's James?" Her husband was always a good guy, and I hope he's doing well.

"Ah, okay. He had heart surgery last year and—"

"No! I had no idea. Is he all right?"

"He's well enough. You know how it is. When you get to be a certain age ..." I listen as Leona drones on about getting older and having heart problems and eating healthy. I was always afraid of all that for Phil, but he just didn't care. I had always hoped he'd take good care of himself for me. He didn't care about me, so he didn't bother—until he had a chance to snag a young girl, and then he started in with going to the gym and flexing his muscles and all that crap.

She finishes abruptly and then blurts out, "I suppose you want to know how Phil is."

I shrug. "Hadn't occurred to me to ask, frankly."

"Now, Kimberly, after all the years you two were—"

"After all the years we two were together, he told me he'd never loved me. I really don't care what he's up to."

"Okay, then, want some juicy gossip?"

Not really, I think, but I say, "Sure. Go for it."

"Well, he's got a new wife. He moved to California. She works out there."

That news hits me in the gut. "Is that so?"

"Yes. And she's a doozie. They've been together since, well ... sometime last year." She stops for a minute like she doesn't quite know what to say. When she notices that I don't look at all surprised, she adds, "She's got a criminal record, according to Davis." That's their other brother.

"Criminal record? That's interesting. What did she do?"

"No one really knows and Phil won't talk about it. But we also know she spent some time in a mental ward."

"He's with a woman who's got a diagnosed mental defect. Nice. So he's managed to find himself a young woman who's a nut job and a criminal. Very nice."

"She's not that young." At first, I think I've heard

wrong, but then she says, "She's in her mid-forties. We're not talking about a kid here."

"Really? I thought this was all about young women. What happened to the young girl?"

Leona snorts. "Seriously? She didn't want him. When she found out he wasn't loaded, she didn't want any more to do with him. And how he found this nut job, I have no idea. She's really something. She's come to a couple of family functions and we all watch the little kids and our purses. And no one wants to make her mad. Who knows what she'd do?"

"Yeah. Wow. That's just, um, wow." I think about that for a few seconds. What the hell is wrong with Phil? It may have been a long eight years since he left, but right now I think I'm glad he's gone. If this is what he wanted instead of me, well, good for him. Sounds like he got himself quite the life.

"So what about you, Kim? Seeing anyone?"

How do I answer that? I'm seeing him, but I'm not seeing him. I'm talking to him. So does that constitute *seeing*? What exactly *are* we doing? I'm confused. The only thing we've actually done is kiss. That doesn't constitute a relationship. No wonder I'm confused. I just answer with, "No."

"Well, you should. You're pretty and smart and nice. There's someone out there for you. You should look around," Leona declares, sipping her cup of tea. I just gaze out the nearest window. There's no point in trying to explain what's going on with me and Jaz. Even I don't know what to think.

We finish lunch and chat about her kids and grandkids, the brother and sister, their mother, who's still in a nursing home, and we part ways after promising to stay in touch. I know we won't. That's just one of those things you do and never follow up on. As I walk away, I think about what she told me.

Phil's married a woman who's certifiably crazy. Good for him. At least I'm not the only crazy one.

Not even back to my car yet, I stop and blink at my phone screen as a text comes in.

Guess what? Got an earlier flight! At the airport waiting. Will let you know when I land.

Can't help it; I smile to myself. Then I send one back.

Be careful. Waiting to hear from you.

His response is simple:

We've graduated to emoticons! How nice. Busying myself with the seatbelt and the radio, I realize I never even asked where he was going on this trip. I'll have to remember to do that. I start my little Ford Focus, pull out onto the street, and tootle home, stopping at the store for something to fix for dinner. But I'm barely in the door when my phone rings and, even though I don't want to, I smile when I see the number. "Hello!"

"Hello to you! You actually sound glad to hear from me." The smirk on his face is visible in my mind. "What's all that noise?"

"Bags. I just walked in and I've got stuff from the store."

"Perishables?"

"A few. Why?"

"Because I pulled in right behind you in your driveway. And I want to take you to dinner, if you want to go."

A breath catches in my throat. "If I, what? You want to take me to dinner? Oh, sir, I'm not dressed for dinner. I mean, I didn't know you'd be in this early and—"

"It doesn't have to be anywhere fancy. But I'm hungry. Oh, and open the door, please."

I sling open the door and there he stands. For some ridiculous reason, I was hoping he'd be holding a big bouquet of flowers. Maybe that's a goofy, old-fashioned fantasy, but there it is. Of course, no flowers, just him in a pair of charcoal gray slacks, a light blue dress shirt, and a gray and navy-striped tie. And a little less scruff than I'm used to on him, but I won't complain. He's still pegging the gorgeous meter. "Hi," is all I can squeeze through my vocal cords.

"Hi." He waits and grins, then adds, "Can I come in?"

"Oh! Yes, of course, sir. I'm sorry." I stand aside until he closes the door behind him, and he drops his overnight bag on the floor. "How do you know where I live?"

"You forget, we have a friend in common." There's a twinkle in his eye. "Are you the least bit glad to see me?"

How should I answer that? I decide that I'll just be honest and see what happens. "Yes. I'm very glad to see you."

Before I can react, he steps closer to me, then right in front of me, wraps his arms around my waist, and growls, "This glad?" That second is sheared away as his lips find mine, and I drop into the kiss without a parachute. Every ounce of restraint I have is gone, and I feel the heat of his skin through his shirt as my hands make their way up his back and his neck, finding their home in his thick, dark hair, my fingers twisting and locking into it. His lips are soft and just a little salty, and I almost giggle thinking about the dry roasted peanuts they most certainly offered him on the flight. When he finally breaks the lip lock, he grins down at me. "Well, I guess you weren't lying. It feels like maybe you did miss me a little."

"Maybe a little," I grin and wink.

"So, do you mind if I change into something more comfortable before we go out?"

I roll my eyes. "Now you're a cliché."

That makes him laugh out loud. "No, I'm someone who squirms in part of a monkey suit. I want my jeans and tee. And my Asics. I'm thinking maybe a sports bar, if that's okay with you."

Now I laugh. "Okay? That sounds unbelievably good. Let me get freshened up a bit while you change. Come on."

I lead the way down the narrow hallway into my modest little bedroom and head on into the bathroom. But before I can shut the door, he says, "Um, before you get started in there, would it be okay if I ... I mean, I just got off a plane."

I know I turn red. "Oh, god, I never thought ... Of course. Help yourself." I sweep my hand toward the bathroom and he heads that direction. It's the second time *I've* seen *him* red-faced, and it makes me want to laugh, but I manage to control myself. With the bathroom door closed almost all the way, I hear that familiar sound that I haven't heard in years, followed by flushing. When he comes out, he smiles. "By the way, I forgot to ask: Where exactly did you go?"

Plopping down on the end of the bed, he sprawls backward, resting on his elbows, and says, "Boring old Topeka. I hate that place, but we've got a very big production facility there and several customers in that region. I'm still trying to match the parts they produce to the customers who need them. It's going to take a while. They're some pretty obscure things, but I know they're necessary in the industry." He points to the bathroom. "I'm hungry."

"Oh. Yes, sir."

I'm almost through the doorway when he calls to me, "Wait!" I turn to see him jump up, run out the door, and then return with a small package in his hands. "I got this for you. When I saw it, it reminded me of you. Here."

Tearing the white paper with metallic silver polka dots from the box, I find a seal on the lid that reads, "Bixby's Gifts—a unique treasure in Topeka." *Well, at least it didn't come from the airport,* I can't help but think, and then yell at my brain, *Shut up, bitch!* But when I get the box open, I gasp.

It's a bracelet, a leather bracelet with a snap closure. And all around it are tiny roses, three dimensional roses, their individual petals wrapped tightly together. They're dyed a dark red, and twisted green leather stems trail between them. I've never seen anything like it, so exquisite and meticulously handcrafted. I want to put it on right that second because it's so amazing. When I look up at him, I hope he can see the delight in my face. My eyes go damp, and I'm embarrassed, but it's been a long time since anyone gave me anything quite so beautiful. In nothing more than a whisper, he asks, "Do you like it?"

"Oh, sir. It's so gorgeous. I've never seen anything like it. Will you help me put it on?"

"You said you wanted to freshen up. Wait until you're done and I'll help you with it." For a brief moment, he looks like a middle school kid presenting his first dance date with a corsage. "Sure you like it?"

"I don't like it. I love it. It's just, well, it's amazing. I can only hope to do work that stunning."

Without warning, he pushes a strand of hair off my

cheek and gifts a tiny, warm kiss to my forehead. "You do. Your work is outstanding. I didn't realize what I was seeing at first but when I realized it was leather, I had to get it for you. That's the coolest little shop too. They have really unusual things. I'm not sure how my eyes fell on this. Guess it was just meant to be."

"Thank you. Thank you so much. It's lovely. And thanks for thinking of me."

"Kimmie," he says, lifting my gaze from the bracelet to his face, "I haven't thought about much else since I left." Oh, god. He's been thinking about me. I feel a little dizzy. "Have you thought about me?"

"Yes, sir," I manage to gasp and, without thinking, I mutter, "once or twice." Then I start to laugh.

"Once or twice?" He's laughing too.

"Yeah. Once or twice. Or twenty times. Something like that. I wasn't counting." Without thinking, I drop my forehead to his chest, listen to the laughter rolling through him, and I feel his breath on the nape of my neck.

His arms encircle my waist again and pull me close, and I flatten my cheek against his chest. A hand comes up and strokes my hair, and I hear him whisper, "Oh, god, little one, we've got so far to go."

I want to cry, but I've got to get pulled together for dinner. Even so, there's something here in that simple statement that gives me a measure of hope I haven't had in a long, long time. Listening to his heartbeat, I admit to myself that I'm really sure about something.

I want Jaz Givens to be my Sir. It's time for being alone to be over.

As soon as the server asks, I shake my head. "No dessert."

I hear Jaz let out a little chuckle before he says, "I'll have the Boston cream pie, and the lady will have the red velvet cake." I glare over at him. "And we'll both have another glass of wine."

"Coming right up, sir." The server beats a hasty retreat before I have a chance to argue.

"You're looking much healthier. I see my admonishment to eat has helped."

I scowl. "More like I eat when I'm hungry."

"You didn't before."

"That's because I wasn't hungry."

It's obvious that he's trying hard not to grin. "So what changed?"

I mock back with, "'So what changed?'"

He levels a faux serious look at me. "Drink your wine."

I play-snarl back, "Yes, sir." It really is good wine, so that's no chore anyway.

"Ah—dessert! That looks delicious," he beams at the server.

"Thank you, sir. Our desserts are very popular."

"I see why." He picks up the clean fork that came with the decadent mess on the plate and smiles. "Eat up, little one." One bite and I have to admit, it's delicious. I'm happily scarfing it down when he says, "Hey, slow down! You're gonna choke!"

I haven't realized I'm gobbling it the way I am. "Oh, sorry. Not very ladylike of me," I mumble, and shoot a few crumbs out onto the table. Now he's laughing out loud at me, and I start to laugh too. When I get it all swallowed down, I open my mouth and stick out my tongue. "Red, huh?"

"Yup!" He's just cackling now. When he smiles, there are these crinkles at the corners of his eyes that make his whole face light up. I'm not sure how that works, but it happens. Hearing him laugh like that causes these funny little sensations to run around in my chest, and it makes me happy to know he's having a good time.

With every minute that passes, I'm surer this man is someone with whom I want to grow something. As we laugh and chat, I feel a connection to him that I haven't felt in a long time with anyone. We're almost finished when I ask him, "So, you know about me because of Michael. Have you been married?"

A dark cloud obscures his smile immediately. "Yes. Some time ago. I have no contact with her anymore. None."

"Oh." I wait for a few seconds to see if the mood lightens, but it doesn't. "So, do you have kids?"

"Yes. A daughter. She's in school at Dartmouth. A freshman."

Thank goodness I've found something that sounds a little cheerier. "Nice! Sounds like she's a good student."

A gentle smile takes up residence on his lips. "She's an excellent student. Studying to be a political analyst. Wouldn't have been my choice for her, but it's what she wants to do, so I support her in that." After taking another sip of wine, he says, "You have a son, correct?" When I meet his eyes with questioning, he laughs. "Michael told me."

Of course; leave it to Michael. "Yes. Jeffrey. He lives in Austin, Texas. He's in electronics. And he's married; has been for a couple of years. Greta. She's a sweet girl."

"No grandchildren?"

"Nope. We try to get together as often as possible, but

I really can't afford to go out there, and they're too busy to come here. She's a nurse."

"Ah. Sounds like Melissa. When she's not at school, she's working with some charity, or planning some kind of trip with her friends, or something that's more important than dear old dad, which is pretty much everything. You know how that goes." I nod. "So we don't get to spend much time together either."

I nod again. "I know. Jeff was the same way in college." My wine glass is going empty. "He won't have anything to do with his dad now, after what Phil did."

He gives me a knowing nod. "Melissa feels the same way about Meredith. I don't think she's spoken to her mother in about five years."

"That's a shame."

He snorts. "Not if you knew Meredith." One more swallow drains his wine glass. "Ready to go?"

"Sure." He's already paid the bill, so we stroll out to the car and drive back to my place.

When he parks the car in the drive, I automatically ask, "Would you like to—"

Before I can finish the sentence, he announces, "Oh, I'm coming in. We have a lot to talk about. Might as well get started."

Uh-oh. I'm not sure if this is going to go the way I'd like or not. After such a pleasant evening, turning it serious seems like a mistake. And it also looks like it's not up to me at this point. I swallow my anxiety and unlock the door, then make a beeline to the liquor cabinet for some liquid courage. "Want a drink?"

"Nope. I want to be completely clear-headed for this conversation, and I'd suggest that you remain the same way." That little pronouncement forces the glass in my hand back into the cabinet, and I head back to sit down and wait for whatever is about to happen. "So I take it you've made a decision about scening with me?"

Straight to the point. I suppose I should be grateful, not only for his straightforwardness, but for the opportunity for me to practice the same. "Well, sir, I—"

"Nope. Tonight you call me Jaz. We're equals in this room right now, discussing where we're going from this point on."

"Okay, si ... Jaz. So, I was wondering, it doesn't really feel like we're, I mean, are we just, um, I'm not sure—"

"Stop." He leans back into the sofa and puts an arm across the back. "Come over here and sit beside me."

That's what I've wanted all evening, but I'm just so afraid. I don't know if we're thinking the same things. Once I've gotten settled in beside him, my whole world spins around and gets set upright in one split second when he says, "We're going to discuss exactly what this is that we're making here and where we want it to go. So, let's do some definitions, shall we?" I nod. I'm afraid it's a little too enthusiastic, but I really don't care. "So, first of all, can we agree that 'scening' is what we're doing either in the club or privately in play?"

"Works for me."

"Okay. Good. That's a foundation. Now, the question is, do you want more than that?"

"Do you?" I counter.

"Answer the question."

Now I'm terrified, terrified of showing too much of what I feel, terrified of saying something that will cause him to jump up and run out the door. What do I do? What do I say? How did I get into this spot? Then I realize: He put me here. He asked me the question. Now

I get to answer however I like. In one blinding flash, I realize this is all in my hands. And I'm going to tell the truth. When The Truth leaves my mouth, it sounds something like, "I don't know. I'm scared shitless."

He echoes me when he says, "The truth?" I nod at him. "I'm scared shitless too." I'm sure he can see the shock on my face. "I mean, we're stepping into a new relationship. That's scary."

Relationship. *That's* what I was wondering about. So it *is* a relationship. Before I can voice that, he says, "Any time two people determine they want to spend time together, it's a relationship. But as a Dominant, it's my responsibility to set the tone for that, and I want this to be an honest, truthful situation."

Tremors wrack my voice when I ask, "So you want to have a relationship with me?"

Leaning toward me, he stares into my eyes as he says, "Actually, I think I already do." He waits. "Well? Do I?"

"Yes, sir. Um, Jaz," I correct myself.

"Good. For a minute there I thought I was in it alone." He gives me a grin that warms everything from the roots of my hair to the tips of my toes. "Now, to the original question—more?"

I nod slowly. "Yes."

"How much more?"

Everything between my legs goes hot. "Much more. What about you?"

With a finger under my chin, he tips my head up to look into my eyes. "Everything. I want it all." A gasp leaves my mouth when he whispers, "Kimmie, I haven't been this turned on in a long, long time. My cock's so hard that it aches, and I want to get to know the woman who's done that to me." An overwhelming urge passes over me to rip down his zipper and take that length straight into my throat. My clit is pulsing. My nipples are throbbing. It's like my brain is going to explode if I don't have him in the next ten minutes, and all I can do is sit there and stare into his eyes. I feel like I'm melting.

Just about the time those thoughts all register in my mind, he drops his hand and smiles. "We're not going to get any discussing done if we keep going like this. But I know this: I want to get this show on the road. I've been attracted to you since the first second I saw you, and I hope you feel the same way about me."

"Yessss," I manage to hiss, albeit weakly.

"Good. Can I make a suggestion?"

"Sure," I wheeze.

"Let's make out."

"Wha ..."

He starts to laugh. "Yeah. Let's make out like a couple of teenagers. I think that'll be fun. Deep kissing, touching over our clothes, dry humping, the whole bit. We've got a chance here to make this relationship whatever we want it to be, and we should want it to be, above all, fun. So let's do it. Whaddya say?"

Mercurial doesn't even begin to describe this man, and I'm so enthralled that I don't know what to say or do. Where does someone like him come from? I feel like I'm sixteen again, going out for the first time with a guy my mom and dad would never approve of. And then I realize something very, very important.

Except for the time I spent with Leona, I haven't thought about Phil a half dozen times during the week. And that's pretty amazing. But the minute I realize that, I feel a twinge of something. Guilt? That's not it. I'm not sure what it is, but it must show on my face somehow because Jaz immediately says, "What? What's going on in your head? I know it's something." When I don't respond, he repeats, "Tell me what's going on."

"I was just thinking about Phil."

The look in his eyes turns to something fierce before he snarls, "I'm going to drive him right out of your head, starting right now."

Like magic, I find myself on my back on the sofa and Jaz above me, my hands pinned above my head by his. Gazes locked, he licks his lips. "Think about me. Don't think about any man but me." Grip tightening on my wrists, he drops onto me and presses his lips to mine.

I see stars and hear bells, and I offer no resistance when his tongue presses my lips open and finds mine, stroking it, curling around it, dancing with it, while my body struggles to coerce his into an act of intense intimacy. He draws my hands down from above my head and around behind his neck, encouraging me to hang on, to pull him in, while he runs his hands down my sides until he scoops them around my ass and pulls my lower body against him. I can feel the length of his hardness against my belly, insistent and pulsing, and the sex rises off us like fog above the water on a cold morning. I'm immersed in the gnawing desire that consumes me and threatens to take me down, and I'm lost in that kiss. The scent he wears, cedar and citrus all mixed into a warm breeze, surrounds us, and the weight of his body makes me wonder if he can feel the thrumming of my blood through my veins as my heart rate increases. God, he's so much man in such an alarmingly handsome package that I'm not sure I can handle this, handle him, handle a relationship with him. He works his way from my mouth down the side of my jaw and on down to my neck, nipping, licking, and sucking, and I writhe with need. I manage to groan, "Oh, god, Jaz, please?"

"Please what, babe?"

"Please. I need you. Please?"

Grinding his pelvis against mine, he nips my lower lip. "I need you too. But we're not going there tonight. We're going to do something a lot more intimate." What could be more intimate than what I want to do? His lips press into mine again, and we kiss for what has to be twenty minutes, hands roaming each other's clothes, fingers in each other's hair. The kisses finally turn into sweet, shallow, quick ones, and then he looks down at me and grins. "Come on. We're going to do something that will teach us a lot about each other." He grabs his overnight bag and then takes my hand to retreat toward the bedroom.

Yeah. This is going where I want to go. At least I think it is.

"You got a robe?" I nod. "I want you to take off everything and put the robe on. I'm going into the bathroom to do the same."

What the hell is he planning? He disappears into the bathroom and I strip off everything, then put the robe on. I think about leaving it gaping open, but I'm fairly certain that's not what he has in mind. He comes out in his robe, three bath towels in his hands. "Come on." I follow him as he starts back to the living room. Once there, he takes one of the towels and spreads it out in the middle of the room on the big rug. He points to it. "Have a seat." I sit right square in the middle, but he says, "No. On one half. Facing out." I move to the end and turn.

Once I'm situated, he sits on the other end with his back to mine, and then he hands me a towel. "You may need this. I know I will. Untie your robe and open it." The cool air hits my nipples and they go even harder than they already were. "Now, you're right handed, right?"

"Yes, sir."

"Okay. Put your left hand behind your back and grip mine." When I do, I find his left hand behind his back and our fingers hook together. "Lean back into me and I'll lean back into you. We prop each other up. Got it?"

"Got it." And there we sit. What next?

"Listen to me, baby. Here's the way it works. I tell you what I'm doing to myself, and you tell me what you're doing to yourself. If we're lucky, we'll come at the same time." Oh my god. He wants me to masturbate again. Seriously? I lean over just a little and he barks, "No. Don't look at me. Just listen to my voice."

I can't help it. I want to see that cock. I've felt it against my belly, and I want to touch it so badly that I can hardly stand it. But I can feel his body moving, and I know he's stroking himself. Then he growls, "Kimmie, I'm so damn hard. I've missed seeing you this week."

There's an inferno setting up in my pussy that can't be ignored. I'm really going to do this. Before I can decide what to do first, he moans, "Play with your nipples, babe. Get 'em really, really hard."

They're already so hard they ache. I pinch one and then the other, and then I get a little brave and twist one. Even though I don't realize it, I must let out a little moan because I hear him murmur, "That's it, baby. Get into it. God, my cock's hurting. How do they feel, baby? Aching for me?"

"Yes, sir. They are."

"Kimmie, tell me how they feel."

Shit. I've never done this before. "Um, they're really hard and, um ..."

"What happens when you twist them? How does that feel? Tell me, Kimmie. I want to hear you say it."

"Um, it makes my clit tingle."

"Yeah." There's a little tiny grunt and he cuts loose a long whoosh of breath. "Tingle and burn?"

"Yeah. Oh, yeah, it does." There's something growing, churning, twisting in my belly, and I want to do something about it. "Can I touch myself, sir? Please?"

"Yes, girl. Do it. Run your fingers down into your slit and find that hard little button. It's hard, isn't it?" He's starting to sound a little stressed, and I hope I don't disappoint him.

"Yes, sir. It's hard." With my fingers grazing across my clit, everything in my body goes on red alert and I groan, "Oh, god, sir, yeah."

"Wet, angel?"

"Yes, sir. Dripping wet. Oh, god, yeah." It's swelling and expanding, my finger working even more feverishly. "God, sir, I want to come, please?"

"In just a little bit. Torture yourself a couple more minutes. I'll tell you when, babe. Okay? Oh god yeah, baby. Yeah. Your hips want to buck, don't they?"

"Yes, sir." Oh, fuck. This is crazy and yet it feels so damn good. I can feel every stroke he's giving himself, and all I can think about is having him inside me. Want is eating me alive, and I don't know how much longer I can hold off. "Oh, god, Jaz, please? Please, I need to come. Please?"

"Get ready, baby. Shit, Kimmie, you make me so damn hard. Ohhhhh, yeahhhhhh, okay, baby, come for me. Come on, Kimmie. Yeah—do it."

I shudder hard and then my body turns loose, my abs in spasms, my legs stiff as boards, my finger working madly. I can feel Jaz behind me, his left hand gripping mine, his right one working his hardness and then the bunching of the muscles in his shoulders as I hear him moan, "Oh, fuckkkkk, yeah. That's it, babe."

We both still, our hands locked together. What just happened? Before I can process it all, he whispers, "Have you ever done that with anyone else?"

"No, sir."

"That's what I thought. Close up your robe. Use your towel to clean yourself up if you need to." That's an understatement. At least the mess I've made was caught by the towel, and I wipe as best I can, then tie my robe closed. I hear something—he had a condom on and I didn't realize it. How neat and efficient. I start to get up, but he says, "No. Sit right there. Tell me: How do you feel about what we just did?"

"The truth?"

"Yes. Absolutely."

"The truth is ..." If the words come out, I'll have to force them. "The truth is ..."

"You want to fuck me?"

I take a deep breath and sigh deeply. "Yes. I want to fuck you."

I expect him to laugh at me, but instead he says, "I want to fuck you too. But not yet. Cleaned up?"

"Yes, sir."

"Okay. Come here." Rolling to my hands and knees, I find him sitting cross-legged on the towel, and I give him a questioning look. And he does the one thing I was hoping he'd do.

He opens his arms. I scurry into his lap and his arms

wrap tight around me, his face buried in my hair. I don't quite know what to do with my arms so I just wrap them around his waist while he hugs me to him, and there's something so sweet and simple about it all. I'm trying to figure out what it is I'm feeling, and then it hits me.

Peace.

The house is silent, and his arms are warm and strong. His heartbeat trips in my ear as I press my face to his chest, and I release a deep sigh. I don't want to move, just want to sit here all night. His breath is hot on my scalp when he whispers into my hair, "Oh, Kimmie. You're so precious."

Relief washes over me and I let the tears course down my cheeks. When he feels me sob against him, he turns my face up to his and kisses me again. There's so much in that kiss, and I can't understand how there's a man here with me to whom I could be so connected, someone I haven't slept with, and yet the bond running between us is so strong that I can almost see it shimmering in the air around us. I'm starting to believe he's right, that there's something long and wide and deep tying us together, and I want to sit here in it and let it warm me from the inside out. That gash in my heart, the one that's been bleeding for eight years, is scabbing over and starting to heal. I can feel it. Suddenly, I have an overwhelming need to see him.

I pull back and put a hand on either side of his face, my palms to his cheeks. Looking straight into his face, I look at those tiny laugh lines I noticed before, the little scar in his left eyebrow, the gray patches at his temples. Those eyes, those sweet, brown eyes, have little hazel flecks in them, and his lashes are long and thick. Narrow nose, and those perfect lips. Just perfect. I trail my fingers from just under his ear and down his jawline, feeling the beginnings of that scratchiness he must've kept shaved while he was gone. When I draw my finger across his lips, he kisses the tip as it passes right under his nose. The smile he bestows on me is gentle and warm. "Sir?"

"Yes, angel?"

"Yes."

"Yes what?"

"I want to scene with you." I can't stop myself. The words start to tumble out of me. "I'll do whatever you want. I want to be with you. You can have me; I'm yours. Tell me what you want me to do and I'll do it."

"I don't want you to sacrifice yourself to me. I want you to partner with me. I want this to be a partnership, something that works for both of us. This isn't about you giving to me; I want to owe you as much as you owe me. I want to scene with you, and I want you as my submissive. But beneath it all, I want us to have a real relationship, not something that's defined by leather or steel or rope. It needs to exist because we're comfortable with ourselves and each other as people, not Dom and sub. I did that for years before I got ... well, before. And I'm not interested in that anymore. It's so fucking shallow. I don't want shallow anymore, Kimmie. I want deep and meaningful."

"Me too, sir."

"Will you do something for me?"

I nod. "Anything. Anything at all."

There's an innocence in his eyes that takes my breath away. "Just once, call me 'baby.' Please?"

My heart breaks for him, but the fissure left behind opens my heart to his. "Yes, baby. I'll call you baby all night if you want, Jaz. Will you stay tonight? Please?"

"I can't. I've got to go home. I've got to be up early

tomorrow morning to go back to the plant and I don't have clean clothes with me. But soon, I promise. I've got something I want you to do."

"What?" Hell, I'll do anything he asks.

"I want you to come over to my place this weekend. I've been here. You should see where I live. That's how you really get to know someone, by being in their living space and seeing what they're really like. Want to do that?"

"Yes! Oh, yeah, I'd love to!"

"Good. Okay, so tomorrow is Friday. How about we meet at the club tomorrow night, see if we can negotiate some little scene, and then we'll make arrangements for you to come over on Saturday?"

"Sounds good! Oh, and your leathers are finished."

"Can you bring them to the club tomorrow night?"

"Sure!" Now I'm getting excited. This is going to be amazing, I'm certain of it.

"Good. I think it's fitting that I wear the leathers you made for me the first time we scene together. Very fitting. So I'm going in the bathroom to get dressed and then we'll do goodnights, okay?"

"Okay." I decide to really go out on a limb. "I'm so glad you're back, baby. I missed you this week."

His smile is a mile wide, and he grabs me around my waist, his hands wide and strong, dropping his forehead to mine. "I missed you too. I'm glad I'm back. And when you come over, I'll cook. Think of something you'd like to have and I'll go get everything Saturday afternoon. How's that?"

"That's great." There are so many things I want to say to him, to tell him how I feel. My heart's crashing into his at breakneck speed, and I want it. I've only known this guy two weeks, and I feel safer with him than with anyone I've ever known. I can't wait for tomorrow night.

When he comes out of the bathroom, he takes my hand and leads me to the front door. The overnight bag hits the floor again, and he scoops me up and kisses me. Then he picks up the bag, gives me a peck on the cheek, and murmurs, "Bye, baby. See you tomorrow night. Six o'clock. Don't be late."

"I'll be early." And I'm sure I will be.

CHAPTER FIVE

Apparently I am indeed early, because he's not here yet. I wait for a few minutes, kind of stand around by the bar, and he still doesn't come in, so I head to the locker room and change.

When I move back toward the bar, he's sitting there, and I'm pretty sure he's waiting for me. He gives me a sexy little smile when I get closer, and my knees feel weak. My outfit isn't horribly revealing, a bustier top and a pair of matching panties, and I wonder if it meets with his approval. I don't have to wait long to find out when he whispers in my ear, "You look delicious," and nips my earlobe.

"Thank you. You look pretty damn fine yourself." I hand him the bag I carried in with his new leathers inside. "You'll look even finer when you put these on."

"Ah! Thanks! And by the way, next time, don't go into the locker room until I get here. The idea that I'm going to leave you sitting here while I disappear in there doesn't sit well with me." I check his face to find that he's telling the truth. There's some stress there that wasn't before. "I'd really like for you to go back into the dressing room and give me time to change. Probably five minutes is all it'll take at most. That way at least I know where you'll be."

"Yes, sir. No problem. I'm sorry." Now I feel bad. I've already messed up and I haven't even done anything yet.

"No, it's okay. Just a thing for me, that's all. Come on. I want to get to it." With that, he sets his glass down on the bar and leads me back toward the locker rooms. He points to the doorway for the ladies' lockers and I stroll back in and sit down on one of the benches. While I wait, I count the tiles on the floor, then try to imagine showering in one of the little shower cabinets with him, soap all over both of us, his body slipping and sliding up and down mine. I look at the clock again—three minutes.

I stand and contemplate peeking out the door, and that's when I pass the big mirror. Something catches my eyes and I turn to see myself there, just a slip of the woman I had been a few years earlier. I've always looked in the mirror and seen the Kimberly I remembered, but reality hits me in this moment and I see what I've become. What little body mass I have is stretched out on my five feet five inch frame, and I'm angular and thin, the dark circles under my eyes accentuating their hazel tone as they stare out from my pale, slack face. Even though my hair is thick and full with almost no gray in its forlorn shade of light brown, it's unremarkable. It's been a long time since I've done anything with it or really paid it any attention. That leaves me to wonder: What the hell does he see in me? I make up my mind that even though I don't know what's caught his attention, maybe I should at least take a passing interest in my appearance, maybe get a new hairstyle—highlight or color or something—and some new makeup, possibly even have a manicure and pedicure. I could at least go to the mall and have my eyebrows threaded so they wouldn't be so dark and thick. If he's kind enough to want to be seen with me, I should be kind enough to not embarrass him with my disinterest in myself. I look like I just escaped from a refugee camp, for god's sake.

Five minutes. Surely he's done. When I sneak a look out the door, I gasp.

He's standing there, leaning up against a post in the room. My god, he's something. There's not an ounce of fat on that body, and he's shirtless. Yeah. Heat starts to pool low in my belly, and it's hard to breathe. It's all I can do to get back to him with my legs shaking and knees practically giving way. The only thing running through my mind is the idea of his hands on my body. That's what I want more than anything.

I'm finding it hard to speak when I make it to him, and all I can get manage to say is a strained, "Sir?"

When he turns, he smiles. In that smile there's want and arousal, but there's also something else too, that thing I can't quite put a finger on. His eyes don't leave mine as he says, "Let's go find a place to sit down and negotiate."

That same sofa we sat on before is empty, so we commandeer it and sit down, and I turn sideways to face him. He sits casually, knees apart and a hand resting on each; he doesn't put his arm across the back of the sofa like before, or lean in toward me, or anything even remotely that intimate. He just sits there for a second before he speaks. "So. What do you need? What do you want?"

I almost say I *need pain*, but for some reason, that's not what I'm thinking. It seems odd but it's also encouraging. All I manage is, "I-I-I-I'm not sure."

His eyebrows drop into a low "V." "You mean to tell me you've known since last night that we were going to do this, and you haven't given any thought to what you need?"

"Well, I have ... sort of."

"And?"

There's a fumbling around in my brain as I look for the words to articulate what it is I feel deep down inside. "I usually need pain. Now, I still need pain. I'm just not sure what kind."

"Let me see if I can help. Do you need the kind of pain that makes you forget, or just the kind of pain that makes you aroused?"

What is it with this guy? How can he read me so well? It's a relief, and yet, it's a huge curiosity. But what he's said helps me collect my thoughts. "I need the kind that arouses, but I need it to have enough of an edge that I concentrate on the here and now. Does that make sense?"

He nods and I'm so relieved I could cry. "Makes perfect sense. I think I can accommodate you. So may I suggest that we start with a warmup? I'll make sure you're ready and your skin is very sensitive, and then I'll do some things that help you to focus while still delivering some pain. How's that?"

"That's perfect!"

"And then?"

"That will be my needs met. What about yours? What do you want, sir?"

"You don't have to worry about me. I can take care of that." As he speaks, he doesn't look at me, and I suddenly have this horrible anxiety rising in my chest. He doesn't want me. Now I'm feeling very, very foolish and stupid. It occurs to me that maybe he's just a caretaker, that he's really not interested in anything except caring for me like one would a pet or a small child. "Kimmie? What's wrong, baby?"

I guess my face must give me away, but I'm not sure what kind of expression I'm wearing. I just know there are so many things I want to do with him, but it doesn't look like he really wants me. "I don't know, I guess I thought maybe you'd want to, maybe, oh, never mind." Heat engulfs my face and I'm pretty sure I'm blood red.

"Kimmie?" Mute as a stone, I just sit there, staring at my hands. "Kimberly? Talk to me." I can't make myself speak. It's too embarrassing. That's when he reaches for my hand. "Hey, look at me." It takes me a little while to meet his eyes, and when I do, they return my gaze with warmth. "You were thinking sex, weren't you?"

"Isn't that what most people do when they come to a club like this?"

He looks around the room. "How many men have you had sex with here?"

I shrug. "I dunno. If they're available, then I've probably scened with them." When I hear myself say that out loud, I feel a pang of humiliation, but Jaz doesn't even flinch.

"How do you feel about having sex with just one?" There's a twinkle in his eyes that I can't miss.

I can feel my entire body relax. "I'd feel very good about it, sir."

"Good. I want you to think about it. And know this: The first time we're together like that, it won't be here. It'll be in the privacy of one of our homes where we're comfortable and feel safe. Understand? If we're doing this, it's not as some kind of freak show. It's to get our needs met and build a relationship. That okay with you?

Is that what you've got in mind? Because we need to be on the same page. Are we?"

"Absolutely."

"Okay. And while we're here, there's something I want you to wear." He reaches in his pocket and pulls something out.

It's a thick curb chain, and it's gold, or at least gold-colored. And it's got a good-sized ring on either end of it. After a second, I recognize it; it's a choke chain for a dog, but it's gold instead of the regular chrome. Once he's got it straightened out, he produces a small gold lock that reminds me of the one I use on my luggage. I guess my eyes are wide in surprise, because he waits until I make eye contact again and states plainly, "I don't share. If you're my play partner, you're *my* play partner. That's non-negotiable. How do you feel about that?"

I swallow hard. "I'm good with that."

There's that smile again. Oh, god, I love it when he smiles at me like that. And I kind of hate it too. It makes me feel like I'm about fifteen, and here I am, a grown woman with my nerves fizzing and my thoughts racing. What is it about Jaz that does this to me? He unnerves me and makes me feel comfortable and safe, all at the same time, and I'm unsure why or how. I just know that parts of me like it, but other parts are terrified.

"So lift your hair." I do as he says, and he drapes the chain around my neck. I hear the lock *click* into place, and there's a fluttering feeling in my chest. "There. That's beautiful. Now, where are we going from here? Scene out here? Private room? What's your choice?"

"We can go to a private room?" That's what I really want. I don't want to tell him that, though, so I'm glad he's asked.

"Of course. Let me see what's open and we'll pick one." I watch his fine ass as he steps over to speak to one of the dungeon monitors and I'm shaking all over with anticipation. "Well," he starts when he returns, "five, four, and two are open. You've been around here longer than I have. Which one?"

"Two, please."

"Two it is. I'll let them know and be right back." He steps away, steps back, and takes my hand. "Ready?"

I rise and shake myself almost like a dog. I can't help it—I'm so damn nervous I feel like I'm going to jump right out of my shoes. "Yes, sir. As ready as possible." I'm used to following a Dom at a respectful distance, but Jaz leads me, my hand in his, through the crowd and down the back hallway. Once we're in the room, he closes the door behind us and I look around. I've been in this room dozens of times, but this time it seems different. Everything looks new and exciting somehow.

He takes my hand again and leads me toward the bed. "Come sit down. We need to talk first." When we're both seated, he gives me his full attention. "Safeword?"

"Pickle."

Than earns me a low chuckle. "Yep. That'll work. I don't usually use a play word. It's not necessary. I just ask if you need to safeword and if you say no, that's good enough. Agreed?" I nod. "So Kimmie, I think this is the time when I need to explain to you my philosophy on being a Dominant. I've watched what goes on here in this club. I know how most of the Dominants here operate. I'm very different from them." He looks down at our hands joined together, and I get that weird feeling in my chest again. "I will discipline, but I'm not quick to punish. I always listen to the sub's side of the story. I'm not as much into pain as I am into restraint and play. I'm far more into surprise. But I want to make something clear: I don't believe there's ever a reason for a Dom to be cruel or unkind. If I administer pain, it's either at your request or to help reinforce a rule or correct a behavior. If it's punishment I'm going for, it's usually psychological punishment I'm going to hand out. But not abuse—never abuse. Getting what you need is the most important aspect of play for me, but I will never take you farther than I feel you can handle or can experience safely. I don't draw blood, and I don't torture. If that's what you want, I'm not the play partner for you. And if and when we move this into the sexual realm, I feel it's as important for my body to be available to you as yours is to me. You have needs to be met, and meeting those needs is my number one priority." He sits quietly and waits. "I need to know your reaction to what I just said. I need to know that you're on board with this."

"I am."

"And now I need to hear your philosophy on being a submissive."

Shit. I hadn't expected him to ask me that, and I'm completely unprepared. I've never met a Dom who cared about my philosophy. They've all had an agenda, and my philosophy wasn't a part of that. I've been so intent on what he's been saying that my brain is in a scramble, trying to formulate the answers he's looking for. "Well, um, I don't see a submissive as a slave. I mean, if you want a Master/slave relationship and it's mutual, then that's okay, but I don't see a submissive that way."

"Good. I don't want a slave."

"Well, that's good, I guess. And then, um, I suppose I see a submissive as one who gives herself to her Dom for his use and pleasure. I get a lot of pleasure out of satisfying a Dominant. That's important to me. If I can trust the Dom, I can surrender myself completely." He smiles and nods. "It takes me a while to get comfortable with that person, but once I do, I'm completely open and honest. And I communicate well. I think that's the key—communicating. It's hard for me at first, but then it gets easier."

"I would think it's that way with anyone," he offers.

"Not for you. You're just out there, if you know what I mean. You just say what you're thinking and feeling and lay it all out there."

"Ah, but there's a difference, babe. The one who stands to be hurt the worst in this relationship is you. Yeah, we're both emotionally invested, but physically, I have the upper hand. You let me bind you and I can do as I please with you. You have no recourse, and if I were the dishonorable type that ignores a safeword, you could be in real trouble. That's enough to make anybody shy and hesitant. But I'm hoping we'll come to trust each other pretty quickly. And I make a promise to you now that I'll do my best to never, ever hurt you in any way. Accidents happen; I don't want them to happen with us."

He said *us*. That makes my heart tremble, but all I can get my tightened throat to say is, "Thanks." This time when I look down at our hands, just the look of our fingers alternating makes my stomach shiver. His hands are strong and comfortable, and I need their heat on my skin. "Jaz, I ..." I swallow hard, unable to force out what I want to say.

Tipping my head back with a finger under my chin to look into my face, he nods. "Whatever you need to say, say it. I swear, I won't run screaming from the room." A silly grin spreads across his face, and I almost giggle—almost.

"Well, um, I ... Do I call you Sir? And do I wear this ..." My fingers go to the collar. "I mean, is it *only* for when we're here? I'm a little confused, and I just don't know ..."

His hands trap both of mine in them, and his voice is warm spiced brandy flowing over my tattered soul. "Kimmie, if you want to wear the collar all the time, please do. I don't have another play partner, and I'm not looking for one. I'll gladly give you a key so you can take it off in case of an emergency or something, and when you shower. But we need to scene together a few times and if things go well, then I'm prepared to offer you a contract if that's what you want."

Oh my god. Heartbeat pounding in my ears, I nod. "It is."

"Then let's get to this. And if we decide on a contract, you won't be wearing that collar. I'll get you something far nicer. But right now, I want you to present yourself to me while I get everything ready."

Dropping to the floor, I settle into my stance and wait. Jaz busies himself with pulling things out of drawers and laying everything out on the bed. His eyes finally land on me and he smiles. "Nice. Very nice. But I want your hands behind you and dropped to rest beside your ankles." I move around a bit until I do what I think he wants. "Comfortable?" I shake my head. "Try other things until it is. Maybe you can actually put your hands on your ankles, maybe grip them, use them to brace yourself? Just experiment. It's fine."

I try a few different things and settle on his suggestion with my hands on my ankles. "How's this, Sir?"

He scrutinizes me. "That's very good, but now you need to pull your shoulders back. Um-hmmm. Very nicely displayed," he says with a nod at my chest. I'm still clothed, and I'm wondering why he hasn't told me to undress. "We'll be getting you fitted with some open-tip demi bras." I blush three shades of pink. "What's wrong?"

"Sir, my, um, gravity is not my friend."

He laughs. "I'm well aware of the effect gravity has on the human body. But yours is exceptional regardless. I'm not worried about it." He leans down next to my ear and growls, "I'm not concerned about how your body *looks*. I'm far more interested in how it *feels*." Awww, holy hell. Now my clit starts to throb unbearably. And apparently I squirm a little, because he follows with, "I'll have you eventually, and it'll be *perfect*. I'm looking forward to it. Tell me: Do you want me?"

Oh no. I'm the one who was talking about honesty and trust. Damn it, I've backed myself into a corner, not to mention that he can see right through me. I just nod. "Say it, sub."

"Yes, Sir. I want you." I look up and my eyes land on his zipper, and there it is, big and hard and just under that ridge of leather. Sweet mother of god. Every thought in my body focuses on everything within my slit, and I can feel the muscles in my pussy ripple. No words can describe the overwhelming urge that smothers me, the need to unzip that zipper and take his hardness between my lips—either set, don't care which. At this point, I think short of shooting me, stabbing me, or shoving me under a guillotine, I'd let him do anything he wants to me. My body has just rendered the rest of me into his hands, and I'm not unhappy about it at all.

"We're working toward that, little one. Stand up." I

comply and wait while he undoes all of the hooks on my bustier and lets it drop to the floor. He picks it up in one swoop, then drags the panties down my legs. Once on the floor, I pick up first one foot and then the other, and he snatches them away too.

I feel his eyes perusing my frame, stopping and staring in all the important places, and I don't know whether to laugh hysterically or burst into tears. Finally, he says, "Now, over to the St. Andrew's and climb aboard. Face to the cross." Once he's bound me in place, I hear him fiddling around over by the bed. "Let me know if this is too much," he says as he steps up behind me.

A lovely scent envelops me as he runs his hands up and down my back, ass, and the backs of my legs and arms. Lavender oil. I'd know it anywhere. He takes a second to run a bit up and down my slit, then dips a finger in and coats my clit with it. The tingling starts immediately, and I can feel the blood rushing to every inch of my body that's carrying the oil. I've used it here and there in the past, but never over this much of my skin, and it's a heady sensation. "You're pinking up. Safeword?"

"No, Sir."

"Good. We'll get started."

That wasn't "started?" I'm wondering what he means when something else comes into play, and I gasp as the pain bites into my skin. What the hell is that? He must realize what I'm thinking, as usual, because he just comes right out with, "Safeword?"

"No, Sir." I'm starting to feel a little buzz from it, and I'm still not sure what it is. In silent explanation, he stops and I open my eyes to find his hand in front of my face. In it? A nylon scrub brush. He uses the fingers of the other hand to drag across it and demonstrate how soft the bristles are, but to my lavender oil-prepped body, they feel coarse and wiry. He brushes over the entire back aspect of my body, and he stops at the areas that have thicker skin, like my shoulder blades, and swirls the brush over them several times to heighten the sensations. As he keeps working, I feel myself slipping into the stillness of the room, listening to his steady breathing as he moves about me. The heat from his body makes contact with my skin several times, and it soothes me in a way I didn't know it could. When he stops, I want to cry out and beg for more, but I stay quiet and wallow in the tickling sensations just under the surface of my skin.

But I shriek when the first pin prick hits me. It takes a second for it to register what I'm feeling, and then I realize: The Wartenberg wheel. I've experienced it and all its little prickles before, but after his preparations, it feels especially intense. I hear his voice say, "Kimmie, concentrate on the feel of the pins. Pay attention and anticipate where they're going next." Giving myself a mental shake, I set my mind on each and every point as it rolls over my back. While it's excruciating, I also feel a cracking open somewhere inside me, and I embrace it and let it roll over me like a steamroller. My brain marvels at this—it's a simple thing, one I've undergone dozens of times, but his expertise has taken it to heights I never could've dreamed I'd reach. He draws intricate swirls and circles on my skin with the points, and my id dances and cavorts with the exercise, offering itself up without a word. No grimaces. No groans. There's just the sensation of floating free in an ocean of relief, and I don't want it to end. In my mind, the swirls he draws are colored swipes, and they come together as an erotic, electric, luminescent paisley print that dips and soars.

I have no idea how long it goes on; I just know that my body is limp and I'm warm all over when I hear him say, "Open your mouth, Kimmie. Come on, sweetie, open wide." He sounds like he's a mile away, but I know what's going on. Ahhhh. I'm finally going to get that cock.

But I'm wrong. A spoon touches my tongue and he says, "Come on, baby. Enjoy it." When I close my mouth, I know I'm going to start to weep. It's warm and soft and sweet and I recognize it immediately.

Butterscotch pudding.

In one blinding flash, I feel like the most loved, cherished, special woman in the whole world. There's nothing I can do to stop the tears flowing down my face, and I swallow and open for another bite. As he feeds it to me a spoonful at a time, Jaz strokes my cheek and my hair, and I desperately want to kiss him, to feel his arms around me, to soak up the warmth of his body and have his lips pressed to my temple. I'm still flying when I realize I'm lying in the big bed in the room, tucked under the covers with him, being held exactly as I'd imagined. His lips press into my temple just as I'd dreamed, and I hear him say, "That's it, baby. Just relax. You did so well, little one. Just rest and come on back."

It takes a while, but finally my mind makes its way back to my body. I blink a couple of times to find his face right in mine, a peaceful smile crossing it and his eyes soft and sweet. "Hey, Kimmie! Feel okay?"

"Yeah. I mean, yes, Sir. I'm fine." I hesitate for a minute, then ask, "Butterscotch. How did you know?"

"Well, those six boxes of instant pudding I saw in the pantry at your house kinda gave it away."

"Wow. You notice everything." At that, he chuckles. "Is my back bleeding?"

"No. I never broke the skin."

"But it hurt so much. How can—"

"It's the lavender oil. Good thing I didn't use peppermint oil. You'd be gone until next week!"

I blink a couple more times. "I guess we should get out of here, huh?"

He scowls. "Nah. They've got other rooms. We can stay as long as you want. Need anything?" I nod. "Yeah? What?"

"For you to keep holding me like this. You're warm." I can feel him shake with laughter, but he doesn't make a sound. "Well, you are."

"And you're soft. I love it. You feel so good."

Tears are right at the surface, and I know why. My heart wants to hear him say, *I love you, Kimmie.* Because I know the truth.

I'm in love with him. There's no doubt in my mind that he's the man I've been waiting for, the Dom I've been hoping to find. I want to tell him that. I can't. Not yet.

But I will.

CHAPTER SIX

I'm not sure what I was expecting, but this wasn't it. I drive through the development, looking at the houses. They're all very nice, but they're all very cookie-cutter. I had Jaz pegged for someone who would want something unique and unusual.

And I find out I wasn't wrong when he opens the front door. The living room is plum with one burnt orange wall, and the furniture is upholstered with fabric that has plum, burnt orange, and gray half circle figures on it. The tables are a gray wood, and I'm impressed by the artwork on the walls and the little touches he's put in place, the gray throw over the sofa, the toss pillows that echo the color scheme but also bring a blue and green into play. I love it all.

The kitchen is just as unusual. The cabinets are a bright blue, and the walls are a light cantaloupe color. Red and yellow canisters sit on one side of the room on the stainless steel countertop, and the glass-front cabinet is home to Fiesta dinnerware in every color they make. It's so cheerful that it makes me want to giggle. "What can I do to help?"

"Nothing. It's all ready. I roasted the chicken this morning, and the vegetables are about ten minutes out. Want something to drink?" he calls to me as he disappears into the dining room.

"Sure!"

"Okay, let's see ... I've got beer, all kinds, and all kinds of mixers. And wine. I've got some pinot grigio, and pinot noir, and merlot, and cab franc, and—"

"I'll take a glass of the cab franc, please."

"Coming right up." In a matter of seconds, he reappears with two wine glasses. "Sounded like such a good idea that I decided I'd join you. A toast."

"A toast!" I repeat as I raise my glass.

"To us. May we navigate the minefield of this relationship and come out with not only exactly what we want, but with all of our limbs intact."

I laugh out loud and exclaim, "Hear, hear!" One sip and I grin. "Oh my god, this is good. So good! Thanks."

"You're welcome." Standing there, leaning back against the counter with the wine glass in his hand, I don't remember ever seeing a more handsome man. He's let that scruff grow back just a little, more like a well-defined five o'clock shadow, gray mixed in with the dark hair there, and on his chest, more dark hair laced with white peeks out the top of his V-neck, pale heather gray tee. Soft, worn jeans hug everything that matters, and he's padding around in a pair of heavy knitted heather gray socks. Everything about him says comfortable and relaxed, and when he drags a hand through that thick, dark hair with the gray frosting heavy at his temples, I want to lick him all over. Just lick until I can't lick anymore. Yum. A band tightens around my heart and squeezes when he says, "You look especially beautiful tonight."

"Thank you. I don't feel very beautiful, but—"

"Well, you should. I mean, look at you! You're just so—" And the timer goes off. Damn it. I wanted to hear the rest of that. "Oops, veggies are ready. If you'll hand me those potholders, I'll—"

"Nope. I'll get it." I grab the potholders behind me on the table and rush over to the oven. The aroma that greets my nose when I open the oven door has me drooling. There, in a large roasting dish, are potatoes, carrots, broccoli, cauliflower, and sugar snap peas in some kind of gorgeous sauce. I place it on the cooling rack he's put out, then turn off the oven before I say, "Oh my god, it smells so good!"

"It's a sauce my mother used to make when I was growing up. It's just simple cream of mushroom soup and some other ingredients, but it really makes the vegetables taste, I don't know, warm and comforting, I guess, like you've spent hours on them when it really only takes a few minutes to put together." Then he adds, "Oh! Grab the bread out of the warming tray, please. Bottom." I turn with the potholders and open the warming tray at the bottom of the stove. What greets me there is a sight for sore eyes.

"Oh, god, ciabatta! What the hell are you trying to do, hook me with food?"

"Is it working?" he grins from inside his wine glass.

"Maybe," I grin back. "I haven't tasted it yet."

"True. Let's fix that, shall we?" He points to the dining room and I hear him pick up the dish as I move that direction. After he's plopped it down on the table with the most beautiful roasted chicken I've ever seen, he retrieves the bread and sits down. Almost immediately, he bounces up again and grabs the bottle of wine from across the room, then pours my glass full once more before sitting and doing the same for his own. Once that's done, he smiles at me. "Well, go ahead. Please. Take what you want."

I sit politely. "Could you serve me, Sir? I'll eat whatever you give me. My dining's at your discretion." It's not about him serving me, after all. It's about me having the portions he wants me to eat, and I want to give him that courtesy.

Hot damn, my heart starts to pound when he lifts my hand to his lips. "I most certainly will. I'd love to." I fight to hold off the tears as he starts to fill my plate, first with a good-sized portion of the chicken, fragrant and juicy and perfectly done, and then a large spoonful of the vegetables. He tears off a mighty hunk of ciabatta and places it on my plate. When he's done the same for himself, he picks up his fork. "I started to make a salad, but I knew this would be plenty. I hope that's okay."

"More than okay. Who needs rabbit food when you've got this?"

He chuckles. "Well, technically, the vegetables *are* rabbit food."

"I don't think rabbits have ever had vegetables in this sauce." I feel him watching me as I fork a bite of carrot and broccoli and slip it into my mouth. The minute it hits my palate, I'm in heaven. "Oh my god, this is so good! I mean, really. It's unbelievable, Jaz."

"Thanks." He takes a forkful of chicken and chews for a second. "Well, the chicken came out pretty good."

One taste and I blurt out, "Pretty good? It's just

scrumptious." Before I can stop it, it hits me and a huge tear escapes one of my eyes, followed by another one and then another, and before I know it, I'm sobbing.

I hear his panic-filled voice and glance upward to see horrified eyes. "What's wrong? Is something wrong?"

"N-n-n-n-nothing's wrong. I'm sorry. It's just that no one's fixed me a meal like this in a long time. I go to Michael and Robyn's and we eat, but a lot of times it's just carry-out. Even then, it's just once in a blue moon. I always eat alone."

"Well, I didn't really go to any trouble either. The hardest part of this meal was peeling the vegetables, and that's no biggie. Kimmie?" When I finish wiping my eyes, I look over at him, and he's smiling. "I don't mind. I'm glad you're enjoying it. I eat here by myself all the time too, and it's nice to have somebody to share a meal with. Really. So eat all you want. And I've got dessert too."

"Butterscotch pudding?" I ask and then burst into giggles through my tears.

"No! Something better." He toys with his food for a second and then, softly, he asks, "Did you enjoy that?"

A half dozen more tears escape as I nod and smile. "Yes. Very much. Thank you. If that's what I've got to look forward to, my future is looking pretty damn bright."

"You're welcome. It was fun." Going back to the food, the quiet that descends on the room isn't awkward, just peaceful. Sitting here at the table with him feels good. When we're done, he clears the table, pulls out smaller plates and clean forks, and then produces the most beautiful Black Forest cake I think I've ever seen. I start to say something when he interrupts with, "Before you ask, no. I did *not* make this cake. I bought it. But I bought one from the same lady right after I moved here, for Melissa's birthday, and it was delicious. She does a great job. So enjoy—I sure plan to." He cuts a wedge apiece for us, and he's right. It has to be the best cake I've ever eaten in my life. As we eat, he asks me if I like to cook, what I like to make, and if I enjoy baking, and I tell him about the sporadic culinary triumphs I've had over the years. I also let him know that the term sporadic is generous, and he laughs at me. That sound, his laughter? Even though he's laughing at me, I don't mind it at all.

With the cake finished, I help him clean up and get everything into the dishwasher, and then he motions me toward the living room. When I sit down, he sits beside me and turns toward me, one leg drawn up on the sofa. "So you said you enjoyed last night."

"Yes. Very much." I draw both knees up to my chest and hug them. I'd love it if he put his arm around me, but he doesn't. I can tell he's determined to have a conversation.

"And I see you're still wearing the collar."

"Yes. I'd like to keep wearing it, if that's all right."

"Quite all right. Now we need to talk about moving forward and what that means."

"Okay. I'm all ears."

"No you're not. You have other parts too—very interesting parts, I might add."

"Why, thank you!"

"You're welcome. Want more wine?" I shake my head. "Me neither." He hesitates for just a second. "I had a good time too."

"Yeah?"

"Yeah. And I want more. You?"

"Yes. Hence the collar."

"Right." He rolls his eyes and I chuckle. "You should

know that I've avoided relationships for a good while now. But I think it's time to stop that. I've met someone I think I'd like a relationship with, and I want to pursue it."

"And who is this lucky woman?" I quip.

"Oh, I think you might actually know her. Beautiful lady, very smart, very talented. And I'm finding out more about her every day, like the fact that she's quite the smartass when she wants to be."

"Is that right?"

"Yeah. That's absolutely right. For the record, I find it charming—for the most part." He releases a laugh. "And I'm hoping she'd like to be in a relationship with me, but I don't know. What do you think?"

"I think she'd love that." Instantaneously, a blush creeps across my cheeks when I realize I've used the word *love*.

"Think so? Hmmm ... Well, I can be very demanding. I like my food to be edible. And I like for my dirty clothes to be washed eventually. I also like for the bed to be somewhat made in the mornings and for the toothpaste spray to be wiped off the mirror at least once a week. I'm very rigid in a lot of ways."

"Well, as long as you're rigid in the most important way." I sense something shift between us, something uncomfortable. "Jaz, is there something—"

"No, no. It's fine. I'm just a little, well, I guess you'd say I'm shy."

Now I'm baffled. A seasoned Dominant? He's been coming on to me since the first time we met, and he's shy? There are lots of ways I'd describe Jasper Givens, but bashful certainly wasn't the first one that came to mind. Before I can stop myself, I blurt out, "Shy? You're not shy. What do you mean by shy?"

"I just ... I am." My mouth opens to say something else, but he interrupts with, "So where did you grow up? Go to school? What about your parents? Siblings?"

Even though I want to know more about this shy thing, I tell him what he wants to know, and he does the same for me with his background. I finish with, "And I was married to a man for years and years before he finally left me and told me he'd never loved me."

"Fuck. That's horrible."

"Yeah. Pretty damn horrible. And you said you'd been married?"

"Yeah. That was pretty damn horrible too."

"What happened?"

"Something pretty damn horrible. Very damn horrible." There's a war of some sort going on behind his eyes, and I want to know what it is. Even though he's not touching me, I can feel him growing tense. It takes a few minutes, but I finally figure out what it is.

It's pain. And I want to take it away. I want it to leave him and never come back. What in the world could this woman have done that makes him shiver as he speaks of her? My mind goes into overdrive trying to come up with something, then I just decide to go for broke. "Jaz, whatever it is, you can tell me. It's okay, I promise."

"It may not be."

"It will be. Do I come across as that judgmental?"

He shakes his head. "No. But it's a lot to take in."

"So give me the benefit of the doubt, please?" How can I make him feel comfortable? "I trust you. Can't you trust me?"

"But this is—"

"Have I done anything—ANYTHING—that would keep you from trusting me?"

Another shake of his head. "No. You've done nothing but be up front and straight with me."

"Then have a little faith in me, can't you? I promise you won't be sorry."

The expression on his face goes from confusion to pure dread. Then, like a lightning strike, he stands, grabs my hand, and says, "Come on. I can't put this off. It's not fair. You should know."

"Know what?" comes rolling off my tongue as he drags me along, and I notice something else odd: He's stroking himself through his jeans. What the hell? This isn't making sense. Pulling me through a doorway, we're in his bedroom, where he points to a comfy little armchair. "Sit." He's still stroking himself like mad when I sit down, and I can see his erection through the soft denim. In a voice tinged with sadness, he says, "I'm sorry, but I can't look at you when you see it. I just can't. It's just too much." He murmurs again, "It's just too much," and unzips his fly. Fingers on the waistband of his briefs, he says, "If you can't take it, just get up and leave. Don't say anything, please. Just leave. I'll understand. It won't be the first time." Running through my mind is the mantra, *What the hell? What the hell? What the hell?* Thumbs hooked in the waistband, he pulls the front of his briefs out and down.

All the air rushes out of my lungs and I fight to keep from making a sound. His erect penis is right there in front of my eyes. It's plenty large enough, but it's kind of twisted in a weird way and makes a bit of an angle, and I'm trying to focus well enough to figure out what I'm seeing when it all suddenly comes into painful focus.

Scars. They're everywhere. They run here and there up the length, and then back and forth too. Some are depressed, and some are raised, most with suture marks. It's obvious they're not fresh; they're well cured, so they've been there for a while. I can't imagine anything that could've done that kind of damage, short of accidentally catching it in some kind of machinery or being attacked by a wild animal, but I've seen his legs and stomach, and they're scar-free. I'm trying to take it all in and make sense of it, and then, without thinking, I look up at his face.

Jaz's eyes are squeezed shut against the sight of me knowing his greatest shame, and my heart breaks for him. A lone tear meanders down one cheek, but otherwise, his face is blank. The thought crosses my mind, *How many women have seen this and run the other direction? Or has he ever shown anyone else? He said it wouldn't be the first time, so it had to have happened to him. Oh, god, Kimberly,* my brain screams, *whatever you do, make it the right choice.*

Something comes over me in that instant, something so clear and pure that I know it's the precise thing to do, and, without warning, I reach out, grab his briefs and jeans, yank them down to the middle of his thighs, and run my mouth down over his cock in one smooth, seamless movement. I hear him gasp, and I grip his thighs with my hands and hang on in case he tries to move away, but he doesn't. Instead, his hands wind around in my hair and something else happens, something that takes my broken heart, dashes it to the ground, and stomps all over it.

He starts to sob. I feel his body shake, feel his tears fall into my hair, and I don't know if I should stop and comfort him or keep going and honor his pain. One hand leaves my hair and grips my chin, but I grab it with my hand and squeeze for dear life. To my great relief, he squeezes back, and I just keep going. I'm not sucking his cock; I'm making love to it with my lips, my tongue, my throat. I want him to know how precious it is to me—I want him to know how precious *he* is to me. Because he is. I don't know how it happened, and I don't care. He trusted me, and I want to honor that trust. I want him to know that trusting me with this secret, this painful truth, was absolutely, positively the right thing to do. I've never had a man give me the gift of such vulnerability, and I wouldn't dream of dishonoring that gift.

My lips leave his hardness for a split second when I murmur, "Oh, Jaz, you taste so good." There's no opportunity to go back to what I was doing before he drops to the floor in front of me, wraps his arms around me, and kisses me.

This kiss. It'll be with me for the rest of my life. My heart expands—I can feel it—and takes in his, giving it a home and a place to rest. Softer than a snow in January, I let my fingertips dance across the back of his neck under his hair, and he moans into my mouth. I manage to break free just long enough to whisper, "I love you, Jaz. Nothing else matters." His mouth covers mine again, and I sink into the kiss like a Dane into the bog. It goes on forever, holding me hostage to its magic, until he finally comes up for air.

"Kimmie, I—"

My finger stills his lips. "It doesn't matter. If you want to tell me, I'll listen. If you don't want to talk about it, that'll be fine too. You, me, now—that's what matters."

"I owe you that. At least I feel like I do."

It seems almost like he's shrinking before me, and I don't want that. He's a good man, a strong man, and I know he didn't do this to himself, so shame is the last thing he should feel. "Have other women really run?" He nods in silence. "Bitches. Weak little bitches. And you don't owe me a thing."

"Yes I do. You said you love me. If that's true, I owe you an explanation, at the very least."

My hair twists as I shake my head. "Yes. It's true. And no, you don't owe me any explanation."

"Even if I can't say it back?"

"Even if you can't say it back." I run a finger down his jaw, and he tips his head toward it. That simple gesture tugs at my heart again, and I press my palm to his cheek.

"I will, Kimmie. I promise, I will. Not right now, but I will."

"S'okay. I can love you without you loving me. Happens to people all the time."

"I didn't say I didn't. I just said I can't say it."

A gentle chuckle rolls from my throat even as my heart leaps in my chest. "Good enough!"

"Come here." He pulls me up from the floor after he stands, and then pulls me toward the bed. Once I'm standing there beside it, he undresses me, then undresses himself, and points to the bed. "In you go." With him right behind me, I crawl in. His arms pull me to him, and I'm awash in the sensations of his strength, his warmth, the softness of his skin, and the scent he's wearing. My cheek registers the feel of the hair on his chest, and one of my fingers meanders through the dark patch, swirling as it goes. "I was married for a lot of years to Meredith."

"Yeah. I remember you said that."

"She got it in her head that I was cheating on her, but I swear to god, I wasn't. My job required a lot from me, and I spent extra hours trying to make my bosses happy so

I didn't lose it. Funny thing is," he says with a snort, "in the end, I lost it anyway. She kept arguing with me and accusing me of being unfaithful, just generally being irrational, and I was getting pretty weary of it. I came home one night, I was really tired, and she just kept yelling at me. Finally, I told her, 'You know what? If you want to believe that, just do. It's not true, but just believe it and shut up about it.' I went in the kitchen and got myself a soft drink, opened it, and went to the bathroom. When I came back, I read some paperwork, finished the drink, and went to bed."

Suddenly, I'm sick and terrified of what he's going to say when he starts again, haltingly trying to recount what happened. "I don't remember a lot else. I remember going to bed, but I didn't take my clothes off. The next thing I remember was waking up in the bed, naked from the waist down, my hands tied to the headboard, ankles tied together and anchored to the bed frame, and she'd gagged me with a piece of cloth tied behind my head. She'd pulled my shoes, jeans, and boxers off, and there was this weird look in her eyes."

"I don't understand how—"

"They ran a tox screen at the hospital. She drugged me. GHB. They said she bought it on the street, and it could've killed me. There's no telling how long I'd been out, but from that point on, time was a blur."

I feel him tremble, and I start to shake. "Please, don't tell me—"

"Yup. By that time, I was wide awake and she was mumbling something about how that weird Bobbitt woman had the right idea. Then she flashed a box cutter."

The images that roll through my mind make me sick. "Jaz, you don't have to—"

"Yes. Yes, I do. Kimmie? Please? Can I? I've never talked about this with anybody except my therapist." I feel him shudder again, and I nod against his chest. "I remember every second of the pain. She ripped and slashed like a maniac. Some of the cuts she did fast, and some of them, she buried the blade and dragged it through very slowly. She was sitting on my thighs and there was nothing I could do but squirm and scream behind the gag. I finally passed out, but not soon enough."

"Dear god, babe. How did you—"

"We lived in a condo. A neighbor heard all the weird noises and called the police. He said he'd never heard anything like it, and it scared him." He swallows hard, and then adds, "Sometimes when I'm alone, I can hear my own screams echoing in my head. The pain was so intense that it was like an out-of-body experience."

"But your daughter?"

"Took me three days to find her. Meredith had just dumped her on some friends. I didn't have my phone with me. We had a landline and an answering machine, though, and my brother went to the condo to pick up some clothes for me and found the message. Her friend's parents were trying to find us because no one had come to pick her up, and when they brought her home, nobody was there, obviously."

"What happened to Meredith?"

"The cops arrested her. She got sent up for a while. It took me over a year to heal. They didn't know if I'd ever be able ... well, they didn't know how it would turn out. I'm lucky it works at all."

My fingers swirl through his chest hair again. "Looks to me like it works pretty well."

"Surprisingly well."

I take a deep breath and sigh. "It took a lot of courage for you to tell me all of that. Thanks for trusting me. Have you been in any other relationships since then?"

"Yeah. One. But she was a few years younger. She had little kids and she and her husband decided to get back together. I think she was just looking for some stability. But I never told her all of this. I just told her it was an accident and I didn't want to talk about it. But I've had several subs refuse to scene with me. I actually dropped my membership at my last club because of it. Once word got out, none of them would even talk to me."

"Then why me?"

"You're different somehow. You're older, not as fickle. And you weren't out prowling for a partner. I just stumbled across you. It's different. You feel like ..." He stops. I wait. Finally, I can't wait anymore.

"I feel like what?"

He sighs and kisses the crown of my head. "You feel like home."

I can't stand it anymore. "You said that thing still works surprisingly well?"

"Yep."

My best coy smile and batting of the eyelashes is directed at him. "I don't believe you. Prove it."

"Is that right? Don't believe me, huh?" He rolls to his side to face me. "Want me to prove it, huh?"

"Yes. Sir." I mock. "I don't think you can really—"

He interrupts me with his lips, and the next thing I know, I'm under him and he's grinning down at me, his upper body lifted by his hands on the mattress. "First, I think I need to return the favor from earlier." He kisses me, then trails kisses down my body, taking in one nipple and then the other, letting his lips and tongue drive me wild. The downward onslaught continues, and he grips a nipple in each hand as he makes his way toward the prize and stops at my mound. "Soft, baby. And you smell so sweet. I've wanted to taste you since the very first second I saw you."

"Oh, is that right? Well, I guess you'll get your chance to ... oh my god!" I cry out as he sucks my clit between his lips, then begins the delicious torture. I'm so wound up and turned on that my brain starts to hum, and I grip the headboard, trying to hang onto whatever sanity I have left.

I hear him murmur, "Over the edge, baby," and then he triples his efforts. I let loose a cry again and he gives me a muffled, "Let go, Kimmie. Let me hear how it feels."

"Oh, god! Oh, I'm gonna come, Jaz. Please, oh, you're driving me crazy. Just crazy. I want it, please? Oh, please? Oh, Jaz, I, I, oh, god, I ..." My hips pick up the rhythm and I'm tipping out over the abyss when he stops. "What the hell?"

"You wanted to see if it really works. Now's your chance." There's the sound of ripping foil, followed by the heat of his body and, in one smooth, rapid movement, he buries his shaft in me.

Between the curves and twists in his cock and the ridges from the scars, I'm feeling things I've never felt before, things that are exquisite and frightening at the same time. Control is a fleeting thing at this moment, and I know when I come, what happens will be new and different. But I want it and, more importantly, I want it with him. His breath is hot and sweet in my ear as he whispers, "God, Kimmie, I've wanted you so much. You feel so good. Oh, fuck, baby, you feel so damn good." His thrusts are solid and then turn almost vicious, and I love the power that comes roaring through with each one. My heart's on fire, my body's in flames, and I don't care if I spontaneously combust, as long as I do it with this guy inside me. I'm meeting his thrusts with my pelvis, rocking with him, learning his rhythm, melding together as one, his body hard but his hands gentle as he grips my hips and moves against me. Jaz completes my soul. I've waited all my life for this.

And the orgasm takes me completely by surprise. The room explodes into colors behind my eyelids and I can't catch my breath, just feel the deep gnawing sensation as it powers through my body and shakes me to my core. I hear him murmur, "Oh, Kimmie, you're mine, girl. All mine," and then he grunts out his release, digging deeper into my hips with his fingers, seeking deeper refuge and finding it at the very last minute.

I've had problems in the past with the weight of a man, that claustrophobic feeling that it sends through me, but Jaz's weight is comforting. I wrap my arms around his waist and take a deep breath, pulling in that scent of our sex and the spicy aroma of his cologne. After what seems like forever, he rolls us to our sides and takes my face in his hands, and then he kisses me. My mind makes every effort to record that kiss so I can replay it later, remember what it was like to lie there with him in the darkening room, the taste of those firm, soft lips, the brush of his scruff against my chin. I breathe a soft little kiss onto his nose. "I love you, Jaz."

He kisses me again, then returns the kiss on my nose and says the words my heart is aching to hear. "I love you too, Kimmie. I'm not afraid anymore."

I feel the smile stretch slowly across my lips, and I

want to stare into those beautiful brown eyes forever. "Hold me while I sleep?"

"All night." The lamp clicks off and we're alone in the dark, me and Jaz and this sweetness that's captured our attention and changed our hearts. "All night long," he murmurs into my hair. "I'm never letting go."

~

The bed is a tangle of legs, arms, sheet, and blanket. And I can't find my pillow, which doesn't matter, because I snuggle up to Jaz and rest my head on his chest. I'm not sure he's awake, but his hand comes up and strokes my hair softly, so I'm guessing he's in at least some form of wakefulness. When his eyes finally open, I smile up at him and he smiles back. "Good morning," I manage to whisper.

He drops a feather-weight kiss on my forehead. "Yes, it is. It really, really is. And good morning to you too, morning glory."

"I suppose I should go, huh?"

He just shrugs. "Got somewhere you've got to be? It's Sunday, after all."

I just shake my head. "Nah. Well, actually, yeah. There's this hot guy, and he's great in the sack, and I want to see him and jump his bones again."

He snickers. "Is that right?"

"Yeah. That's right. You might know him. Tall-ish, kind of—"

"'Tall-ish?' Really? You just called me tall-ish?" He doesn't play incensed well.

"Yeah, you're what, five eleven?"

"I'll have you know that I'm six even."

I snort. "Oh, well then, sorry. My mistake, Jolly Green Giant!" Next thing I know, he's tickling me. "Hey! You should probably stop that! I've gotta pee!"

He throws his hands back in mock surrender. "Noooo. Don't want any of that. Go get rid of it and come back. Geez, girl. I'm not into that."

"Me neither. Be right back." I run to the bathroom and almost don't make it. I make a mental note: If I'm going to be here very often, I need some baby wipes under the sink. And a toothbrush. Shit—I don't have a toothbrush here. I call from the toilet, "Hey, do you by any chance have an extra toothbrush?"

"Um, not unless I've got an extra one that the dentist gave me at my last checkup. Check the drawer on the right-hand side of the vanity." I look. Nope. No extra toothbrush. "You know, you've had your tongue down my throat countless times in the last however many hours. If you use mine, it really won't bother me."

After staring at it for a few seconds, I just grab it, shoot some toothpaste onto it, and start brushing. I can hear Jaz laughing in the bedroom. "What's so funny?" I come strolling out of the bathroom, naked as a jaybird, and he's still laughing.

"You. Silly woman. Come here and sit down beside me." He's propped up in the bed with the pillows—apparently he found mine—and he pats the mattress beside him. I slide in and lean into him, and his arm wraps around me. I feel protected and loved with that one simple action. "I'm glad you're here."

"I'm glad I'm here too. With you."

He smiles and kisses my forehead again. "I see you're not wearing your collar. I thought you wanted to wear it."

"It kept getting hung on the neckline of my top yesterday, so I took it off. But it's in my purse."

"That's not good. If you want to wear it, I guess you need something a bit nicer, huh?"

"You gave it to me. It's plenty nice enough." Our hands are intertwined and lying on his thigh, and the sight makes my stomach do little flip-flops of joy.

"Listen, last night was great."

I nod. "Yes. It was." I'm scared to death of what he's going to say next.

"I don't want it to be the first and last time by any means."

Whew! my inner voice whispers. "Well, I should hope not!" I declare, trying to sound jauntily offended, a big, dopey smile on my face.

"Good. Kimmie, last night was just a man and a woman. Do you really want some kind of D/s relationship?"

"Do you?"

"Answer the question, please."

I huff. "Yes. I'd like that. It makes me feel ..." I'm fishing for the word.

"Secure?" he offers.

"That's it. Secure."

"Okay, then. I'd prefer it too. It makes me feel more manly," he says, using his best lumberjack voice.

"You don't need any help in that department."

"Oh, don't think so?"

I shake my head with a huge grin on my face. "Nope. You're plenty manly enough."

"And just how manly am I?" He's looking at me out the corner of his eye, and he sticks his hand down under the covers and starts to stroke himself.

Whooooo-boy, I'm liking this. "Pretty damn manly. Want me to show you how manly?"

He grins like a little kid. "Yes, please!"

"I think I can handle that." I drag the covers back and, yep, there it is, winking at me. Honest to god, I look at it and think how lucky I am that I get to see it, that he trusts me that much. I manage to flip myself over and between his legs, and I open wide and draw his semi-erectness right in. I love his musky smell, and I'm thoroughly enjoying myself, listening to him groan just a bit with each stroke.

And then I hear a voice say, "Hey, Daddy! What's going ... OH MY GOD!"

There's this scramble that I can't even describe and before it's over, I land on my ass on the floor on the far side of the bed. I hear Jaz's voice say, "Melissa! What are you doing home?"

"I just thought I'd ... were you ... oh, god, I'm leaving!"

"Melissa! Wait!" Then he says, "Kimmie? What the hell? Where are you?"

I wave an arm from the floor. "Down here. Hiding. Go. Don't worry about me. I'm fine." *No I'm not*, I think. *I'm humiliated. Oh, god, maybe the floor will open up and swallow me.* No. I couldn't be that lucky. I hear Jaz rustling around, probably for his jeans, and then the sound of his feet hitting the floor as he runs down the hallway.

I just drag the sheet off the bed and roll up in it like a burrito. What else can I do? I was sucking a man's cock when his teenage daughter walked into the room. True, she should've let him know she was in the house, but I guess she thought she'd surprise him.

Well, it worked.

My face is so red that I'm pretty sure if I put it to the floor, it would burn a hole in the hardwood. I wait for what seems like forever, and I can hear their voices occasionally. I catch the following phrases: "had no idea you were coming;" "can't believe I saw that;" "so horribly, terribly gross;" "wish you'd at least called to let me know;" "scarred for life;" and "not apologizing for what I do in my own bedroom." *Yeah, Dad, you tell her.*

I want to get up and put my clothes on, but I'm terrified the door will open and there she'll stand. Shit. I don't know what to do, so I just lie there. The mix of voices dies down and, after about twenty minutes, I hear a soft "Kimmie?"

"Down here."

I look up and Jaz's face is sticking off the side of the bed and staring down at me, and it's wearing a grin that stretches from cheek to cheek. "Hey, baby! It's okay. You can come up here."

"I don't think I can. I'm all tangled up in this sheet." In trying desperately to get myself unwound, I think I'm becoming more tightly wrapped, like one of those finger cuff things you get as a party favor.

"Here. Let me help you." Jaz plops down on the floor and helps to unwrap me, and I wait for the circulation to return to one of my arms. "I'm so sorry, honey. I had no idea she was coming home. She never said a word."

"Is everything okay?"

"Yeah, I think so." He pulls me into his lap and smooths my hair. "Her girlfriend broke up with her and she's really down. She just needs some 'dad' time." I guess he gets a good look at my face because he smiles at me. "Listen, don't be embarrassed. It's okay, really. She's cool with it."

"That's not what I heard coming down the hallway."

"I think the shock's worn off. Want to get dressed and come in here with us?"

"I really want to get dressed, climb out the bathroom window, and sneak off."

"Look, go into the bathroom, brush your hair, wash your face, pull on your clothes, and get on out there. We'll go get some breakfast somewhere and I'll take you home afterward."

"Sure." That's what I say anyway. Deep down inside, I want to die of embarrassment, but I do as he says. Before he leaves the room, I ask, "Hey, do you have a ponytail elastic?"

"Do I *look* like I'd have a ponytail elastic? I'll ask Melissa. Hey, Melissa, do you ..." he's saying as he leaves the bathroom. In a minute or two, he comes back. "Here you go. She has no hair. I have no idea why she had it, but it's your lucky day." By then, I've gotten my clothes on, gotten myself pulled together, and I brush my hair back, then wrap it with the elastic. "Pretty as a picture," he declares and kisses my forehead. "See you in a minute."

When I step into the living room, I have no idea what to expect, but Jaz is sitting on the sofa, his feet pulled up and one knee up, the other dropped to the cushion. He's got an arm draped casually over the knee that's up, and he's talking to a girl sitting in a chair adjacent to the sofa. She's late teens or early twenties, and her dark hair is short-short. Through her plaid button-front men's shirt I can see that she's wearing a compression garment to bind her breasts. Her jeans are baggy, and she's got on Chucks. There's a rainbow pendant around her neck, and my fingers go to my throat, but my collar's not there—it's still in my purse. "Kimmie! Hey, I'd like for you to meet my daughter, Melissa. Melissa, this is my friend Kimmie."

"Nice to meet you," I say as I hold out my hand.

She takes it and squeezes it comfortably. "Hi. Nice to meet you too."

"Babe, come here." Jaz is patting the sofa cushion beside him, and I sit down and wait while he drapes an arm over my shoulders protectively. "I was just telling Melissa that this is a new relationship and we're working things out."

I have no idea what to say, so I just choke out, "That's right."

"That's cool. Relationships are tricky," Melissa warns, sounding like a sage relationship expert. "They don't just happen. You have to be intentional about them."

Jaz nods. "And we're doing just that. We're being very sure to be open and truthful with each other."

She levels a look at him before she says, "So she knows—"

Before he has a chance to answer, I chime up. "Yes. And it doesn't matter a bit. Not one bit." That nets me a kiss on the temple, and I beam up at him.

She asks quietly, "So should I go?" Jaz said Melissa just broke up with her girlfriend, and I think he's right—she needs some "dad" time.

I shake my head. "No. I probably need to go anyway."

"Don't you want to go get breakfast?" Jaz looks upset, like he thinks I'm leaving and never coming back.

"Are you sure? You could probably use some time together without someone else around, don't you think?"

Now Melissa starts to plead. "Please come to breakfast with us, Kimmie. Listen, I'm sorry I surprised you like that. Please don't be embarrassed or anything."

Bless her heart, her face is so sad that I feel bad now, even though I didn't do a damn thing wrong.

I sigh. No way out. "So where are we going?"

Next thing I know, we're on the road. Melissa drives his car and he rides with me. "So what do you think of my little girl?"

"I think your little girl is quite the mature woman."

"I think you're right. I'm a lucky man in that regard."

"Only that regard?" I quip.

"Oh, and in other ways too," he answers quietly, then leans over and kisses me on the cheek as I drive. I want to stop and crawl up into his lap right there.

An hour and a half later, Jaz and I park in front of my little house. I turn off the car as Melissa pulls in behind me, and Jaz turns to me. Something in his eyes tells me he doesn't want to leave with her. "Want me to walk you up to the door?"

"Yes, please." We leave the privacy of the car and Melissa puts down her car window. I decide to be first. "Bye, Melissa! It was fun."

"Yeah, it was! Thanks, Kimmie. Hope to see you again sometime."

"Oh, I hope so too." When we reach the door, I turn, my eyes searching his face. "Did I do okay?"

His arms wrap around my waist. "Baby, you did great. I think she really likes you."

"I really like her too. She seems like a great kid."

"She is. She's had a really rough time of it since Meredith ... well, ancient history. Anyway, I'm glad you went with us. Although I was hoping that we'd ..." He nuzzles my neck and I suppress a little giggle.

"I know. There's time for that. In the meantime, why don't you work on that contract, Sir?"

"I'll do that, sub." As his hand sweeps a stray hair off my face, I draw my hands behind me and lean against the door, and he reaches around to hold my wrists together tightly. "I meant every word, angel. I love you. We're just getting started."

I breathe a silent sigh of relief. Everything's okay. "Good. Because I love you too. And I think we've got something to work with here, don't you?"

"Absolutely. Call you later?"

"I'll be upset if you don't." I lean out and give him a peck on the lips. "Get back to Miss Melissa out there. Talk to you in a bit."

"You know it. Bye." With that, he gives me a peck back and heads to the car, and I stand and watch as they drive away, everyone waving.

There's laundry to be done, and the dishwasher to unload, and the bathrooms to clean. But I spend most of the day on the sofa, napping and daydreaming about Jaz. I hate that he's just a dozen or so miles away but I can't see him. Thinking about all of it, I can't believe it's all happened so fast, but I also can't imagine not being with him. I basically just mope about all afternoon and evening, and when my phone rings at around eight, I snatch it up and answer without even looking. "Hello!"

His voice is pure silk. "Hey. Have a good day?"

"Spent most of it thinking about you. Did you and Melissa have a good visit?"

"Yes. And we were right: She needed some 'dad' time. Her girlfriend left and spread some really nasty rumors about her. She's pretty torn up about it." There's silence for a few seconds before he adds, "She needs a mom."

I nod to myself. "I'm sure she does. Every girl does, straight, gay, or bi. They all need a mom. Although I'm betting the two of you were pretty close while she was growing up."

"Always. Still are." He starts to chuckle. "She said, 'You know the only reason I thought what she was doing was gross is because I'm a lesbian.' Her way of smoothing it over, I guess. But it's still a shock when your college-age daughter comes in and finds your girlfriend sucking your dick."

I smile there, alone in my living room, and say, "Girlfriend, huh?"

"Unless you don't want to be."

I purr into the phone, "I love you, Jaz Givens."

"And I love you, Kimmie Hendricks. I guess I should hang up. I've got to put my bed back together before I can get in it for the night. You wrecked it."

I feign indignation. "I had help."

"Yes you did. Will you come over and wreck it again soon?"

"I absolutely will." I try my best sexy voice. "Or you can come here and wreck mine."

"I'd like that a lot." My eyes close and I sit and enjoy that feeling of warmth running through my veins at the thought of being in his arms. "So I'll talk to you tomorrow. Night, babe."

"Night, Sir. Kisses."

"Mwah, little girl."

Clutching the phone to my chest, I sigh and smile. If someone had told me ten years ago that I'd be in love in my fifties, I would've told them they were insane. But it's true. Ass over teacup—I'm all in.

CHAPTER SEVEN

Club? 6:oo?

I text back quickly: *See you there.*

We'll go out for a drink after if you want.

I send one of those cute little "thumbs up" things and think about his warm hands all over my skin. Little snaps like popcorn popping run up and down my spine as I imagine it.

At five 'til six, I walk into the club and sit down on a stool. As soon as my butt hits the vinyl top, he walks in. Watching him stroll across the floor toward me makes my whole body sing, and I want him desperately. Reaching for me, he gives me a little peck on the lips. "Scene with me?"

"You bet."

"Go change. I'll snare us a room when I come out." He takes my hand and leads me that direction, then turns me loose in the doorway with a smile.

Laying out the new things I've bought, I smirk to myself. Boy, is he going to be surprised, and that's what I want, so I slip on my short satin robe to make sure that happens. Dressed and ready, I wander back out to find him at the bar. His eyes are locked on my neck as he watches me come up to him, and he whispers, "Room three," and leads me away and down the hallway.

This room isn't as familiar to me as some of the others. I've only been in here maybe three times. It doesn't have a lot of equipment in it, and I wonder what he's up to. When the door closes, his first act is to take me in his arms and kiss me. "Wow. Do all Doms do this with their subs?" I ask with a giggle.

"Only the good ones. Come over here and sit down." Before I do, I untie and drop the robe on the floor, and he's treated to a view of my new fuchsia shelf bra and crotchless panties. His eyebrows shoot up in delight and a huge grin spreads across his face. "Well, sub, thank you for that view. It's spectacular. Guess there's no need to book a sightseeing tour of Europe—I like the sights here a lot better!" In a low, sexy growl, he adds, "After all, these are totally interactive." Once we're perched on the edge of the bed, he takes both my hands in his. "The contract. Do you want to see it?"

I don't even have to think about it—I'd already decided. "Yes. I do."

"Okay then. I made up one that's pretty generic. We can add or delete before the final one is drafted. See what you think." He reaches in his gig bag and hands me the folded paper.

He's right—it is pretty generic. It's mostly who's in charge and how, meaning the knowledge of and say in what I eat, where I go, what I do. There's an agreement over sharing of the housework; I like that. There's a section governing disagreements, as in being respectful, listening to each other's opinions, working toward compromise, and what we'll do if no compromise can be reached. Simple and clear. Problem solved. In thinking about it, I think it might be nice to not have that much responsibility for a change.

This section makes me feel comfortable about the whole thing:

Upon the decision to cohabitate, the Dominant will make every effort to maintain an account for the submissive which includes any monies she brings into the contract, as well as regular contributions to increase the amount. This account will be surrendered to the submissive at such time that the contract is broken.

So I'll be taken care of if he breaks the contract. I like that. And then I see a section that takes my breath away.

Upon being presented with the Dominant's collar, the submissive will wear the collar at all times except when not practical (showering, heavy manual labor, hair cutting/coloring, etc.) or at the discretion of the Dominant. Return of the collar by the submissive will be perceived as a breaking of the contract, rendering all agreements null and void. Requesting the collar's return shall signify a breaking of the contract by the Dominant, and the submissive's services are no longer required.

He's basically negotiating a marriage. Stopping myself

isn't an option when I realize what he's outlined. "So are we going to live together?"

Jaz just shrugs. "I don't know. We haven't gotten that far. Those sections are so that if we do, we'll both be protected. Do you think that's adequate?"

"It's more than adequate. I can see you put a lot of thought into this."

A sweet smile crosses his face. "I put a lot of thought into this because it's really important to me."

"Thanks." I fold it and hand it back. "I don't see anything that needs to be changed. I guess it's just a matter of you deciding if and when you want this to take place."

"When *we* want this to take place. Sounds good to me. I'll make up clean copies for signing so that both of us have one." With that, he stuffs the contract back in his bag, then returns his attention to me. "Now, as in the contract, show me your presentation pose and we'll work out the kinks. Oh. I think I just made a joke," he snorts. I giggle and do as he instructed before, kneeling, leaning back, and grasping my ankles with my hands. He instructs me further, telling me that I can rest my weight on my hands and ankles as I lean back. "Let's be honest here. Neither of us is twenty-five anymore. If that's not comfortable for you, it can be modified until it is. The only kind of discomfort I want to cause you is the type you want. So if something hurts unnecessarily, you need to say so."

"Yes, Sir." I can't help it—I giggle again.

"What?"

"I guess it's official." Seeing his brow furrow in puzzlement, I offer, "You're my Sir."

His eyes close and the corners of his mouth turn up

almost imperceptibly. "I guess I am. I hope you don't live to regret that."

"I doubt that I will. Is this good, Sir?" I ask when I've got the presentation to a point where I think I can tolerate it for a long period of time.

"Very good. You look beautiful. Eyes downward. Now, I've got to get everything else ready. I'll only be a couple of minutes." He heads back to the bed and tinkers around with some things laid out there. I'm not sure what all of those things are, but I do sneak a peek to see a bundle of rope and something with a long electrical cord. I have no idea what he's planning, but honestly, I'm not afraid. I trust Jaz. Everything he's done with me has felt so right that the idea of something new is exciting, not frightening. Being patient and waiting is hard when I know he's going to blow my mind.

When he comes back to me, he has rope. "Stand up and everything off." And I spent some money on this getup too. Oh, well—who cares, right? Once I've complied, he turns me with my back to him. He reaches around me and begins the process of tying around my torso in various patterns, isolating each breast, securing me in every direction. Then I realize: For all intents and purposes, he's made a sling out of rope, a sort of on-the-body hammock. I start to guess what he's going to do.

And I would be right. There are already ropes with hooks hanging from eye bolts in the ceiling, tied off on a cleat on the wall. Unwinding the rope from the cleat and pulling it down, he passes two of the hooks, large chrome S-hooks, through his rope creation and hooks them into something at my shoulders. The other two are hooked to something at my hips. He tightens the ropes and then says, "Kimmie, trust me. I won't let you fall. Do you understand?"

"Yes, Sir. I believe you."

"Good. Here we go." I watch as he ties off the ropes at my shoulders, then begins to tighten the ones on my hips. In a matter of seconds, my feet rise off the floor. As soon as my hips are at the level he wants them, he begins to lower my shoulders. I'm trying to figure out what he's going to do next when he pulls my arms behind me and ties them. Curiosity about what will be done for my legs is satisfied when he pulls one up and secures it with rope to the suspension rope coming off that hip. He goes to the other side and does the same, and suddenly, I realize I'm trussed up like a hog on a spit. There I hang, swaying gently like a bird feeder in the breeze. And I'm pretty sure this is when the fun begins.

I couldn't have been more right once again. Out of nowhere, a black scarf appears and wraps around my head, covering my eyes. When he's satisfied that I can't see, I hear him doodling around with something. The minute he turns it on, I hear it crackle to life.

But when it touches me, I'm completely unprepared. The electrical charge, like a light switch on a cold winter evening, snaps my skin alive and makes me shriek. "Hush. Keep silent." It makes contact again, and it takes everything in my being to keep from screaming. "Safeword?"

I don't have to think about it. Whatever he's planned for me, I want to experience it. "No, Sir."

"Very good." As he's speaking, Jaz draws a hand over every spot he's zapped, calming the nerve endings as he goes. It's then that it occurs to me: He has very soft, warm hands. It's like being calmly and quietly stroked into oblivion, and I remember what he told me before with the Wartenberg. As he starts again, I try hard to concentrate only on the point where the wand makes contact. Now, instead of just zapping random spots, he begins to trail the wand over my skin, gently wandering about on my body, leaving behind a tingling path over which he runs those hands. Before I realize it, I'm lost in the sensations, the electricity lighting up my nerve endings until my skin's hypersensitive, followed by the soothing warmth of his palm. Just tingle, smooth, tingle, smooth, and a cadence develops. My breathing has started to fall into rhythm with his movements, and I feel myself anticipating the next touch of his fingertips, longing for it.

Before I know it, I'm gone. My mind is somewhere else, waiting for the next touch, aching for it, and then silently rejoicing as it materializes. Over and over he completes the dance between electricity and hands until I thank the universe for the colors rippling through my mind and the sound of wind chimes inside my head. I'm so wrapped up in it all that I barely notice when the strokes become slower and farther apart, and I just let myself go with it. When the wand goes silent, I'm sad until I feel his hands touching me everywhere, my cheeks, my chin, my shoulders, my breasts as he pulls downward to my nipples, down my belly and my back simultaneously, drawing big circles on my ass, then down both legs, fronts and backs. I want to cry out, *God—don't stop!*

And then he draws his hands up the insides of my legs until he comes to the crease between legs and labia, and I shiver all over with arousal. I had no idea I was aroused—I was concentrating so hard on the sensations I was experiencing that I hadn't noticed. I wiggle a little and he murmurs, "Easy, baby. I'm taking care of you. Tell me what you want. Are you ready for me?"

I try to answer but I can't make my mouth move. I manage an "Uh-huh."

"Very good. You need this. You'll be satisfied when I'm finished with you, and so will I. You want to please me, don't you?"

I force out another, "Uh-huh." Everything's so foggy that I'm having trouble putting it all together, and I feel like I'm floating—then I realize I *am* floating in those bindings.

"Good girl. You're about to be rewarded. And so am I." I feel his fingers slide into my pussy and start to stroke, a fast and furious stroking. Before I know what's happening, I feel a warm gush and my whole body stiffens. A wildness comes over me and I just want more, want to feel him inside me, want to come over and over. If I could speak, I'd beg, but all I can do is moan and whine. God, I want his length in me, to feel him fill me and pound into me. Squirming in my bonds, I want desperately to press back against him, but I'm neutralized and there's no way for me to propel myself. I have to trust him to do that.

And he does. With his hands turned palms up to grip my thighs, Jaz steps up between my legs. I feel the head of his cock pressing into my slit, and in one smooth, gentle move, he's buried inside me. My every thought is directed at that one place where he connects with me like no one else, so erotic and deliciously painful in the first three seconds, and so satisfying and thrilling in the next. His hands grip my thighs, then slide up to my hips and pull me back against him. In the next movement, I'm sent forward until just his tip is left in me, and then pulled back again. My hands ache to touch him, but they're bound tight. I'm completely at his mercy, and knowing that turns me on in ways I've never been turned on. He can do whatever he likes to me and I'll take it. The sound of a slap registers a split second before I feel it on my ass, my brain dopey and slow, and I moan, not from pain, but from sheer want.

Jaz Givens is commanding my body. And he's stealing my heart. Any reservations I might've had about him up to that point just fly away with the swing of my body in the ropes. My brain struggles to hear the words he's murmuring to me. "Oh, yeah, Kimmie. God baby, I wanna fuck you all night. Do you know how beautiful you are? Do you know how hard I am for you? Kimmie, oh god, Kimmie. I want you, babe. I want you always."

It all rolls over me like thunder in the night, and all I can manage is a strangled, "Come? Come? Please? Pleeeeeease?"

"Not yet, babe, not yet. God no, hang on." And he stops, buried in me up to his balls. I want to scream, *What are you doing? Why are you stopping?* and then it becomes clear when his fingers find my clit. He leans over my back as he strokes, kissing here and there while his fingers work magic, drawing sweet, tantalizing little strokes around and around to make me shiver and moan, then backing off just enough to give me some relief before starting again. He knows exactly how to capitalize on my sensitivity, and every time he starts again, I'm more certain that the intensity will be my death. I'm working at waiting, I really am, but my body is giving way rapidly and I know it won't be long before I can't hold back anymore. Begging is what I want to do more than anything, but I can't; I can hear myself mumbling, my mouth unable to form words, trying so hard to plead with him and wishing he could read my mind. Before another thought comes, he whispers, "Okay, Kimmie, anytime you're ready."

My body convulses and I bounce on the ropes as the orgasm swallows me like a black hole. I hear myself scream, "JEEEZUUUUUUSSSS," the first semi-intelligible thing I've said in twenty minutes. "Oh, please, oh, please, oh, please," I manage to pant as he just keeps stroking, and a low growl breaks from his throat.

"That's it, baby. Get it all out." When he finally stops, he growls, "I'm gonna fuck you like you've never been fucked before. If you want me like I want you, you're on fire right now." Drawing back, he plows into me.

Like an alien voice from a sci-fi movie, from my mouth comes, "OhhhhhHHHHH GAWD!" and I give in to the friction of his shaft. I can't remember any other man ever making me feel this way, wanton and needy, begging pathetically for more of his cock. Sweet lord, he's all the man I can handle and then some.

As he strokes into me, I hear him start to groan, in rhythm with his strokes, "You. Are. Mine. All. Mine. Kimmie, you're so fucking tight and wet, and I'm so fucking hard. Damn, baby. I know you can feel it. You can feel how much I want you. Fuck, fuck, fuck. I'm gonna fuck you until neither of us can walk. Oh god, oh god, oh god, I'm, I'm ... OH YEAH!" Even through his condom, I can feel the heat of his cum, all the while wishing I could know what it's like to have it inside me, warm and wet and comforting. He's enjoying me, wanting me, letting me want him and giving me what only he can give. This is bliss, and I float along on it as surely as I float on these ropes. It's magical, being here with him in this moment, sharing our bodies and our hearts and our souls. Then he stills, and the next words he speaks freeze the moment for me forever.

"You're mine. I don't want another woman—ever. Oh, Kimmie, please ..." His hands engulf my bound ones, slide up my arms, and tangle in my hair, and he pulls my head back and whispers, "What did I do to deserve you?"

All I remember from that point on is the sensation of my body lowering and the ropes loosening. When I open my eyes, his are looking straight into them and he smiles. I try to move my arms and, when I understand that I can, I put a palm on his cheek. Reaching for it, he pulls it away from his face with his own hand, turns it, and kisses my palm. Every sweet minute from before is in his voice when he says, "Hi, beautiful. Welcome back."

"Was I good?"

He kisses my forehead, a light little kiss that sends shivers up my spine. "You were okay."

I'm still trying to make sense out of everything. "What did I need to do to be better? I only wanted to please you. I want you to be happy, Jaz, really." Without warning, I start to cry and I feel like a complete idiot.

Thank god, he blurts out, "Baby, baby! I was just joking! I guess I shouldn't make jokes when you're just drifting back from the zone."

I sniffle hard. "No. You should not."

"I'm sorry." He kisses my forehead again, this time more purposefully, and his lips linger a bit longer. When he pulls back, he smiles. "You were perfect. No, perfect plus. We're very, very good together. You know that, right?" I nod and start to cry again. "Oh, honey, don't cry! It's okay. It was awesome—*you* were awesome. Just rest, okay? We'll go in a little bit."

"Jaz?"

"Yes, darling girl?"

I start to sob again. "I want to sign the contract."

And I cry even harder when he answers me. "Know what?" I shake my head and peer up at him in time to see his eyes mist over. "I do too."

～

"You look like you're feeling well," I tell Candy when she comes into the workshop on Tuesday.

"I am. For being preggers, I feel pretty good. But it's getting harder and harder to get up from kneeling in presentation pose."

I've worked to try to get a good fit for her corset and I finally came up with exactly the right thing. She looks adorable, even though it's not a traditional kind of thing. "So how is Mr. Augustino?"

"He's well. And we're getting married!"

"Really? You finally said yes? Congratulations! So when are you going to do this?"

A wistful look crosses her face. "Next Wednesday. It's his anniversary."

"Anniversary?"

"Yeah. His and his late wife's. He says it will honor their relationship."

I'm sort of appalled, I guess you'd say. "*Their* relationship? This is about the two of you."

"Oh, I know. But if that makes him happy, I'm okay with it. She's dead. It's not like she's going to be in attendance or try to break us up or anything."

Hey, you know, if she's okay with it, who am I to say? "So are you planning to wear the corset to the wedding?"

"Oh, no! I'm wearing white!" she smiles with obvious pride.

Good lord. I don't know what to say to that. "Okay, then, let's see if we can get this thing finished up for you." I start working around her. "Are you excited about the baby?"

"I sure am! I never thought I'd have children. You know, after everything." I guess I look pretty puzzled because she adds, "You know, with all the abortions and everything."

Uh-oh. This is none of my business. "I see."

"I've had six or seven." Six or seven? She's not even sure how many. Holy shit! Since I'm determined not to ask, I'm glad when she offers. "I was an adult film star. And I did a lot of bareback. I tried to time it when I wasn't ovulating, but to do that *and* miss out on filming when I was having my period didn't always work. So I got pregnant several times."

"But weren't you on the pill?"

"No! I'm a good Catholic girl!"

Well, now, that's the beatingest damn thing I've ever heard. Porn and abortions, but no birth control. I'm trying to figure out the logic and I realize—it's pointless. There isn't any. It's not about religion. It's just, well, quirky, and it can't be figured out. So I just manage, "Oh, well, of course. No birth control. That would be so wrong."

"I know, right? So I just had them removed." She talks like it's a surgical procedure, which I suppose it is. "And my doctor told me after the fifth one that I'd probably never be able to get pregnant. But I did. That guy at the club who bred me has like eight or nine kids, so we knew he could get the job done." And I realize: She's talking about Blaze. He and his sub have a houseful. At least two of them belong to other subs who didn't want them once he got them pregnant, and he and his sub—she's actually his wife as well—are raising them as theirs. It's a crazy mess that, oddly, seems to work for them.

About this time, I think to ask, "Boy or girl?"

"At my last ultrasound, they said it was a girl. But sometimes they're wrong, you know." A sad look crosses her face. "He really wanted a boy."

"Oh, I'm sure he'll be fine with it, er, her, as long as she's healthy."

"I hope so. But he already has a daughter."

"Oh? How old is she?"

She laughs. "She's forty-six."

I should've seen that coming. His daughter is about twenty years older than the girl he's getting ready to marry. Holy shit. I hope the old bastard takes his vitamins, that's all I've got to say.

As she's leaving, Candy smiles at me and asks, "Can I hug you?" I open my arms and she walks right into them, wrapping hers around my neck. "Thank you, Kimberly."

"For what?"

"For letting me talk. I don't have anyone my age to talk to." She hugs me really tight and it's hard to breathe. "I know you're older than me, but you're nice to talk to."

In an instant, I'm sorry for this girl. She's barely in her twenties and getting ready to marry a man in his seventies. Yes, he's filthy rich and yes, he's good to her, but she's got to be horribly lonely. I'm glad I can lend her an ear while she's here. The whole situation is strange, but she's a good person. "Anytime, Candy."

"Thanks. Bye. Next time I'll bring a copy of my ultrasound so you can see her!"

"I'd love that. See you soon!" As I'm speaking, she

closes the door and disappears. I pick up my phone and send a quick text: *Busy? I miss your voice.*

My phone rings almost instantly. "I miss your voice too. You okay?"

I sigh as I drop into my chair. "Yeah. I just had a client who, well, she's having a baby with her Dom."

"Oh yeah?"

"Yeah. And she's barely in her twenties and he's in his seventies."

I hear him sigh too. "Well, nice to know he's still 'got it.'"

"Nope. Had her bred by a guy at the club."

"No shit?"

"No shit."

"Wow." He's quiet for a few seconds, then he asks, "So do you want more kids?"

"God no! I'm too old."

"You are not—"

"Yes. I am. I had my last period five years ago. And my son is grown. So no. If that's something you really wanted, I wish you'd—"

"God no!" He starts to laugh. "I was terrified you'd say yes just a minute ago! I've got Melissa. She's all I need. And I'm hoping someday she'll have a partner who wants a child and I'll have a grandchild. Or two. And hopefully that's a few years down the road, seeing as how she's not in a relationship now."

"She doing okay?"

He sighs again. "Yeah, I guess. She has no idea why Adelaide is being such a bitch. She thinks Addie's involved with another girl and she's being bitchy to try to deflect from what she's doing. I told her she just needs to get out of a poisonous relationship."

"Poor girl." I'm picking up and cleaning up from the day's work as we talk. "So what are you doing for the rest of the day?"

"I'm driving back from St. Louis. I should be in by seven. Want to come over?"

I think for a second. "Why don't you come to my place? I can start cooking and by the time you get there, it'll be done and waiting. I'll try to have it ready by seven. If you're late, it'll keep; if you're early, you can wait!"

I love the sound of his laughter. "Works for me! Want me to bring anything?"

"Your gorgeous smile." I can see it now, and I'm almost giddy thinking about it.

"Got it with me. I'll see you around seven. Can't wait."

"Me neither. Jaz?"

"Yeah, babe?"

"I love you."

I can hear the smile in his voice when he says, "I love you too, Kimmie. See you in a bit."

"Be careful!" I yell into the phone.

"Okay! Okay! I will! Bye, babe." With that, he's gone.

I dance around the workshop, anticipation coursing through me, rising like sap in a maple and just as sweet. Everything in me wants everything about him. It really seems that, for the first time since Phil left, I have a chance to have a happy future. And I want it with Jaz. He's everything I've ever wanted in a man, and he wants me too. That makes me more than happy.

That makes me ecstatic.

CHAPTER EIGHT

There's a rap at the door, and I turn the sauce down before I head that way. I pull it open to find him standing there, bottle of wine in one hand and a huge bouquet of roses and carnations in the other. Ah—my old-fashioned fantasy realized! I take both out of his hands, set them on the table by the door, and kiss him before I ever close it. "Wow. I like that," he grins.

"Yeah. Me too. And thanks. Let me put these in water." Without me having to ask, he follows me to the kitchen.

"I just wanted to bring you something. The last few days have been busy and we haven't gotten to see each other," he says as he stands behind me, his arms wrapped around my waist, and he kisses me on the side of my neck. I feel the hair at my nape rise. "I've missed you, Kimmie."

"I've missed you too." I get the flowers into the vase and spin toward him. When I do, he pins me against the edge of the countertop. "God, Jaz, I want you," I manage to mumble into his mouth as he kisses me.

"I want you too. But we're not wasting this food. Let's

eat first. I'm sure we can work something out afterward." He pulls me away from the cabinets, only to smack my ass hard with his open hand. "I'm going to warm that cute little backside up tonight."

"Promises, promises!" I giggle. "Okay, dinner first. Then don't make me wait."

"Not on your life, beautiful," he whispers into my mouth and then kisses me again. There are no sweeter lips on earth. But he interrupts the kiss with, "What's that smell?"

"Oh shit! Oh shit, oh shit, oh shit," I squeal. When I pull the roasted potatoes out of the oven, I find it was just the butter in the bottom that was getting a little hot—the potatoes are perfect. "Oh, god. I thought I'd ruined them."

"Look pretty damn good to me. Can I help you with anything?"

"Sure. Open the bottle, please?" I point to the wine bottle sitting on the counter, the one he brought in. "Corkscrew's in the drawer under it."

"So, Kimmie, I've been thinking." I hear him doodling with the corkscrew and then that *paahhhh* sound it makes when he pops the cork out. "You asked me if we were going to live together."

The sound I hear in my ears is my own blood whooshing through my veins, and my heart starts to slam so hard against my ribcage that I'm afraid it'll break loose and skitter across the floor. "Yeah?" I manage, breathless and weak.

"So maybe we should consider that. I mean, if we were in the same house, we would've seen each other every night instead of going several nights without. Seeing each other, I mean. Not just sex. I mean just spending time together. You know what I'm talking about, right?"

I nod, trying to make words form. "Uh-huh." I swallow a couple of times and take a deep breath. "I mean, yes, Sir. I know what you mean. And you're right. We would've seen each other every night that way."

I hear the *glug-glug-glug* of liquid pouring from a bottle and a glass appears in front of me. "So let's think about what that would mean, if we'd want to do that, how we'd do it. If you want to, I mean."

I nod again. "I want to."

"Okay. Sounds good." He leans against the countertop right beside me, turned toward me while I cook. "By the way, Melissa called me today."

"Yeah?"

"Adelaide's pregnant."

My eyebrows shoot up. "Oh, is that right?"

"Yeah. That's what this was all about. She's pregnant and wants to marry the guy. Melissa told her that it was fine, but she had a lot of people she needed to confess to about the lies she told. I don't know if that'll happen, but at least the mystery's been unraveled. And Melissa had nothing to do with any of it. She's still heartbroken, but now she knows she had no part in the breakup of the relationship."

"Poor girl. When will she get to come home again?"

"Probably not for a couple of weeks. That's quite a trip from there to here."

"Sure is. I'm glad you weren't gone out of town the weekend she showed up."

"Me too. But I don't think she'll surprise me again," he says with a wicked grin that makes me laugh.

"So how's work?"

He takes a sip of wine before he answers, and his face

goes flat. "It's work. It's not as good as my last job, but it's a job."

I hate the look on his face. "What did you do at your last job?"

"Basically the same thing, only just one side of it. I found the plants that used the products we manufactured, and I coordinated with their buyers to develop new ones so they had what they needed, something made specifically for them that totally covered their requirements." Before I get a chance to ask any more, he adds, "One year my bonus was over two hundred thousand dollars."

"Oh my god!" That's more money than I've ever seen. "That's just, well, I don't know what to say."

"Say goodbye, because it's gone. They let three of us go, and then shut down. Now I do the same job, plus I have to go to the damn factories to see what they do with the parts, and then coordinate with the engineers to find ways to make them better. I'm doing twice the work. I'm getting half the pay. And no bonuses—none. I was excited when Melissa got accepted to Dartmouth. These days I'll just be glad when she's done and I'm hoping I have a little savings left." Now he's not looking at me as he speaks, just staring out into space.

"But the cost of living is cheaper here, right?" I offer.

"Yes. That's true. But it's still hard to take." He takes another swig of wine and looks over at me. "You know, guys identify themselves by what they do. When a woman's asked, 'What do you do?' she typically says, 'Oh, I'm a mom and I'm married to so-and-so.' But a man? He says, 'I'm a chemical engineer' or 'I'm a crane operator' or something like that. He identifies himself by his job. And when we lose that job? It's emasculating." Now he's staring back down into his glass, swirling the wine, watching it coat the inside of the bowl.

I just put my spoon down, take the glass out of his hand, set it on the countertop, and wrap my arms around his waist. "I don't identify you by your job. I identify you by *you*. And you're a helluva guy, Jasper Andrew Givens." After thinking for a few seconds, I look up into his face. "So if you could do anything in the world that you'd like to do, what would it be?"

"The truth?" I nod at him. "I'd be a farmer. I'd love to plow and plant and cultivate. I'd love to have cows and pigs and a horse or two." Now I'm shocked, and I guess I look it, because he shoots down my unasked question with, "My grandparents had a farm in Oklahoma. I loved spending time there, feeding the chickens, going with my grandpa to drive the cows up to the feed lot. I loved it all. I loved the dust when the combine was running in the soybeans in the fall. I begged my parents to let me live there, but they wouldn't. They loved southern California. But I always wanted to go there, to live there."

"I assume they've passed?"

"Oh, yeah. Many years back."

"And what happened to the farm?"

"It's still in the family. The house is really run down and I'm guessing the fields are in bad shape. Probably overgrown with weeds and shrubs. But I remember what it looked like when I was a child, and it was a magical place, Kimmie. The creek. The big trees. The tire swing hanging from the big oak out in front of the barn. Magical." There's a far-away look in his eyes that steals my breath because I can tell it hurts him to talk about it. Then his face meets mine, and it's almost like a light has flickered out in his soul. "But I grew up, got a business degree, got a good job, married the woman of my dreams, and watched as it all went to hell in a handbasket. My dreams, up in smoke." He kisses my forehead and my lips reach to his for something stronger. Instead, he gives me a little peck and then says, "So let's eat this wonderful meal you've cooked. It smells delicious!"

"I hope it is." I busy myself with getting everything on the table while he pours more wine and sets our places with the things I've left stacked up. I've made pork chops cooked in wine and shallots, roasted potatoes, and steamed asparagus with my signature Hollandaise sauce, and I let him serve me again. We eat and laugh and talk, and a firm plan entrenches itself in my mind.

Jaz Givens wants to be a farmer. And I still have a few tricks up my sleeve. I'll just play along and see what happens but, if I'm right, I may be able to make that dream come true.

With dinner cleaned up, we sit in the den and talk until late. I didn't realize we had so many things to talk about, but we do. We talk about religious theories and the global market and the defunct space program—we just talk and talk and talk. At eleven, I say, "Oh, god! It's late. Are you staying or going?"

"I'd like to stay."

"Good! I didn't want you to go!" I giggle. We've been sitting there on the sofa, my legs draped across his lap, and he's rubbed my feet practically the whole time. His shoes lie beside the sofa, one on its side. Even though the uppers look almost brand new, the soles are very worn, and a pain shoots through my chest. Looks can be so deceiving, and the leathers I made for him must've been quite a luxury. Then I realize: He wanted to meet me. That's what the leathers were about. That was Michael, telling him about me. It was his way of having an excuse to meet me. That's one very expensive dating service, but it worked. I smile to myself, thinking of how much he sacrificed to order those leathers. Probably dipped into his savings. He should've just introduced himself! But I probably would've just ignored him.

Look what I would've missed. Oh, god, I look at him and my heart just melts. We're so good together, and I can't wait to see where this goes, to know what it's like to be with this man all the time. Without thinking, I ask, "So what about that contract?" I instantly wish I'd kept my mouth shut in case he changed his mind.

He places a palm on my cheek. "I'm ready to sign anytime. What about you?"

"Yes. Anytime."

"I'll arrange some kind of special celebration. I think we owe ourselves and each other that. What do you think?"

"I think I love it."

"I love you."

I giggle again. "I love you too."

His hand wanders up under the front of my top and when his fingers pinch my nipple, I squirm. That gets my top pulled right off, and my bra follows. He pulls out his belt and I wonder what he's going to do with it, but I don't have to wonder for long. Making a figure eight out of it, he wraps it around my wrists behind my back and tightens it, and a throbbing sets up in my clit. I just sit and wait while he pulls his slacks down, followed by his boxer briefs, and the hard, sexy object of my affection greets me with a heartbeat-induced wave. "Stand up, sub." When I'm standing, he stands too, slips his pants and briefs completely off, then strips mine off so I'm bare. He levels a smoky gaze at me. "Present, sub." I kneel without the benefit of my hands, and he helps me with a hand under my elbow. Then he steps directly in front of me. "You'll suck me until I come. I'll be taking it deep, so be warned. I expect complete compliance." He steps up until his manhood is resting against my lips. "Open wide, sub. Prepare to please me." My mouth drops open and in a long-practiced move, he buries his cock in my throat.

It takes me about five strokes to adjust and then I'm good. I'm concentrating on keeping up some suction as he uses my mouth and throat, his hands wrapped tight in my hair, and he moans every so often as he strokes into me. He smells of soap, his cologne, and the musk that defines a man, a heady blend that hardens my nipples and makes my pussy weep. The faint taste of pre-cum sets my heart racing, and I double down my sucking efforts, longing for that moment when my mouth is flooded and I'm overcome by the taste of his desire. And I don't have long to wait; I feel him rise up onto his toes, his back arching, and he pours into me with a strangled gasp of, "Fuck, Kimmie!" I'm waiting to breathe with his hardness lodged tight in my throat as he grinds in to wring out the last few drops, and I draw in a ragged breath when he moves back, then start trying to swallow it as fast as I can.

His hands run down my cheeks and his fingers curve under my chin as I lick him, lap at him, make every effort to capture every drop. Pulling my chin up to look down in my face, he smiles at me as I lick my lips. "Very good, baby. So good. Stand up." He helps me up with hands under my elbows again, then kisses me, his own hands wrapping around my bound wrists behind my back. When he pulls back, he whispers, "Your turn."

I'm extremely glad I cleaned off the dining room table

when we were finished eating, because he pushes me back through the doorway and against its edge, then lifts me and sits me on it. Spreading my legs wide, he pulls up a chair, sits in it in front of me, and buries his face in my slit. A million things run through my mind: The roughness of his tongue; the heat of his breath; the sounds of the wind chimes on the back porch; the smell of the leather in my workshop; and the vision of a young boy with brown hair and brown eyes, running through a field of winter wheat, his corduroy jacket missing a button and his eyes dancing in the sunlight. Quick as a wink, my body shudders and I come with my hips pumping toward his face. The sound of his laughter from between my legs brings me back into the room, and he stands and leans over to look into my face. All he manages to choke out is, "Kimmie, I—"

"Please, Sir, fuck me, please? Oh, god, I need you. Please, Sir ..."

He just scoops me up and heads down the hallway to the bedroom. Once there, he plunks me down unceremoniously on the bed and crawls up with me, then rolls me to my face. "Draw your knees up under you to lift your ass." As I do, I hear the familiar sound of ripping foil, followed by, "God, girl, you're so fucking wet. I want to pound an orgasm right out of you. You're going to come for me, and you'll do it fast." My face is jammed into the mattress, my collarbone resting on it, and he grips my hips and forces his dick straight into my wetness. When I shriek a little, he slaps my ass with a hot palm and growls, "You want it, don't you, sub? Say it."

"Yes, Sir! Please fuck me, Sir! Oh, god, pleeeeeeease ..." The heat of my desire is almost more than I can stand, and there's an ache deep inside my pelvis that feels like a roaring forest fire.

"That's it, beautiful." His hands grip my wrists to hold me just as he wants me, and he's slamming into me, hissing and groaning as his hardness stabs into me over and over, occasionally drawing back to slap my ass again, hard. That insistent, expanding gnawing deep inside me is coming to the surface faster than I ever thought possible, and I'm waiting for him to tell me it's okay, that I can let go, when he says, "Not yet, sub. Stay with me."

I start to wail. I can't help it. His shaft grates over my G-spot until I'm writhing, my arms still held firm by his hands, and I'm pleading for release. I need it. I have to have it. It's eating me alive. And then I hear the magic words.

"Let go, sub. Come for me. Now!"

I swear, everything turns black. The things I'm feeling don't consist of anything I have words for, and I don't know how long I can take it. I feel that sensation again, the warm gush down my legs, and a faint humming sets up in my ears. In what has to be only seconds, but seems like an hour, I feel Jaz's fingers dig into my hips as he pounds into me and releases with a shout of, "FUCK, KIMMIE! God damn, girl, you're so fucking amazing!" There's the sensation of something falling beside me, and then I topple over, but I don't care. Everything's a jumble for me, and my body is still jerking, my hips still bucking and pumping. I want more; I need more.

Apparently I drift off, and when I finally open my eyes, I'm lying in the bed with my hands unrestrained. My face is damp and my hair is stuck to it, and I'm lying in a huge wet spot. Flailing around, I find Jaz, and he's still panting and just as fucked up as I am. Everything's still a blur and I'm trying to sort it all out. And that's when it happens.

There's a flash of lightning and a clap of thunder, and the sound of rain pouring down fills the whole house. As the rumble of the thunder fades, I feel it—it's like the very air in the room ripples and expands, and the gasp that comes from his lips matches mine. Strong arms drag me across the bed and grip me tight, and I squirm until I'm turned to face him. With one hand tangled in my hair, he clutches me so tightly that I can barely breathe and kisses me so hard he'll bruise my lips, I'm sure. But I find myself clinging to him too, kissing him back, trying to draw him into me so he can't get away. When he finally presses me back and looks down into my face, his eyes are so dark and serious that even the next lightning strike can't illuminate them.

Something has happened between us, something so profound that I can't explain it, and I know he feels it too. His body and my body—I don't think I can tell where one ends and the other begins. It's exciting and comfortable at the same time, and I don't ever want to leave this room and not have his hands on my skin. He whispers hoarsely, "Touch my face, Kimmie. I want to feel your fingertips. God, I love you, girl. I can't turn loose. I have to have you with me. Please, god, Kimmie." He sounds so desperate and afraid when he whispers, "Please love me. Don't leave." When I start to cry, I hear him say, "Oh, god, please ..."

"I'm not going anywhere. I don't belong anywhere else, just here with you. If everyone else in the whole world slipped away and it was just you and me, that would be fine. As long as I have you, it's all okay. Always. I don't care about the past or anything in it, just you and me and here and now." My nose is running and I'm choking and I don't care. I don't care about anything but this man and his arms around me. This is my whole world. This is all that matters. "Just hold me. Please, just hold me tight." Thunder shakes the house again, and I sob in his arms. For the first time in a long time, I feel safe and loved. Someone loves me. Jaz Givens loves me. And I love him.

I fall asleep with him whispering, "Oh, Kimmie, oh, Kimmie, oh, Kimmie," into my hair, warm and sated and overwhelmed with joy. Our connection is complete. It's total. It's deep and firm and never-ending. I'll be whatever he wants me to be, do whatever he wants me to do, go wherever he wants me to go. I belong to Jasper Givens. And I know he belongs to me.

There's rustling in my little bedroom, and I squint into the lamp light. "What are you doing?"

"I have to go to work. I don't want to, but I have to. Promise me something." He's scrambling around to get into his clothes. I look at the clock—it's five thirty in the morning.

"Okay. Whatever you want. What?"

"I know we talked about going to the club and signing the contract, but promise me we'll talk this evening instead. I don't know what happened between us last night, but whatever it was, it was important, too important to ignore." He runs his fingers through his hair to straighten it out, then takes both my hands. My sleepy eyes are fighting to find his and when I do, they're so full of love that it takes my breath away. One of his hands leaves mine and comes up to brush my hair away from my face. "I love you, Kimmie. I've never loved a woman this way. We need to figure out what's next, but this, whatever this is that we're growing, it's consuming us both and I want it to. I want it to grow and bind us together."

With a sleepy smile, I nod. "I want it too."

"Okay then. I'll see you this evening. Me here or you there?"

I look around at my bedroom. "You here. I want you back here. In this room with me, your arms around me."

He leans down and kisses my forehead. "You've got it, babe. Got clients today?"

I chuckle. "Oddly, no. No one's on the schedule."

His lips meet mine, and then he pulls back and smiles. "Then stay in bed. Rest. I wish I could, but I've got a damn meeting. I've got to go home and shower and change before I go in. But I want to be here with you."

"And I want to be here with you, Sir," I whisper back and stroke his cheek with my finger.

"Good. I'll bring something to eat so we don't have to waste time cooking, okay?" I nod. "So I'll see you as soon as I can get back here. Love you, baby." He rises and heads to the door, then turns and looks back at me.

"I love you too, Sir."

"Go back to sleep." With that, he closes the door and I'm alone.

The bed is still warm where his perfect body had been, and I scoot into the warm spot and wrap the covers around me tight. I want to feel his arms around me. As I drift back off to sleep, I remember the night before, the power and intensity of our coupling, the orgasm and the way it shattered the room, his fear and desperation, his pleading and my own. The phone wakes me at five 'til eight, and I pick it up and smile. "Hey."

"Hey. I love you, Kimmie."

"I love you too, Jaz. Come back to me?"

"As soon as work is over. Can't wait."

"Me either."

"Bye, baby."

"Bye, Sir."

After we hang up, I go to the recent calls list and stare at the entry showing that he called me. I can still hear his voice and see his smile, feel his lips on my skin. I'm just gone.

No matter what, we're going to do this and it'll be spectacular. And I've got a lot of phone calls to make. I should probably get started.

Not too long before he should be off work, I run to the hardware store and have a key made. I want him to have it. I've no more than gotten in the door when there's a knock and I find him standing there, his arms open, waiting for me to leap into them, and I do. "God, I missed you," he moans into my neck.

"I missed you too."

"I brought ribs. Hungry?"

I grin and wink. "Yes! I have quite an appetite tonight! Wonder why?"

"Hmmm. Maybe because you got the hell fucked out of you last night?" he snickers.

"Yeah. I'm guessing that's it. Come on. Let's eat and figure this all out."

While we sit with our ribs, baked beans, and slaw, Jaz

starts. "So last night was, well, I don't know what to say. It was one of those nights I needed to videotape so I could play it over and over because, trust me, that's all I thought about all day. I'm sure I looked like a lovesick fool to anybody who ran across me today, but I don't care."

"Me either. I'm glad I didn't have any clients. I don't think I've could've functioned well enough to take care of them."

He gives me a tired smile. "This is what I want. Being with you. It's all I want. If there were somewhere we could go and be alone together all the time—and I'm not talking about sex, I'm talking about just *being*—then I'd go right now and take you with me. I just want you as part of my world."

I nod as I chew on a bite of rib, then swallow. "I feel the same way. I don't know a lot of things, and I don't pretend to, but I know I love you and want to be with you. If I have you, I'm complete."

"Okay." He wanders across the room to the messenger bag he brought in, pulls out some papers, and comes back. "I rewrote the contract. Read it and tell me what you think. I thought we'd go and scene at the club tonight, but I really want this to be far more intimate."

I start to read it and it sounds like the previous one. He agrees to take care of me, help me reach my full potential, and see that my needs are fulfilled, with special emphasis on the sexual ones, of course. I agree to follow his lead, to make myself available to him mentally, emotionally, and physically, once again with the sexual aspect emphasized. There are parts about rules, like greeting him naked in presentation pose at the end of the day if I get home before he does, not giving myself sexual pleasure unless I have his permission, and working toward a physical response to simple verbal instructions from him. And then I get to a part I haven't seen before.

The Dominant and submissive shall agree that the initial contractual period of six months shall constitute an engagement, and that, after said initial contractual period, a marriage will take place which will make the contract permanent and binding. Thereafter, all rules of legal marriage will apply.

I stop and stare just in time to see him drop to his knees in front of me, reach into his pocket, and draw out a ring. "Kimmie, this is what I want. I hope you want it too. A D/s relationship is fine, and a contract is fine, but that's not enough for me—not anymore. I want to know this is permanent, that during the time before it is, to know that we both know it's what we're working toward and planning. What do you think?"

I'm smiling so hard my face is hurting. "I think that's exactly what I want too." Then I stick out my hand.

His fingers are trembling as he slides the ring onto my finger and before I can stop myself, I'm in the floor in his lap, kissing him, touching him, pressing myself to him as his arms wrap around me, strong and possessive. Without hesitation, I whisper to him, "I want to marry you, Jaz. I want to be with you forever."

"I want to marry you and be with you forever too. I've been waiting for you for a long time, little girl." He kisses my nose and I melt into him. "So start looking at the calendar. Six months. You can have whatever kind of ceremony you want, as long as we're both there."

Six months. In six months I'm going to be even happier than I am now? I don't think that's possible, but I'm certainly willing to find out.

It crosses my mind that we've got to decide what we're going to do about the housing situation. "So what about the living arrangements?"

He shrugs. "What do you want to do? I'll do whatever you want."

That makes me laugh aloud. "Spoken like a true Dominant!"

He chuckles a little. "Well, really, it doesn't matter to me. I don't care one way or another, as long as we're together."

"The truth?" I hesitate until he nods at me. "I'd just as soon live with you at your place. I like it there."

"That's fine with me. And that makes it not my place—it's *our* place. Come on. Get up. Let's iron this out." Up and out of his lap, I wait while he rises too and takes my hand. We sit down on the sofa, my legs across his lap again, and talk about where we're going to live and how. I keep my house for two years, and then, if I want to, I either sell it or I rent it out for extra income. That sounds good to me, except I've got plans for it. Finances are discussed, how we want to arrange paying our bills and all of that sort of thing. Finally, he says, "And promise me something?"

"Sure! What?"

"If you have a Dom coming in for a fitting and he's someone you feel even the least little bit attracted to, you'll let me be there to protect my interests, if you know what I mean?"

I just shake my head and give him a smirk. "You don't have anything to worry about. Nothing. So don't."

"Promise?"

I let out a huge sigh. "Yes. I promise. But don't doubt. There's no one on earth I'd rather be with. Okay?"

"Okay." He ruffles my hair and gives me a silly grin. "You're the only woman for me. I've waited for you. I didn't think I'd ever find you, and here you are."

"Let's celebrate. Let's go out to dinner or something. Want to?"

Jaz's eyebrows shoot up and he grins. "I'll take you dancing!"

"Oh! That would be so much fun!"

"Yeah? Let's go. Tomorrow night. I'll find a place. You just dress up and have a good time."

"I can do that." I lean in and give him a peck on the lips. "And can I ask a favor?"

"Sure. What, baby?"

A shy smile creeps across my face. "Can we just sleep tonight? I'm exhausted. Whatever that was that happened last night, it wore me out!"

Peppering a light kiss on my forehead again, he gives me that warm smile that makes me blush all over. "That's fine. I'm pretty tired too. You wore me out, girl!"

"I wore *you* out? Seriously? Jasper Givens!"

"Well, you did! I'm exhausted!" He's laughing so hard that he's wheezing.

My expression turns serious, I'm sure, when I finally ask him, "Jaz? What happened last night? I mean, it was strange. And awesome. And a little scary."

"I know." Looking into my eyes, he shrugs. "I don't know for sure. But I know this: I felt things I've never felt with anyone else. And when that clap of thunder came rolling through? It was like some kind of electromagnetic field passed over that just drew us together. It was incredible. I don't believe in a lot of things, Kimmie, but that was no accident. It was meant to be. I'm convinced of that."

"Me too." Something is right there behind my teeth and on my tongue. "Do you think this is happening too fast?"

Jaz's gaze is serious. "Does it feel like it's happening too fast?"

"No."

"Then there's your answer. Babe, I asked myself that several times today, and the only answer I could come up with was that I couldn't wait to get back to you. I finally decided that was the only answer I need." With a long pause, he jumps back in again and asks me a question that surprises me. "When I met you, you pretty much wanted to be beaten to death by anybody who'd do it. Do you still need that?"

That one question almost causes me to fall off the sofa. He hit the sweet spot. "No. I don't. I hadn't given it any thought until now, but I don't even have that craving anymore. It's gone." Now I'm just bewildered until my tattered brain understands the importance of this.

I don't need it anymore. The pain? It's a thing of the past. I don't see it as necessary, haven't thought about it, haven't asked for it, and if anyone approached me right now and offered, I'd look at them like they were loony, I'm sure. That hunger has just disappeared. That's how I know this is right. Whatever has happened between Jaz and me, it's something healthy and healing for me—for us both.

"Come on, baby girl. Let's go to bed. My arms feel empty." Jaz motions for me to get up and off his lap, and then he joins me and leads me down the hall to the bedroom. Fifteen minutes later, we're snuggled together and whispering back and forth to each other about how much we love each other and never want to be apart. I think the life I've always wanted has arrived.

I wake in the wee hours of the morning to a sensation that's unfamiliar. It takes a little while, but I realize that there's something over my face and what I'm seeing is not the dark of the room. It's the darkness of what seems to be a hood. But when I reach for whatever it is that's covering my face, I find my hands restrained outward and to the sides, stretched wide. I try my legs and find they're tied the same way, out and flat. Panic is creeping in when I hear Jaz's voice. "I'm right here, sub. Just breath. You're safe."

"Jaz?" He doesn't answer. "Sir?"

"Yes, sub."

"What, I don't ..." I'm still groggy from sleep and trying to make sense of it all.

"I want you to understand what signing that contract and accepting my ring means. It means your body belongs to me, and mine to you. This will be difficult for you, but you'll be fine. I want to see how far I can push you. Safeword?"

Streaking through my mind are the faces of all the sadistic bastards I've submitted to, men who didn't give a shit about me, and all the times I should've safeworded with them and didn't. It takes me exactly two seconds to decide: I belong to him. He loves me. This is his place as the Dominant in my life, and I accept my place as his submissive. My decision is clear: "No safeword."

"Are you sure?"

"Yes. Absolutely, Sir."

"Then you're mine for the duration. I hope you're

prepared." He's moving around on the bed and I'm trembling as I'm waiting. What's he doing?

I hear the sound of a mechanical device, and I recognize it immediately. It's one of those huge vibrators, the big professional kind they use at the clubs. Then it snaps back off. His lips encircle one of my nipples and suck it to a hard point, then the bite of a clover clamp takes over. When he's treated the other to the same, he pulls hard on the chain between the clamps and I moan loudly. "Guess I got them seated perfectly. Can you possibly understand how positively fuckable you look like this? You've got the most exquisite nipples I've ever seen. They're perfect, and I know they're aching now." I feel his fingers on my lips. "Open wide." When they part, he slips the chain in and says, "Hold it with your tongue and lips. No chipped teeth." The chain is just long enough that it puts a constant tension on the clamps and makes my nipples throb. "You'll be tugging it soon enough."

The sound starts again, and I feel him spread my lower lips with his fingers. Before I can even twitch, he retracts the hood of my clit and presses the head of the vibrator directly onto it.

My body knots immediately and I feel my breath catch in my throat. Just as I think I can't stand any more, he growls, "No, sub. Don't come. You'll hold that orgasm. This will be difficult but not impossible. Concentrate on the feel of my fingertips."

His fingertips gently brush up and down my abdomen and ribcage, then circle my breasts, skipping over the chain almost seamlessly. I try to concentrate on his touch, but every muscle below my waist is beginning to spasm, and I'm not going to be able to hold off my orgasm. I whine loudly, and just as my hips are about to give in, he removes the vibrator.

The chain doesn't keep me from crying, "Oh, god! No, Sir!" My scream is followed by a hard, sharp slap to the inside of my left thigh.

"I'll give it to you when I please, submissive. You'll hold it. Understood? Otherwise, there will be more discipline." He waits. "Do you understand?"

"Yes, Sir," I groan around the chain.

The vibrator returns to my clit, and so does his hand to its tracing up, down, and around my body. I'm fighting the orgasm, fighting the restraints, fighting his touch and the vibrator. God, I'm fighting everything. I hear him whisper, "Give in, sub. Just let me have your body. Do as I say and experience it." He whispers the same thing three or four times.

I get lost in the sound of his voice, in the sound of the vibrator, in the goose pimples his touch raises on my arms, legs, and everywhere else on my body that can generate them. My hips want to buck, my pussy clenching and releasing, and just when I think I can't stand another split second, his flat palm lands firmly in the middle of my stomach and he tells me, in that authoritative voice of my Dominant, "Come for me, submissive."

Everything explodes, my body reverberating with the humming of the vibrator, and my head lurches backward, taking the chain in my lips with it. The instantaneous pain in my nipples intensifies the orgasm, and I feel like I'm levitating off the bed, the power of my muscles and the endorphins in my body carrying me above what Jaz is doing to me, forcing on me, refusing to let up. I pray the vibrator will shut off, but it doesn't. My head is jerking now, yanking over and over on the chain attached to my nipple clamps, and I can feel my hands thrashing, my fingers clenching and releasing almost like I'm pleading. I hear him murmur, "That's it, baby girl. Keep it going. You're about to float away. Just a minute or two more ..."

And it happens. He grinds the second orgasm out of my over-sensitized clit with the vibrator, and I feel the disconnect between my mind and my body. Sounds seem to move away and there's a dull ringing in my ears that fills my head. My back arches and locks, and my body just trembles all over in a way it never has before. Everything is dark and warm and quiet, and I hear a tiny, quiet voice say, "That's it, baby. Fly for me. Just let go and let it take you. That's right, Kimmie. Keep it up, baby."

Abruptly, the vibrator stops and I feel his hand on my stomach press me back down into the mattress. The chain disappears from my lips and I feel an almost unbearable pull on it, pulling my nipples up and out hard, and I can feel my mind drifting back down and into my body, the pain bringing me back to earth. I release a gasp and feel the tension disappear. In just a second, I shriek as the blood rushes back into my clampless nipples, and he announces matter-of-factly, "Here we go, babe. Turn loose."

I feel two fingers slip into my pussy and start to stroke furiously, and I hear myself cry, "Noooooo! Oh, god, nooooo. Oh, pleeeeeeease, oh, no, please. Oh, fuck, fuck, fuck ..."

"Let it go, Kimmie." I clench down, trying hard to prevent what I know is about to happen, but it's in vain. His voice changes and he growls, "Come for me, submissive."

I feel the gush and the relief, and Jaz slows and massages inside my warmth and wetness. In just a few seconds, I feel his hardness pierce me. His strokes are powerful and insistent, and I sense his increasing hardening and lengthening. "God, you're so beautiful like this, left totally to my will. Your body belongs to me. I want to use it until you can't take any more, and then use it just a little more. Look at you, submissive. My cock is so beautiful moving in and out of that sweet little pussy of yours." Even though I can't see him, I can tell he's looking down at me, feel his eyes moving over my body, and I want him to use it, use me, until he's satisfied. I can tell that he's nearing his own orgasm but without warning, he stops and pulls his cock from me.

I feel him loosening the restraints on my arms and legs, and then the hood disappears from my face. There's no chance to process what's happening before he snarls at me, "Climb on and ride me. Ride me hard until we both come. Now." I'm scrambling and when I straddle him, he grabs my waist and yanks me down on his hardness. His cock head slams into my cervix and jolts everything inside me, and I scream. "Fuck me, sub. Now." I rise and when I drop, he slaps both my tits with his hands. "Fuck me. Hard. Now." I start riding him in earnest, and after a couple of minutes, he slaps my ass with both of his hands, then slaps my tits again, and I shriek. "Fuck me! Hard! You can do better than that, submissive. I want my cock to hurt you when it hits bottom. I want you to know how hard I am for you, how I want you. I want to know how you want me." He slaps my tits again. "Fuck me! Harder!"

The pain is so intense and amazing that I'm incoherent. Even though I want to tell him how good it feels, I can't. All I can do is babble. I can feel myself slipping into another orgasm, and quick as a wink, I find myself on my back again and Jaz above me, slamming into me pile driver style. His balls slap against my ass, his shaft pounding into me, everything in my belly shifting and swelling with the increased circulation of arousal, and when he leans down and nips my shoulder, I scream out and come, clawing at his chest, begging him to stop, to go on, to fuck me until I can't move, can't breathe, can't think. In just a few seconds, he mutters, "Oh, yeah. I'm giving it to you, girl. That's it, little one. You've never been fucked the way I'll fuck you, all day and all night." His body shudders and he grinds his dick into me, his hips digging in and pressing me upward until I'm sure my head will pound the headboard.

When he finally stills, his weight resting on me, he props himself up on his hands and looks down at me. There's a wildness in those brown orbs that consumes me, and he smiles down. "You let me love you. You let me fuck you into oblivion. Who are you, Kimberly Hendricks? How did I find you? Are you an angel? A witch? Who are you and how do you do this to me? Why do you let me do this to you?"

My hands wrap around the back of his neck and my hoarse voice croaks out, "I belong to you, Sir. I'm yours. Fuck me. Fuck me twenty-four hours a day. Fuck me until I can't walk. I want it, Jaz. I want you buried inside me."

Nose buried into my neck, he nips me gently, then traces from my collarbone up to my earlobe with his tongue. When he's sucked my lobe in and released it, he whispers in my ear, "From this day forward, my cock is the only one you'll know. Your pussy is the only one I'll plunder. I won't let you get away from me. You belong to me."

"Yes, Sir. I belong to you. Only you."

"Good." He kisses me gently and runs a finger down

my cheek. "You're my one and only, Kimmie. We've honest-to-god bonded. Tell me it's real."

"It's real, baby. It's so real."

"Good. Get some sleep. I'll fuck you again in the morning before work. You'll start to need it more and more, and I'll do my best to supply. This is our life. We work, we eat, and you submit to me. You need it, I supply it. That's my job. I need it, you submit. That's your job. And we fall deeper and deeper in love."

I can barely speak from exhaustion. "Deeper and deeper in love. I love you, Jaz."

"I love you too, Kimmie." Those are the last words I hear before I drift off.

I hear him in the bedroom. "Kimmie?"

"In here." I'm already in the shower, getting ready for the day. The shower door opens, and his face is dark. "What's wrong, babe?"

"Any bed we're in together is my bed. You'll ask permission to get out."

"I'm sorry, Sir. I didn't—"

"You'll learn. You need to read that contract more closely. Move over." He climbs in with me. "Back to me. Bend over and fold your arms on the bench." I anchor my forearms on the bench and wait.

Sure enough, in a matter of seconds he forces himself into me and starts to stroke. "Sir? Oh, god, Sir. Oh, god. Sir, please—"

"I don't care when you come. I'll just keep going until I come. Whenever you want, as many times as you want."

My body turns loose and I can barely stand, but he

doesn't even slow down, just keeps fucking me and fucking me hard. I slide forward enough that I brace my head on the wall of the shower at the back of the bench and he just keeps going. After what seems like forever, I feel him speed up a little, then slam me hard half a dozen times until he finally rises up on his toes and forces himself up against me, gripping my hips and pulling me back against him. One of his hands slips up my back, wraps around my throat, and pulls me upward, my back to his chest. "Beautiful girl, I love you."

"I love you too, Sir."

He kisses the side of my neck. "Good morning. Sore?"

I giggle a little. "Yes, Sir, very sore."

"Good. What's your day look like?"

"Um, an appointment at eleven and one at three. Between them, nothing." Something clicks in my head. "Are you working in town today?"

"Yes, my dear submissive, I am." Even as his cock softens against me, his fingers tighten on my throat and his other hand reaches around to stroke the softness of my lower belly. At my tiny gasp, he whispers into my ear, "I'll be there to take you to lunch at twelve fifteen. Skirt, button front blouse with an underbust corset over it, ankle-high books with heels. No panties. Be ready."

"Unless my client makes me late, I will be, Sir."

"If your client makes you late, tell them that's very rude and you have a prior engagement at twelve fifteen."

"Yes, Sir." The hand that was on my belly is now tweaking one of my nipples and I groan. "I will, Sir."

"Very good. Now, soap up your hands and wash my cock and balls. Thoroughly. You can finish your shower after I'm out."

I do as he says, and he steps out. Standing there in the

steam of the shower, I think about what's happened since he walked through the door last night with that bag of ribs, and everything in my body feels electrified. It's done. I'm Jasper Givens' submissive, and he's my Dominant.

I make sure I take everything he wants me to wear. When the buzzer sounds at twelve fifteen, I'm trying to tie one of my boots. Hitting the button, I listen to the door buzz and then open. He strolls in looking perfectly edible in a pair of black slacks and a grey oxford cloth button down shirt, the sleeves rolled up to show off his perfect forearms and hard, wiry wrists. His stainless steel watch glistens in the fluorescent lights of my workspace, and he smiles down at me. "Hey, angel."

"Hi." I'm not sure if I should reach for him, but he reaches for me first, drawing me up against him, my face pressed against his hard chest. I can hear his heart beating, and I have an undeniable urge to strip bare and beg him to pound me. "I missed you."

"I missed you too. Kiss me, girl," he orders, and I turn my face up so he can press his lips to mine. In a matter of seconds, we're locked in a kiss so scorching that the temperature in the room goes up by about eight degrees. When he pulls back, he stares down at me. "I hope I wasn't too hard on you overnight. You okay?"

"Yes, Sir. Very okay, Sir. You've left me with a deliciously painful reminder."

"Good. Let's go. We're meeting someone for lunch."

"Oh? Who, Sir?"

"Don't worry about that. You'll find out soon enough." I lock the door behind us as we head down the street.

Instead of steering me toward the parking lot, he turns and walks down the sidewalk with my hand in his, and I fall into step beside him, grinning like an idiot as we walk along. We chatter about various things, the weather and work and the like, until he stops in front of a little French bistro I've passed dozens of times and leads me inside. The hostess seats us and Jaz makes sure that I'm on his left. Guess I'll eventually find out why.

In a few minutes, I hear a familiar voice say, "I hope we're not too late. The lot where I usually park was full."

"Michael! So glad you and your submissive could join us. Robyn, you look lovely." Jaz presses me out of the booth and we both rise. He kisses Robyn on the cheek after taking Michael's hand and shaking it heartily.

"Thank you, sir," she gushes as she turns pink.

"Kimmer, I'm glad to see you looking so well." Michael reaches for my hand and takes it, then wraps both arms around me and hugs me tight. I wonder if Jaz will say something, but I feel his hand on my lower back as encouragement, and I hug Michael back, then hug Robyn and kiss her cheek. When we're all finished, we take our seats and Michael orders a bottle of wine.

I'm wondering what this is all about, and I don't have to wait very long. Once our orders are placed, Jaz says, "Any time you're ready, Michael." Now I'm really confused.

For about a minute.

Michael looks directly at me. "Kimberly, pull up your skirt until your bare ass is on the seat of the booth." I glance over at Jaz, but he nods without a word, so I do as Michael has said. I'm sitting up against the wall of the booth where I can't be seen from the floor, but it's still uncomfortable as hell. "Done?"

"Yes, sir."

"Now, throw your right leg over Jasper's left one." I do as he says, and my lower lips gape open wide, exposing everything between them to the air and making me gasp just slightly. "Done?"

"Yes, sir."

He looks at Jaz. "To your satisfaction?" Jaz nods. "Kimberly, Jasper will begin to stimulate you. I want you to tell me what he's doing and how it feels as he does it. Do you understand?"

My eyes fly open wide and I turn to Jaz, sure that my jaw has dropped, but he says, "Do you understand Michael's instructions, submissive?"

Wide eyes rotating back to Michael, I answer, "I do, Sir." I direct a stare toward Robyn, hoping she'll throw me a scrap here, but she just looks down and smiles.

"Very good. Let's begin. Jasper, I'd like for you to use your right hand. Index finger and thumb, on the sides of Kimberly's clit, and stroke it as though you were jacking it off. Do you understand?"

"Yes. Very clearly." Without even looking at me, Jaz reaches across, finds my nub, and begins to do exactly what Michael described.

I'm growing uncomfortable—very, very uncomfortable. I don't really understand the exercise here, but I don't want to fail or question my Dominant, and yet I don't want to have some kind of screaming orgasm right here in a restaurant which, since we arrived, has started to fill up. People are sitting all around us, and I have to wonder if they can tell what's going on. As he strokes my clit, Michael asks, "Are you comfortable, sub?"

"No, sir."

"Why are you uncomfortable, sub?"

"I need to come," I moan in a loud whisper.

"You know the rules," Michael grins. "Tell me how it feels, sub."

I almost choke. "Like I'm on fire. Like I'm going to pass out."

"What's the physical sensation, sub? His fingers on your nub. What does it feel like?"

"Oh, god." I can't even think. "Like satin and sandpaper. Like my bladder's about to explode." That makes him chuckle. God knows I'm not laughing.

Jaz makes small talk with Michael, and I feel like the top of my head is going to blow off. My right hand comes down off the table and searches out Jaz's left hand, lying dormant on my thigh. When I grip his wrist, he leans toward me and whispers, "When I tell you to come, you will, but you'll be absolutely silent. Do you understand?"

A strangled, "Yes, Sir," escapes my pursed lips. Oh, god, I'm not sure I can do this. Squirming is forbidden, I'm sure, so I'm trying not to, but my hips have other ideas. As the tension builds deep in my sex, a sweat breaks out on my upper lip, and I steal a glance to see Michael look me dead in the face and smile. They continue to talk and Jaz ramps up his movements, sending my body into a spasm denied until I think I'll pass out.

Staring at the table and concentrating on keeping myself together, I hear Michael say, "I think it's time."

Jaz's voice drifts into my thoughts. "Sub, look at me."

I lift my head and my eyes meet those intense brown ones as they burn into me. Without a sound, he mouths, *Come.*

My body vibrates and gives a huge shudder. But just as it does, he slows his finger and thumb until they're almost still, just barely brushing my sensitive flesh, and the climax that engulfs me warms me from the crown of my head to the soles of my feet. It rolls and meanders through my body, making me feel limber and light, and I'm pretty sure if anyone were to look over at me, they'd find me glowing with pure joy. I desperately want to fold into Jaz's side and, almost like he's read my mind, he pulls his left arm from between us and drapes it across my shoulders, pulling me up against him and kissing my forehead as his right hand finally stops moving. He leans back slightly and looks down into my face. "Look up at me, Kimmie."

My eyelids flutter. All I really want to do at this moment is sleep, but I whisper, "Yes, Sir?"

"I'm so proud of you. That was excellent. There's even more of a treat waiting for you, angel." More than his praise, that promise sends a *zing* through my body like a violin string being plucked. Our food comes, and I just pick at mine. I know he's watching me, and he interrupts his conversation with Michael to say, "Baby, you need to eat."

I shiver a little as I lean toward him and whisper, "I'm trying, Sir, but my arms don't want to work."

A low chuckle comes from his chest. "Oh. I see. Well, then, let me feed you, why don't you?"

"Oh, no, Sir, please, don't interrupt your meal for me. It's okay. I'll manage."

"Sure?"

"Yes, Sir. I'm sure. It may take me a little longer, if that's okay."

"Take all the time you want. You have an appointment at three, right?"

I'm glad he remembered my client, because I sure as hell didn't. "Yes, Sir. Thank you, Sir, for remembering."

"Part of my job. If I render you mindless with sex, I should at least be responsible for getting you back on track, don't you think?" The peek I sneak at him finds him smirking at me.

"Your call, Sir. But thank you, Sir."

"You're quite welcome." He kisses me on the forehead again. "You'll get dessert in a few minutes."

He and Michael go on talking. I manage to get another glimpse of Robyn, and she's grinning down at the table. Then it hits me: Have they done this with her? I'm betting they have. No wonder she wouldn't come to my aid. These two have been in cahoots all along, and I'm fighting laughter. I'm caught between thinking I'm probably in big trouble with the both of them and wondering if I'm in for the time of my life. The latter part of that thought has probably already been established. Hanging on for the ride is all I have left to hope for.

I get down almost all of my lunch before I put down my fork and give up. The server comes, cleans up the plates, and asks about dessert. Michael orders for Robyn and himself. Jaz looks at me first, then tells the server, "I think we'll have the triple chocolate cake and the sawdust pie." Sawdust pie—my favorite. I learned about it one time when I went to Kentucky, and I've loved it ever since, that mixture of chess pie and coconut. I'm wondering which I'll get when he whispers to me, "We're going to share. But first, your real dessert. Excuse us for a few minutes, please," he directs at Michael and Robyn, and Michael nods. Robyn never looks up.

Taking my hand, he draws me out of the booth and pulls me toward the back hallway where the restrooms are. "Stay right here," he growls, then disappears into the men's room. In a split second he's back, and he grabs my hand and drags me into the room and straight into the handicap stall. He points at the toilet. "Climb up." I manage, with his hand steadying me, to climb onto the toilet seat. "Squat." Arms braced on my thighs, I wait while he pulls something from his back pocket.

In a flash, he restrains my wrists to my thighs just above my knees. Before I can ask a question or protest, he unzips his fly, pulls out his hardened manhood, rolls on a latex sheath, then lifts me with hands under my thighs and pins me against the bathroom wall inside the stall. "Not a sound, baby girl," he breathes out in a coarse whisper as he shoves his hardness inside me without warning. Soaked and needy from the orgasm out in the booth, it's all I can do to keep from crying aloud as he starts to shove in and out of me, his speed and intensity almost alarming. Over and over, hot in my ear, his breath carries the words, "Mine, Kimmie. You're mine, Kimmie. Mine. Always mine. Forever mine. All mine. Mine, Kimmie." I hear the door open a couple of times, a splash in the urinal, a stall door closing and then reopening and a toilet flushing, but it's all extraneous. I can't concentrate on anything except the feel of his cock piercing me, hard and insistent, his tempo increasing until he's frantic and practically hunching me. I'm holding back, sure that's what he wants, and then, in a split second, he grunts out "Now!" and nips my neck.

My arms go rigid in the restraints, and I think my legs stiffen until they're sticking straight out behind him. I'm not sure. All I'm really sure of is that he's pleased with me, the heat of his cum warming me inside even through the condom he's wearing. Still pinned against the wall, I'm crushed against it by the weight of his body, and he leans back enough to catch my eyes.

I'm shocked to see his eyes moisten and turn red as he whispers to me, "Do you have any idea how proud I am of you right now?"

All I manage to stutter is, "N-n-n-no, Sir. Thank you, Sir."

A sweet little smile turns up the corners of his lips. "I think that title is past. Say, 'Thank you, Master.'"

Hot tears fill my own eyes. "Thank you, Master."

His lips meet mine in a kiss that I hope is never-ending. It's not one of those frantic, crazy things, just sweet and warm and comforting. And when he draws back this time, he smiles again. "I love you, Kimmie."

"I love you too, Jaz."

"Okay. Let's see if we can get you out of this predicament," he says with an almost-inaudible chuckle. Leaning me back into his chest, he carries me over to the toilet again and perches me on top of it. "Before I take the restraints off, pee."

"What?"

"Pee. Right now."

"In front of you?" I'm sure he can see the horror on my face. Hell, I can't see it, but I can most certainly feel it.

"Yes. In front of me. Get it over with." He stands there, facing me, and folds his arms across his chest, determined to wait.

So I try. I really do. But it just doesn't want to come out, not with him standing there. In a minute or so, he announces, "I can stand here all day."

"I'm trying, Si ... Master. Really, I am." I've got my face all screwed up and I'm thinking it's never going to happen when, finally, I feel a trickle and then a gush as my bladder empties. As soon as it does, he rips the hook and loop on the restraints and removes them, folding them and sticking them back down in his back pocket.

"Good girl. Wipe yourself up and let's go." With his help, I climb down from the toilet and clean myself up, only leaving a couple of drips on the floor. When I'm finished, he takes my hand, smiles at me, and opens the stall door.

The man standing at the urinal when we waltz through turns and pretends he doesn't even see us, and my face goes crimson. Jaz just acts like it's an everyday occurrence as we wash our hands at the basins, leave the restroom, and make our way back to the table, stopping outside the door to pour on the hand sanitizer he pulls from his pocket and rub it in. Michael and Robyn are sitting there, desserts placed neatly in front of them, and there's a look on Robyn's face that tells me she was treated to her own orgasm while we were gone. Once we're settled back into the booth, Michael smiles at Jaz. "Everything work out okay?"

"Everything worked out better than okay. It was amazing. Wouldn't you say so, submissive?"

My heart flutters when I say aloud, "Yes, Master."

The look Jasper Givens gives me blows me away. It's lust and want and need, but it's also something else, something that looks a lot like pride and even somewhat like gratitude. This is it. The commitment's made. I hear Michael clear his throat, and when I turn away from Jaz's face, Michael gives him a look that I can't read. To my amazement, Jaz nods, and Michael pulls from his jacket pocket a document sleeve. When he flattens the papers out, I know what it is.

It's our contract. Oh, god, this is real. I feel a tear roll down my cheek as I look back to Jaz, and he lifts my hand and kisses the back of it. "You ready?" he chokes out.

Trying hard not to sob, I sniff back, "Yes. Very, very ready."

Michael nods to us both. "Jasper, you'll sign first as Master. It's your responsibility to lead her, and this is your first official act of doing so." Jaz takes the pen and, to my surprise, his hand isn't shaking at all. Steady as a rock, he signs his name at the bottom of the contract, then turns to me and hands me the pen.

Wordlessly, I take it and sign my name. I'm bursting with pride. I can't imagine why this man loves me, but it sure looks like he does. Finished, I cap the pen, hand it back to Michael, and then fold the document neatly and turn to Jaz. When he grasps it, instead of turning loose, I hold on and look him straight in the eye. Then I say something I didn't expect, something that's spontaneous and right. "Master, my life is in your hands."

His eyes are warm and soft when he murmurs to me, "I'm going to do everything in my power to never let you down." Jasper reaches into his pocket and brings out a beautiful chain—well, three actually, woven together, a yellow gold, platinum, and strawberry gold, with a ring at both ends. It's not a traditional collar; it's far more discreet, and I love it for that reason. He wraps it around my neck with the rings at the front and from his pocket produces a pretty little gold heart-shaped lock. When it snaps shut, I know that I'm his.

Michael raises his wine glass aloft. "To Jasper and Kimberly, Master and submissive. May the bond between you always bring you joy."

"Joy," Robyn reinforces, lifting her glass.

Jaz hands me my glass, then takes his and presses his

forehead to mine. "More joy than we've ever known," he whispers. Then he raises his glass with Michael's and Robyn's, and mine joins theirs. The clinking sound they make is like bells pealing, at least to me. It rings in what I now know will be the rest of my life, and it's going to be amazing.

~

Jaz comes in from work that evening to find me naked and kneeling by the door, waiting for him, just like the contract stipulates. To my surprise, he says, "Don't do that again."

"I read through the contract as you said. I thought this is what you want." I pout.

"I thought I did too. But know what?" I shake my head at him. "I love it when I open the door and you just launch yourself at me. Now, if you want to do that naked, that'll be fine, but you don't have to." He swallows hard, then adds, "It's good to know somebody's happy to see me at the end of the day."

"Always!"

"Good. Because I promised you I'd take you dancing, and we're going. Go get dressed and ready." He slaps me on the ass as I run down the hallway to pick out something to wear. I'm so excited that I'm not sure I can stand it.

An hour and a half later, I'm grinning from ear to ear and feeling like a kid at her first boy/girl dance. "My god, that was a blast!" I sit down, huffing and puffing. It's been a long time since I've danced, and I'd forgotten how much fun it could be. "You're really good!"

"You're not shabby yourself," Jaz tells me with his

wine glass up to his lips. "I'm impressed. You make me look good out there."

"You make me feel like a star!" I giggle and take another swallow of champagne, then look down at the ring on my finger. Now I *feel* like a star with this rock on my hand. No, it's not huge, but it's big enough to suit me. I would've been happy without a ring, but I really, really like that I have one. Looking at it makes me feel like a twenty-five-year-old bride again. But this time, the groom's drop-dead gorgeous and I'm the luckiest woman on the planet. And my collar isn't hurting my feelings either. I'm pretty damn proud of that.

"Don't have to—you already are one, babe." He leans over to kiss me and I see a couple of other women in the room roll their eyes. I want to yell, *Suck on that, bitches!* but I don't. Not yet anyway. Maybe later. "How was your filet?"

I beam at him. "Perfect. Delicious! This place is wonderful." The restaurant used to be an old supper club, and it's just beautiful, all art nouveau with big, plush booths and decorative, wall-mounted torchiere uplighting everywhere. When he promised me weeks earlier that he'd take me dancing, I wondered where we'd wind up, and this place is absolutely, positively perfect. "How did you find it?"

"I asked one of the guys at the plant for the name of a place that was really romantic and this is the one he gave me. I think he kind of outdid himself. I owe him lunch or, at the very least, a bottle of wine." His wine finished, Jaz reaches for my hand. When our fingers intertwine, something deep inside me clenches tight.

I feel like I'm going to cry. "Can I tell you something?"

His smile is gentle. "Of course."

With a deep sigh, I manage to choke out, "I love you so much that it hurts."

His eyes close and he nods. "I know exactly what you mean. I want this to work. I want us to be together forever. I know everything's happened really fast, but I just feel like we fit together like puzzle pieces, you know?"

"I know exactly."

"I'm not rich, but I want to give you everything. I want you to be happy. That will make *me* happy. And I want you to tell me when you're not. I want us to trust each other. We have to talk openly and honestly to do that."

"I know. I'm being honest with you all the time. I haven't told you a single lie about anything, or covered anything up. And I feel comfortable being honest with you." His fingers tighten on mine, and my heart sings. I've got my secret, but I think when he finds out what it is, he'll be glad.

"Good. Because I've done the same with you, and I feel the same way. Six months." He chuckles low in his throat. "I'm not sure I can wait that long."

"Me either." I'd marry him tomorrow if he wanted that. Right now. This minute. I wouldn't wait. "So do the stipulations of the contract carry over to the marriage?"

"If you want them to." He's refilled his glass from the bottle in the chiller on the table. "But honestly, it suits me."

"Suits me too." I think for a second. "So the house has three bedrooms, right?"

"Yeah."

"And is one of them fixed up for Melissa?"

He shakes his head. "No. She hasn't lived with me since I've been here."

"We should fix one of them up for her so she'll come and visit more often. I'd love to have her around."

To my surprise, his eyes grow misty and he clears his throat before he answers with, "That would be okay with you?"

"That would be more than okay. I really want to get to know her. She's a big part of your life, so I want her to be a big part of mine too. And with the third bedroom, Jeffrey and Greta can come and visit whenever they want. I want you to get to know him."

"I want that too." He sits for a minute, staring off into space, his wine glass in his hands, and then he looks straight into my eyes. "Kimmie, I just ... I don't know what to say to you. You're everything I ever ... you just ..."

"I love you. I want this to work too. And the only way that's going to happen is if we have a meeting of the minds on everything."

He pulls my hand to his lips and kisses it. "I love you too. This is going to work. I have to believe that. You should too."

"I do. I really do." I want to say a real *I do* to him right now. Six months. That's a long, long time when you're as in love with a man as I am with Jaz.

CHAPTER NINE

"So?"

"So what?" Jaz is grinning from ear to ear.

"What did you think?"

"I think," he says, hugging me close as I wave goodbye toward the car heading down the street, "that your son is a great guy and we had a really, really good visit." He stops for a second and then asks shyly, "Did he like me?"

"He thinks you're amazing. I think that run to the liquor store was what did it for him. His dad would never have done that with him. He thinks you're unbelievably cool."

"Good. I think he's unbelievably cool too." He nuzzles my neck. "But I have to admit, I missed fucking you all weekend while they were here."

I giggle when I say, "I almost asked you to go to the garage with me and do it in the car."

"I would've! You should've said something. If I'd thought of it, I would've asked you." When the front door closes behind us, his hands are all over me. "God, Kimmie, I missed your body like crazy."

"I missed yours too. Let's make up for lost time, shall we?" I grin and grab his hand as I head down the hallway toward the bedroom. "Come on! I'm hungry for you!"

"Okay! Okay!" He's laughing as we wander down the hallway. I just fall across the big bed and pull him down with me, and he's still laughing as he drops kisses all over me, stripping me bare as he goes. Trapped under his weight, I'm helpless as he grabs my hands and pulls them over my head. A sinister grin spreads across his face. "Get up there in the bed. On your back. And grab the headboard." While I do as he says, he crosses to the other side of the room, then comes back. Climbing onto the bed and still fully dressed, he ties my hands to the headboard before I even realize what he's doing, the slick, satiny cord softly reflecting the light. His eyes roam my body as he licks his lips, and heat radiates out from between my legs and pools low in my belly. God, I have no idea what he's going to do with me, but I can't wait to find out. I cross my thighs and grind the air. It's maddening, the way my body responds to him, and I love everything about it.

I watch him strip off his tie, then slowly unbutton his shirt. After he pulls his shirttails from his slacks, the shirt drops to the floor and I'm left with an unobstructed view of that chest, that gorgeous, muscled chest. An ache invades the lower half of my body and spreads to my nipples, and I writhe in anticipation of his hands on my skin. But he just stands and watches me as he unzips his slacks slowly and lets them fall to the floor, and I wilt under his gaze. "What do you want, sub?" he snarls at me, and I hesitate. "Tell me or I swear I'll walk out of here and rub one off. And I'll leave you lying there wanting. What do you need?"

"Oh, god." I can barely speak. My tongue seems thick and I can't catch my breath. "Oh, god, Master, I want you to lick me, and then I want you to fuck me. Please?"

"Very good. I can probably accommodate you." Just watching him slip his briefs down crazes me, and when he adds an aggressive stroking of his cock, I almost come undone. I've never come just from the sight of pure sex, but I'm so damn aroused that I'm not sure I can control myself anymore. Good thing my hands are tied. No telling what I might do if they were free. He interrupts my thoughts with a slow smile. "Do you have any idea what kinds of things I'd like to do to you?"

My voice is strained when I try to answer. "I hope I have some ideas, but you can do whatever you want with me, Master. I'm yours."

His eyes soften and a small smile turns up the corners of his mouth. "You belong to me, sub. I want to drive you wild with my fingers and my tongue and my cock. I can make you scream and shake, and I plan to. It's all I can do to keep my hands off your tits. God, you're gorgeous, breathing heavy like that, squirming and wiggling. Did you know I can see your clit throbbing?" Shaking my head, I bite my lip and wait. "I can. And your pussy's almost dripping. You're so damn wet that I could fuck you right now, just slide right in. But I want to watch you come undone first." His cock bobs with its own pulse when he releases it so he can crawl deliberately toward me on the bed, looking like a tiger stalking his prey. "Spread 'em," he snaps, slapping the insides of my thighs. On his knees between my legs, he puts a hand behind each of my knees and forces them up toward my chest, and the thought that I'm spread wide open for him makes me cry out. A low snicker rolls through his chest just before he buries his face in my pinkness.

"Oh, gawwdddd ..." I'm so wound up that the touch of his tongue on my nub makes my temples pound. "Sir, please. I need to come. Please?" There's that chuckle again, and it vibrates against my skin as he just keeps working my nerve endings into a frenzy. "Oh, Master, oh god. Please, Sir, please? I can't stand it anymore. I really ... Oh, please? No! I can't! I don't know ... god, Master, please?" My brain is turning to mush and I can't think, only feel. And I feel like I'm going to explode.

Stopping for a split second, he replies, "Any time you want. And know that I won't stop."

My god, he'll drive me insane, I just know it. I'm trying to hold off, and I can't, I just can't. My voice sounds like it's coming from somewhere else when I hear myself crying, "Nooooo! Oh, god, nooooo. Please, Master, I don't think I can take it. It's too much!" For the first time in my life, I'm terrified of coming. Everything inside me is so tuned up that I'm not sure I'll survive it. My mind is spinning out of control when, without any further warning, the orgasm slams into me and I see stars and hear bells. My whole body goes rigid, shaking and knotting, and I scream into the silence of the bedroom as Jaz never even slows. "Oh, fuuuuuuck." I'm hitting critical mass, my hips bucking so hard that I'm shaking the bed, but Jaz holds them down and keeps going.

I fight for my hands. If they were free, I'd push him away, but they're tied fast, and I feel the second one building in my belly. This is one I'm not sure I'll survive. He knows exactly what he's doing to me and he just keeps going while I writhe in ecstatic misery until I can't process it anymore. And when that misery grows and expands the way I know it will, there's a moment there when I think about calling my safeword, but I don't. In the next second, I know why.

Every nerve ending in my body carries heightened sensation from the first orgasm, and when this one hits, it slams into me like a wrecking ball. It's a fight to stay conscious, and I'm gasping when Jaz slows his strokes. I can feel my mind slipping away and I'm barely aware when he crawls up between my legs and drives his manhood straight into me with no hesitation. I feel him; I know what he's doing. But my body feels like it's a million miles away as I float on the endorphins his skill has released for me. My eyes are closed and I'm sure if I opened them, I'd see clouds and sunshine and maybe even angels. There's a buzzing in my ears, and a sensation's expanding in my pelvis that I welcome and embrace. The vaginal orgasm hits hard, and the deep, powerful rhythms of the muscles buried in my channel pull my already-overloaded brain farther out into subspace. I can feel my body jerking as it convulses and I don't care. It's so amazing and powerful that I release any control I was fighting for and let go, let him take my body where it needs to go.

This is bliss. A big fur-lined parka of warmth and peace surrounds me and I don't want to be anywhere with anyone else. His hands on me seem to impart some kind of energy to me, and I want him to touch me all over, every inch of my skin, until I can't tell where I end and he begins. His voice seems far away when I hear him cry out, "Oh, fuck, baby! That's it, Kimmie. We're both there, precious. We're one. Oh, god." And then he stops.

Time stops. I can't move, and even if I could, I don't want to. Trying to make sense of everything, I feel his arms around me, holding me tight, and it occurs to me that my hands are free. When I try to wrap my arms around him, they're limp—my whole body's limp. His lips fall on mine, but I can't kiss him back. All I can do is lie there in his arms and, frankly, that's all I want to do. He kisses my forehead, my temples, my eyelids, my nose, my lips, my chin, and then tweaks one of my nipples with his fingers. That gets a response out of me because I shiver like I'm cold, and I hear him chuckle. His voice is sweet and warm when he sing-songs, "Kiiii-mmie. Kimmie, baby, wake up. Hey, honey, come on back to me." I grunt and shake my head, and the next sensation that hits me is his lips around one of my nipples. I groan and he laughs. "Come on, girl. I'm here waiting for you, baby. Just snuggle up."

When I finally force my eyes open, I'm still in Jaz's arms, and he's sound asleep. His breathing is silent, and there's a calm look on his face that reminds me of the face of a sleeping child. I rouse a little and his arms tighten around me, followed by his eyes blinking open and a huge smile splitting his face. "Hey, little one! I was starting to get a little concerned about you."

"Ah, I'm okay." I yawn—loudly—right in his face and he really laughs. "Were you trying to kill me?"

"Are you dead?" he snickers.

"No."

"Then no, obviously I wasn't trying to kill you. You were, after all, tied to the head of the bed. If I'd wanted to kill you, you'd be dead now, right?" He's still laughing.

"I guess." I try to make sense of everything. "Was I good?"

He shakes his head in frustration. "Why do you

always ask me that? You were more than good. You were unbelievable. Do you feel okay? You were really gone."

"Yeah. I'm fine, I think." Things are slowly coming together for me and I'm checking all of my limbs to make sure they still work as the fog starts to lift. "Jaz?"

"Um-hmmm, babe."

"I love you." When I manage to get a look at his face, I'm shocked.

His eyes are gleaming with unshed tears when he murmurs, "Baby, I love you too. I'm so glad we found each other. I can't imagine being without you."

"I can't imagine being without you either. But I want to sleep."

He grins and pinches the end of my nose. "Sleep. You earned it. And Kimmie?"

"Yes, Master?"

"I'll be thankful that you're mine every day for the rest of my life. I won't ever take you for granted."

"I won't ever take *you* for granted either." I put my hands on his cheeks and look into his eyes. "You're the greatest gift I've ever been given." One of his hands clasps mine and drags it to his lips so he can kiss my palm. "Thank you."

"No. Thank you." His hand rises and rests on my head, and he drags his fingers through my hair absentmindedly as he breathes into my crown. As I drift off, I hear him whisper, "You're everything to me, Kimmie. Everything." I don't know if I manage to get a smile to show on the outside, but I'm definitely smiling on the inside.

∽

We have a long talk and decide that we'll try to go to the club every Thursday night. Being there has been important for us, at least for me, for a long time. Now my position is different. I have a permanent Dominant, so other members now have to show me a different kind of respect, especially the unattached Doms. One of the things we discuss is the fact that, because of the performance areas and the furnishings, there are opportunities to explore things there that we can't at home. Some day we might have room for a St. Andrew's cross, or a bondage table, or a whipping horse, but right now, that's not an option. We also have nowhere for him to practice suspension with me, and the club can offer us that. It just makes sense. Along with all of that, it cements our union in the eyes of the kink community here, and that's one thing we both want.

I warned him that I might be running late—my last client had to come after work and she's very, very hard to fit—so he knew that six might be impossible for me to make. When I pull into the parking lot of the club and stroll into the building with my backpack in hand, his car is already here, and my heart gives a little jump knowing that he's going to be just inside, waiting for me.

It takes me almost a minute for my eyes to adjust to the darkness inside, and when they finally do, I do a sweep around the room for Jaz. And I have one of those red-letter, white-hot rage, what-the-fuck moments.

Jaz is sitting on a sofa across the room with a blond, and I'm not talking about your average blond. I'm talking about a bombshell. She looks to be barely over thirty, and not only do I see red, but I have flashbacks of Phil and all the shit he put me through. I stand there, not quite sure what to do or say, and I'm shocked when he turns, looks at me, and then goes right back to talking with her.

A shrieking sets up in my brain and I feel like the top of my head is going to blow off. I know he can hear me stomping across the room toward him, and yet he never turns to look. When I'm finally standing stock-still at the end of the sofa, I wait, but he *still* doesn't turn to look at me. I finally clear my throat loudly and add, "Aaaa-hemmmm. Jaz?"

He turns and smiles, a passive smile that makes my blood boil. "Submissive?"

I know my voice is shaky when I blurt out, "Would you like to tell me what the hell is going on?"

Rising from the sofa, he takes the two steps to me and stands right in front of me, looking down into my flaming face. There's no anger or malice in his voice when he says, "You'll not speak to your master that way, submissive. Go to the locker room, dress out, and wait for me at the bar."

My eyes go so wide that I'm pretty sure my eyelids completely disappear. "What the fuck?"

His next words are a little more forceful and dispassionate. "Submissive, you'll not speak to your master that way. One more disrespectful address and you'll suffer punishment. Are we clear?"

"Crystal clear, Master." I just stare at him as, without a smile or any hint of an expression, he turns and sits back down to resume his conversation with the blond.

It takes me about thirty seconds to process what's just happened, and I turn on my heel and head for the dressing room. More than following his directions and dressing out, I really want to just walk back out, get in my car, and drive away. I have three-quarters of a tank of gas, and I wonder how far I could get before I just run out.

When the bag's unzipped, I find what he packed for me that morning: an emerald green lace shelf bra with a matching flounced garter belt. No panties. That seems to be his thing. And a pair of silver stiletto sandals, strappy and sexy. He even found green stockings to go with the outfit. If I weren't so fucking furious, I'd be impressed, but it's all lost on me at the moment.

Suddenly, it occurs to me that in looking over that contract, I never saw anything allowing more than one submissive, but I never saw anything forbidding it either, and my heart sinks. Is that what he's up to? Fifteen minutes earlier, I'd been the happiest woman in Chicago. Now, I'm just trying to figure out how to save face and get through the evening as my hopes and dreams lie crushed and mangled before me.

Numb and shaking, I make my way out to the bar. I can see Jaz and the blond still across the room. He's pretty still, but she's animated and smiling. It's taking all I have to sit there when I feel a presence beside me.

Well fuck me. It's Angus.

"Hello, slut. What are you looking for tonight?"

"Hello to you too, asshole."

His eyes pop open wide and he jerks back. "Well, well, well! For somebody who's begged me to fuck her senseless and use her like a common whore, you're full of piss and vinegar tonight."

"Yeah, well, sorry for your luck, but I have a Dominant."

"Yeah, and looks like he's got himself some hot ass tonight," Angus says with a belly laugh. I can feel my face burning and I'm working to keep the tears at bay. It takes me by surprise when he reaches over, pinches my nipple, and says, "I think you're really going to need a fucking tonight."

"Stop, Angus," I manage to snort and push his hand away.

He's laughing outright at me now. "You weren't saying, 'Stop, Angus!' a bit ago, now were you?" Before I can move away, he grabs the back of my neck and smashes his lips against mine. I thrash around to find something, anything, to grab hold of. Stationary, I'll pull away from him; moveable, I'll smash him in the back of the head with it. I'm clawing around when I hear this odd sound against my lips and open my eyes to see his bulging back at me. His face pulls away from mine and I see a hand around his throat.

Then that voice like molten metal says, "Keep your hands off my submissive." By now, Angus's face is blood red and he's grappling at the hand around his neck when it just tidily sets him on a bar stool and turns loose. I watch in horror as he immediately takes a swing, but a neat upward-bound fist knocks him right off the stool and on his ass. When I turn, Jaz's eyes are glowing at me and he grips my upper arm. "You okay?"

"What the hell do you care?" I spit out and try to wrest free of his grasp, but he's got me tight.

"Your submissive?" I hear Angus growl as he's scrambling to stand. "Looks to me like you're looking to trade up."

I watch Jaz's eyes flicker darkly as they rotate to Angus. "You'd do well to watch your mouth. If you ever touch her again, I'll kill you with my bare hands. Do you understand me?"

Angus sing-songs back toward Jaz, "Well, if you weren't so busy chatting up Goldilocks over there—"

"Who I talk to and what I do is none of your fucking concern. You've got two minutes to vacate the premises or I'm going to clear the room with pieces of your sorry ass. Got that?"

Angus snorts, then turns to me. "Well, slut, you know I can deliver when he's *otherwise occupied*," he chortles. "Show up without your *Dominant*," he says, almost spitting the word, "and I'll supply what you've always wanted."

"Go to hell," I snarl back at him.

"Ungrateful bitch." Those words are followed by the sound of skin against skin, and Angus goes down again.

Jaz towers over him. "Speak to my submissive that way again, and you'll never utter another word."

When Angus stands, he holds his arms up in the air. "Well, you all heard him! This *Dominant* just threatened me! So if anything happens to me, well, here's your man!" He laughs, a nasty, grating sound, but no one joins him. They all just stand and stare, and I want the floor to open up and swallow me. "Okay, okay, I'm going. But I'll be back." He turns to me. "I'll fuck you soon, you can bet on it."

I toss back, "Piss off." We all stand and watch as his back disappears into the darkness of the front hallway on his way out.

Jaz turns back to me. "Are you okay?"

I don't even look at him. "Yeah. I'm fine."

"Did you invite that in any way?"

That just pisses me off to no end. "No. I did not."

I hear a voice from the bar say, "No. I was sitting right here the whole time. She's telling the truth."

Jaz's hand lands on the back of my neck, pretty much

in the same spot Angus's did, but it's gentle. "Okay. I just need to know you're okay."

Now's my chance. "No. I'm not okay. I'm being ignored by my Dominant who's over there ..." And it hits me. "You're negotiating a scene with her, aren't you?"

"Yes. I am."

I'm hit by something that I can only describe as nausea. I'm not sure what it is, but I feel my heart start to hammer so hard that I can hear it in my ears. All I can think is, *Oh, god, please don't let this be happening to me. Please. Not again.* I try to get up and walk away, but my legs are like lead and I can't feel my feet. If I could figure out what to say, I still couldn't say it. When I finally make it to my feet, his hand is still on the back of my neck, and I try to shake it loose, but I can't. The only thing I can get to come out of my mouth is, "Don't."

There's an edge to his voice when he orders me, "Follow me, submissive. Now." He turns toward a performance platform and I follow, blindly and silently, my heart breaking in a thousand pieces. I hear him talking to someone, and then there's movement around me. When I manage to catch a glimpse, a bondage table has been moved up onto one end of the platform, and Jaz points to the floor in front of it. "Present yourself, submissive."

So this is what I am. I'm a sex slave. I knew it was all too good to be true, and here I am, finding out that's correct. I kneel and I'm getting as comfortable as possible when he leaves the platform and returns with the blond. They stand right in front of me, and Jaz orders her, "Strip."

I watch in horror and humiliation as she removes every article of clothing, and her toned, tanned, perfect body is on full display for Jaz and everyone else to enjoy. A burning sets up in my gut, and I'm having trouble breathing as I watch him readying things off to the side. To my utter amazement, he turns to me and says, "Submissive, watch and enjoy." I'm feeling a lot of things at this moment, but pleasure is definitely not one of them. And, because of his command, looking away is not an option.

From seemingly out of nowhere, a photographer steps into the light, camera ready. Rope in hand, Jaz begins to bind the woman in intricate, beautiful work that spreads around and across her body. It isolates her breasts until they begin to redden, and I know they'll soon be throbbing in pain from the binding at his hands. As he works, she beams at him, her eyes sparkling and clear, and I feel a tear start down my cheek, followed by another. The whole club gets to witness my embarrassment and, throughout it all, the photos will bear witness to the whole scene. I notice with confusion and then shame that the guy's making a special effort to *not* get me in any of the photos. How nice. I don't even rate that. That's the icing on the cake for me, and all my efforts to keep my shoulders from shaking with sobs are breaking down and abandoning me.

Jaz continues on, seemingly unaware that I even exist, and I grow numb in a short while. It helps—it lets me watch them as though I don't know either of them, as though they're strangers I haven't even met, and right now, that's how I feel about the man I pledged my life to. Out of the corner of my eye, I see movement and I notice Michael and Robyn standing there, just out of the light. When Michael sees me looking at them, he nods and points back toward Jaz and the blond.

They knew. They're my friends and they knew this was going to happen. Had it all been arranged beforehand? Obviously so. The photographer, the crowd that's here tonight, all no coincidence. But my friends?

I'm alone. I'm utterly, completely alone. Jeffrey and Greta live far away. I have no family here. Apparently, I have no friends. And any dignity I might've had has evaporated. I had some savings, but I've spent it all trying to do something important for him, and now I know it's all been wasted. It seems to me that the best thing I can do when this debacle is over is go to the locker room, change, get in my car, and just leave.

I wonder briefly about Alexander, but I'm pretty sure that, after watching me dressed down this way, no one at this club will ever want to touch me again. I'll be that submissive who fell in love with the Dominant, the Dominant who made a fool of her in a very intimate yet public way. Not a good line on a submissive's resume. My mind goes in all kinds of directions, none of them healthy or helpful, and I just sit there and watch her ecstasy grow.

The one thing I do notice that seems odd to me is the expression on Jaz's face. Complete dispassion. He doesn't seem to be enjoying it at all, just performing some kind of task, kind of like sweeping a floor or drying his hair—like it's not a big deal. He's paying close attention to the rope, straightening it, adjusting it, but as for her body, he hasn't really touched her anywhere. I do note that he uses his fingers to spread her labia apart, but then he draws a rope up her slit and never touches her again. I find that strange. Maybe he's at least going to be that merciful to me by keeping his hands off her. If I have to watch him fuck her, I'll die. That'll be the end for me.

She's bound beautifully, I'll give him that. When he

seems to be satisfied with the arrangements of the knots and lines, he attaches lines to her just as he had me and begins to hoist her upward. Unlike me, however, when she gets to a certain point, the ropes in which she's bound are used to secure her, their long, tendril-like extensions apparently tied into the pattern for that purpose. The original lines are undone and removed, and she hangs there, one arm up and pointed forward, the other crossed across her ribcage. Her legs are wide open, and one arches upward toward her back, while the other is straight and pointed downward at an angle toward the floor. Unlike when he bound me in the hammock-like arrangement, she looks very graceful, almost ballerina-like in her pose. After he takes a minute to stand back and admire his work, he moves back to her and, taking a smaller, thinner cord, braids it into her hair, then secures it to one of the ropes on her back, drawing her head back with it. She's completely immobilized, barely able to breathe, and even though my heart is broken, I have to admit, he's done a beautiful job. She's a gorgeous, alluring woman, and his work is amazing.

Jaz turns toward the crowd and begins to speak. "At the request of the management, I have been honored to give this demonstration tonight. Known in various forms as shibari or kinbaku, you are witness to a form of Japanese rope bondage in which I was instructed by a kinbaku master on the west coast, Master Morris Davidson. I usually perform this art only with my own submissive, but tonight I employed the assistance of Master Davidson's daughter, Amelie. Raised in a household where her father worked out intricate knot arrangements using her mother as his submissive, Amelie is quite accustomed to the practice and not prone to the panic that an inexperienced submissive might suffer. While I have worked with my own submissive to begin her familiarization with the art, this particular demonstration is far too rigorous for someone who does not practice on a regular basis. I'd like to thank Master Aaron," he says, and points to an equally attractive blond man standing in the shadows, "for allowing me to work with his submissive tonight. This scene is far from over. For my part, I will complete it with my own submissive to allow her to experience it as well."

Jaz turns to me for the first time and I have to wonder what he thinks about my tear-stained face. Does he even realize what he's done? How much he's hurt me? He steps in front of me and simply says, "Submissive, rise." Once I'm on my feet, he points to the girl in the ropes. "Kimberly, please step in front of the bound submissive." Great. She gets to laugh at my discomfort. That's going to be fun for me, I'm sure, and I can't imagine what he hopes to accomplish by breaking me down this way. Addressing her, Jaz states, "Amelie, eyes on me." Her eyes open and she looks directly at him. He turns back to me and asks, "Are you ready?"

I have no idea what I'm supposed to be ready for, so I just stand there, mute. He puts a finger under my chin, tips my head up, and kisses my forehead, then turns back to the girl. "Amelie, tonight I finish this scene with my own submissive. Her name is Kimberly, but to you, she is Mistress Kimberly. For the rest of this scene, Mistress Kimberly is in control of your orgasms. You will not climax unless she allows it. Disobedience will result in punishment. The safeword we negotiated earlier in the evening remains in play." He turns to me and says, "Her safeword is sky." Returning his eyes to her, he states firmly, "Submissive, address your Mistress."

In a shallow, breathy groan, her ribcage restricted in its expansion by the ropes, Amelie looks at me and says, "My orgasms belong to you, Mistress Kimberly. I beg your mercy."

I'm dumbstruck. I don't understand what's happening. Nothing is making sense until he looks back to her and announces, "I will finish the scene with my submissive and you will watch. Although you will want to come, you will not do so until Mistress Kimberly approves." Without another word, Jaz takes my hand and leads me to the bondage table. He climbs up, sits down, and reaches out toward me. "Come to me, Kimmie." I don't know what to do. Part of me wants to run, and part of me wants to be with him. When I reach the edge of the table, he smiles. "Shoes off." I toe them off and climb up, wondering what to do. He takes my hand and I stare down at him. "Stay standing. Okay, stand astride my legs. Move right up in front of me, baby, up, up, right there—stop. Put your hands on my head. And don't worry for a single second—I've got you. I won't let you fall." With that, he buries his face in my slit and drags his tongue upward.

I almost collapse. After everything I've been through this evening, it's too much, and I feel my spirit wilting even as my body comes to life. I cry out and he grips my ass tighter, pulling me in closer, sucking and tugging at my clit until I'm whining and panting. My hands wind into his hair and I know I'm yanking hard on it, but I can't stop myself. And every time I pull, he just sucks and tugs harder on my tiny little pearl until I'm a mess, a writhing, squirming, sweaty mess. I'm losing ground, giving in a little at a time, until one last moment when he slides his hands from the globes of my ass to the insides of my thighs, then slips two fingers into my pussy and one into my tight, dark back entrance.

Everything around me explodes as my entire core clenches and spasms, and my knees buckle to almost let me fall but, true to his promise, he holds me tight, torturing me until I think I'll faint. When he finally stops, I'm gasping and shaking. His hands leave me and I feel him moving around until he says, "Look down, Kimmie."

Leathers unzipped and tucked back, Jaz's rock-hard cock and full, tight balls are on regal display, and I look into his face. "That's yours, girl. Belongs to you and no one else. I'm going to let you down on me. Wrap your legs around my ass and just enjoy. I'll do all the work." I'm so overwrought that I still can't speak. "This is your reward for being the best submissive any Dominant has ever had." I'm limp as a noodle as he lowers me, and when he gets me close enough, he drops me on his length and I scream through the deliciously painful stretch.

"Here we go, Kimmie. Rock your hips, baby, and I'll do the same." His hands under my ass, we rock together as he raises and lowers me slightly, and I've never before felt the things I'm feeling. Holding me almost as though I were a rare treasure of antiquity, he strokes down my upper arms, then curves his hands around my breasts and cups them, teasing my nipples with his thumbs. "I love you, Kimmie. Only you. No other woman. Ever. Do you understand?"

I start to cry. "But Jaz, I was so ... it felt so ..."

"I know, precious. I did this to teach you something. I wanted you to watch me with her, know that I never touched her, know that I'd never betray you that way.

Your hackles were up from the very minute you saw me talking to her, but there was no need, my angel."

"But why—"

"Because you didn't trust me, you put me in a position where I had to do exactly what I did. If you'd just trusted me, you would've been her mistress from the very beginning." He kisses me lightly, then deepens it, and the hands I've put on his chest in indecision finally find their way around his neck and I kiss him back, tears flowing unrestrained. *That's* why Michael and Robyn never said anything. They knew exactly what was happening. I still feel betrayed, but not in the same way I originally thought. My eyes are so full that I can't see, and Jaz whispers gently to me, "Kimmie, I love you, baby girl. Just you. Do you finally understand that?"

I start to cry so hard that he just stops and holds me. "Yes. But Jaz, I was so afraid."

"I know, and I'm sorry. I think I probably went a little too far. I was trying to make a point, but I think the point got lost in the fear. That'll never happen again. I don't want you to ever doubt me. I belong with you."

I'm so confused. "You didn't want a picture of me? Just her?"

He shakes his head. "Baby, the photos are for demonstration purposes for Master Davidson. I would never, never take photos like that of you. I'm too afraid of them finding their way out and around, and I don't want anyone gawking at you. You're mine. We may scene here, but if I caught anyone taking pictures of you, they'd probably need a new camera or phone when I got done with theirs." From a few feet away, there's a groan. "I think you need to check on your sub." He leans in and whispers directly into my ear, "Be firm with her. You can do it."

Gazing in the direction of the suspended woman, I see her writhing in her ropes as she watches Jaz and me together. When she sees me looking toward her, she moans, "Mistress, please?"

"No. You'll wait until I tell you that you can come. If you do so beforehand, you'll be punished." I turn back to Jaz and search his eyes.

"Very good. Now I want to make *you* come again." With no fanfare, he drops me to my back on the table and rises above me, then does the one thing I never expected him to do.

He makes love to me. This is not frantic. He's not performing. Arms wrapped under my shoulders, he kisses me hard, our tongues winding together, teasing but satisfying. I think about all the times I've been in these performance areas, letting first one idiot and then another use me like a bitch in heat, and wonder what they must think now. And in the next second, I forget that there's a club full of people watching us and my world narrows to me and the man towering over me, powering into me and giving me his heart with every stroke of his shaft. His breath grows more ragged, and he murmurs, "God, Kimmie, you give me everything I ever needed. I'm all yours, angel. Oh, god, please, Kimmie, come with me, please?" Two more strokes and I feel his body shudder out its release. Without hesitation, I knot up and buck against him, feeling the head of his shaft slamming into the top of my channel, moving everything in my belly as it drives home all his passion and promises.

Still gasping, I look over at Amelie, watch her eyes tear, see her body writhing and bucking. She doesn't make a sound, but the pleading in her eyes is enough. I nod to her and call out, "Submissive, come for your mistress."

And she does. I'm amazed as I watch her, her body jerking and shaking, and Jaz turns his head to watch as well. I could only hope for my body to be as well-trained one day. Then he looks down into my face. "Tell me that you know I belong to you. Say it, Kimmie."

"I know you belong to me, Master."

"Again."

"I know you belong to me, Sir."

A knowing smile spreads across his face. "Again."

"I know you belong to me, Jaz. You belong to me, Jasper Andrew Givens."

"And you belong to me, Kimberly Elizabeth Hendricks. We belong together. Don't ever doubt that again."

"No, Master." Light as a breeze over the water, my fingers trace his face. I see in his eyes a reflection of me, not the me I see, but the perfection he sees, and my heart is full to overflowing. As sure as I've ever been of anything, I whisper back to my lover, "I'll never doubt again."

I've gotten dressed and I've got all of my things back in my backpack when I hear someone come out of the showers and out walks Amelie, naked and glorious. When she looks up and sees me, she smiles. After glancing at the doorway, she asks, "Can I talk to you for a minute?"

I just shrug. "Sure, I guess." She pats a seat on the bench next to her, and I join her.

For some reason, she almost looks embarrassed, and I don't understand why until she says, "I'm so sorry."

"For what?"

"For making you feel the way I'm sure you felt. I didn't like it, but when you got so angry, he told me he had to teach you a lesson."

"And did he explain that lesson?"

"He said you were angry because he was talking to me, and the only reason for that would be if you doubted your relationship with him. He said he never wants that to happen again. He loves you, Kimberly. I want you to know this: When I submit to kinbaku, submitting to the kinbaku master comes with the territory, and I know this. Every kinbaku master I've ever worked with has fucked me, as was their right. Except Jasper. He never touched me any more than he had to in getting the ropes right. That guy is one hundred and fifty percent faithful to you. There's something pure and kind and genuine about him. You're one lucky woman."

"Thanks." I can kind of feel my poor wounded heart scabbing over with her words. He told her the exact same thing he told me, and it worked. I'll never doubt him again. "I appreciate you telling me that. It just hurt so much and I didn't understand."

She wraps an arm around me and pulls me up against her. It's the first time I've ever been embraced by a naked woman, and it's kind of weird, but it's also kind of nice. "I like you, Kimberly. And you're a good submissive too. He's really proud of you and proud to be seen with you. And you make a cute couple." Towel in hand, she stands and smiles down at me. "I guess I'd better get dressed. Aaron will be looking for me."

"He's pretty damn gorgeous too," I grin at her.

"Yeah, and fucks like a racehorse. Plus he shares me with anyone I want. He's pretty cool." But a sad look crosses her face and she sighs before she says, "Still, it would be nice to have what you have with Jasper."

I watch her shapely ass wander away and think about the things she said. It's encouraging to know she could see all of that between us, and I hope everyone else did too. Kimberly the slut is gone.

Mistress Kimberly is in the house. And she'll bow to Master Jasper any time—any time at all, whatever he wants. I'm his and his alone.

CHAPTER TEN

I can tell something's going on in his head, but he's really not giving me any clues. It's been a long day. I had a submissive who couldn't stand still while I measured her, a Dominant who couldn't decide what he wanted, and another guy in his eighties who wanted a pair of leathers "that'll make my junk look perky." I wanted to tell him that I'm a leatherworker, not a magician, but I bit my tongue and told him I'd do my best. I honestly don't know what that means, but whatever—I'll figure it out.

But it's not one of those days where I feel like playing twenty questions to figure out what's going on with Jaz. I'm pretty sure he'll tell me eventually and, as usual, he doesn't disappoint. As soon as we've cleaned up the dinner dishes, he grabs my hand, leads me to the sofa, and turns to me with a big grin. "How would you like to take a little trip?"

"With you? I'll go anywhere!" I gush. Well, I would. I'd go to hell with him if he'd promise to fuck me when we got there. Might as well admit it: I'm in up to my earlobes, and I'm as happy about it as the Queen of England in a high-end haberdashery. "So where and when?"

"Tomorrow. Got any appointments through the end of the week?"

"None I can't reschedule."

"Good. Get on it." He knows damn well I want to hear more, so he hum-haws around and finally says, "Do you like St. Louis?"

Inside my head, there's shrieking and clapping. "I don't know! I've never been there! I get to go?" Yes, I'm bouncing up and down like a first-grader, and I don't give a damn. This is just too exciting.

"Yeah. I talked to my boss. I'm driving it like always, and I booked a suite at the Ritz-Carlton."

That doesn't sound right. "The company's paying for a suite at the Ritz-Carlton?"

"No, but they're giving me the money they'd spend on a room for me, and I'm just applying that to the room tab."

Now my heart sinks. I know he can't afford that. "Sweetie, you don't have to do that. The Ritz-Carlton? That's pretty expensive. I'd be happy in a Holiday Inn or ..."

His hand lifts my chin and tips my head back to look into his eyes. "I want to do this. I want to take you there and have a good time. My work will be three days; we're staying five nights, leaving on Tuesday and driving back Sunday. I'll have to be at the plant on Wednesday, so we'll arrange for someone to come and take you around, show you some sights. I'm sure I can find someone to chauffeur you around for three days."

"But Jaz, are you sure—"

"I'm positive." He kisses my forehead and I just drop onto his chest, my arms wrapping around his waist. As he strokes my hair, he whispers, "Please don't worry about money. I just want us to go there and have a good time, okay?"

No man has ever wanted to go that kind of distance for me. I'm excited about going, but I'm more excited about being with him, about having someone who thinks I'm worth the time and money to go to this kind of trouble for me. I'm not exactly sure what I think, but I know I love him more every minute that I'm breathing. "Okay. I won't, I promise. But can I take some of my own money, you know, for spending money, to buy souvenirs and stuff like that?"

I feel the vibration in his chest when he laughs. "Sure. That's fine. Maybe you'll buy me a present!"

I lift my head and gaze up at him. "Maybe I will." He leans into my face and gives me a peck on the lips. "I'll get you something nice, something that I can only get there. How's that?"

"That sounds perfect. Whatever you give me, if it's from you, I'm sure I'll love it."

My head drops back to rest on his chest. I'm going to St. Louis with Jaz. The Ritz-Carlton. How exciting! Wonder if they have those big fluffy white robes like in the movies? Wonder if I'll even need one? That makes me laugh out loud.

"What?"

"Oh, nothing. Just something silly. Wondering if they have those fluffy white robes like in the movies."

Just as deadpan as possible, he answers, "Doesn't matter. You won't need one."

Now I'm shrieking with laughter. "Oh my god! That's exactly what I was thinking!"

"See?" He drops a little kiss on the crown of my head. "We understand each other pretty well, don't you think?"

I just sigh. "Yes. And I think I love you more every day."

"I *know* I love you more every day!" He lets out a little sigh. "Kimmie, I've never been this happy in my whole life." Without warning, I just burst into tears. "Baby, what's the matter?"

It's hard to talk while I'm sobbing. "Nothing. I just never dreamed any man would ever say anything like that to me. Why, Jaz? Why do you care anything about me?"

Still stroking my hair, he answers simply, "You're beautiful. You're funny. You're smart. You're a great cook, and you appreciate my cooking too. You're as happy with a bottle of beer as with a glass of fine wine. You have great fashion sense, but you're not out spending like a drunken banker. But you know what the most important thing is about you?" I'm still blubbering as I shake my head. "You love me. And I *know* that you love me. You don't just tell me; you show me with everything you do. When you add to that your submission, there's no man on this earth who's luckier than I am. Kimmie, I don't think you have any idea what an extraordinary woman you really are."

I just can't stop crying. My heart was so damn broken, and now it's so amazingly full. If I'd even had the notion to pray for someone, this man would've been more than I could've ever hoped for. I manage to stammer, "Jaz, please, please don't leave me. Please?"

There's that rumble in his chest again when he says, "Baby girl, I'm not going anywhere. I don't think you could get rid of me if you tried. Come on, let's go to bed. It's been a long day."

With a shudder and a sigh, my tears finally end. "Hey, can I ask you something?"

"Sure."

"How could I make a pair of leathers that would make a guy's junk look perky?"

After staring at me for a full fifteen seconds, he starts to howl with laughter. "You're kidding, right?"

There's a huge grin on my face as I answer, "Nope. Got that request today, and I have no idea where to go with it."

"Well, seeing as my junk's still perky," he gasps, "I have no idea what to tell you!"

I play-snarl back, "Well, you're just no help at all."

Before I can even shriek, he stands, grabs me up, and throws me over his shoulder, slapping my ass when I come to rest there. "I'll show you what I'm a great help at!" he bellows as he carries me down the hall.

I'm kicking my feet and screaming and laughing, "Put me down! Put me down!"

He drops me across the bed like a giant bag of coffee beans and then braces himself above me. "Want some help?" he growls down at me.

I'm still laughing like a hyena. "Yes! You can help me all you want. I can use all the help I can get!"

Like lightning, he strips off my jeans and shoots me a malevolent grin. "Oh, I'm gonna help you, all right. I'm gonna help you until you're begging me to stop. Get hold of that tee and that pretty, lacy bra that I'm sure I'll love and get them the hell off, baby girl. That body of yours is mine."

"Yes, Master!" I grin and pant. While I take everything off, I watch, delighted, as he does the same. I'll never get tired of that body, no sir. It's amazing. Oh, god, I know I'm going to love this. I'm wondering what he's planning to do and, as usual, he surprises me.

Two pairs of cuffs. He puts a set on each of us, on our left arms, then cuffs us together, my right hand to his left and vice versa, so we're facing each other. Pressing my wrists into the mattress and looming over me, he stares down at me. "Just look into my eyes. Don't look away. We need to be together in this world, and I want you to know how much I love you." With no fanfare, no foreplay, no prelude of any kind, he rolls his hips forward and buries himself in me.

I've never seen a more intense pair of eyes as they capture me and hold me hostage. I couldn't look away if I tried, and yet it's difficult to keep my gaze locked with his. I've always needed clitoral stimulation, but there's something rising in me that I can't describe. It's almost like the whole world has dropped away and it's only the two of us, our bodies drawn together almost painfully. I feel like an addict waiting for the rush to hit, and I want to wrap my arms around him, but his hands holding my wrists to the mattress trap me there and keep me prisoner. One at a time, he takes a hand from my wrist, presses our palms together, and wraps his fingers through mine. As we continue to stare into each other's eyes, something amazing happens.

An orgasm unlike anything I've ever experienced settles in. It's quiet but powerful, and I'm drawn into it like the pull of a magnet. His eyes bore into my soul and he whispers, "Kimmie, I love you more than anything else in this world."

I can barely speak as another climax hits me, but I manage to groan out, "Oh, god, Jaz, I love you too. You're my everything." In just a few more minutes, another one knots me up, and I grip his fingers so tightly that I'm sure I'm hurting him, but he just squeezes back gently and keeps going, that rock-hard shaft making my body sing.

But staring into his eyes this way? I can honestly say I've never felt this connected to another living soul. It's almost like our life forces have combined, and I feel like I'm slipping into forever with him. When I look into those gorgeous brown orbs, what I see reflected back is pure joy, and I just want us wrapped up in each other's arms. I want to drown in the passion and beauty that this relationship is steeped in. "Can you feel it, baby? Feel it?" he whispers to me.

"Oh, god, yes. Yes, Jaz, I do, and I don't ever want to stop. Promise me you'll always love me."

"Always, baby." I start to say something when he moans, "Oh, god, I'm coming. I can't hold back anymore."

"Then don't. Just let go." Another orgasm hits me just as he grinds into me, setting my body on fire, and his climax is complete. He drops his body weight down onto me and buries his face in my neck, his breath hot on my skin. I murmur to him, "Can we undo these cuffs? I really want to touch you."

With a little nip on my neck, he rises and starts unhooking the cuffs. When they're off, we roll to our sides and just hold each other. I've never felt so complete before, and it's sweet and precious. "Better?" he asks with a warm smile.

"Much better." I hesitate for a few seconds, then say, "I'm so glad we don't have to use a condom."

"Me too. Never again, except for anal," he says, then adds, "always for anal. Always."

Wonder when we'll do that? I ask myself, but I don't

say anything. There's always tomorrow. I want tomorrow with Jasper. I want all of my tomorrows with him.

~

"Ready?"

"Yeah! I think I've got everything. How long is it going to take us to get there?"

"About five hours. I figured we'd stop along the way and get some dinner." Jaz reaches down and picks up my bags. "Good lord, girl, what've you got in these?"

"Bricks," I grin.

"Feels like it." Once he gets them in the car, he comes back for his own.

I notice his gig bag sitting by the door. "What's in the bag?"

He grins. "Stuff."

I grin back. "What kind of stuff?"

"Good stuff."

I like the sound of that.

Once we're on the road, I turn on the radio, but Jaz reaches over and turns it off. "Why'd you do that?"

He smiles without looking at me. "I want us to be able to talk. Can't do that with the radio going."

"Oh." I'd never thought of that. Phil didn't ever want to talk. He just listened to the radio. Half the time when I tried to ask him something, he couldn't even hear me. Of course, I've wondered if he just pretended he couldn't. "So what are we going to talk about?"

Jaz just shrugs. "I dunno. I just thought it would be nice if we could."

"Oh. Okay. So, um, I had a new client today."

He grins. "One of those Doms I asked you to call me about?"

"No!" That makes me laugh. "No, just a sub who wanted a new corset. She doesn't have a Dom. I think she's planning to look for one and she wants to look good."

"Makes sense to me." I watch him as he's driving. God, he's a looker. I still can't believe he'd have anything to do with me, but I'm sure glad he has. "So have you heard anything from the young sub with the older Dom?"

"Not lately. I'm guessing she's getting pretty big. But she's so cute. I bet that baby will be cute too."

We just keep chatting, and I get a surprise: Jaz's oldest sister, Marlene, lives in St. Louis. And it appears I'll be meeting her. That makes me extremely nervous, but I guess it's inevitable. Then I think of something else. "So are we going to a club while we're there?"

"I'll let you decide that. Let's see what happens, shall we?" I'm watching his face and there's something there that I can't define. He's up to something; I just don't know what. "So I found someone to show you around."

I just know what he's going to say. "Marlene, right?"

"Nope."

Well, that's a surprise. Once again, it's not safe to assume. "Oh? Who?"

"Misty. My friend Reggie's wife. She said she'd be glad to. Is that okay with you?"

I shrug. "Sure, I guess. I like meeting new people. That'll be fun."

"Yeah. I think it will be."

Why do I get the distinct impression that there's something going on there? That he's not telling me something? It's right there on his face, but he's not giving anything away. I decide to not ask and just wait instead. If he wants to surprise me, there must be a good reason.

We take a couple of breaks and, because it's late, we stop in Springfield and eat on the way. There's a little mom and pop Italian place, and it's really good; Jaz says he stops there when he's going to and coming from St. Louis, and I love that we're getting to do the things together that he does while he's traveling alone. We manage to roll into the *porte-cochère* of the hotel at eleven thirty. What a place! I may not be much of a traveler, but I've got a feeling it'll be a long time before I see another hotel this beautiful. The fountain out front alone would impress anyone, but the inside of the hotel is like another world. Wandering about in the lobby, I take in the furniture and artwork while Jaz checks in. Lost in my observations, I'm startled when he slips an arm around my waist from behind and says, "I've got the key. Let's go." He leads me toward a bank of elevators, and I start to ask about our luggage, but I'm guessing there's someone bringing it up for us, so I just say nothing and grin. I feel like a princess.

"Home sweet home," Jaz says with a sweep of his arm when the door to the room opens. My god—I've never seen a more opulent room. It's amazing, from the beautifully-appointed draperies to the big, regal bed. I note immediately that the headboard is solid, damn it. But I know Jaz. If he wants to play, he'll find a way to do it. I'm greeted by a bathroom that's gorgeous, all granite and chrome and glass. There are fresh flowers everywhere, their scent wafting about as we walk the room. "Like it?"

"Oh, god, Jaz, it's incredible. I feel like royalty." Without warning, he grabs my arm, yanks me up against him, and wraps his arms around my waist.

The sudden sadness on his face freezes my heart. "You are royalty, baby girl. You're my queen. This is the kind of life you should be living, not some two-bit existence with a manufacturing specialist who can't give you the things you deserve. This is what I want you to have."

"I have everything I need," I whisper and give him a peck on the lips, then add, "and everything I want. More. I have more than enough." My hands find his face, my thumbs stroking his cheeks, and I murmur into his mouth, "If all I had was you, I'd never want for anything more." The second the words are out, he crushes my lips with his in a kiss that makes little flames lick up and down my spine. I'm losing myself in it when there's a knock at the door.

"Ah, opulence has its downfalls too!" he snickers as he goes to the door. The bellman—yes, he's wearing one of those suits, to my delight—wheels the cart with our luggage into the room, and I behave myself while Jaz flips open his wallet and hands the man a bill before the gentleman retreats to the hallway. "So everything's here. And it's midnight. I've got to be at the plant tomorrow morning at eight, and your ride is coming at nine. I'm thinking we should just get some sleep. Whaddya think?"

"Oh, I don't know," I singsong back and give him my best coy smile. "I was kinda looking forward to making this bed ours."

"Oh yeah? We can do that. I'm just not up for our usual Olympic decathalon." He's coming out of his shirt and slacks, and seeing him standing there in nothing but his briefs and socks makes my tummy do little flip-flops. Before I can get comfortable with that view, he whips off the briefs, slips off his socks, and turns to me. I reach for the bottom of my top, but he barks out, "No. I'm undressing you. Stand still." The top comes off first, followed by my jeans and socks. I stand there in front of him in my bra and panties, a racy little number that I bought at the big lingerie store in the mall about a week before. They're extremely frou-frou, and I suddenly feel stupid. Someone my age standing here in something like this? Really? I should be wearing cotton granny panties and a fifties cone-shaped bra.

"You look delicious, angel," he hums into my neck as he nips it, and suddenly I'm glad I wore the set.

"I don't look ridiculous?"

"Ridiculous is the *last* term I'd use to describe you." His teeth graze my neck again before he sucks hard on it.

"No hickeys," I mumble.

"Love bites. Please. We're not in high school anymore," he snickers.

"Hickeys. Love bites. Whatever. I really don't want to wear them around St. Louis. I think my tour guide might be a little uncomfortable with that, not to mention what your sister will think."

"Trust me, they'd be fine with Misty, and Marlene couldn't care less." His hands wander from my waist up my back, and when they find the closure on my bra, they snap it open and he releases a sigh. "There we go," he whispers as he slips the straps down my arms, and I stand there in nothing but my panties as he stares at me.

I guess I squirm a little because he growls, "Stand still. What's wrong?"

With a little shrug, I mumble, "That's a little uncomfortable, you looking at me that way."

"Why?" In a second or two, he says, "Kimmie, look at me. Eyes up here, baby." When I manage to meet his gaze, he chuckles. "I've fucked you to kingdom come and back, lay face to face with your yoni, licked and sucked your clit until you're screaming, and you're embarrassed to stand in front of me naked?" He shakes his head and chuckles again. "I'll never understand women if I live to be a thousand. Never."

That makes me giggle. "We're a curiosity, I guess."

"You *guess*? Yeah, a curiosity. That's one way to put it." I get the impression with the way he's looking at me now that he's planning something, maybe something I don't want to know about, at least not yet. Then he leans down and drags my panties down my legs, stopping on the way back up to kiss my mound sweetly before standing in front of me again. "Now, go over and stand in front of the bed." I do as he says and watch him go to his gig bag, rummaging around until he pulls something out. Turning back to me, he holds out the objects he's pulled out and I almost snort.

My blue platform stilettos. He hands them to me and snarls, "Go to the bathroom, do whatever you need to do, put these on, and get back out here." Without a word, I grab them from his hands and make a bee-line for the bathroom.

It's amazing in here. There's a toilet and a bidet. Never got the hang of those things, but I decide to try it. Not bad—not bad at all. That eliminates the need for personal towelettes, I must say. I find my toothbrush and toothpaste and brush my teeth, then grab my hairbrush and brush my hair. A quick look in the mirror says that I look okay, so I slip on the shoes and head back out into the bedroom to find him waiting. Lamps and lights turned off, there are a half-dozen candles burning around the room to illuminate it. "Give me just a few seconds and I'll be right back," he says, and I hear the sound of the water running, probably for brushing his teeth. When he returns, he goes back to his bag and digs around again.

When he steps toward me, I see that there's some kind of box in his hands, a good-sized, wooden box. Gesturing at me, he entices me to reach for it, and I take it in my flattened palms, his hand resting on the lid of the box. Once I'm holding it, he opens the lid and takes out something sparkly.

It's a massive necklace covered in what looks like diamonds, and when he fastens it around my neck, it fans down and across my chest like a huge collar. Next comes a pair of earrings to match it, their dangles brushing the tops of my shoulders, followed by two large cuff bracelets, which he snaps around my wrists as I continue to hold the box. I can't imagine that there could be anything else in the box.

I'm wrong. The last item he pulls from its depths is a tiara, and it's huge and gorgeous. He places it gently on my head, then clips it in place. Even without shaking my head, I can tell it's more than secure enough to stay on through … well, whatever it is that he's planning to do. My jewels firmly set, he takes the box from my hands and places it on a small table to the side, then spins back to look at me.

What I see in his face takes my breath away. It's as though he's mesmerized by the sight in front of him, and yet it's just me, just plain, boring me. Before I can move or even think, he takes my hands and leads me out to the balcony.

I'm horrified. I know logically that the rest of the city is probably asleep—well, most of it anyway—but still, I'm naked, dripping in jewels, and standing on a balcony on the fifth floor. If it were the sixteenth, I might feel better, but it's just the fifth. Anyone driving up in the drive could easily see us up here, and yet it doesn't seem to bother him one bit. Hands on my shoulders, he turns me to face the outside, then sinks to his knees in front of me. "Hands on my head," he orders, and when I comply, he parts my lower lips and presses his face into me.

The intensity makes me gasp as his tongue finds my clit and teases it to misery, making me squirm and wiggle. A yelp escapes my lips as his hand comes down with a firm slap on my ass. "Hold still, princess. And not a word." I concentrate on not only staying still and quiet, but also on staying upright in those shoes. They weren't meant for sport, but it seems that's what we're into tonight. I'm getting closer and closer, and I groan when he stops. He stands and, with a wicked glint in his eye, he just says, "Turn around. Hands on the railing and legs shoulder width apart."

I know what's coming, and I grip the metal tightly, listening to the now-familiar sound of latex snapping. I know what's happening, and I'm torn. Part of me wants his cock buried in me, and part of me is terrified that someone is going to see us, see me because I'm on the outside and closest to the railing. That terror just feeds my arousal, and I struggle to stay steady on my feet and in my mind. His body is hot and hard when I feel him behind me, and he moans, "Take it like royalty, princess."

He takes me like I'm a common whore, and my body responds to it like a lit match to gasoline. Behind me, pounding into me, he's muttering, "I'm gonna fuck you, girl. I'm gonna fuck you until you can't walk, you hear me? I'll come in you so hard I'll lift your feet right off the ground. Like my big, thick cock in your pussy, girl?

Hmmm? Like it? Want it?" He told me to be silent, so I just wait. "Answer me, princess. Do you want to be fucked like a whore?"

"Yes, Master, fuck me like a whore," On a breath I manage say, "Oh, god, fuck me like a whore. Fuck me hard, Sir."

"I'm going to fuck you so hard and so long that your teeth will rattle. I'm gonna tear that pussy up with my hard dick. Take your hand off the rail and play with yourself until you come. Pinch and pull on those nipples and then flick that clit. And I wanna hear you telling me about it, girl," his voice snarls, and everything in my body concentrates on that one sensation of his cock dragging out and plunging back into my channel.

When I manage to pinch one nipple, I groan. "Say it, slut. Tell me how it feels to touch yourself."

"Oh, god, Master. Oh, god, I'm so turned on," is all I can squeak out.

His thrusts are hard and relentless. "Turned on? You're not turned on. You're horny, that's what you are, whore. Horny as hell. You're a horny little slut who wants me to fuck her."

"Yes, Sir, I'm so horny I can't stand it." That's no lie at all. I've never wanted to be fucked more in my whole life. "I want you to fuck me hard. Fuck me hard, Master, please? Please fuck me so hard it hurts."

He shifts positions and I realize he's stooped a little bit and fucking up and into me now, his hands on either side of me on the railing to brace himself, his breath hot on my spine as he slams into me, nearly lifting my shoes from the concrete. I'm all decked out like a proper princess, and I'm getting a world-class fucking on the balcony of the Ritz-Carlton. Holy hell. Talk about a fantasy come true. Suddenly I'm overcome with the desire to somehow see his back as he uses me. I can just imagine the muscles bunching and releasing, the contours of his skin, the sweat glistening on it as he pours such a huge amount of energy into pounding my pussy raw. It's got to be an amazing sight. I've been mindlessly pinching and twisting one of my nipples, and he snarls, "Get those fingers down to your slit and find that hard little button of yours. I want to hear you scream when you come. Get to it, slut."

I send my hand downward until it finds my wetness. For just a few seconds, I reach on downward to my cunt and lay a finger against his cock so I can feel it as he works in and out of me. There's a nip on my shoulder and he growls, "Don't be feeling my cock, girl, just diddle yourself until you come. Hear me? Don't make me punish you."

"Yes, Sir." I trail up from my introitus to my clit and start to circle it with my finger. The pressure is rising as I gasp, "Oh, holy hell."

It's doubling back on itself, his dick still ripping into me, and he calls out, "Stop! Don't you dare come yet. Your orgasm belongs to me. You won't come until I tell you to." I don't know what to do now, so I drag my hand back up and pinch and pull my nipple. "Good girl. You're a good slut. You know how to keep yourself horny for me. You like this fucking, girl? Hard enough for you?"

"Harder, Sir," I pant. "I want it harder and faster, Sir. Fuck me hard and fast, Sir."

"Fingers back to your clit, girl. Work yourself fast and hard."

"Yes, Sir." I go back to stimulating myself, and it takes almost no time for my body to respond.

And just when I think I'm going to tip over the edge, he stops me again with, "Hand to your nipple, whore. No coming for you yet. Understand?"

"Yes, Master." I'm so needy that I feel like I'll explode and I half whisper, half groan, "Oh my god. I need to come." The orgasm is right on the surface, and yet I can't have it. God, I want it so bad.

"Not until I tell you to. Work that nip. Stay hungry for it. Like this cock, girl? Want more?"

"Oh god, yes, Sir. More, please, more," I plead. I feel his finger dip into my juices and, to my surprise, he rims my asshole with it. I just moan loudly and beg silently for him to force his finger into me, but he doesn't, just rims me and fucks into me with that amazing cock.

Finally, when I'm so wound up that I feel like I'll collapse, he growls, "Hand back to that button. Ramp it up. And when I tell you to come, I want you to do it and keep stroking. Don't stop. Understand, whore?"

"Yes, Master, I understand." Oh, god. This is going to tear me apart, I can just tell. I tease and torment my swollen nub while he pounds me so hard that I'm having trouble staying on my feet. Just when I think I can't take another minute, he barks, "Come with me, slut! Do it!" and slaps me on the ass.

My pussy clamps down tight and stars burst in balls of fire behind my eyelids. My hips are churning beyond my control, and I hear Jaz remind me, "Keep going. Don't stop until I tell you to."

I can't help myself; I shriek and cry, "Oh god, fuck me, Sir! Fuck me so damn hard, Sir, please!" My finger's still working my clit when I stammer, "Oh, please, Sir, please let me stop? I can't stand it anymore, Sir, please. Please? Oh god, no more, no more, please?"

"Keep going. You want it, you know you do."

I shake my head violently, my hips still bucking. I can barely speak when I answer, "I. Want. It. Sir. Please. Oh god, please, let me, oh, oh, OH GOD!" My body convulses for a second time, and all lucid thoughts stop. It's like my fingers are working of their own accord, and the sensation of his shaft piercing me so hard and so fast intensifies everything. I'm getting lightheaded and weak, and the contractions in my belly are so strong that I'm bowed into myself, my mound pumping forward, my body trying to fuck him harder and deeper. With no warning, he grabs my hair and yanks my head backward, sending me over the edge again.

It's all rewarded when I hear him cry, "Oh, god, god, god, baby, I'm coming. Fuck, girl, I've got a gallon for you. Some day soon ..." His fingers grind into my hips as he gives me a half dozen slams that really do bring my feet up off the concrete, and then he grinds into me, the head of his dick buried in the end of my silky depths, pressing upward on my cervix and shifting everything inside my pelvis until I almost faint. In my climax-induced stupor I hear him say, "Hey, stop, babe. You can stop. Kimmie? Kimmie, stop."

My hand drops from my slit and dangles, limp and spent. Knees trembling so hard I can barely stand, I wait while his hands hold me steady, his cock still buried in me, and I try to gain something that might look like composure. I don't want him to pull out; I want him buried in me forever, but when he finally does, he tries to spin me to face him and my hand won't turn loose of the railing. That makes him snicker, and he spends a few seconds prying my fingers free, then turns me. "Baby, look at me." I'm trying to make sense of everything and he repeats, "Baby, look at me. Kimmie? Baby? You okay?"

"I, um ... uh, I," I stammer. The words just won't come out of my mouth; they're right there, but I just can't get my lips to form them.

"Kimmie, look at me." When I finally get my head to cooperate and force my gaze to his face, he's got this amused look in his eyes that sends a smile careening across my heart. "Hey, baby, I love you."

"I love you too." Finally—my mouth's working again. "That was ... um ..."

"I don't know about you, but it was awesome for me!" He's grinning like a loon, and I find it absolutely charming.

"Jaz, holy shit. I mean, holy shit. What the hell? That was crazy!" Now I'm sure I'm grinning like a loon too.

"But did you enjoy it?" There's a bit of concern on his face, and I almost giggle.

"Enjoy it? Yeah. You could say that." I keep him dangling for a few seconds before I snicker, "Can we do it again?"

He laughs out loud and sweeps me into his arms. "Next time maybe you can be a prisoner and I'll be a guard. How 'bout that?"

"You fuck me like that and I'll be whatever you want me to be," I whisper and curl into his chest. I can hear his heart beating and its rhythm reminds me of how much I love him and how much I never want to be without him.

"I'll fuck you like that every time I get a chance. And may I say, you in those jewels and heels, naked and on this balcony? Oh my god, baby girl, I've never fucked a hotter piece of ass in my life. I think the only word that'll do you justice is glorious."

Me. Glorious. He can fuck me on the lawn of the Field Museum in a chicken suit if he'll call me glorious again. Holy hell. All I can do is wrap my arms around him and press my face to his chest. And then, out of nowhere, it hits me and I'm so weary I can barely stand. I think he feels me sag and he says, "Let's get you into bed. It's been a long day and I'm pretty tired too." In one smooth motion, he lifts me off my feet and carries me to the big bed, placing me there and, if I'm not mistaken, arranging my body to his liking.

I listen while he blows out the candles and snaps off his condom, and I can feel him working to take my shoes off and then my jewelry. That reminds me of a question. "Hey, can I ask you something?"

"Yes, baby."

"Is that jewelry real?"

He chortles. "Yes. It really is jewelry."

"No, no, I mean, are they real diamonds?"

"Do you want them to be?"

I shrug and grin. "Yeah. I want them to be."

"Then they are. They're real diamonds and you're a real princess. I don't know what that makes me, but—"

"You're the king who fucked the princess and turned her into a queen," my semi-lucid mind directs my lips to say.

"And gets to keep her?"

I giggle. "And gets to keep her."

"Yay me! Scoot over, babe." When I've managed to wiggle over a bit, he crawls into the big bed and pulls me up against him. It's become automatic—my cheek rests on his chest, my free hand coming up to stroke the dark patch of hair spread across those hard pecs and down the center of those amazing abs. In the darkness, his arms holding me tight, Jaz whispers, "I love you, Kimmie. I never want another woman. You're all I'll ever need."

"Thank you, Master. You're all I'll ever need too."

A sweet, soft little kiss finds its way to my forehead and he whispers, "And you're the absolute best submissive any Dominant ever had." His hand comes up to rest on my cheek, and the heat from his palm sends a shiver of arousal through my exhausted body. "Get some sleep. Morning comes early."

Lying awake there in the darkened castle of a room, I snuggle into my king's arms and bless the universe for letting me be his queen.

CHAPTER ELEVEN

"Holy shit." That's all I can find to say. The cart sitting in the middle of the room when I wake is the most fantastic display of culinary excess that I've ever seen. Nestled on overflowing serving platters are strawberries and cream, sticky buns, eggs, sausage, bacon, biscuits and gravy, bananas, tangerines, pineapple, kiwi, and some kind of sauce to dip the fruit in. *Oh, wouldn't it be wonderful if it were butterscotch?* my half-asleep brain giggles.

"Yeah. They put out quite a spread. Okay, listen," Jaz says as he ties his tie, "I've got to run. Misty will be here in a little over an hour for you. Nine o'clock. Be ready. She's got a lot planned for you today. And here," he says, handing me a handful of folded bills. "Make sure you pay for her lunch. It's the least we can do."

"Got it. Misty. Nine o'clock. Pay for her lunch. Big day. What should I wear?"

"Got a little dress and maybe some flat sandals?"

"Yep."

"That's what I'd suggest. And take some athletic

shoes and socks with you, in case she wants to take you somewhere that'll require a lot of walking, like the zoo or somewhere like that."

"Good idea! So what time will you be done?"

He shrugs as he fastens on his watch and slips everything into his pants pockets. "I'm not sure. Sometime between five and six, I hope. I'll be working alongside her husband today, so he'll call her when we're wrapping up so you two can meet us for dinner."

"Oh! That sounds like fun!" As I talk, I chew up a sausage link and sprinkle pepper on my eggs. "What's the sauce?" I ask, pointing at the little tureen.

"Caramel." I guess I make a sad face because he laughs. "Let me guess: You wanted butterscotch."

"Bingo!" I yell, then shriek with laughter. To my surprise, he crosses the room to me and sinks down on his knees in front of me. My mouth drops open.

"Kimmie, last night was incredible. It was so much fun and, god, girl, I can't believe how well you took that fucking."

"I wanted more," I assure him, my eyes staring into his.

"Oh, you're gonna get more, to be sure, and probably this evening."

"Good." I look up at the clock. "How far away is the plant?"

"I'd better go," he says in answer to my question. "I'll call you a couple of times during the day. But have fun, please?"

"Yes, my liege," I intone in my most serious voice and do a fake bow from my chair.

"Good god, you're silly. And I love it." Jaz rises to his feet and then kisses the top of my head. "I'll see you this evening. Have a fun day and enjoy yourself. Please have Misty take some pictures and send them to me. I'd love to see what you're up to."

"Yes, Sir, I'll do that. Bye, baby." I rise and make it to the door before he has a chance to get out. When my hand reaches out and touches his arm, he spins around and grabs me up in his arms.

"Bye. I love you, Kimmie."

I smile into his eyes. "I love you too, Jaz. Have a good day and don't work too hard." He leans in, gives my lips a little smack, and then the door closes behind him.

All I can do is stand there and hug myself. I know I should be getting ready to go, but I wander out onto the balcony and stand there in the morning sunlight, looking out across the city and thinking about last night. God, that was so fucking hot. Poor Robyn. She was going on about how gorgeous he is, but she'd just die if she knew how he fucks me. I'd have to fight her off with a big stick. Unfortunately, I have a feeling I'm going to have to fight off a lot of women with a big stick, but I don't care. As long as he makes it clear that he wants me to, I'll send 'em all packing. He's mine and he's going to stay that way if I have a say in it.

It's not until the hot water in the shower is pouring down over me that I realize how tired and sore my muscles are. I think about all the things it takes to survive an encounter with his body. Stamina, balance, muscle control, strength—the list goes on and on. I don't know if I've been in his bed or the athletic department of the nearest university. I catch the scent of my perfume, his cologne, and our sex, and I want to stand there and breathe it in all day, but she—someone named Misty, apparently—will be here soon, and I've got to be ready. I find the little dress that I brought with me, some panties and a bra, and a little pair of sandals that I bought at a consignment store. I decide in that moment that I'll buy my clothes at consignment and thrift stores from now on. I want to help him have the things he needs and wants, and he deserves to have nice things to wear to work. I can work in anything.

I've gotten the last of my jewelry on, including my collar, when there's a knock at the door. I expect room service, but instead, a cute, buxom redhead stands there with a huge smile on her face.

And a collar around her neck.

Holy crap! This is turning out to be a spectacular day! my brain screams. "You must be Misty?"

"Yes! Hi! You're Kimberly, right?" she gushes with her hand outstretched.

"Yeah! Come on in. I keep thinking room service will come and get the breakfast stuff," I say in way of apology.

"Oh, they will." She looks over the food. "May I?"

My eyebrows shoot up and I smile. "Sure! Take whatever you want."

"Oh, this is good sausage," she mumbles around the link she's chewing.

"Yes it is. I loved it. The bacon's pretty good too. Shame the eggs are cold. They were wonderful. Oh, and try those strawberries with that sauce. It's delish," I tell her as I put on my last earring. Then I decide to step out on a limb. "I like your collar. It's very pretty."

"Thanks! Yours is too." She sweeps a strawberry through the sauce and grins. "Yum!" Then she asks, "Do you know how I came to be here?"

"I'm sorry. I don't quite know what you mean."

"You know Jaz and my Sir know each other from California, right?"

"No! Really?" Well, that mystery is now solved. That was going to be my first question for him when he got back.

"Yeah. They both worked at the plant out there. Jaz was severed, and then Reggie had to go when the plant closed. Reggie found this job and let Jaz know about it; we were hoping to be at the same location, but they put Jaz in Chicago. I really like it here, but I've never been to Chicago. What's it like?"

We spend a few minutes talking as I tell her about the museums and zoo, the ball parks and stadiums, and all of the shopping. I'm sure to throw in, "But you have much better winters here. Ours are vicious. I dread them, and I'm happy to see them go."

"I bet, although we can have some pretty bad weather. I wish Jaz could've been here instead of there. But then he never would've met you. Sir says the guy's head over heels in love with you."

"I know I'm ass over teacup in love with him," I grin.

"Of course you are! He's gorgeous, fit, and sexy as hell. What's not to love?"

"Exactly." I pick up my bag and rifle through it. "Damn. I forgot to ask him for a key."

Misty's licking her fingers. "Oh, well, just make sure you've got everything. We'll be meeting them tonight anyway."

"True. So where are we going?"

"Thought I'd show you around a bit. Come on. It'll be fun!" Misty leads the way and I look around the room before I close the door. Hope I didn't forget anything important. If I did, I'm screwed.

We start out at the Gateway Arch—and I flatly refuse to ride the elevator to the top. Not happening, and she manages to snap a picture of me that makes it obvious exactly what I'm saying as she tries to talk me into it. Busch Stadium where the St. Louis Cardinals play baseball is amazing. Our lunch stop is at a little café at LaClede's Landing, and there's a really cute magic and costume shop there. Wandering around, I find a costume for a farm girl, give it just a few seconds' consideration, and buy the damn thing. Wonder what Jaz will say to that?

We spend the afternoon in Forest Park at the art museum and the planetarium. I've always loved planetariums, and theirs is especially fun. There's a place called the Jewel Box that's like a huge terrarium, and I love that too. We stop down near the mall and have a coffee—I have chai—and I spend my time asking Misty about things Jaz and I could enjoy together on Saturday.

"Is he a big science person?" she asks me. Good question. I have no idea. When I shrug, she says, "The science museum is incredible. And the Missouri Botanical Gardens is beautiful. You'd both enjoy that. If you like zoos, the zoo is really nice too." I know at that moment that we're not going to have enough time to do everything I'd like, so we'll just have to pick something. But when she says, "Oh, and Grant's Farm. The Clydesdales are there, you know," I know exactly where we'll be going.

I like Misty so well that I find myself hoping we can come back, and I wonder what Reggie's like. "So have you got a picture of you and Reggie?"

"Sure! Wanna see?" Misty gushes, and I nod

enthusiastically. She whips out her phone and pokes around on the screen, then hands it to me.

Sure enough, there's Misty, not much shorter than me, standing beside the most enormous black guy I've ever seen. He's got to be seven feet tall. "Holy hell. How tall is he?"

She starts to giggle. "Seven feet two inches. He used to play professional basketball."

"I bet he did! How on earth did you two meet?"

The story is wonderful, how they found each other online. Reggie was in California and Misty was in Florida. They talked back and forth, but it wasn't until he had a chance to move to St. Louis that they got to finally meet each other. "We were careful because we didn't really know each other, well, you know, in person, so it was kinda scary the first few times. But he was just like he seemed on the phone and the internet, and I was comfortable with him pretty quickly."

"And the lifestyle?"

"We talked about that before we ever actually met. We met on a website for kinksters. He liked me because I didn't have naked pictures of myself posted, and I liked him because when he sent me the friend request, it wasn't a dick pic. Of course, I got one of those later!" she laughs.

I just have to ask the question that's burning in my chest. "So is there a club around here?"

"There are several, but we really like the one where we're members. It's clean and the people are friendly, and they're very non-judgmental. Believe it or not, one of the clubs wouldn't let us in because we're an interracial couple."

I wrinkle my nose. "What the hell century are we in again?"

"I know, right? Idiots." She turns up her upper lip in disgust and rolls her eyes. "If that's how they feel, we don't want to be members there anyway."

"Exactly. So what do we do the rest of the afternoon?" I'm looking at my watch and I think we've still got a couple of hours to kill.

"Come on. I'll take you to my favorite store." This should be fun. I'm sure they have cutesy dresses and sexy shoes and all that stuff.

Oh, yeah, sexy shoes and all that stuff. It's an adult store, The Painted Lady. I don't think there's a single thing anyone could want that they don't have. Craziness, that's what it is. And then she takes me to a big wooden door with huge iron hinges. "Here's the fun stuff," she whispers and throws the door open.

It's a warehouse full of dungeon equipment. My god. There are things in here that I've only seen in pictures, and I've been a member of the club for years now. One of the ones I really like is a huge bondage bed, and I make a mental note to see if I can find them online. But there, in the store, it's about twenty-three hundred dollars, and we can't afford that. Plus I don't want to have to move the damn thing, and that's exactly what would happen.

We putter around in there for a couple of hours, and I buy some blow job candy—it's really like pop rocks—plus some throat numbing spray and a gel that's guaranteed to make my clit tingle. Like I need that ... and then my phone rings. "Hey, Sir, how's it going?"

"Good! You girls about finished up?"

"Yep. I got some fun stuff too. Wait until I tell you about everything we did."

I hear him snort with laughter. "So I hear there was no way you were going up in the arch!"

"Absolutely not. Never gonna happen."

"Never say never, baby girl."

"Never. Never, never, never."

"Okay, all right. Point made. So what's for dinner?"

"Where do you and Reggie want to go?"

"We want seafood or Italian. Which one would you—"

"Italian! Please!"

Now he's really laughing at me. "Okay, Reggie says to tell Misty to go to Guido's Trattoria. She knows where it is."

"Okay. I'll tell her. Hey."

"Yeah?"

I try to whisper loudly enough that he can hear me. "I missed you today."

"Same here, baby. Love you. See you in a bit."

"Love you too. Bye." I turn to Misty. "Guido's—"

"Trattoria. How did I know?" she laughs. "We'll be there in fifteen."

The restaurant is elegant beyond belief. And I hate that. I'm sure it's expensive, and Jaz really can't afford this. Both guys greet us with kisses, and I'm instantly impressed with Reggie. He seems like a fabulous guy who's just positively smitten with Misty. She watches him with google eyes all evening like she just can't get enough. God help them, they're in as deep as we are.

Dinner is incredible, starting with lovely wine-steamed mussels. I let Jaz order for me, and he orders a *pasta al pomodoro*. I love the tomatoes but, unlike a lot of dishes with tomato sauce, this is very light and refreshing.

He has the biggest lump of lasagna I've ever seen in my life, and I'm thrilled to see it has a healthy layer of spinach and toasted pine nuts in it. Bless his heart, he tries.

We sit around afterward with our wine, sipping and talking. Finally, Jaz asks, "So do they let visitors into your club?"

"With me they will or I'll knock some heads together!" Reggie says, laughing into his wine glass. If he asked me to let someone in, I'd say yes. I wouldn't want to be on the other end of his wrath, no sir.

Jaz turns to me. "Would you like to go?"

"I sure would! Can we?"

Jaz looks at Reggie. "Tomorrow night?"

"Thursday nights are usually pretty quiet. I'm sure that won't be any problem at all. Let me call the manager and explain the situation to him. Would you be willing to do a shibari demonstration?"

"Kinbaku and, yes, I'd be glad to." Jaz turns to me. "Do you think you can do that?"

"I'll most certainly try but I don't want to embarrass you." I'd die if he were embarrassed by me freaking out.

"You'll do fine. I won't do anything too terribly restrictive, and I'll take my time and let you take yours to settle into it." He looks at me and says, "I know you're thinking about Amelie. It's okay. I don't expect you to be her, Kimmie. You're a different person, and you'll react differently. And we'll adjust." I just nod. "Good. Make the commitment, Reggie. We'll do it if they want."

"Good deal. I know they'll let you in that way. And you'll be able to do whatever you please after the demonstration. Do you need a third or fourth? Because we've got some guys at the club who're really good at—"

Jaz's eyes flash. "No. I don't make it a habit to share. Ever."

Reggie nods. "That's cool. Just thought I'd offer."

"Thanks, but no." Jaz turns to me. "More wine?"

"Nah. But thanks, Sir." I try to stifle a yawn but I can't.

"Looks like you need to take someone back to the hotel and put her to bed!" Reggie chuckles.

"Looks like I do! Hey, listen, thanks for dinner. And Misty, thanks for showing Kimmie a good time. You guys got something fun to do tomorrow?" Jaz asks her, and her face lights up.

"I think so. But she'll have to call you several times during the day." She turns to Reggie. "Is that okay, Sir?"

"Perfectly okay. So you two can find your way back to the hotel?"

"I have nav," I say and hold up my phone.

"Then see you in the morning, Jaz." The guys exchange handshakes and then Reggie hugs me and Jaz hugs Misty. I like these people. They're comfortable to be around, friendly, warm, everything I'd want in friends.

Friends. I have new friends. I've spent years with just Michael and Robyn, too afraid and damaged to go out and meet anyone new. But today I've had fun. On the way back to the hotel I tell Jaz, "They're so nice. I wish we lived closer."

"Me too. But you have Michael and Robyn."

"Oh, yes. I'd never trade them in for anything."

He pats my thigh as he drives and I watch various landmarks go by. St. Louis is a pretty place. I'm so happy to be here with him.

Once we're back in the hotel, the very first thing he does is gather me into his arms and kiss me—hard. When he pulls back and looks at me, he grins. "God, I missed you. All I could think about today was last night. You're a magnificent fuck, missy."

"You're a magnificent fuck too, Master." The minute the word is out of my mouth I can feel him hardening against me. "I hope I get to experience some of that magnificence tonight."

"Absolutely. Got anything new for me? Did you buy me a present?"

"Well, sort of. Wanna see?"

He laughs aloud. "Sure! Hope it's good!"

"Oh, I think you'll like it. I'll just be going into the bathroom now," I say as I pick up my bag of new stuff. "Nothing going on in there. Absolutely nothing."

"Of course not." As I walk away, he starts stripping off clothes, and I know he'll be naked when I come back out. And that's fine with me.

I get all dressed and stick my head out the bathroom door. "Ready?"

"Um, yeah, I suppose. What am I supposed to be ready for?"

I step out of the bathroom and I get a, "Sweet mother of god, look how fuckable you are!" I just grin. I'm barefoot, and I'm wearing the tiniest pair of little Daisy Duke shorts ever made and a red and white checked shirt that's tied at my midriff. My hair's up in pigtails, and I've got a rope belt around my waist. Did I mention my push-up bra? Yeah, the girls are high and huge, and Jaz's eyes almost pop out.

"Hey, Sir! How y'all doin'? Y'all wouldn't know somewhere that a little ol' country girl could find a man, now wouldja?" I'm trying hard not to start giggling. He's not. He's staring at my tits.

"I think I might know one who'd love to meet you. How 'bout you come on over here and let me see how purdy you are, little girl." His outstretched hand is met with mine, and I'm more than ready for him to take me and tear me down with that yummy cock of his. I swear, I think he's sexier right now than he was the night before, if that's possible. "Um-um-ummmm, look at you, darlin'. You got yourself quite a rack there, don'tcha?"

I thrust my chest out. "Yes, Sir, I do. And I'm lookin' for a man who can handle 'em. Know any around these parts?"

"Actually, I do. Let's see what we got here, girly." He unbuttons my blouse but leaves it tied, and then pulls it open to expose my red check bra. "Nice bra. Very nice." He slips a hand into each cup and just hefts my breasts out of them, leaving them supported by the cups but completely exposed. There's a rattle in his pocket and before I can respond, he snaps a clover clamp on one of my nipples and I shriek. "You wanted a man, you've got one. Take it like a big girl."

"Oh, Sir, please ..." I moan as he clamps the second one on. "Oh, shit! Oh, god, please ..."

"Please what?"

Now I'm panting. "Please, Sir, jerk that chain."

He gives the chain a sharp tug and the clamps tighten. In that moment, I go wet. "Yesssss," I squeeze out.

"Down on your knees, country girl. I'm gonna fuck your face something fierce." I think about the exploding blow job candy I bought, but I don't want to stop in this moment. It's too good. "Take off that belt," he barks, so I untie it and hand it to him. He moves in behind me and ties my wrists together with the rope run through the back belt loop. "There. At my mercy, and I have very little," he lets out in a menacing whisper. "Open wide and take this cock, girl."

Straight down my throat. I cough the first time, but after that, I'm fine. I add in a little hum and he really gets into it, his hands tangled in my hair and his face a study in ecstasy. This is what I live for. This is what I want. Being used is my calling *if* I'm being used by a man I know cares for me. I'm lost in thought, my nipples tingling and my pussy dripping. Pulled out of my reverie by his voice, he growls, "Take my offering, submissive. Swallow it down." In a split second, my throat is flooded and he lodges his cock in it, grinding in and then holding still.

I don't fight him. I can't breathe, and it's okay. Things start to get very, very dark, and then suddenly I'm gasping as he pulls out. As soon as I've caught my breath, he slaps me—not hard, just a wake-up call kind of slap. A groan escapes my lips. "Had enough yet?" he asks, and he's answered with the shaking of my head. "Is that right?" Leaning down, he grabs the chain on the clover clamps and gives it a sharp jerk, enough to make me squeal. "I think we need to play rough tonight, don't you?"

"Yes, Sir. Please."

"Good deal. Tonight I own your body. It's mine to play with however I want, and I want to give you a reminder of who you belong to." This isn't the Jaz who usually plays so sweetly with me, and I like it. "Get up off your knees," he orders, and helps me by pulling upward hard on the chain. That makes me almost leap to my feet, which is difficult, seeing as how my hands are tied. "To the bed. Lean over it." He doesn't join me, and I hear him rustling around—the gig bag. When he comes back, he reaches around me, unbuttons and unzips the shorts, and pulls them down and off. Something is rubbed all over my ass, and I recognize the scent of the lavender oil from before. As soon as he stops rubbing, he says simply, "I can't wait to see your ass red." The next sound I hear is the swish of a flogger's falls, and then he makes contact.

There's no way to hold it back—I yelp. The pain takes me completely by surprise, and it warms me from head to toe. The strikes keep coming, and I'm shocked that Jaz would do this, even though I need it. What the hell's gotten into him? Mind you, I'm not complaining, not one bit. It just seems so out of character for him, and yet I'm so excited I can barely breathe. By the time the last strike hits, I'm a panting, wriggling, writhing mess.

He follows with, "I really think it's time we did something different, don't you?"

I have no idea what he means, but yeah, bring it. "Yes, Sir. I'm here for your use."

"Good. Stay put." I feel him step away and then he's back, and there are two snaps—one of latex, and one of a bottle cap. And I know what he's about to do. This will be it, the final frontier of our sexual realm, and he's about to explore it. I can't wait. God, I wish I'd known he wanted to do this so I could've done some prep, but I have to trust that whatever happens, it'll be okay. "Kimmie, safeword?"

"Pickle, Sir."

"Very good. If you need it, use it, but I hope you won't." The trickle of lube is cold, and I wait expectantly while he works it into my rosette. I wasn't sure this was something he'd ever want—we've never really talked about it—but looks like it is, and that's fine with me. And just like in the men's room that day, he orders, "Not one sound. You'll be punished for non-compliance." It crosses my mind to defy just to be punished, but this all seems so odd for him that, on second thought, defiance might not be the best idea.

And then he shoves in. Maybe shove isn't the best word; he does take his time with the first two strokes, but after that, it's game on. Jaz isn't the largest guy I've ever been with, but he's plenty big enough, just a bit above average, and I'm having trouble staying quiet. Most of the guys I've done anal with wanted me screaming, so this seems even more odd than before. I really can't figure out what's going on with him, but I'm turned on to a fucktastic level, so I decide to get into it and worry about the emotional stuff later.

That's when I realize: He hasn't made a sound either. Not one peep except to direct me. After about ten more strokes, he grabs my hair and leans back into it, pulling my head up more than enough to restrict my airway. The only way I can describe this ass fucking is aggressive. He's not intentionally trying to hurt me, but he's not intentionally trying not to either, just pounding away like there's no tomorrow. Because of the scars and curves, his cock is challenging for this. It's rubbing every spot I need it to, and I want so badly to come that I can't stand it, but I don't think I can. It's just not possible. I know my juices are running down my legs and there's nothing I can do about it except ride it out. I'm about to just give up when he stops, his shaft buried in my ass, his tight, full balls against my pussy, and leans around me. Oh, god, is he going to do what I think he's going to do?

He absolutely is. Finding my hot spot, he strokes like a maniac and pretty soon I'm wishing I could cry out. The orgasm isn't pleasant; it's violent and over-the-top intense, and I jerk and convulse with out-of-control spasms. He just keeps stroking wildly, and I feel another one coming right behind the first. The second one is just downright scary and crazy, and I'm losing my battle to stay on my feet. Just as the realization hits that I'm going down onto my knees, he stops stroking my clit and starts pounding my ass again.

I shudder and come, and he just keeps going. He wrings at least three climaxes out of me just from the stroking of my G-spot through that thin membrane that separates my pussy and my ass. For me, the question becomes how long he can keep it up—literally. He's got great staying power, but this is unlike anything I've ever seen. He goes on and on and I find myself lifting off into subspace, drifting along as I wait for the next orgasm to hit and for him to finally come.

His climax brings my flight to a plummeting halt. In all the years I've spent in the lifestyle and all the things I've done, I've never known a man to have an orgasm like that. He turns loose of my hair, grips my hips, and bows his back over me, hunching me like a maniac, like some kind of wild animal.

Through it all, he's never made a sound. Finally still, he rises up behind me and I can feel him trembling, hear him panting. Then he pulls out of me, unties my hands, and simply says, "Go shower." That's all. It's all I can do to straighten up and, when I do, it's to watch him strip off his condom, pull on his shorts, and walk slowly out onto the balcony.

Too weird. I really don't understand what's going on, so I head on into the bathroom, take off my shirt and bra, and climb in. Other than the butt plug that one night, it's been a long time since anyone fucked my ass, and that tiny little ring is now on fire and sore. Once I've washed it gingerly with some antibacterial soap, I take my usual shower, dry off, comb out my hair, and wrap a towel around it. To my amusement, there *is* one of those fluffy, white robes on the back of the bathroom door, but I bypass it and instead walk out into the suite naked.

Through the sheer draperies, I can see him, still sitting in one of the chairs on the balcony, and I tiptoe out that direction. He never told me I could talk yet, so I'm not sure what to do. I decide to do the one thing that seems right.

Silent and waiting, I sink to my knees beside his chair in the pose I finally developed. The concrete of the patio is rough and cold, but I don't care. Something's up and I don't know what it is, but I want to find out. If he needs something, or someone, I want to be there. After what seems like forever, he whispers, "I'm sorry, Kimmie." Apparently he realizes why I'm not responding and he says, "It's okay. You can talk now."

"Thank you, Sir."

"No, thank you. Your body was just incredible, as it always is." The silence grows thick between us again, and I finally can't stand it anymore.

"Sir, is something wrong? Have I done something wrong? Because if I have, if you'll just tell me, I'll be glad to apologize for—"

He holds up a hand to quiet me and sighs before he speaks. "No, baby, you haven't done a thing wrong. I'm so sorry. You know I love you, right?"

"Yes, Sir." I just go back to sitting there, waiting, and even though I fight them, big tears start welling up in my eyes and then trickle down my cheeks. Then my nose starts running, damn it. I guess he hears me sniffle because he turns and looks down at me, and the look on his face is pitiful.

"Hey, come here. Sit on my lap. Oh, baby," he whispers to me as I climb onto his legs and he wraps his arms around me. "It's okay. I'm sorry. You haven't done one single thing wrong. You're perfect."

"Sir, I'm a long way from perfect."

"You know what I mean. But it's not you." He lets out another big sigh. "Do you know why I'm really here this week?"

"To work."

"Yes, but there's another reason."

I shrug. "All I know is to work."

"Yeah. Well, the real reason I'm here is because I was up for a promotion to another position." He said *was*. Oh, god, no. Before I can ask what happened, he says quietly, "They passed me over for someone who's been with the company longer. Problem is, they have half my skills and they've made messes of the last five projects they've done. And I had to help straighten them out."

"That's not fair, Sir. It's not fair at all."

"Life's not fair, Kimmie." I sure as hell know *that's* true. "But I was really counting on that promotion. It would've been more money, it would've cut down on my travel, and," he says with sadness in his voice, "it would've put me here with Reggie and Misty. I come here a lot and I really like this town. I would've loved to be here with them." My heart starts to hurt until he adds, "I would've loved for *us* to be here with them." He didn't mean alone, and my panic starts to subside a little, but I still hurt for him.

"Can you just find another job? Something here instead of in Chicago?" My mind is churning with all my ideas now, and I know I've got to get busy.

"I'm trying, but there isn't that much around here,

believe it or not. There's an automotive plant here, but they don't have any openings. Trust me, I know; I've checked with them about a dozen times."

I try to think of something that'll brighten him up a little. "Well, you certainly hid all of this very well during dinner. I had no idea there was anything wrong, and I think we both had fun, didn't we?"

A soft little chuckle rises from his throat. "Yeah, we did. I mean, Reggie knows what's going on. He's the one who pressured them to consider me. It was down to me and the other guy, and Reggie's still in shock that they chose him. Doesn't make any sense, but that's what they did."

"I'm so sorry, baby. I really am." I put my hands on his cheeks and give him a little peck on the lips.

Thank god that makes him smile. "It's okay. I've still got you. And I'm sorry I was so rough on you, but I needed to blow off some steam. Are you okay?"

"Yeah, I'm fine. And that's fine too. If there's a way you can use my body to relieve stress or make your world a little better, that's one of the things I'm here for. That and to love you."

His arms tighten around me and he presses one cheek to my chest. My arms are wound around his neck, and my hands automatically drag upward into his hair. I scratch his scalp gently with my fingernails and run my fingers through that thick darkness, feeling its silkiness. As I do, I can feel him relax and sag against me, and my heart is so full that I think it'll explode.

After we've sat there for a very long time, he whispers, "We should go to bed. I'm sure you and Misty have some things to do tomorrow. At least you're having some fun."

"Yes, I am. She's a hoot, and we're having a really

good time. Thank you so much for bringing me, for this beautiful room and the wonderful food and the great company." Now I start to sniffle again. "And thank you for loving me and wanting me here with you. I just wish you'd told me from the beginning why we were coming here."

"Shhhhh, don't cry. Thank you for loving me, precious. And I didn't say anything because I didn't want you to be disappointed if it didn't work out, but I didn't factor in how disappointed I'd be. I don't think I realized how much I was counting on this until it didn't happen. I don't think 'crushed' is a strong enough word." He draws back, looks at my face, and then kisses me. "Let's get some sleep. Tomorrow will look better, I think. Stand up." Climbing off his lap, I wait until he's standing and take his hand. As we step back into the bedroom, he pats me on the butt and says, "I'm going to get a quick shower. Get on in the bed. I'll be right out."

I know he wasn't in there long, but by the time he comes out, I'm sound asleep. Somehow I feel his weight shift the bed, then feel his warmth behind me, his skin against mine setting me right. I dream, and in my dreams, I see that little boy again, and he's leading a calf down a road. He asks, "Hi, ma'am. Would you like some fresh milk? I'm not big, but I will be someday, and so will my cow." In the dream, I scoop up the boy and kiss him on the cheek, and he smells like clover and old-fashioned lye soap. Then he asks, "What's your name?"

"My name is Kimberly. What's yours?"

With a smile full of sunshine and promise, he says, "My name's Jasper. Nice to meet you, ma'am."

After my trip to the bathroom at three o'clock, I make my way back to the bed and look down at the man there.

His face is smooth and relaxed, and there's something so innocent and pure about him, his chest gently rising and falling with his breath. When I scoot back in beside him, his arms reach out to me, and I cuddle into them. His breath is warm on my neck when he whispers, "I love you, Kimmie."

"I love you too, Jaz," I whisper in reply just before his warmth lulls me back to sleep.

CHAPTER TWELVE

When Misty shows up on Thursday morning, I'm dressed and ready, but I'm in the middle of The Most Important Thing, as I've come to think of it. "Ready to go?" she chimes.

"Nope. I've got something going on. And please keep to yourself anything you hear while I'm doing this, okay? It'll only take me a few more minutes, but I need to get this done. Mum's the word?"

She does a pretend lip-zipping. "Not a word to anyone, I promise."

"Good." I look at my notes and punch another number into my phone.

When they answer on the other end, I ask for Miss Babcock. "Hi, Kimberly! How are you?"

"I'm good. And you?"

"Can't complain. You ready to list?"

"I think so. Can you get it ready for about a month from now?"

"Oh, sure! Want to wait a little, huh?"

"Yeah, just a little. But something's happened that

makes me think I should just go ahead with it. How long do you think it'll take to sell?"

"Not long. You live in a quiet neighborhood, but you're really close to downtown, so it should go pretty fast."

"Even though it's only two bedrooms?" When those words leave my lips, I see Misty's eyes go round.

"Oh, yeah. No one will balk at that. It's all about the location. How about I come over, take some pictures, things like that."

"I'm not there. I'm in St. Louis, but I'll be home Monday. Will that work?"

"Sure!"

We make arrangements to meet on Monday, and I'm pretty excited. When I hang up, I make another phone call, this time to the offices of Wilson, Wilson, and Green, Attorneys at Law. Working my way through secretary after secretary, I finally get Kevin Wilson, the second Wilson in the name. "Ms. Hendricks! Hope you're well."

"I am. Quite. And I hope you are too."

"I am. And I have some very, very good news for you."

"Yeah?" Now my heart starts to race.

"I found the relatives and talked to them. Believe it or not, they're so excited that someone might be living there again that they don't want anything. Every one of them has given me a clear title. So you want this to go into Mr. Givens' name?"

"Yes, please. Send any tax bills to me. Does he have to sign it?"

There's a chuckle on the other end. "Actually, I think I can work a way around that. Shouldn't be much owed in taxes either."

I'm still in shock that none of his relatives want to lay claim. "Okay, so what are your fees?"

"You know, I'm so impressed that you'd do this for him that I'm going to make it a flat thousand dollars. Is that within your reach?"

Now my heart is pounding out of my chest. "Oh, absolutely! Oh, thank you so much, Mr. Wilson! I can't believe this. He's going to be so excited!"

"Great, great. I'm so glad. So I'll get everything drawn up and let you know when it's done. Sound good?"

"Sounds wonderful. Thank you so much, Mr. Wilson." When we hang up, I let out a big sigh. "One more call," I tell Misty, whose eyes are getting bigger by the minute.

When his secretary answers, I ask for Mr. Jennings. "Hello," he barks.

"Mr. Jennings? This is Kimberly Hendricks. We spoke on the—"

"Oh, yes, the old Stevens place. I remember. So have you made a decision?"

"Yes, sir. The paperwork is being done now. I'm trying to sell my house in a few weeks, so as soon as that happens, I'll give you a call and we can talk about what needs to be done. Now I have to tell you, I won't be there—no one will—so I'll have to trust you as far as repairs go. I got your name from the chamber of commerce there in town, so I'm hoping you'll live up to your reputation for honesty and dependability."

"I most certainly will. I've lived here all my life. I've watched that old place just start falling down and it made me so sad. I'm glad someone's taking an interest in it. Mr. and Mrs. Stevens were wonderful folks."

"So I hear. Well, thanks, Mr. Jennings. I just wanted to give you a heads-up."

"Thank you, Ms. Hendricks. Talk to you soon."

When I put the phone down this time, Misty's eyes are bugging. "What are you doing?" she whispers as though there's a crowd and everyone's listening in.

"I'm making arrangements to make Jaz's biggest, wildest dream come true."

"Are you talking about his family's farm?"

"Yeah. How did you know about that?"

Misty grins. "I've heard him talking to Reggie about it. He gets all dreamy-eyed when he mentions it."

"Yes, he does. So you can't say a word. I'm doing everything I can to keep it secret until I can get most of the work done on the house, at least until it's liveable."

"What about work?"

I shake my head. "The farm will *be* his work. He dreams about doing this, and it's doable. I've already talked to the people at the extension office there, and they say there's more than enough land there to make a decent living off of. I've got to have the money from my house so we have something to live on initially and money to buy a few things to get started, but I can always get a part-time or full-time job to help out."

She gives me a wistful smile. "You really love him, don't you?"

I let out a little giggle. "Honey, there isn't a word for how I feel about Jaz. It's just so ... he's just so ... oh, I don't know. I just love him."

"Well, then, we've got quite a day ahead of us! Ready to go?" Misty stands and heads toward the door.

I grab my bag and follow her. "Ready to go!"

~

"Oh, god, girl, this is amazing!" As I sit there in my fluffy mint green robe, the mud mask tightening on my face and sipping a mimosa while a gorgeous French guy named Gérard does my nails, I try to relax. It's hard to be pampered.

"He gave me quite the budget for you today, so we're going to have it all!" she coos.

Inside my head I tell myself, *He really can't afford this. I should pay for it.* Unfortunately, I don't have this kind of money either. But this mimosa is damn good.

Two hours later, the girl says, "And I think this grey eyeshadow will look good on you."

"How much is this?" I squeak.

"Kim, doesn't matter. If it's what you need, get it," Misty calls back as a girl in a black cape-like dress brushes bronzer on her face.

"Margot," the taller, older hairdresser says, "I need to borrow Kimberly for a few minutes. It's time for her shine treatment to be rinsed and conditioned."

"Sure." She helps me down out of the chair. "I'll be right here when you get back."

I follow the tall woman, Kathleen, back to the hair area, but it's hard to keep up with these little cotton thingies between my toes. Misty calls to me, "Love that toenail polish, girl!"

"Thanks," I call back. Good god. I'm afraid when this is all done, I'll look in the mirror and won't recognize myself. Sheesh.

But I get a huge surprise when my shine treatment is done and dried. Kathleen spins me around for a peek, and I gasp at my hair. It's sleek and shiny with just the right amount of curl, and the way it tumbles around my shoulders is gorgeous. I can't help but smile. Jaz is going to love it.

I leave with my face all made up surprisingly well—no clown look here, thank god—and carrying a sack full of all kinds of products. There's stuff for my hair, and new nail polish, and all kinds of makeup. I look beautiful but feel horrible. That was an enormous amount of Jaz's money that I just spent. I sure hope he thinks it was worth it.

We're headed out for some lunch when I yell, "Stop! Turn around!"

"What? Why?"

"I want to go to that little shop over there. Please?" I point to a yellow- and orange-striped awning.

"Okay. Looks cute. I've never been in there before." Misty wheels into the parking lot and I practically jump out of the car.

It's the dress in the window that catches my eye, and I can't wait to try it on. First thing I do, out of habit, is look at the price tag, and I can't believe it—it's eighty-five dollars, which is a very good price. I put it on, step out of the dressing room, and Misty gives a long, low whistle. The clerk stops what she's doing and turns to say, "Oh, that's gorgeous on you!"

With a deep plunging V-neck front and back, the bodice is criss-crossed and all ruched in a dove gray. The skirt is sleek and fitted and comes to just below my knees. All I need is a pair of black heeled sandals and I'll look elegant. "Here. Try on this jewelry with it," the clerk says and fastens the necklace around my neck.

I look in the mirror and gasp. Standing there looking back at me is a woman I almost don't recognize. She's thin, but her bustline is full and her hips are curvy. Her long hair is glossy and healthy-looking, and her skin is rosy and clear, not to mention her shining blue eyes. My eyes tear up and everything is blurry. I'm surprised when Misty comes over and puts an arm around my shoulders. "You okay?"

"Yeah. It's just that I used to look so awful, so run-down and tired and raggedy. I didn't know I could look this good. I mean, I'm no beauty, but I don't look so bad." I'm almost crying just standing there looking at myself.

"What do you mean, you're no beauty? You're lovely! Just a doll! Now, here," Misty says, handing me a tissue the clerk gave her, "dry your eyes before you ruin that beautiful makeup job." About that time her phone rings. "Hi! Okay. Yeah, in just a few. Okay. Yeah, about thirty. Okay, babe. See you. Love you too." She turns to me with a huge grin. "You need to find some sandals ASAP because we're meeting the guys at Café Étienne and I can't wait to see Jaz's face when you walk in."

"What size, honey?" the clerk calls back to me. When I give her a confused look, she says, "Shoes! Shoes! What size?"

"Uh, seven and a half."

"Here. Try these." She hands me the cutest pair of heeled black sandals I've ever seen, and I put them on. Their gladiator straps make my legs look long and lean, and I know right then that they're the best choice. She rings up the dress, the necklace, earrings, and bracelet set, and the shoes, and I put them on my card. Then she and Misty set about taking all the tags off before we leave.

Café Étienne is a tiny, fancy kind of place, and when Misty opens the door for me to enter, I'm taken aback by the chandeliers and silky tablecloths and beautiful, hand-rubbed wood fixtures. But what really takes me aback is the look on Jaz's face when he spots me. His eyes go round, his jaw drops, and he rises from the table like a man who's seen a ghost. I have to stifle a laugh, and I hear Reggie say long and low, "Wow. Looks like we hit the jackpot, my friend." Jaz doesn't say a word in return.

In a voice as sweet as cream I coo, "Hey, baby. Have a good day?"

The fog must be clearing because he stammers, "Uh, it was, um, it was a pretty good day. Holy fuck, it's a lot better now. Sit down, babe, please," he says as he pulls out a chair for me. I sit and let him help me scoot the chair up, then realize he's staring at me like I'm some kind of alien.

"Is everything all right?"

Instead of answering me, he turns to Misty. "I don't know how much of my money you spent on her, and I don't care. It was worth it. Every. Fucking. Penny." He turns back to me. "Honey, you look incredible."

"Don't get too used to it," I quip. "I'll still turn back into a pumpkin at midnight."

"A beautiful pumpkin. You're just ... I'm just ... Kimmie, I just don't know what to say."

I grin. "Say you love me?"

He snorts. "Oh, god, girl, yeah. I love you anyway, but oh my god." A waiter appears and Jaz blurts out, "Oh, yeah, I guess I should order us some wine, huh? Uh, got a good pinot gris?"

"We do. Two glasses?" Jaz looks at me and I nod. "Two glasses of pinot gris."

"Thanks," Jaz manages to mumble. "God, Kimmie, where did you get that dress?"

"A little place called Melanie's. Like it?"

He sneers at me. "I'd like it better on the floor."

I snicker back. "I think we can arrange that."

"Eat. You'll need your strength," Reggie laughs. I can't help it; I start to belly laugh, and Jaz follows suit. In seconds, Misty's laughing too, and when we finally get calmed down, I look into the eyes of my beloved and sigh.

"Thank you. You didn't have to do all of this for me," I gush and bat my eyes coyly.

"I didn't." He lets out a chuckle. "I did it for me!"

"You're impossible!" I huff and play-slap his arm.

"Yeah, but I'm cute," he grins back and gives me his best little-boy charm look.

I reply, "Yes. You are," and pinch his cheek.

"Owwww!" he fakes with a laugh.

The whole dinner is that way. We laugh and talk, and I realize I haven't felt this comfortable with other people around in a long, long time. But I feel …

Secure. That's it. I'm not waiting for someone to hurt me by saying something rude or mean. I'm not expecting someone to put me down or criticize me. The other three people at this table like and respect me, and yes, I mean Jaz too. He loves me, but he also likes and respects me, and I feel the same way about him. If I'd met him under other circumstances, I think we'd still be good, good friends. He's just a likeable person, and I enjoy spending time with him. It's not just about sex. It's about companionship, and I can honestly say I've never been as comfortable and relaxed with anyone else as I am with him.

We say goodnight and drive back to the hotel, chattering and laughing the whole time. "So what are we doing Saturday and Sunday?" he asks me just as we're pulling into the valet parking.

"Whatever you want to do. I've been going and doing

the last two days while you've been cooped up at the plant. We'll do what you want."

"I'd like to stay in bed all day," he growls into my ear as the valet is walking up.

"We can do that at home," I laugh and climb out of the car.

But when we step into the room, I hear the door close and his voice behind me snaps, "Strip. Keep the shoes."

I'm out of that dress in a flash, only to find that he's shed everything. I wait as he drapes a towel onto the sofa, sits down sans clothing, and points to his cock. "Mount me."

I clamber up onto the sofa on my knees and lower myself onto his rigidness. And once again, I'm stretched to bursting and weak with the pressure of his hardness in me. When I start to ride him, he places his hand down low and in front of me, his fingers cupped, knuckles turned in my direction, and with every movement I make, my clit rubs across them and I moan through my need. Ten minutes in, I'm ready to come and working to keep it from happening. "Are you close, Sir?"

"So close, baby girl. So close. Come whenever you're ready and I'll be right there with you."

He doesn't need to tell me twice. In mere seconds I shudder and my hips begin to buck, and ten seconds later, he grabs my waist, forces me down on his cock, and grunts his climax into me. Suddenly, we're kissing and groping and stroking and moaning, and I'm just lost in him, in his lips and his arms. I finally whisper into his mouth, "Jaz Givens, I love you more than I thought it possible to love anyone."

"I love you that much and more too, Kimmie. And this

body, girl, I swear. You're going to fuck me to death. And I'm going to die a happy man."

"Good! Want some more?"

"Hell yes! You got more in that honey pot?" he laughs.

"Lots, lots more. More than you'll ever be able to stand!" I giggle.

"We'll see about that!" He runs his hands under my legs, stands with me still on his lap, and carries me to the bed, with me shrieking and laughing all the way. Once he drops me there, he strips off his condom and drops on all fours on the bed in front of me. "Spread 'em, darlin'," he snarls, and I giggle and open my legs. Next thing I know, his face has disappeared in my mound and I'm writhing in ecstasy. God, this guy knows how to eat pussy, yes he does. I come with a scream, my hands wrapped in his hair and pulling for all I'm worth, and he slides up and into me in one smooth move.

"Oh, Jaz." I can feel the hot tears pouring down my cheeks and I don't care. "I want you for always too. Just make love to me, please? I need to feel you moving inside me."

It's sweet and tender and perfect, and I'm engulfed in the joy of making love with a man who truly loves me, someone I can fully give myself to. His hardness moves inside my softness, and then there's that moment when the heat and wetness of his cum fills me and I know we're one.

We lie there in the dark as he goes soft inside me and I look into those eyes. God, I'm so in love with this man. I can't imagine my life without him and, almost like he's read my mind, he says, "I never want to live in a world without you in it, angel."

"I hope you never have to."

He drops a soft little kiss on my forehead. "I hope I don't either.

∼

"We need to talk before I go today." We're sitting there enjoying another one of those amazing breakfasts they keep bringing. Today it's cherry crepes with a shit-ton of real whipped cream and enough fresh fruit to keep a monkey happy for a week. "We're going to the club tonight for the demonstration. Kimmie, if you're not comfortable with this, I can—"

"No. I'm going to do it. I have to. I've got to learn it sometime, and this is as good a time as any. I know you're going to do everything you can to make it successful, so I'm not worried." I take another bite of the crepe. Hot diggity damn, those are some fine crepes.

"Okay. If you're sure ... good god, these crepes are delicious. Do you know how to make these?" he asks around a mouthful.

"No."

"Well, then, learn. I want these again, and if you make them, they'll be even better."

I just laugh. "Why, thank you for your generous but grossly misplaced trust in my culinary skills. You'll rue the day you said that."

He lets out a big belly laugh. "Girl, you're really something! Okay, I've got to go. Let's meet for a very light meal beforehand and then we'll head on over. I want Misty to bring you to me and then go on with Reggie. I really want to be alone with you for a little while before we go over there and do this. We need that connection."

I nod in agreement. "I'll ask her to take me to meet

you somewhere that serves soup and salad, light things like that."

He grabs his wallet and keys. "Sounds perfect. Love you, baby. I'll see you this evening." His hand is on the doorknob, but he turns and comes back to me, then kisses me square on the lips. I'm still chewing crepe and he says, "Ummm. You taste good!" I pinch his cheek and he yells, "Owwww!" again, then heads back for the door.

"And you're cute as a button, Mr. Givens. Love you too."

My mission today is different. I'm spending the day looking for a gift for Jaz. It's got to be something really cool, something I can only get here. Misty insists on taking me to Grant's Farm, and I finally acquiesce, only because I want to see the Clydesdales. We're walking around, looking at the animals and rides, and walk down to the horse barn. The Clydesdales are out in the pasture today, but over to the side of the center aisle, there's a cart manned by a park employee and lots of people crowded around. "Wonder what's going on over there?" I ask Misty.

"Dunno. Hey, 'scuse me!" she barks to another employee. "What's going on over there?"

"Oh, last day. We've got a colt to name and we're drawing the name at two o'clock. Everyone's trying to get their name into the drawing at the last minute."

And something shoots across my mind. "I've got to do that, Misty. Help me get in there." I head toward the group, gently shouldering people who are just gawking so I can get close to the cart. When I finally push my way to the front, I pant, "Can I make an entry, please?"

"I don't have any more slips, ma'am. Just ran out. Sorry," the young guy says. And just as I turn to walk away, he calls toward me, "Wait! There's one on the floor. Can you reach it?"

I drop to my knees—I don't care who sees me scrounging around down there—and finally find it. He hands me a pen when I'm upright again, and I blink at the form.

Name: Kimberly Hendricks
    Proposed name: Jaz
    In honor/memory of: Jasper Andrew Givens

Then I circle *honor* and drop the slip into the barrel. I know it's ridiculous—there have to be ten thousand slips in there—but what the hell, right? You never know unless you try.

Misty and I make our way back through the crowd and out the door. "Fingers crossed?"

I just shake my head. "Nah. I just wasted five minutes, but you can't win the lottery if you don't buy a ticket."

"Exactly! Gotta have faith," she says with a grin.

We eat a funnel cake, something I haven't had since I was a kid, and then wander around the different little areas where there are animals. There are so many kids around, and I have to smile as I think about Jeffrey and some of the places I took him when he was little. There's a little girl with a patch over her eye, and I remember when he had a little classmate who had to wear a patch for a "lazy eye," poor little guy.

At five after two, the public address system in the park crackles to life. "Ladies and gentlemen, we'll now have the drawing to name our newest colt. Let's see what it is." There's a pause, and then the voice says, "And the name drawn is Shazam. Believe it or not, we already have a horse by that name, so we'll have to draw again." There's another pause before the voice blaring over the loudspeaker says, "The name drawn is Suzy Q. Unfortunately, that's a girl's name, and this foal is a colt, meaning he's a boy. We'll have to try again." Misty grabs my hand and squeezes so tightly that I'm afraid she'll break my fingers. "And this time, the name drawn is Felix. Congratulations to Wendy Montgomery! Please come to the park office, and thanks to everyone who participated."

"Well, that's that. Let's go find some postcards." As we start toward the little gift shops, the PA system rattles again with the sound of someone clearing their throat, and then the same voice from before announces, "Ladies and gentlemen, it's just been brought to our attention that there was a foal born this morning, another colt, and because we've already got all of these names, the management has decided to go ahead and draw a name. Let's see, what have we got here ... Chester." There's some background noise and the man says, "Not again. Unfortunately, we already have a Chester. Guess we'll draw another." Misty's standing there holding her breath and I start to laugh at her when he says, "And we have a winner! The name drawn is Jaz! Kimberly Hendricks, please come to the park office."

I'm standing there speechless while Misty jumps up and down, squealing like a three year old. "Come on! Let's see what they say!" she yells and grabs my hand. "Where's the park office?" she yells to an employee picking up trash nearby.

"I'll take you," the girl calls back. "Follow me." We

run to catch up with her and she leads us down a little narrow alley-type corridor. It opens into a bright, modern office where a rather rotund gentleman is already talking to someone. He turns and smiles.

"Miss Hendricks?"

"Yes, sir!" Now I'm getting excited—this is really happening!

"Congratulations! We don't give much for this kind of thing, but you do get a certificate and we'll take your picture with the plate beside the door, and with the foal if it's awake."

Before he can say anything else, I ask politely, "I turned in that name because it's the nickname of my fiancé. Is there any way possible that we could come back tomorrow so he could have his picture taken too?"

He smiles so hard his eyes crinkle shut. "Absolutely! Here." Reaching down to the desktop, he hands me back a business card. Printed on its face is *Arnold Foster, Park Manager*. "Show this to them at the gate tomorrow and tell them you're here to see me. They'll bring you right in."

"Oh, thank you so much, sir! He's going to be so surprised and excited!" He shakes my hand with a warm, firm grip, and Misty and I head back out into the park. We stop and get the postcards just like I wanted to, and then we spend some time feeding a kid, the goat kind, before we head to the car. She drops me at a little place called The Salad Bowl where she picks up Reggie and I find Jaz sitting inside, waiting for me.

Over the soup and salad, which is excellent, we talk about tonight, what's going to happen, everything he can think of to prepare me. He seems excited about it, but the more we talk, the more apprehensive I become. His face is serious when he says, "Okay, Kimmie, listen closely. If you get into trouble, you let me know, understand?" I nod. "I mean it. Don't just keep going. I want to know if you're having trouble. Let's use the red light/green light thing tonight. If you need to call a yellow, you do it, don't hesitate. I'll stop and we'll talk and decide if you can keep going or if you need to stop. We clear on that?"

"Yes, Sir."

"Tonight it's Master."

"Yes, Master."

"Good girl. Let's go."

We make it to the club in plenty of time, and Jaz checks in with the man at the front window. "Yes, sir, Mr. Dolan is waiting for you. Right that way," he says and points to a door, then buzzes us through.

Sure enough, Reggie is standing right there on the other side. "I'll show you two around, and Jaz, I want to show you the performance area I booked for you. If it's not what you need, we'll find something that'll work." This club is amazing. It makes ours look like a warehouse. We spend a few minutes looking around, then look at the alcove. Jaz pronounces it perfect, and Reggie shows us to the locker rooms. I get a peck on the cheek and a promise that Jaz will be standing outside the ladies' area when I come out.

Oh, god, this place is fabulous. The locker rooms look like the kind you'd see in a high-end athletic club, and there are a couple of submissives already in there who introduce themselves. They're both sweet and friendly, and I have a good feeling about the clientele.

I come out in my satin robe to indeed find Jaz standing there, looking scrumptious as always, bare-chested and in his leathers. "You ready?"

"Yes, Master."

He grins at me. "You sure?"

"Yes, Master."

"Okay. Not our hometown, so protocol is in place. Here we go." I walk two feet behind him as we'd discussed prior. That's not usually something he wants, but for tonight and in this position, he feels the need to have everyone acknowledge his expertise, and I'm happy to help that happen. We step up onto the platform, which is lit only with ambient lighting, and he makes sure everything is ready while I fall into the presentation pose I've come to find most comfortable. No need to stress myself out with a simple pose when the night's going to be so stressful for me anyway.

He's sure that everything he needs is there just about the time a dungeon monitor stops by and says, "Lights up in two minutes."

Jaz smiles at him. "Thanks." Then he looks to me. "Kimmie, remember: You get in trouble, you say something, understand?"

"Yes, Master."

"Okay. We're up." As though they'd heard him, the lights in the alcove come up, and we're there in front of everyone. Apprehension is starting to take up residence in my throat, but I just choke it back down.

I listen in awe as Jaz does a small introduction piece about what we'll be doing and the art form itself. My mind is running in circles as he speaks, and he jolts me into the moment when he says, "Submissive, rise and come to your Master."

I rise gracefully and, as he nods, drop my robe. Without a stitch on, I walk straight up to him and stand there, looking downward respectfully, until he tips my head back with a finger under my chin and kisses my lips lightly. "Ready?"

"Yes, Master." His smile is the only reward I need.

He begins easily enough, wrapping the rope around my ribcage just under my breasts, and I hold my arms out at forty-five degree angles as he showed me earlier. As he wraps, he criss-crosses and knots, and my breasts are isolated and bound tight. That makes them start to redden, and I could swear he licks his lips as he looks at them. He continues by binding my right arm tightly to my torso, and I start to feel the first niggles of panic hit as the ropes tighten around my chest. Perceptive as he is, he stops and looks into my face. "Color?"

"Green, Master," I choke out.

"Remember, Kimmie, slow and easy breaths. No panting. No breathing through your mouth. Got it?"

"Yes, Master, I do."

"Good girl." He goes back to binding and, when he seems to be finished with my torso, he takes the long ropes tied into my bindings and uses them to hoist me upward. When he does, my weight in my torso falls against the ropes and I feel the first constriction. It's a fight to keep from gasping, and he notices and gives me a look, but I shake my head gently and he goes on.

Once I'm tied upright, he begins binding my lower body. He draws rope around my waist, then between my legs, criss-crossing it directly on top of my introitus. On the second pass through, he pulls the rope between my lower lips and I go wet, and he uses that rope to begin binding my legs. My left leg is bound straight out and then secured in that position by drawing the rope up to one around my waist, but my right leg is bound up and over my back. Then he connects it to my right arm, which he draws behind me and up. As my foot and hand are bound together, my spine arches and my chest presses even harder into the ropes. I struggle to breathe correctly, and he stops and bends down to look into my eyes. "You okay, subbie?"

"Yes, Master." Funny, I don't *feel* okay.

"You don't look okay." *You're damn funny, Jaz*, I tell myself.

"I'm okay, Master. I promise."

"Okay. If you insist. But I'm watching you, and if you go on when you should stop and I find out, you'll be punished. Know that going in."

"Yes, Master," I nod in understanding as I concentrate on my breathing. But that's getting harder to do.

His last act is to use some trailing ropes to hoist up the lower part of my body to the level he wants it, then adjust my torso to match. The one thing he hasn't done is to bind my head back by using my hair like he did with Amelie, and I'm thankful for that. I knew she struggled, and I'd struggle even more. Once I'm suspended there, he bends down and looks into my eyes. "Kimmie, you hanging in there?"

"Yes, Master." I'm trying hard to follow his instructions for breathing.

"You sure?"

"Yes, Master."

"Good girl. It'll all be over soon."

He turns and begins to speak to the crowd, but I'm having trouble concentrating on what he's saying. Time seems to have stopped, and everything is blurry and muted. I do, however, hear him say, "This is my collared submissive, Kimberly. I'd like for everyone to know that this is her first time doing a full-blown kinbaku demonstration, and I think she's done an excellent job. Could you give her some encouragement, please?" People start to cheer and clap, and I know it's for me, which makes my face flush red. When the applause dies down, he says, "As is the Master's prerogative, I will now use my submissive for oral pleasure."

I had no idea he was going to do this. And then it strikes me: His scars. Is he crazy? How could he have forgotten? I try to speak but sort of choke. Fortunately, he hears me and leans down again. "You okay, baby? Color?"

"Green. Sir, don't."

He gives me a quizzical look. "Don't what?"

"Jaz, please. Your scars. Have you forgotten? I don't want them to hurt you by—"

His smile is so warm that it lights up my skin. "Shhhh, baby. No. I haven't forgotten. Kimmie, listen to me carefully." My eyes go straight to his and what I see there makes me weep. "Baby, I'm a better man because of you. If you can love me and my body, then I don't give a rat's ass what anyone else thinks. I want them to see how much we love each other, and to know that no matter what, we always will. I want them all to know what a strong, brave, loving woman you are. Do you understand?" I can only nod and cry. "Shhhh, don't cry, angel. It's okay. This is our one chance to show the world that they can go fuck themselves because we love each other. You with me?"

I take the deepest breath I can manage and, my voice clear, I answer, "Yes, Master. I'm with you."

"Thank you, precious." He kisses my forehead, and then I watch with wonder and arousal as he unzips those beautiful leathers I made for him and frees that cock I adore.

I hear a couple of gasps from the audience, but I don't

care. They mean nothing to me, to us. This is *our* time, and I'm thrilled that this man has chosen me to make it known to the world that he's alive and whole. His hands grasp the sides of my head and he whispers down to me, "Open wide, baby. I'm going all the way down."

I let him take my throat and don't make a sound. In a couple of minutes, I start a very low, quiet humming, and I feel him tense and struggle to maintain. I'm sucking as well as I can while he's stroking, and his fingers dig into my scalp and wind through my hair, letting me know he appreciates the work I'm doing to keep him satisfied. I want desperately to cup his balls, but I don't have a free hand, and it's difficult to tell where he is in the process, but I think I feel his cock harden more and lengthen just a little. All I hear is, "Ah, ah, ah, ah, ahhhhh. Yeah, baby," and he fills my throat, then grinds his pelvis into my face and stills with that hard shaft blocking my airway.

Dots start to form behind my eyes and things are getting dark when he finally pulls out and I take in a ragged gasp. I'm shaking so hard that I forget to swallow, and cum runs out of my mouth and down my chin, dripping onto the floor below. Faster than I can process, a towel wipes my face dry and the next thing I know, I'm standing on the floor, rope lying all around me. Everything is moving and spinning, and I'm so dizzy I don't know what's going on. I can feel myself being lifted and then everything goes dark.

When I awaken, I look around and find myself in a room every bit as opulent as the one at the Ritz. Jaz is beside me, and I stare into those beautiful brown eyes. With a soft hand, he strokes my face and whispers, "Hey, baby, you okay?"

"Uh-huh," is all I can manage to squeak.

"Kimmie, you did so great out there. Amazing, really. I'm so proud of you."

I try to kiss him but I'm shaking so hard that I can't. In a few minutes, Misty wanders in. "Can I get her something?" I hear her ask, but things still aren't making sense. In just a couple of minutes, she's back.

"Baby, sit up. Come on." But I can't. He lifts me up to sitting and puts a glass to my lips, but I only manage a couple of sips. I hear him say, "I need to take her back to the hotel. She needs some rest."

"Rest," I breathe out.

"Yes, baby. I'm taking you back to the hotel. Let's go get some sleep."

There's movement and then muggy night air. I hear the click of a seatbelt, and then feel the car moving. Next thing I know, I'm snuggled down into the bed in the beautiful room at the hotel, and I can feel Jaz's warmth beside me.

When I take my three o'clock bathroom trip, I come back to find Jaz sitting up in the bed with a glass in his hand. Once I'm back in the bed, he holds the glass out. "Wine. Drink it. It'll make you feel better."

I gulp it down, hand the glass back, and then just moan, "Sleep."

"Okay. Sleep," he chuckles. Falling back to sleep with his arms around me is no trouble—no trouble at all. I have another dream, but this one has corn growing in a field and no people, just the rustle of the silks and husks in the wind.

CHAPTER THIRTEEN

Sunshine pouring through the window wakes me, and I squint and groan. Then there's an annoyingly cheery, "Good morning, sleepy head! Wake up!"

"What the hell?" I pull the pillow over my eyes and mumble, "Fuck off."

"Now that's no way to talk to your Master!" Jaz laughs. I'm not laughing. "Come on and get up. It's Saturday. Let's go do something fun!"

"Sleep."

"No. No more sleep. Get up. Breakfast is here." That's when I recognize the aroma—bacon. I need some.

"Okay. Bathroom, then breakfast."

He just shakes his head. "Sounds like a plan. I'll be right here." I stumble into the bathroom, then come back out to find him filling a plate for me. Today's offering is a beautiful pile of bacon and hash browns, and plenty of colorful fresh fruit. "So," he pipes up cheerfully, "what are we going to do today?"

"I dunno." I stuff another strip of bacon into my mouth.

"What do you want to do?"

"Uh-uh. No. I've been going and doing fun stuff for the last three days. You have to choose today."

He sits there thoughtfully, then asks, "What do we have to choose from?"

Suddenly, I snap back to myself and realize what's going on. I have to work carefully, so I mention a half-dozen mediocre things we could do and then add, "And there's always Grant's Farm."

"Grant's Farm. Where the Clydesdales are?" His face lights up at the thought.

"Yep. We could go there, I suppose."

"Hey, yeah! That would be great! I'd love that. Let's do that. Hurry, eat your breakfast so we can get ready and go." He's bouncing around like a three year old and it's really irritating.

"What happy bug got up your ass overnight?"

He just plops his fists onto the bed and leans over into my face. "I love you, Kimmie."

I just grouch and grumble, "I love you too, you fucking irritating cheerful bullshit damn it to hell son of a bitch."

That just brings on a laughing fit. "Do you remember *anything* about last night?"

"Very little, thankfully." And I mean that.

"No, I wish you did. Sweetheart, you were amazing. Everyone thought so. They were all so impressed."

Then I remember the face fucking and his dick out there for everyone to see, and I'm horrified. "Did anyone say anything mean to you about your scars? Because if they did, I'm going to hunt their asses down and kick the shit out of them. Did they? I mean it, Jaz, I won't have that shit. They'd better not have—"

"Hey, Penis Avenger, chill out! No. No one said one mean thing. Matter of fact, a couple of people told me that it really helped them see themselves in a better light and be more self-confident. So thanks for that, baby."

"Okay. You're not lying, are you? You'd better not be lying because if you are—"

"No! I'm not lying! Shit, Kimmie, you're in a foul mood." A big frown is directed at me.

Now I feel bad. "Sorry. I just don't want anyone being mean to you, that's all." When I see the mirth in those brown eyes, I have to smile. "I love you, Jaz."

"I love you too, babe. Now let's get ready to go. I want to go to this farm!" He's pulling out clothes as he's talking. "What do they grow there?"

"Beer."

Now he starts laughing again. "This I gotta see!"

It is mega impressive to walk up to a gate at a place like Grant's Farm and just walk right in, but that's exactly what we do. "Yes, I'm here to see Mr. Foster?"

"Name?" I give her mine and she looks at a list, then says, "Go right on in, Ms. Hendricks."

"Thanks!" I take a peek at Jaz, and he's totally bewildered. "Come on, let's go."

"Where are we going? There are goats over there," he says, pointing.

"I know. We'll see all that stuff later. Come on."

"But Kimmie, what's this about?"

"You'll see," I grin and give him a wink. We walk down the little alleyway between two of the buildings, and then I open the door and we step in. The bright, well-lit, modern office is a contrast to the older buildings around the park, and we both blink a couple of times.

A young girl at the desk asks why we're there, but before I can tell her, Mr. Foster comes barreling out of the office. "Miss Hendricks! So good to see you! I take it this is Mr. Givens?" Jaz's eyebrows shoot up and he looks at me like I'm a Martian.

"Yes, sir, this is my fiancé, Jasper Givens. Jaz, this is Arnold Foster. He's the park manager here."

"Um, hello, Mr. Foster. Nice to meet you."

"Very nice to meet you too, Mr. Givens. If you'll give me just a minute, I'll get the photographer headed toward the barn and we'll walk over there to meet him."

"Sure thing." I shoot another glance at Jaz, and now he looks like he's going to pop a blood vessel. It takes everything I have to keep a straight face.

Once the walkie-talkie squawks out that the photographer is at the barn, we head out with Mr. Foster leading the way. On the way, he tells us things about the different buildings and crop programs they've got going on. Even though he's confused, Jaz is enthralled with everything Mr. Foster says and asks a lot of questions about the farm. His interest is just further proof that I'm doing the right thing.

Inside the barn, we can see the photographer near the far end of the aisle, and we march straight down there. Mr. Foster's been carrying something, and now I see what it is—the certificate. We step up near the photographer and Mr. Foster reaches out to slide open the stall door.

From inside its shadowy, cavernous depths, a large mare stares at us, a lead snapped to her halter and tied to a cleat on the wall. And standing beside her is a foal which would be considered tiny, except that he's a

Clydesdale, so he's pretty big. His big brown eyes are curious and a little wary, but he takes a couple of steps toward the door and stands there, eyeing all of us. The mare lets out a little nicker of warning but doesn't make any attempt to stop him, and he watches, front legs splayed out, while the photographer gets everything set up.

"Okay," he calls out to us, "now Miss Hendricks and Mr. Givens, one of you needs to stand on one side of the plates, and one on the other." He points to the wall, and we both turn to look. That's when Jaz finally figures it out.

There, on the top plate, is *Agatha*. And underneath it is another plate that reads *Jaz*. "So he's ..."

"Named after you. I wanted to give you a present that would be unique to St. Louis, and I think I succeeded, don't you?"

Jaz actually looks like he's going to tear up. The photographer snaps our picture and as soon as he's done, Jaz starts to say something but he's propelled forward and almost falls. We both turn in shock and, when we do, a furry face with a big white blaze straight down the middle butts him in the belly and he starts to laugh. He puts a hand under the little guy's chin and says, "Hey there, kid! Look at you! You're a big boy, aren't you?" The colt responds by nibbling at his fingers and blinking those big brown eyes with those giant eyelashes at him. It's beyond adorable, and I'm tickled pink when I hear the camera snap again.

So we take more pictures. There's Mr. Foster standing beside me, and I'm holding the certificate. Jaz is on my other side and, there between us, there's a brown and white head sticking out. Jaz's right arm is thrown across the colt's neck, and he's scratching little Jaz Junior's right ear. The foal seems to be enjoying himself immensely, and so does my guy.

We're told the pictures will be up at the photo shop whenever we want them, and I thank the photographer and Mr. Foster again, as does Jaz. He says goodbye to his little buddy and we walk back out toward the park. "I suppose I should go buy us some tickets, huh?" I smile at Mr. Foster.

"No, ma'am. You two are our guests today. Have a good time and I hope you'll come back to see your little namesake, Mr. Givens. Wouldn't it be great if he became the lead horse in the team?"

"Yes, it sure would! Hey, thanks so much, sir," Jaz tells him as we part, and we drop off the certificate at the photo shop so we're hands-free to wander.

I take a potty break and come back out to Jaz, but he's nowhere to be found. After looking around for a few minutes, I find him, foot on the lower fence rail and arms folded on the top one. He's staring out across the field at the horses grazing there, and beyond them is some kind of crop. I'm not sure what it is, but it's really pretty and green. Moving up beside him, I take a good look at his face and see a sadness there that takes my breath away. My hand lands on the small of his back and I ask quietly, "Hey, honey, whatcha doin'?"

He just shrugs and says, "Looking at the life I wish I had."

I try to be cheerful. "It could still happen. You have to have faith."

His head drops and he shakes it. "Nope. Never gonna happen. My dreams are over." Then he turns to look at me. "But I've got you. Having you to love and to love me makes up for all of that shit, baby. It really does."

Oh, god, my heart breaks for him. He's so miserable in what he's doing now, and I want to change that. I hope I can get everything set up so we can move forward. I want him to have the life he dreams of and if I can make that happen, I'll be happier than I've ever been.

We walk back through the park, pet the goats, buy a beer and a hot dog apiece, and just sit and enjoy the afternoon. Little kids play around, squealing and laughing, and it's just a fun, relaxing place to be. When we leave, I'm genuinely sad to go, and I make him promise that we'll come back soon.

And he drops the bomb.

"Marlene's meeting us for dinner."

Shit. I knew I'd have to do this eventually, but I really don't want to. I don't have any family to speak of—when they found out I was in the lifestyle, they just shunned me—but I know his family is important to him. "Okay. I'll be on my best behavior."

"I'm still screwed," he laughs.

"Oh, hahaha. You're a really funny guy, Mr. Givens."

"I try." He waits for a few seconds and tries to look at me as he's driving. "Look, she's a nice person. Actually, she's my favorite of my siblings." I know he has another sister in Texas and a brother in California.

I have to know before I accidentally put my foot in my mouth. "Does she know about your lifestyle choices?"

He's slow to answer. "Yes. And she doesn't understand, but she also doesn't judge. She pretty much raised me."

I'm confused. "What do you mean?"

"I mean she pretty much raised me." I wait, and finally he says, "She was on the upward side of her twenties toward thirty when I was born."

"What?"

"I was a change of life baby, Kimmie. My mother was forty-nine when I was born."

"And your other brother and sister?"

"In Marlene's age bracket. I was more like their child than their younger brother."

I'm shocked. He never told me *any* of this. "So, your parents ... did they both ..."

"My mom died when I was twelve. Breast cancer. But I was in my early thirties when Dad died. He lived to be eighty-five."

"Wow." I don't know what else to say.

"So Marlene loves me almost like a son, and she's always been a mother figure to me."

"So she's in her sixties?"

"Yeah. She's, um, I think she's sixty-six now."

"Married?"

"Jack. He passed away a few years ago. Heart attack. She's a retired school teacher, so she has a good pension, plus his savings and investments. He was a pediatrician."

"I see." How can I ask what I need to ask? Finally, I just blurt out, "So if she doesn't like me, is that the end for us?"

Jaz just snorts and shakes his head. "I'm a grown man, Kimmie. She'll like you, but if for some reason she doesn't, well, that's her problem, not mine. Won't change a thing."

Yeah, you say that now, I think, *but I bet reality will be a lot different.* I just sit quietly after that, staring out the window and trying to think about other things. Then I think about the day I met Melissa. *Oh, god, if this meeting is anything like that one, I hope I die right there at the table.*

She's waiting for us when we get to the restaurant,

and I'm struck by how attractive she is. She's really, really lovely, and even though she's much older than Jaz, she's very youthful and fit. "I'd like for you to meet Kimmie. Kimmie, this is my sister, Marlene."

"I'm so glad to meet you," I gush, hoping I don't sound like an idiot.

"I'm happy to meet you too. I've heard a lot about you." *Oh, god, I'm sunk*, my brain screams. "I hope you like seafood. This place is amazing."

"I love it." A host shows up to lead us to our table, and we have a seat and commence with the small talk.

Dinner is light and pleasant. I have mahi mahi while he has sea bass, and Marlene orders crab. They serve a whipped spinach that's delicious, and I order a baked sweet potato, while Jaz gets a big helping of whole kernel corn. He talks about the colt and how much he enjoyed all of that, and I'm so glad I had just a little smidgen of luck yesterday. Marlene seems delighted with the story, and she even pats my hand and says, "Bravo, Kimmie!"

But when dinner is over and we're waiting for dessert, Jaz stands abruptly and says, "I'm headed to the restroom. Be right back." I don't get a chance to yell out *Please don't leave me here with her!* before he disappears down the back hallway. He did this on purpose, I just know it. You just wait until we get back in the car.

And, sure enough, Marlene turns to me immediately. "So, Jaz has told me all about you. You don't really have any family?"

"No. Not really. They shu ..." No. I can't say that. She'll wonder why if I do. "Um, they live pretty far away." Yeah. Peoria. Because that's *sooooo* far away.

"I see. It wouldn't have anything to do with your, um, lifestyle choices, now would it?" Damn. How do these things happen to me? I start to say something to defend myself when she adds, "I see the collar around your neck. Don't think I haven't read up on all of that. He's my baby brother, and I want to understand what he's doing, if I can." She takes another sip of wine as I sit there, my eyes getting wider by the minute. "Of course, it's kind of uncomfortable reading about the kinds of things your little brother is doing in his bedroom, but that's really none of my business, now is it?"

What's the right answer? I just mumble, "I suppose it's only your business if you make it your business."

"I'll tell you what *is* my business," she snaps, her voice forceful. "Jaz is my business. I don't want to see him hurt. I know you know about all of that, but you weren't there. He almost didn't make it. He was suicidal for a couple of years." He didn't tell me *any* of that. "We were afraid for him, really afraid. He had a friend, Reggie, who kind of kept tabs on him and watched him. Reggie lives here now."

"Yes. I spent the last few days with his submiss ... wife. He's a great guy."

"Yes, he is. I think in a lot of ways, he saved Jaz's life. My baby brother was so destroyed. That bitch of an ex-wife went off to the loony bin, and he was left to take care of Melissa all by himself, not to mention the fact that he was recovering physically too. And he wasn't sure if he'd ever fully recover, so he was terrified of what that would mean. He really thought his life was over."

"I'm glad he had you and Reggie to look out for him." The thought of Jaz possibly not being here now makes my heart hurt.

"Me too. But I want you to know that if you hurt him, I swear, I'll hunt you down and—"

"I'd never hurt him! I love him more than anything in this world. Look, you don't know me, but I've been hurt too. You have no idea. So before you go threatening me, you need to know that my life hasn't been rosy either." I want to tell her what happened to me, make her understand, but Jaz picks that moment to come back to the table.

"You girls have a nice chat?"

I pat his hand and I'm getting ready to tell him what a pleasure it's been when Marlene blurts out, "Yes. Oh, and by the way, someone's been asking about the farm."

Shit, shit, shit! I have no idea what the attorney told her, so I just stare at my food and take a big bite, hoping I don't choke.

I hear Jaz say, "Oh? What do you mean?"

"Some attorney. Wanted to know if I had any interest in it. When I said no, he asked if I'd sign a quit-claim deed."

"And?" Jaz's voice is strained.

"I asked who wanted to know about it, but he said that was confidential." I have to fight a *Whew!* so he won't know I'm involved. "He sent it and I signed it. Attorney in Chicago, actually." In that instant, I realize: She knows. She's torturing me. I'm sure of it.

Now the tone of Jaz's voice changes. "Chicago? Who do we know in Chicago who'd want anything to do with the farm?"

"Only you," Marlene shoots back and takes another bite of crab. I glance up at her and she gives me a wily smile. I am so fucked it's not even funny. "No one else I can think of."

"That's weird. Wonder why they haven't contacted

me?" As soon as he says it, I choke on my tea and start to cough violently. "Kimmie? Honey, you okay?"

"Yeah, yeah," I wheeze out between coughs. "I'll be right back." I jump up from the table and practically run down the hallway. Once I make it into the bathroom, I lock myself in a stall, lean against the stall door, and try to catch my breath.

I haven't been in there three minutes when a feminine voice says, "Kimmie?"

Well, might as well get this over with, I tell myself as I open the stall door to find Marlene leaning back against the vanity on the other side of the room. "Yeah."

"You okay?"

"Yeah, I'm fine, thanks." I walk to a sink, take a look in the mirror, and dab under my eyes with a wet paper towel.

"Kimmie, I know it's you. You're the one with the attorney sniffing around. If you want him for that farm, know that it's in poor shape and the house is falling—"

"NO!" A rage is rising in my chest and my face is getting hot. I'm sure it's brilliant crimson. "I want that farm for HIM! When he talks about being there as a kid, there's so much pain in his face that it takes my breath away. I want us to be able to move there, for him to be able to live there and have the life he's always wanted. I'd do anything to make him happy." As I've talked, my voice has gone from strong and indignant to wilted and soft. "Anything to make him happy. I'm selling my house to have the money for renovations." I finally look over at her to find her mouth hanging wide open. "What? Can't believe anyone would love your brother enough to do something like that for him? He's a fine man and a fine Master, and I'm lucky to have him. I'd walk through fire for him. If he needed a heart, I'd give him mine, because it wouldn't be worth anything if he weren't here with me." She still doesn't say anything. "So please, *please*, don't ruin this, please? I want this to be a wonderful surprise. The attorney's drawing up the paperwork in his name. It'll be his. My name won't be on it anywhere. But I'm doing this for *him*, Marlene. If he were to decide he didn't want me anymore, my only consolation would be knowing that he was there and had a happy life."

Her eyes go soft. "You really do love him, don't you?"

A huge sigh escapes with the rise and fall of my shoulders. "Why the hell is that so hard for you to believe? Yes. I really, truly do love him, and he loves me."

"You're selling your house?" Apparently she's still having trouble with that detail.

"Yes. I'm selling my house. But he doesn't know it yet. So please, Marlene, please—"

"No, no, I won't say anything. He loved it there with Grandma and Grandpa. I remember him begging our parents to let him live there with them, and they wouldn't, but he would've been right there if they had." She stops and stares into my face. "Kimmie, all I've ever wanted for Jaz was for him to be happy. He seemed happy with his job and Meredith, but I know there were lots of problems there. And now, he seems happy with you. I hope it's more than an illusion."

"It is. We're very happy together."

"Good. Then let's go back out here and sit down. I think there's dessert waiting for us." She strides across the restroom and opens the door, holding it for me. "Well, come on. We don't want to waste cake."

Jaz rises when we come back to the table, and he leans his head down and stares into my eyes. "You okay?"

"Yeah. Just got a little choked," I answer in barely more than a whisper. I just know Marlene's going to spill the beans.

But she doesn't. We finish the meal in conversation, and when it's time to go, Jaz gives her a big hug. "Oh, I just miss you so much! It's so good to see you," she whispers to him.

"I miss you too. Tell the girls I said hello. And that grandson of yours."

"Will do." She turns to me and I get the shock of my life. "It was so nice to meet you, Kimmie," she murmurs as she hugs me.

I give her a little extra squeeze. "Nice to meet you too, Marlene. I hope I get to see you again soon."

"Me too. You two be careful going back tomorrow. Love you both."

"Love you, sis," Jaz calls back. I see how sad he is to watch her walk away, and I'm sad for him. "Well, guess we should call it a night, huh? I'm exhausted." He helps me into the car and we head back to the hotel. All the while, I'm praying silently that Marlene keeps my secret.

When we get back to the room, we both strip off and take a shower together. We make love in the shower, my hands on the glass while he enters me from behind, and between the hot water and the scent of the bath gel, it's intoxicating and erotic. Finally falling into bed, we lie there awake for at least two hours, talking about the trip, the things we enjoyed, how much we'd like to come back, and what's going to happen when we get back. He wants to keep looking for a job here. And I want to tell him what I'm up to.

But not yet.

~

They wave goodbye and so do we as we drive away the next afternoon. "I have to tell you, I really like Reggie and Misty," I say as we pull onto the interstate.

"They really like you too. I wish we could spend more time with them. I miss Reggie a lot. We were good friends in California. We've tried to stay in touch, but it's hard when we're both working and we live several hours apart."

"But you've managed. That's to your credit. You understand the value of friendships, and it shows. And they're great people."

"You know," he says, watching the road but his voice focused, "we really should spend more time with Michael and Robyn. I mean, you've known them a lot longer than I have, but they seem like the real deal."

"They are. Without them, I don't know what would've happened to me when ..." I realize in that moment that I haven't thought about Phil the whole time we've been gone, and it's been liberating at the very least. "Well, while I was really down. They were there for me in some of the worst times of my life, and Michael would've graciously taken over as my Dominant, sex-free, if I had let him. But I wouldn't."

"Yeah, he's a caretaker for sure," Jaz grins.

"Just like you." I lean over and drop a kiss on his cheek.

"I'm a caretaker?" he scoffs.

"Yes. You absolutely are. And I love you for it."

"Well, thanks then. And thanks for sharing this trip with me. I've enjoyed having you along."

"Thanks for inviting me. I loved it—all of it. Except

300 | DEANNDRA HALL

the part where they promoted the douchebag. That sucked."

Jaz starts laughing loudly and glances over at me. "Douchebag, huh? You're hysterical. I love you, Kimmie."

"I love you too. Watch where you're going," I bark and he starts laughing again.

If this is the rest of my life, I'm a lucky woman.

〜

"Oh, god, I'm so tired." I drop onto the sofa like a limp noodle. Our luggage is strewn around, and I don't even care. When he tries to pick it up and move it, I just say, "Leave it. I'll take care of all of it tomorrow."

"But I've got to have my toiletries. I have to go to work tomorrow, remember?" He's digging through his small personal bag, trying to find everything he needs.

"I know. I wish you didn't."

"Me too." He finally just gives up and plops down beside me. "Can I ask you something?"

Nodding, I answer, "Sure. Anything."

His eyes roll upward as he stares at the ceiling. "If you could change anything about your life, what would it be?"

I think for a few minutes. "Well, I started to say meeting and marrying Phil, but that wouldn't be true. If it weren't for him, I wouldn't have Jeffrey." Jaz nods. "And I wouldn't change the fact that we split up, but I would change the *way* he went about it."

"I can see why you'd say that."

"Yeah." After a few seconds, I say, "Well, I would change the fact that I spent the last few years alone. If I could change things, I'd find a way to meet you a lot sooner. And in between, I'd take Michael up on his offer, you know, protection and guidance. I would've been a lot better off over the last few years if I'd let him watch out for me and handle my pain management." That's how I've come to think of it and, in reality, that may be pretty close to correct. "So what about you?"

"I wouldn't have gotten my degree."

"What? I can't believe you'd say that! I'd give anything to have a college education, and you'd skip that?"

"I didn't say I'd skip college. I just would've gotten a different degree. I would've gotten one in animal husbandry or agricultural land management or something. I could've gone back to the farm and lived there. Now that's not even a possibility." *Oh, yeah? We'll see about that!* I want to scream, but I fight the urge.

"So you wouldn't have met Meredith?"

"I didn't say that either. I met Meredith after college."

I haven't heard this story. "How *did* you meet her?"

"My first job after I graduated. Her father owned the company."

"What kind of company?"

"Big logistics firm. I hated that job, stuck in a cubicle day in and day out. But then there was the boss's daughter. I have to admit, she was a looker. I suppose she still is. I have no idea; I haven't seen her in years."

"Is that where you were working when you, well, when she—"

"No. God, no. I hadn't worked there in years. I took the job I had before I came here and stayed there for a long time. When the automotive industry started going sour, that's when our company tanked. They did me a favor by letting me go; I got a much better severance package than the employees who were let go when they closed. But it still sucked."

"I bet." I yawn but just as I do, he grabs me and kisses me. There's that look in his eyes, and I have no idea what's coming next, but I'm betting it'll be sexier than hell. "So what would you like to do for the rest of the evening?" I wait a second. "Sir?" I tag on the end.

"Stand up, sub." Uh-huh—just as I thought. I'm about to get used, and I'm going to like it, I can tell. "Undress. Slowly. I want to watch you."

Stripping right there in the living room, I put on quite a show for him. I know I'm no raving beauty, but he seems to like it, so I give this and that a shake and watch his eyes light up. When I'm completely naked, he stands too, reaches out, grabs both my breasts, and sucks first one nipple and then the other. With my hands on his shoulders, I brace myself, and his licking and sucking get more and more aggressive until he starts to bite. When I wail, he bites even harder, and he intentionally gets closer and closer to the tips of my nipples. That makes me scream and when I start screaming, he bites and then slaps my ass.

I'm starting to feel more than crazed; I'm on overload and I need some kind of release, but instead, he barks at me, "Go to the bed. Lie down, head hanging off the edge." I know what that means, and I run down the hallway and put myself exactly where I'm supposed to be.

Following me into the bedroom, he stands and lets me watch him undress until that body is on full display in front of me, and my pussy and mouth both water. The bed is nice and tall, and when I look up, there's his cock, right in front of my face. And I'm surprised—instead of burying it in my mouth, he leans down over my body, plants his face in my slit, and takes a long, hard suck on my clit.

I'd just assumed I was about to be face fucked, but instead, he brings me closer and closer to coming, my hips trying to buck as he holds them down tight. And just when I'm about to come, he stops. "Oh, god, Sir, please—"

"My scene. My submissive. You'll do as I say. Do. Not. Come. Don't. I'll tell you when you can." With that, he stands up and in front of me. "Open your mouth. I want to bury this thing deep down in your throat. And you'll let me."

"Yes, Sir." Without another word, he makes good on his promise and I feel that huge cock go straight down my throat. I do the old gag reflex trick—squeezing the left thumb in the left fist—and let that massive shaft just slide on in. He goes slow at first, and then picks up the pace.

It's the very next thing he says that nearly does me in. I've got my eyes closed when he growls down toward me, "Holy hell. Look at that throat bulge. Shit, girl, I wanna fuck you so bad." And I can't help what happens next.

Without warning, I come. I don't mean to, but I do it. This has never happened to me before, coming like this without even being touched, and it takes me completely by surprise. My whole body convulses and he snarls, "Now you've gone and done it. I'll have to punish you." Instead of just watching his cock going down my throat, he starts to stroke into it and I feel the pressure with every slam. I'm trying to push him away, but he just hangs onto my arms and fucks into me like mad. By the time he comes, his hot seed shooting down my throat, I'm writhing and squirming and trying to loose myself from his grip, but I can't.

With his climax done, he yanks his cock from my

mouth and stands there, staring down at me as I heave in big shuddering breaths. I don't know what's going to happen next, so I just lie there. But the need to have him inside me is making me sweat. I finally whine, "Please, Sir, fuck me? Please?"

There's something—a smirk, maybe?—on his face when he says, "No. That's your punishment. There'll be no fucking for you tonight. Come with me." He pulls me up from the side of the bed, slides me up into it properly, and then grabs the cuffs. Before I can protest, he cuffs my hands to the headboard and smiles down at me. "Now I won't be fucking you, and you won't be taking care of yourself either. I specifically told you not to come."

"I didn't mean to! I don't know what happened, but I'm sorry, Sir! I couldn't help it! It just happened. That's never happened before, Sir, and I'm not sure how it did, but I just—"

"You need to be quiet." He buries his face in my slit again and I'm so relieved that I try to press into his face, but just as I come to the edge, he stops again and I cry out. That gets me a sharp slap on the inside of my thigh. He repeats the process until I'm screaming and crying, begging and pleading, and he just does it over and over, never quite letting me come, just torturing me.

And when he stops the next time, he takes that big, meaty dick of his in his hand and starts to stroke right there in front of me. I want him so badly that I'm crying, "Oh, please, Sir, please fuck me! Oh, god, please! Please, please please! I need it so bad! Oh, god, oh please ..."

But he keeps stroking himself and I watch as he loses himself in the act, forgetting that I'm even there, panting and moaning. My eyes never leave him and suddenly, to my great dismay, he stiffens and shoots his load onto my belly. The minute it happens, I scream, "Noooo! No, I need that inside me! Oh, god, please, Jaz, fuck me? Please?"

Balls completely emptied, he turns and heads for the bathroom, then comes back with a wet cloth. He wipes the cum off my belly, then wipes himself down, and I hear the water come back on in the bathroom when he's returned there. He comes back, crawls into the bed, and turns off the light. There's no move made to touch me at all, and I wonder if he's really, really angry with me.

That question gets answered when, there in the dark, he says, "Kimmie, when I tell you not to come, I mean it. I'm not kidding around."

"But I didn't mean to. I was just so turned on and—"

"You're going to have to learn some self-control. We can talk about this tomorrow."

"No. I want to talk about it now."

"Okay." He sighs. "What do you want to say?"

"I want to say that I couldn't help it. I've never come like that before, without even being touched, and I don't know how I could've stopped it."

"You could've. Next time you'll do better. Anything else?"

"Yes." I'm embarrassed to go on, but finally I whisper, "Please, Jaz? Please fuck me? I want it so bad."

"That's a good way for you to remember. Goodnight, angel."

"But Jaz!"

"I've got to get up and go to work. Please go on to sleep. I love you, baby girl."

I can't believe this. He's going to leave me like this? There's nothing for me to do, my hands bound to the headboard, and I just lie there and cry myself to sleep, my body still humming and my belly heavy with the increased circulation there.

I finally drift off, only to be awakened by Jaz as he gets up to go to work. Before he gets in the shower, he unbuckles the cuffs and turns my hands loose, then leaves the room. In minutes, I hear the shower start, and I get up and go to the bathroom to pee.

When I'm all finished, I stand to leave, but a hand grabs my arm and pulls me toward the shower. The water's hot and steamy, and the look in his eyes tells me he wants me now just like I wanted him last night, just like I want him right now too. I don't even have to look; I know his shaft is steely. He whispers to me, "Don't do it again, Kimmie. All I thought about all night was your body." In an instant, he pushes me up against the shower wall and buries his hardness in me, and I gasp and cry out as he takes me, one leg up and over his forearm, my arms around his neck. "God, Kimmie, I love you, little girl, and I love to fuck you. Do you know how much I want you?"

"Not as much as I want you," I whisper back, then groan as his hardness fills me almost violently.

"I doubt that. This time, come as soon as you're ready and I'll be right there with you." He pushes me back against the wall, keeps stroking into me, and then begins to tease my clit with the fingers of his other hand.

"I'm, I'm, oh, god, I'm going to come, Jaz, I'm going to ... Oh gawwwwddd," I moan into the steam, and my body shakes, my pussy pulsing around his manhood. His muscles bunch under my hands, and next thing I know, hot, thick cum warms me from the inside and runs down my leg.

When we're both still, he kisses me on the tip of my

nose and smiles. "That was a hell of an orgasm, girl. Feel better?"

I press my forehead to his chest as best I can. "Yes. Much. I was hurting for you."

"I was hurting for you too. Get dried off and go back to bed. I've got to get ready for work." As I turn to step out of the shower, he kisses my shoulder and my heart melts.

Spinning around, I smile and tell him gently, "I love you, Sir. Thank you."

"You're welcome. Back to bed with you. Go back to sleep."

"Yes, sir." My body sated and my heart full, I make my way back out to the bed with my towel wrapped around me, slide in, and fall sound asleep.

CHAPTER FOURTEEN

"Hi!"

"Hey, baby. How was your day?" Jaz's voice is warm and sweet in my ear, and I know he must be on his way home.

"It was pretty good."

"You at your place packing?"

"Yeah." I wrap another figurine in newspaper. "Did you get some boxes for me?"

"I did. The liquor store told me to take all I want, so I got quite a few. I broke them down. Got packing tape?"

"No. I didn't even think about it."

He chuckles. "I'll stop and get some. Anything else I need to pick up?"

I think for a few minutes. Since we started doing anal, we've really blown through a bunch of latex. "Yeah. I think we need a couple of boxes of condoms, one apiece for each house."

Jaz laughs aloud. "We're burning through those things pretty damn fast, aren't we?"

"I'll say! I think we should buy them in bulk."

"Wonder if they've got them at the buyer's club? I'll check. Okay, then, packing tape, condoms, and I think a carton of rocky road ice cream."

Now I laugh. "What a weird combination!"

"Yeah. If they ask, I'll tell them we're putting the ice cream in the condoms and taping them shut. It's a new serving suggestion. Wonder what kind of looks I'll get?"

"Crazy looks. Come home. Hurry. I miss you." I shiver all over, wanting his arms around me for even a few seconds.

"On my way. Damn."

I hear a sound in the background. "Train?"

"Yeah. It'll pass soon. I'll be there as fast as I can get there. I love you, baby girl."

"I love you too, Sir. See you soon." The sound of the train disappears as he hangs up, and I go back to pulling things out of drawers. I'm glad he got the boxes so I can keep packing.

I work along, stop to go to the bathroom, drop an earring and spend a few minutes looking for it, take a load of clothes out of the dryer, and basically just lose track of time. I hear the door and, since I know he's probably got his hands full, I hurry to open it.

But when I throw it open, a hand reaches out and grips my neck. In my confusion, it takes me a second or two to figure out what's going on, but then I recognize him.

Angus.

"Fucker! What are you doing here! Turn me loose!"

I'm propelled back through the room by the hand on my neck, and I hear him kick at the door to close it. A ringing sets up in my ears, and his breath reeks of alcohol when he growls at me, "Stupid slut. Think you're too good for me now, huh? We'll see about that!" I'm trying to claw at his face, but his arms are so long that I can't reach him, and I can't bite him because he's got my throat. Pinned against the wall with his knee between my legs, I can't kick him, and I'm squirming to no avail. Worse yet, I can't scream. How in the hell does he know where I live? While I continue to kick and squirm to no end, he grabs the front of my jeans and starts working on them. That's when I know: The bastard's planning to ... oh, god, what do I do? I try to think, but everything's a scramble and nothing I come up with will work.

He manages to get my jeans unzipped and down, then plunges his hand down in my panties and shoves fingers inside me, and I know his nails must be ragged because I feel a scratch and instant pain. Things are starting to get dark and I know something is moving in and out of me. Is it his fingers? Did he really manage to get his penis out and force himself inside me? I can't breathe and panic is starting to take over, his hand tightening around my neck, crushing and pinching off my blood supply, and I can hear my heart thrumming in my ears. He's laughing and smashing me against the wall, and it dawns on me that I'm going to die. This is it. What'll happen to Jaz? I hope he knows how much I love him. All I'm thinking about is Jaz and us and how I won't get to say goodbye.

There's a flash of light behind my eyelids, and the burn is horrendous as I suck in fresh air, my lungs deprived for too long. That leads to uncontrollable coughing as I fight to see and hear what's going on. Hands grab me and lift me, and I start to kick and scream, still choking and coughing and fighting, until I hear that voice:

"Baby girl, calm down. It's okay. It's me, sweetie. Kimmie! Kimberly. Stop, baby, just stop. It's me, it's Jaz."

"Jaz?" I'm crying and coughing so hard that I can't really talk. Before I can speak again, his arms wrap around me and pull me in tight. "Oh, god, Jaz! Oh, Angus. I think he—"

"He tried, babe, but he didn't succeed. It's okay, baby, try to relax. Just relax. I'll look at your neck in just a second." I'm still coughing so hard that it's difficult to stand, so he scoops me up and carries me to the sofa, then sits with me in his lap. But I can't stop—I cry and scream and wheeze and cough.

"Where is he? Where is he? He'll hurt you! Jaz, please! He's crazy! He, he, oh, god, no, please!" Now it's all coming at me in a rush and my heartbeat is out of control. "Oh, shit! I think I'm having a heart attack! Oh, god, Jaz ..."

"Baby, you're hyperventilating. Just try to calm down. Hey, Kimmie?" A hand flattens on both my cheeks and when I manage to focus, he's looking straight into my eyes. "Listen to me, Kimmie. It's all okay. He did *not* rape you. He tried, but the stupid son of a bitch was so drunk he couldn't get it up."

"But I felt him—"

"He did violate you, baby, but not with anything below his waist. He couldn't, and he sure as hell can't now."

Oh, god, what did he do in trying to protect me? Is he going to jail? I don't want Jaz in jail because of me, because of my slutty ways and how stupid I am. "No, Jaz! Oh, no, no, don't, I don't want them to take you away, oh, please ..."

"Shhhh, baby, the police and an ambulance are

already on their way. It's okay." Pushing hair out of my face, he calmly says, "Let me look at your neck. Come on, sweetie, it's okay. I need to look at it." As he speaks, sirens scream in the background drawing closer, and in a few minutes an authoritative voice says, "Is this the Hendricks residence?"

"Yes, officer. I'm Jasper Givens. This is Kimberly Hendricks. And that man forced his way into her home and sexually assaulted her."

I can make out someone in dark clothing squatting in front of me, and the same voice sounds again. "Are you okay, Ms. Hendricks?"

"I-I-I-I-I think so. My neck hurts." I close my eyes again even though I know he's looking at my throat.

"There's an ambulance on its way, but I think it'll be needed to take the perpetrator to the hospital. Sir, can you tell me what happened?"

"She was expecting me. When I got to the door, I noticed it wasn't pushed completely closed, and I could hear scuffling sounds inside. I opened the door and that's when I saw them. He had her pinned to the wall by her throat, his knee between her legs, and his free hand down her pants. I'm positive he intended to rape her, but I got here in time to stop that."

"And what exactly happened to him, sir?"

"I smacked him in the head with the only thing I had."

"And what was that, sir?"

"That carton of rocky road ice cream over there."

With all the adrenalin coursing through my system and my nerves raw and jangled, that strikes me as just about the funniest thing I've ever heard in my life, and I start to laugh hysterically. I manage to look across the room, and the plastic grocery bag is lying on the floor beside a still and quiet Angus, smashed-looking and gooey. I hear Jaz say, "I think she needs a sedative," and I laugh even harder. I can't stop. Now I'm having trouble breathing because of the laughing, and I'm still coughing, and, oh god, this is a weird-ass evening.

Two hours later, we leave the hospital, my neck already turning black and blue. I've been turned upside down and wrong side out and deemed okay but needing rest. At Jaz's insistence, they gave me a sedative, and I can't walk straight, so he just picks me up and carries me. Even though I feel okay now, he buckles me into the front seat and by the time he makes it around to the driver's door, I'm bawling my eyes out. "Awww, baby, it's okay," he croons, stroking my cheek and pressing his forehead to mine. "Come on, let's go home and relax, okay?"

"Oh, no, ice cream ... it'll be everywhere!" I wail.

The chuckle that rolls from his chest soothes me somehow. "It's fine. You'll see." He starts the car as my head lolls back, and I stare out the window into the darkness.

I rouse when he carries me through the front door, and I stare around to see Michael and Robyn. "What are they ..." I manage to stammer.

"We cleaned up everything, honey. It's okay. Let Jaz put you to bed. We love you," Robyn murmurs to me, stroking my forehead. As she speaks, Michael takes my hand and kisses it. I feel safe and loved and overwhelmed with gratitude. I try to tell them that I love them, but my mouth won't make words and I'm having trouble thinking. The bed is soft and warm when Jaz settles me into it and undresses me slowly.

"Please don't hurt me," I hear myself mumble.

"I'll never hurt you, angel. Let me go and tell Robyn and Michael thanks and goodbye and I'll be right back to you." His lips are feather-soft on my forehead and I hear him leave the room.

The next thing I know, sun is streaming through the window and Jaz's arm is wrapped around me, protecting me. I snuggle back into his side and rest my cheek on his hard, broad chest. A sigh escapes his lips, and he curls his body around mine, shielding me from the world. This is my life, and this is my love. I don't need another thing.

"So have you gotten any farther along with the packing?" We're cleaning up from dinner. I've been here every night for weeks, ever since the mess with Angus, and moving has become kind of a joke between us. I just keep going and getting things a little at a time, and Jaz keeps telling me to just go ahead and pack. But I haven't had time. Things have been busy at the workshop. Seems everyone wants some kind of leather garment right now. I think there's a festival or something coming up and everyone's going. I don't know and I don't care; all I know is I'm making money. And that's good. I need every penny I can scrounge up right now, and if things keep going and I can sell my house, everything will fall into place. And I can't wait.

Jaz is busy with work too. He'll go for a good while without having to go out of town, and then he'll have two or three trips back to back. I don't like it when he's gone, but that's just how it is.

Melissa came to visit and picked out things for her room. I'm working on that a little at a time. She was planning to come in one weekend when Jaz had to be gone and she almost cancelled, but I asked her to come anyway. We had a good time, cooking and eating and going to movies. She's fun to be around, and I think she really likes me. I know I like her. It was nice to have her here, especially since he was gone.

Jaz has been gone for two nights—he thinks he has two more to go—when I get a phone call I couldn't have anticipated. Phil's sister, Leona, calls me right after dinner that night, and she's crying when I answer the phone. "Kimberly?"

"Leona? What's wrong?"

"I know you said you don't really want to talk about Phil, but I felt like I should call you and at least let you know." Before I can ask what she's talking about, Leona says, "Phil passed away this afternoon."

"Oh god! Oh no! Oh, Leona, I'm so sorry! Was it an accident? Had he been sick?"

There's a choking sound before she continues. "Abdominal aortic aneurysm. Just dropped dead."

"That's horrible! I'm so sorry. Is there anything I can do?" I really don't know why she called me, but I guess it makes sense that she'd want me to know.

"No, no. Nothing you can do. I just wanted you to know in case, you know, you wanted to come for the service or something."

She wants me to come—*that's* why she called me. I'll have to think about that. "Tell you what. Give me the address and the day and time and I'll talk to my fiancé. If he doesn't mind, I'll try to come. How's that?"

"Oh, would you, Kimberly? Oh, I'd really, really appreciate that. I know Mama would love to see you." Their mother is a kind, sweet soul. She's the person I'd most likely do this for. I make up my mind that if Jaz says it's okay, I'll go.

"I'll talk to Jaz and ask him if it's okay. I'm sure he won't mind. So when's the service?"

"Seven tomorrow evening."

Wow. They aren't wasting any time getting him in the ground. "Um, I'll try to be there, Leona, but that doesn't leave me much time."

"I know. But please, if you can ... Here's the address." She rattles off an address in Los Angeles and in a few minutes, with a handful of pleasantries behind us, we hang up. I immediately call Jaz.

"Hey, baby! What's up?"

"I just got a call from Phil's sister. He died."

"Oh, god! Oh, I'm so sorry, Kimmie."

"Don't be. I mean, I hate it for his family, but I don't really care one way or another. But they're hoping I'll come for the funeral."

"When is it?"

"Tomorrow."

"Tomorrow? I don't think I can be back by then—"

"I'll just go by myself and come right back."

I don't have to see his face; I can hear the strain in his voice. "I really don't like the idea of you traveling alone. Where is this?"

"Los Angeles."

"No. I don't like that one bit. I'd rather that you didn't."

I sigh—loudly, I'm sure. "Babe, it would just be one night. And I wouldn't stay with them. But I feel like I should go and pay my respects for his family's sake. They were *my* family for years, and they never did anything against me. Matter of fact, they supported me when he, well, you know. I really feel like it would be the right thing to do."

There's silence on the other end of the phone before he asks, "Are you sure you want to do this? Because I really don't like it."

"I know. I really don't like it either, but I do feel that I need to go. Look, I'll leave and be back before you get here. You won't even know I'm gone," I laugh.

"Yes I will. Book your flight and let me know your flight schedule. I mean it, Kimmie. I want to know where you are and when."

"Okay, okay. I promise I'll stay in touch. I love you, Jaz."

"I love you too, babe."

"I feel like this will give me complete closure."

"Well, then, by all means, do it. But please, be careful."

"Always, babe. I'll let you know my plans as soon as I know."

"Okay." His tone has changed from indignation to worry. "Please do."

"You'll know every step of the way." As soon as we hang up, I call around and get a flight, then start packing. While I'm packing, I grab my planner and start calling clients I had scheduled for the next two days. Before bedtime, I've got my plane tickets, my clients have been notified, and I'm packed. I head off to bed, knowing tomorrow will be a difficult day.

God, what a horrible flight. I got stuck in a seat beside a guy who could double as an elephant for the circus, and he honked like one too. I hope his problem is allergies or I'll be sick before I can get back home.

I booked a cheap motel near the funeral parlor and I manage to get checked in by six so I can fix my makeup and freshen up a bit. It's not the Ritz-Carlton, but it's a place to sleep. I took a rental car with a navigation system, so I have no trouble finding the funeral home.

The sight in front of me is beyond my imagination. There are camera crews everywhere and TV station vans, and people are lined up out the front door of the funeral parlor, waiting to get in. I ask one of the women in line, "Is this the line for the Hendricks funeral?"

"Yeah. Sure is," a little blond tells me.

I see a side door and head that way, but the man standing beside it stops me. "Sorry. You can't enter there."

"But I need to see Leona."

"Are you family?"

I think about that. Technically, I'm not. "Uh, no, I guess not."

He points back to the back of the line. "Then you'll have to go to the back of the line and wait like everybody else." The stern look he gives me makes me decide that I'd be best off to just do what he says.

So I go back to the back of the line. What are all of these people doing here for Phil? He hasn't lived in Los Angeles all that long, maybe a couple of years, so he can't know very many people. I stand and wait, stand and wait, stand and wait. While I'm standing there, I hear conversations all around me, just snippets of them anyway. I hear "hasn't worked since she left the show" and "met through a friend" and "what he saw in her except dollar signs." I really don't know what to make of it.

It takes almost an hour before I make it far enough up the line to get into the actual chapel where the family is gathered. There are photographers trying to snap pictures everywhere, and a reporter with a microphone and a notepad talks with people standing in line. There are so many people that I can't see up to the front to see his wife and to see if Leona is there, so I just entertain myself watching the people I *can* see from my little pocket of space. My eyes sweep the room when I see something that puzzles me.

There's a girl across the room and close to the front, and she looks a lot like Melissa. I'm marveling at their similarities when the girl turns, scans the room, and then looks right at me. And then I know for sure.

It *is* Melissa.

What the hell? Why is she here? It doesn't make any sense. As soon as her eyes land on me, she stands and makes her way across the room to me. The first thing out of her mouth is, "Kim! What are you doing here?"

"The dead guy is my ex-husband." A weird look passes over her face, so I ask, "What are *you* doing here?"

"The dead guy is my stepfather." Her eyes search my face. Even as we speak, I'm moving forward in the line, and I finally get a glimpse of the woman at the center of everything.

Meredith. Meredith Renzada, the soap opera star; well, former soap opera star. Meredith Renzada is Jaz's ex-wife. I'm still having trouble grasping it when I choke out, "Meredith Renzada is your mother?"

"Yes. I thought you knew that."

"No. I had no ..." In one blinding flash, it hits me in the gut.

Jaz. His ex-wife was married to my ex-husband. And

then I remember. He lived in Hollywood. And Phil moved out here because his wife worked out here. Phil married Meredith Renzada, Jaz's ex-wife. They've been together about a year.

Something in my chest tightens and it's hard to breathe. I manage to stammer out, "Your dad. He came to Illinois because—"

"Because he needed a job. Kim, are you okay?" I can't imagine the expression I'm wearing when she says, "Maybe you should sit down. You don't look too—"

"No. I have to leave. I have to get out of here. Please tell Leona that I was here and that I, I had to leave. I have to go." I've already turned and I'm heading toward the door, toward fresh air and the night sky and anything and everything that'll make my head stop spinning and my stomach stop churning. Somewhere behind me I can hear Melissa calling after me, but I'm not going to stop. I can't.

Jaz came to Illinois looking for me. Was this some kind of weird revenge thing for him? Find his ex-wife's husband's ex and ... and what? Marry me? And then divorce me? Hurt me? Maybe cut me up like she'd cut him up? What? What was he trying to do? To prove?

I knew it was too good to be true. I couldn't understand why a man like Jasper Givens would want to be with me, and now I know he didn't. This was all some kind of weird plot, some twisted, convoluted shit that he dreamed up. I make it to my rental car, gasping for breath. Once I'm inside it, I lock the doors and sit for a few seconds, but when I see Melissa coming out the doors, looking around for me, I start the car and pull out. I don't know where I'm going or what I'm doing, but I can't stay here.

I drive for hours, not knowing where I am, just

driving and thinking, barely able to see for crying. I wander into some pretty dicey areas of town, but I look around at the people standing on street corners, hooking and dealing drugs, and all I can think is, *So what if they shoot me? Kill me? Pull me out of the car and beat me or rape me? Nothing can be worse than this. Nothing.* I keep driving and realize I'm out in the suburbs or something. I'd turned off my phone out of respect, so I turn it on and turn on my navigation system, then put in the motel address which, of course, I have to look up on the internet because I have no idea what it is. And sure enough, I've got about a dozen voicemails. The trip back to the little budget motel is a blur as I turn whenever and wherever the nav system tells me to. I don't look around. I don't know where I am, where I've been, or where I'm going.

I don't know anything anymore. Finally in their parking lot, I park and turn off the car. As I start to get out, I put my hand on the wheel and there it is: The ring.

That's when I dissolve. How could anyone play such a horrible trick on me? How could he use me so carelessly to prove whatever point he's trying to prove? Was there *no* concern at all for my feelings? And I realize that there wasn't. This wasn't about me at all. I was just lonely enough and trusting enough to play the game. All the things he said to me, all the ways he touched me, all a lie, just a big, nasty lie.

Stumbling through the motel room door, I manage to make it to the bed before I collapse. My whole world is crumbling around me, and in this moment, in the silence and unfamiliarity of the ugly little room, I just want to die. What did I ever do to deserve this? Was I so horrible in a past life that this is my comeuppance? And what do I do now? We've linked our lives together with a home and other financial things. I have nowhere to go but back to my tiny little house and my tiny little life. The life I thought I had with Jasper Givens?

It's gone. It's all over. How long did he think he could keep this a secret from me? Was he planning to slash me in the night, maybe drive me into subspace and then mutilate me? Running ninety miles a minute, my brain is throbbing with all of the hideous things rolling through it like tumbleweed in Death Valley. I don't know what to do or who to call. I'm trying to figure out what my next move should be when my phone rings.

It's him. I can't. But I have to. I answer the phone and I don't say anything. "Hey! Hi, sweetie." I can't make my mouth form words. After what I'm sure is only a few seconds but seems like hours, he asks, "Kimmie? Are you okay, baby? Kimmie? I've called you like ten times."

All I can do is growl out, "I know."

There's silence, followed by, "Then why didn't you call me back?"

"No, Jaz. I know. I know all about it."

"About what?"

"Jaz, I'm in California."

I hear him chuckle. "I know! I was worried about you. I haven't talked to you all day. You okay?"

"No. I know, Jaz. Quit pretending."

The silence comes back, followed by, "Pretending about what? Kimmie, you aren't making any sense."

"No, let me tell you what doesn't make any sense. Why would you do this? You told me you loved me. I love you. You let me fall in love with you. Why would you do this, Jaz? I don't understand."

His voice is stern when he says, "Kimmie, what the hell are you talking about? I have no idea what you're—"

"Oh, stop it! How stupid do you think I am?" I'm shrieking into the phone and I'm sure I'm waking up the people in the room next door, but I don't care. "You're one helluva actor, I'll give you that. So what was the plan? Find me, woo me, and do what? Kill me? Cut me up? What was the plan, Jaz? I want to know before I say goodbye for the last time."

Now *he* starts shrieking into the phone. "Kimmie, what the hell? What are you talking about? What's going on out there? Kill you? Cut you up? That's insane! Where would you get that idea?"

He doesn't have to know that I didn't meet his ex-wife. "Oh, I don't know. Maybe Meredith?"

He just sounds pissed when he asks, "You talked to Meredith? How in the hell did *that* happen?"

"Gee, Jaz, why don't you tell me that, huh? Is that why you didn't want me to come out here? Are you back there packing up to disappear before I get back?" I'm growing more agitated by the minute. "And the worst part? I might've never figured it all out if it hadn't been for Melissa."

"What the hell does Melissa have to do with anything?"

"Because she's here, Jaz. She's how I found out."

"Found out WHAT? Good god, Kimmie, you're talking in circles. I can't make heads or tails of anything you're saying. Where is Melissa and what is she doing there?"

"She was there, Jaz. She was at the funeral parlor when I got there."

"I don't understand—"

"She was there for her mother."

"Kimmie, I'm sorry. I have no idea what you're talking

about. You went to your ex-husband's visitation. What does that have to do with Melissa or Meredith?"

"Really? This is how you're going to play this?"

"Look, I'm really confused here. You're screaming into the phone at me, and you're talking about Meredith and Melissa and I don't know what either of them have to do with why you're in California. I'm sorry. I must've missed something important in this conversation. And by the way, little girl, those are some pretty serious accusations you're leveling at me, whatever the hell they are. I'm not even sure about that."

"Stop it, Jaz. I know. I went to my ex-husband's visitation." There's silence. "And his wife was there." Still silence. "You know, his wife. The soap opera star. Meredith Renzada."

"Whaaaa ..."

"You're going to tell me that you didn't know my ex-husband was married to your ex-wife?"

"Uhhh, yeah. That's exactly what I'm going to tell you because it would be true. Are you sure? Phil and Meredith? Seriously?"

A blind fury passes over me. "Stop it. Just stop. What was this about, Jaz? Some kind of weird retaliation? Revenge? What? Why would you do this to me?"

"Kimmie, I haven't done anything to you. I'm as surprised about this as you were. I had no idea—"

"I'm sorry. I don't believe you."

There's dead silence on the other end of the phone. Minutes tick by, and he still says nothing. Finally, I can't stand it. "Well?"

"Well what? What do you want me to say? Do you want me to confess to some kind of strange plot against you or Meredith or Phil or, hell, I don't know who?

Because I can't. It's not true. I'm still trying to process the fact that they were married."

"You're going to tell me that Melissa hadn't told you?"

"No. We don't talk about her mother. I don't want to. I told her a long time ago that she could do whatever she wanted, but I didn't want to see Meredith, talk to her, hear her voice on the phone, even hear her damn name. I'm surprised Melissa's there. They haven't spoken in years, as far as I knew. And besides, I doubt she knew Phil was your ex-husband. How could she?"

"So you expect me to—"

"I expect you to come home. I expect you to remember that I love you and I've never lied to you about anything—*anything*. I've always been straight with you, Kimmie, you know that."

"I thought you had been."

"What would make you doubt me?"

I'm so beyond furious that I don't even know what to call what I'm feeling. "Because there is no way this is a coincidence. Absolutely not. It couldn't possibly be." My phone starts to beep. "I've got to go. Someone else is calling me. I'll get my things when I get back. And I don't want you there while I'm doing it."

"But Kimmie, please –"

I just hang up and look at the phone, then hit ACCEPT. "Hello?"

"Kimberly?"

"Yes."

"It's Leona, honey. Phil's stepdaughter told me you'd been there. Why didn't you stay to see me? I was hoping you'd come—Davis was too. And James was looking forward to seeing you."

"I couldn't stay. Did you know I was engaged?"

"Yes. I remember you said you'd check with your fiancé. Congratulations, by the way."

I wait to drop the bomb. "I was engaged to Meredith's ex-husband. Melissa's dad."

"Seriously?"

"Yes. I didn't know until I saw Melissa there. And Jasper never told me anything except Meredith's first name. He never told me that she was married to Phil."

"Wuh, uh, well, is it possible that he didn't know?"

Now I'm really suspicious. "Are you in on this too?"

"In on what?"

"Leona, I can't believe that he had no idea his ex-wife was married to my ex-husband. Can't believe it. Just can't."

I hear her snort before she says, "Now listen here, Kimberly. I have no idea what you're talking about, but I don't have anything to do with it, whatever it is. I've never wanted anything bad to happen to you. Matter of fact, I was pretty pissed off at my brother for a long time after he left you. And I certainly wouldn't conspire to hurt you in any way."

I just stand, phone to my ear, patting my foot impatiently on the floor. Someone's lying. Everyone's lying. This is mind-bendingly freakish. "Look, Leona, I can't talk anymore. I don't really know what's going on, and I need time to think. I'll talk to you later." Before she has a chance to argue with me, I hang up. And damn it, I haven't more than thrown the phone down before it rings again: Melissa.

"What do you want?"

She's crying. Wow—a whole family of thespians. Great. "Kimmie? Please, Kimmie, Daddy told me what you said. Kimmie, he didn't know. I never told him her husband's name, and he didn't know, I swear! Please, he's so upset, please talk to him. He'd never hurt you, Kimmie, never. You have to know that."

"I don't know anything anymore. Were you in on this too?"

"Wha ... what? In on what? I don't understand."

"What was the plan, Melissa? He won't tell me. Maybe you should."

"There was no plan! I'm telling you the truth! There was no plan. Kimmie, honest to god, if you think my dad would do something like this, you really don't know him at all."

That's it, right there. "You're right, Melissa. I think you're absolutely, positively, one hundred and fifty percent right. I think I don't really know him at all." She tries to interrupt, but I just tell her plainly, "You're a sweet girl. I've enjoyed spending time with you. But this is so, so, so fucked up that I don't know what to think anymore. I've got to go. I'm upset and confused too."

"But Kimmie –" I hang up on her just like I did the other two. My brain is in a tailspin, and I really don't know what to do except sit and stare at the floor.

My phone keeps ringing—Jaz. I'm not answering it. Every time he calls, he leaves a voicemail. I don't want to listen to them. Then Michael calls. "Kimmer, for the love of god, would you please tell me what's going on?" he barks into the phone.

So I explain everything while he listens silently. When I'm finished, he just says, "I'm sorry, Kimmer. I can't believe Jasper would do anything like this to you. Have you talked to him about it?"

"Lies. All lies."

"Honey, you should at least hear him out. The two of

you have gotten along so well, and you've been so happy together—"

"And all the while he was planning something horrible. I'm positive of it."

"Kimmer, that's just ridiculous. I know how it looks, but it's ridiculous. It's just a simple coincidence. I have to believe that."

"Simple coincidence? Well, I don't. It's too much. Will you at least support me in this? Please? I could use someone I can trust, because it sure seems like I don't have anyone right now."

"Only on one condition."

I feel it coming. "Yeah? What's that?"

"That you come to our house and meet with him. Talk to him. I just don't believe he'd do something like that to you. I can't. I mean, if he wanted to do you in, he's had ample opportunities. Why didn't he just go ahead and do it?"

I shrug to myself. "I don't know. Maybe he was waiting to get my insurance money."

"So he took out an insurance policy on you?"

"No. But maybe he was going to."

A huge sigh comes out of the phone. "Do you hear how ridiculous you sound now?"

"Oh, now I sound ridiculous. Thanks. Thanks a lot." I can feel the anger leaving me and a big ball of hurt and exhaustion taking its place. "I need to go. I've got to get some rest. I've got a flight back tomorrow and I'm going to have to move back to my house."

"Promise me you'll talk to him. And get some professional help. I think you need it."

"I'll think about it." And just like with Jasper and Leona and Melissa, I hang up on him.

Weird shadows fall on the ceiling and walls during the night, and the quiet is interrupted off and on by people laughing or yelling, or a dog barking, or a car horn. I lie awake in the dark, staring at the ceiling, and listen to my phone buzz. I turned off the ringer, but it keeps vibrating with every call, and I know who it is. I finally start listening to some of his voicemails.

"Kimmie, baby, please, I don't know what's going on, but whatever it is, we can fix it. I love you, Kimmie. Please come on home. I love you. Bye." I hit DELETE and go to the next one.

"Kimmie, it's me. I just talked to Melissa. I can't believe you think I was plotting to do something to you or get some kind of weird revenge. Have I ever hurt you? I've never hurt you, baby. Please come home and we can straighten all of this out. Please? I love you so much, baby girl. Call me back, please? Bye." Once again, DELETE.

The next one takes me by surprise—a little. "Kimmie, baby, I called Meredith and we talked. Honey, she didn't know I was engaged to Phil's ex-wife any more than I knew she was married to your ex-husband. Neither of us knew. Baby, please come home. It hurts me to know that you think I'd do something like that to you. What have I ever done to make you think I'd do something like that? What? I've never done anything. Look, you don't have to stay here. You can stay with Michael and his wife until we get this worked out, okay? But please come home. I miss you. Please?" His voice breaks as he says, "You're the most important thing in my world. I just want to hold you and kiss you and make everything all right. I'll be waiting here for you. I love you, Kimmie. Bye." And again, I hit DELETE.

And if I thought that one was a surprise, the next one

blows me away. "Is this Kimberly Hendricks? Kimberly, this is Meredith Renzada. I just wanted you to know that I've talked with Jasper. First, you need to know that after what happened between us, it took a lot to get him to call me and talk to me, but he did, and he's very broken up about whatever this is that you think is going on. The things that happened between us were a long time ago, and I was very sick. I've had a lot of therapy and a lot of treatment and I'm doing very well. But I wanted you to know that I had no idea he was engaged to Phil's ex-wife, I mean, you. Well, you're Phil's ex-wife. But you know what I mean. Look, I don't know what you think was going on, but neither of us knew who the other was involved with. So please, talk to him. He didn't do anything wrong, really. I wish you'd stayed at Phil's visitation. I would've loved to meet you. Melissa says lovely things about you. Well, okay then. Sorry to bother you. I hope the two of you work this out. Goodbye." I start to erase it, but it's Meredith fucking Renzada, the soap opera star. No one will believe me if I tell them.

The darkness is like a big, fluffy blanket, hiding me from the world and keeping the world away from me. I try to sleep, but I can't. I just lie there in my cocoon, waiting for dawn, so I can go back to Chicago and face my ruined life.

CHAPTER FIFTEEN

When I get back to town, I go straight to my little house. I don't want to talk to anybody or see anybody. I don't even go to the workshop the next day. After canceling every appointment I had, I just hide out. Jaz tries to call me several times during the day; matter of fact, everybody does. I guess no one understands that my brain is overtaxed and I can't deal with anything. Even a conversation seems too hard. I just lie in bed and wish I could die.

The next day, halfway through the day, someone knocks on my front door and I go to it and yell through, "Who is it?"

"Kimmie, baby, please, let me in?"

"No. Go away."

"Kimmie, I have a key. I could—"

"And I'll call the cops, I swear I will."

"Baby, please, just talk to me?"

"Not yet. I need you to go away." I wait, and then I hear the sound of a car starting and pulling away. I peek out the curtains at the window over the sofa to see his car leaving. I think about what it feels like when he holds me and I want him so much, but I can't trust him now. Maybe no one else knew anything about this, but he certainly did. Maybe he acted alone. That makes no difference. It's still just as bad, and my heart's just as broken.

The following day, he calls three times; the next, twice. Finally, on the fourth day after the trip, he doesn't call at all. I breathe a huge sigh of relief, and I start to wonder what will happen when I sit down and talk to him finally. I know he's waiting for that. I'm feeling better and stronger, and not quite so afraid of him. He hasn't come over and tried to knock down my door or anything. To me, that's a sign that he knows I'm onto him and I won't take any shit from him.

Several days pass without a call, and I decide it's about time that we talked—at Michael and Robyn's, of course. I don't want to be alone with him. That's not going to work. While I put away my work for the day, I make the decision to call Michael when I get home and see if we can arrange for a meeting the next evening. I stop and pick up a sandwich on my way home and then head in for a quiet night. And when I open the front door, I get a big surprise.

My things. Everything I had over at Jaz's is there in the living room. It's all neatly packed in boxes and stacked there. On top of it is a note:

I hope this is everything. After I lock the door, I'll put the key in the pot holding the marigolds. If anything is missing, have Michael call me and I'll take it to him. You can keep the ring.

Jaz

. . .

Something twists in my gut, and I call Michael's cell. When he answers it, instead of saying hello, he just says, "Before you say a word, let me just say that I support his decision."

"Michael, what the hell's going on?"

He sighs. "He called me last night and told me he couldn't be with someone who thinks of him what you do. I guess all your stuff is there?"

"Yes." My voice sounds hollow in my ears.

"That's what I thought. He tried to talk to you, Kimmer. He wanted to talk to you. You accused him of some horrible things and just shut him out, and I don't think he could handle that. I don't blame him for feeling that way. He loves you, but he doesn't want to be treated like that."

"I was planning to call you tonight, ask if we could come over to your place tomorrow night and talk. Maybe if I call him—"

"I don't think it'll do any good. You can try, but I don't think so."

My heart is about to pound out of my chest and I'm getting lightheaded. This was not what I thought was going to happen—at all. I thought we'd meet, talk, maybe iron it out, maybe not, but he'd at least try, and maybe he'd confess what his plan had been so I'd know what his intentions were. "I'm calling him now, Michael. If we meet, can we do it there?"

"Sure. Let me know."

"Thanks." My hands are shaking so hard that I can barely hold the phone, and for the first time I find myself thinking, *Maybe I overreacted.* I hit his contact and it rings long enough that I'm pretty sure it's going to voicemail before he finally says, "Hello?"

"Jaz?"

"Yes?"

I wait. That's all he says. I thought he'd start asking me to talk to him, to come home, to believe him, but he says nothing else. "Um, Jaz, I was going to call Michael tonight and ask him if we could meet at their house tomorrow night to talk."

Just as evenly and matter-of-factly as I've ever heard, he says, "No. But thanks anyway."

No, but thanks anyway? "Listen, I just needed some time to think about everything and—"

"Kimberly." I stop dead in my tracks. He hasn't called me that in forever, and I know the next sound I hear will be the other shoe dropping. "I needed some time to think about everything too. And I came to the conclusion that I don't want to be with somebody who would believe those kinds of horrible things about me. I'm sorry. I just can't."

"But Jaz, you have to understand, that's an awfully big coincidence and I couldn't—"

"Doesn't matter. I can't do that, be with somebody who might think that kind of thing about me. You wouldn't even talk to me. You just pushed me away. I'm sorry. If you think of anything else you've left behind, like I said in the note, just let Michael know. He'll tell me and I'll get it to you through him."

His tone, the passivity of it, the detachment in it, lets me know that I've committed a grievous error. Trembling and in little more than a whisper, I croak out, "I love you, Jaz."

"I love you too. But I can't be in a relationship like that. So it's over. You're welcome to the ring, and I'm sorry everything turned out this way. I was looking forward to a lifetime with you. I hope you find someone you can love and trust in ways you couldn't love and trust me. Goodbye, Kimberly."

"But Jaz, I—" And the phone goes dead in my hand.

A feeling of dread unlike anything I've ever known winds around my body. What have I done? What was I thinking?

I make a decision to go over there, so I grab my purse and run to the car. When I knock on the door, no one comes at first, so I knock again. After the third round of knocking, the door opens.

He's standing there in those worn jeans and a Cubs tee-shirt, barefoot. Instead of the Jaz I know, this one is pale and drawn, and his eyes are sunken and dark. He just stands there, door open, arm resting on the facing as he blocks the doorway. After a little bit of fidgeting, I quietly ask, "Can I come in?"

"No." I start to say something, but he interrupts. "Kimberly, there's nothing to say. There's no reason for you to be here."

Without thinking, I reach for him, but I almost gasp when he backs away, a horrified look on his face. "Jaz, please—"

"Please, call me Jasper. And no. Don't touch me. This is over. I'm sorry it has to be this way." With that, he closes the door in my face.

All I can do is stand there in stunned silence. It's over. If he'd been planning something dreadful for me, he wouldn't have handed over everything I had here. Yes, I overreacted. I was so afraid, so shocked and terrified, that I let my imagination run away with me. But the emotions I'm experiencing now are even more terrifying. I can't even draw a breath—my heart and lungs are just frozen. I've thrown away the love of my life, a man who never did anything but love me and try to please me. All I wanted was a little time to think things through.

Looks like I waited a little too long.

I have to go to the courthouse for Angus's arraignment, but he pleads guilty, so there'll be no trial. I look around to see if Jaz is there, hoping he'd at least come to support me, but he's nowhere to be found. At least I know where Angus is and that he won't be bothering me.

At Michael's insistence, I find a counselor. I had no idea how much damage Phil had done, and I'm still paying for the way he treated me. It hadn't been obvious to me before, but now I see that, for all my yearning to move forward, his verbal abuse and neglect held me back and made me afraid and paranoid. Jaz never offered me anything but truth and love, and something inside me didn't want to see that; it couldn't trust. Exposing his worst behavior was what I was seeking, and I couldn't make that happen, so I let my imagination run away with me. All I could do was be fearful that history would repeat itself. And it has. Unfortunately, this time, to my shame, it's totally my fault.

And it's come back with a vengeance, that need to hurt. I've been afraid to go to the club for fear I'll run into Jaz; even so, I can't hold out anymore. I need it so badly that I can't think.

For the first time since I met Jaz, I scene with someone else. Alexander is handy, and I tell him what I need. His point of negotiation is simple: He gives me the pain I need, and I give him the sex he wants. Hell, why not? No reason why that can't happen. After working me over with a stiff flogger, he takes me to a private room and fucks me like I'm just a dog. After he's fucked my pussy until he's come, he fucks my ass for another thirty minutes. Even though I'm not sure I can take it, the pain and degradation are welcome. And that's okay. I deserve whatever I get.

But during the scene, I turn my head, gasping in pain, and there he is. When our eyes meet, the agony I see in those brown ones pierces my gut just as Alexander is lashing me so hard that I can't breathe. Then Jaz does the one thing that crushes my heart—he shakes his head ever so slightly and just walks away. It's final confirmation that what we had is gone, pulverized like old bones and blown into the wind. When Alexander releases me and drags me toward the private room, I silently pray that whatever he does to me, it'll kill me. Going on is something I don't really want to do.

Striped and aching, I leave the private room for the dressing area and pull on my jeans and an old tee. The cotton of the shirt is abrasive on my raw skin, and something trickles down my back. Blood? I don't care, really don't. What happens to me now doesn't matter.

As I leave, I see him. He's across the room with a redhead and, just like that time before, he never acknowledges me as I walk through. Even though I try to catch his eye, he's resisting it, and there's something different about him, but I can't figure out what it is. I just go home and cry myself to sleep, the pain of my punishment faint compared to the misery in my heart.

And that's what I do every night. Days turn to weeks and weeks to months and, as time goes by, I see him at the club less and less frequently, then finally not at all. In the meantime, Mr. Augustino has a heart attack and dies, and I hear that Candy's been evicted from their home. His kids claim she only married him to get his money. They're all rich enough to pursue a judgment against her and she doesn't have the finances to defend herself, so she's homeless. I worry what will happen to her and her baby—a beautiful little girl—and I make a mental note to ask Michael about her.

It's been five months since I've seen Jaz, and the days are getting short, the wind picking up off the lakes announcing winter's approach. I settle into the sofa after dinner with my tablet, and I've just gotten into the story in the book I'm reading when my phone rings. "Hello, Michael. How are you, sir?"

I don't get my usual admonishment; instead, I hear him blurt out, "Kimmer, you need to come."

There's an urgency in his voice that frightens me. "Come where?"

"To the hospital. Please, Kimmer."

"What's wrong? Oh, god, Michael, is Robyn okay?"

"Robyn's fine. It's Jasper."

The room starts to spin. "What's wrong? What's going on?"

"He was picking up his car from long-term parking at the airport about nine hours ago and a guy jumped him. Stole his wallet. Took them all this time to find Melissa. She's at the hospital with him now."

"What? NO! God, Michael—"

"Knifed him in the back. He was bleeding out when an airport employee found him. They've had to remove a kidney. Liver lacerations. He's in bad shape, Kimmer. I didn't know if you'd want to ..."

Struggling to keep from fainting, I choke out, "Where? Where do I go? Oh, god, Michael, where do I need to be?"

I write down everything he tells me and run out the door, even though I hear him yelling how he wants me to call a cab to keep from having an accident. I'm in such a hurry that I forget my bag and have to go back for it because I don't have my keys. In the process of getting there, I run three stoplights and two stop signs. True to Michael's fears, it's a miracle I don't get myself killed; at least once, a car slides sideways in the intersection to avoid me, but I don't care. I've got to get there. Seeing him is all that matters. To my surprise, on my arrival they tell me at the front desk that they've been told to bring me right up—Michael must've called ahead. He's been moved to the intensive care unit, and no one will tell me how bad it is or how he is. I'm just escorted to the room. When we get close, the nurse points and says, "Right there."

Dread fills me when I see the door up ahead. If I do this, go in there, there's a really good chance that he'll send me away if he sees me, and if he does, I'll die. Shaking from head to toe, I creep to the doorway and I can hear voices. Melissa's soft one says, "I know, but I don't care. College can wait. This is my dad. I can get another semester; I only have one dad." There's another soft voice, one that seems familiar but I can't make it out, and then Melissa's again when she says, "I know. He's been so down. He just won't fight."

Rounding the doorway silently, I'm stunned to find Melissa sitting there next to Jaz's bed and, of all people, Candy sitting on the other side, holding his hand. I suddenly feel completely out of place, but when Candy looks up and sees me, she whispers, "Kimberly! Oh, thank god you're here. Come—sit down."

Melissa stands and hugs me. "I was afraid you wouldn't come. Thank you so much for coming."

"I had to. I couldn't stay away. Look, Melissa, about—"

She holds a hand up in front of my face. "Forget it. Forget it all. It's water under the bridge. The only thing that matters right now is Dad. I don't know if he'll be able to hear you or not, but please, try to talk to him."

Stuttering, I blurt out and motion to Candy, "But if the two of you are in a relationship, I should just—"

Candy's blond hair whips as she shakes her head energetically. "No, Kimberly, it's not like that, not at all. Michael and Robyn introduced us. Jaz gave Petunia and me a place to live. We've been there since Mr. Augustino died. He's been really, really good to me. Hasn't asked me for a thing, just wants me to have a safe place to raise my daughter. He's such a good man." A lone tear trickles down her cheek as she turns to look back at the still form in the bed, pats his hand, and repeats, "Such a good man."

For the first time since I entered the room, I let myself look down at Jaz. He looks twenty pounds lighter and so frail in that bed. His skin is white and pasty, and his lips are barely parted. I can hear his tiny, shallow breaths as they whistle in and out through those lips that kissed me and delighted me. Try as I might, I can't help it.

I start to cry. I look into his face and I see all the times we laughed, all the kisses we shared, and all the times he whispered, "I love you, Kimmie," in the dark. Regret and remorse burn behind my breastbone with nothing to soothe them. This is karma come to exact its vengeance, but why Jaz? Why not me? Guilt overwhelms me, and I know it won't go away anytime soon.

I'm sure my eyes are anxious when I turn them to Melissa. "What do I do?"

"Just hold his hand and talk to him. He may or may not hear you. But try."

My fingers take his gently, and then I feel the warmth of his palm against mine. I hope all the love and longing I feel for him is passed along in that simple touch. I did a terrible thing. I thought horrible things of him. Looking back, I'm not sure why I was so willing to do that. Sure, the counseling is helping to bring that to the surface, but Jaz never deserved that. Did I really believe I wasn't entitled to the joy he brought to my life, all the passion and happiness and security? And I know that was it. I felt he was too good for me.

I felt he was too good to be true.

And now the man I love, will always love, lies here fighting for his life and he's spent all these months alone. But I realize he hasn't been alone, not really. He's had Melissa and Candy and her baby, and Michael and Robyn. It's not the same, but he hasn't been alone, and I'm grateful to them for the love they gave him when I abandoned him. Still, some part of me hopes that some feeling remains for me, even though knowing it does will haunt me for the rest of my life. As I hold his hand, Melissa picks up a cloth, dips it into some ice water in a bowl by the bed, and wipes it across his forehead and all over his face. When she finishes, his eyes open and he smiles at her. Through chalky lips, he whispers, "Thank you, baby."

"I love you, Daddy. Look who's here to see you." With that, she points at me and his eyes swivel in my direction.

I hold my breath. Even though I halfway believe he'll summon the strength to yell at me and order me out of his room, I pray that's not what happens. It's as though it takes him a minute to figure out who I am.

But my heart breaks when he croaks out, "Kimmie? Is that you, baby girl? Please, god, tell me it's really you."

On my feet in an instant and leaning over him, I whisper against his forehead, "It's me, Master. I'm right here. Oh, god, Jaz, please tell me you love me."

He squeezes my hand gently and whispers back, "I never stopped, angel. I never stopped."

They can hear me sobbing out in the hallway, and I don't care. I don't care who hears me, sees me, even takes a picture of me doing my ugly cry. My broken heart empties out onto his chest as I sob and clutch his hand, and all I can think about is all the time I've wasted and all the years we would've had if I hadn't been so crazy and stubborn. One weak hand comes up and strokes my hair. "I love you, Kimmie. It'll all be okay. You'll be fine."

"No. Not without you. You can't leave me, you hear me?"

"I'm really, really tired and it hurts a lot."

"I don't care. You listen to me and listen good. There aren't words to tell you how sorry I am." He tries to shush me, but I grab his hand. "No, I need to say this. When I think about how I treated you, I'm so damned ashamed that I can't look at myself in the mirror. I treated you like you were some kind of criminal. Do you know what Meredith said when she called me?" He gives his head a little shake. "She left a very nice message. She told me that the two of you had no idea who the other was involved with, and that she hoped we hadn't had problems over it. I realized later that if the woman who had hated you enough to, well, you know, would go to such lengths to clear your name with me, she must be telling the truth. And then when I came home and my stuff was there, and I went to your house and—"

"Kimmie." There's an authoritative quality to his voice even though he's weak, and it stops me in my tracks. It's not the voice of Jaz Givens. It's the voice of my Master, and everything in me automatically throws itself at his feet. "I love you. We'll not speak of this again. I don't know what you did with it, but I'd like it if ..."

The ring on my left hand sparkles as I hold it up so he can see it, and I see a feeble smile stretch across his face. "I never took it off. I couldn't. Even when I scened at the club, I wore it. No matter what happened, my heart's belonged to you the whole time."

"Good. Because mine belongs to you." He gazes up at me with such love and adoration that I tune up again, weeping out loud. "Now listen to me. I've got to rest. And if I don't wake up, I love you, Kimmie. You and Melissa were the brightest spots in my whole life. If I could go back and do everything over, somehow erase all the things that tore us apart, I would. Now sit down and get some rest. If I wake up, we'll talk again, okay?"

"O-o-o-okay. Okay. I love you. I'll be right here." Before I can get into the chair Candy's pushed up to the bed for me, Jaz's eyes close and he's out again.

I sit there all night. It gives me plenty of time to think, and I decide right then that if he doesn't make it, I'm done. He'll be the last Dominant I ever commit to. There'll be no more. The thought of submitting to another man makes my bones melt and turns my heart to mush. A couple of times I get up and go to the bathroom, but I rush right back to his bedside, terrified that something will happen to him and I won't be there. Melissa tells me she's going out to the waiting room to lie down on the couch and to come and get her if I need her. Candy takes her place. When I ask where the baby is, she tells me that Michael and Robyn are keeping her while she sits with Melissa and me.

At around seven the next morning, as I'm alone sitting there by his bed, an alarm goes off and nurses come running from every direction. A doctor comes in, and there's a lot of whispering between the doctor and the nurses who've been tending to Jaz. He asks, "Where's the daughter?" and I sprint down the hallway to get her.

Her face falls when she walks in and sees the doctor. "What? What's wrong?"

"He's not improving. We're not sure what's going on, but he's getting weaker instead of stronger, and his blood pressure's dropping. There's got to be more internal bleeding. Another surgery could kill him, but I really think he'll die without it."

The weight of the world falls on me when Melissa turns to me. "Kimmie? Do you want them to do this?"

"What are his chances without it?"

The doctor looks up at the ceiling for a few seconds like he's calculating, then looks back to me and says, "About five percent. Truth be known, probably a lot less."

My stomach clenches with those words. "And with it?"

"No real way of knowing, but I'm pretty sure it's better than five percent."

I fix him with a glare. "If this were your wife?"

"I'd do it."

I nod, sure of my decision. "Then do it." I see Melissa

nodding out of my peripheral vision, and I know it's the right thing to do. "When will we know?"

The doctor answers, "As soon as I do. You'll be kept in the loop." Melissa and I both slam ourselves against the wall as they whisk his bed out the door and down the hall.

We're sitting there, waiting, for about six hours. Nurses come in and out, telling us what's going on. More bleeding found. More repairs done. More time.

At four thirty, they tell us he's in recovery. It's seven o'clock that evening before they bring him back to an ICU room. And we wait. We wait for him to wake up, to seem to be coming around, to get some good news on his vitals. I hold his hand and wipe his face with the cold cloth, and pray over and over that his eyes will pop open and he'll tell me that he loves me. Nurses wander in and out but say nothing.

The next day is just as quiet, and we keep silent vigil. I realize I haven't had a shower or brushed my teeth in three days, and I really don't care. At four o'clock, the nurse comes in and does what nurses do, then leaves just like always. But in fifteen minutes, the doctor's there, and panic blooms in my chest as I watch them conferring, looking at his chart, and checking various machines and monitors at his bedside. With no hint of Jaz's status on his face, he motions for Melissa and me to come out into the hall. Once we've leaned up against the wall and taken each other's hands, the physician pulls off his glasses, slips them into his pocket, and says with a tiny smile, "His vitals are stable. If this trend continues, he'll be out of the woods in forty-eight hours."

My knees are wobbly and my heart is pounding in my ears when I breathe out, "Thank you, sir. Thank you so much." Melissa and I grab each other and hug.

We're on the road up.

~

"Are we about done? Because I want to get out of here."

"And I want you to get out of here. Nothing personal," the nurse says, growling playfully.

"No offense taken," Jaz snarls.

"Yeah, yeah. You can't go anywhere until your doctor comes in to see you. So you might as well just chill out."

"Thanks, Nurse Ratched."

"You're welcome, McMurphy," she tosses back along with the wave over her shoulder as she heads out the doorway. He's become a favorite on the urology floor. The nurses all flirt with him, even the male ones, and he makes everyone laugh.

I roll my eyes and shake my head. "You are incorrigible, Mr. Givens."

"And you're precious, Ms. Hendricks." When he manages to catch my eye, he winks at me and I just melt. "I sure wish he ... well, hello there, Dr. Larsson!"

"Hello, Mr. Givens. How are you feeling?"

"Like I want to go HOME," Jaz almost shouts.

"Well, trust me, I want you to go home. Nothing personal," Dr. Larsson adds.

"No offense taken," Jaz laughs.

"Oddly, I don't care," Dr. Larsson replies and, just as Jaz starts to say something, the doctor starts laughing. "Gotcha that time!"

"Damn. I'm losing my touch."

"Yeah, must've gone with that kidney," the doctor quips. "Okay, here's the deal. Remember, you've now got one kidney doing the work of two. So watch your sodium intake. Watch your calcium intake. Watch your carbonated beverage intake. Watch your sugar intake. You also have to make sure you stay well hydrated. Oh, and beer is your friend, but not too much. One a day is good for your kidney. Couldn't hurt your sense of humor either."

"Oh, hahaha," Jaz snorts.

"Exactly. Otherwise, you're on probation for at least four more weeks. Got that, missy?" Dr. Larsson slings in my direction.

"Got it. Although I don't know how I'm going to make him do *anything*. He's kinda hard-headed."

Jaz sits right straight up. "Hey, wait a minute ..."

"Yeah, I see that," Dr. Larsson deadpans. "Maybe you should get yourself a ball bat to threaten him with."

"Right here. Sitting right here. I can hear everything you're saying," Jaz play shouts.

"Maybe I should." I turn and look him dead in the eye. "Are you going to give me any trouble, mister?"

"Not if there's ice cream."

Dr. Larsson is laughing at us. "You guys crack me up. Got any other questions?"

"Um, so what kind of restrictions do I have? You know, like climbing ladders, or mowing grass, or sex. You know, stuff like that."

"You're not climbing or mowing. That's not what you're wanting to know about. I *know* what you're wanting to know about. And as long as you feel like doing it, do it. No gymnastics, but regular sex is fine."

"Define 'regular,'" Jaz says with a smirk.

"I'm not painting you a picture. Just try to use some common sense and if you're in doubt, ask her. She seems to have all of hers and most of yours."

Jaz grimaces. "Wow. Thanks. I love you too."

"Nice to know. Well, okay, I think that's it. Make an appointment for four weeks from now and I'll see you then. And I'd better get a good report on you or I'll take that other kidney."

Jaz cuts his eyes at Dr. Larsson and his brow furrows. "Over my dead body."

"Yep—that's the way it's worked in the past, as I recall. Good luck. And special good luck to you, ma'am. I think you're going to need it."

I nod. "Thanks." As soon as he's gone, Jaz starts packing up everything in the room. "Going somewhere?"

"Yes. I've got to get out of here. I'm convinced they're trying to poison me."

"Jaz?"

"Yeah, babe?"

"We need to talk." That gets his attention.

"Okay. I guess we do." He sits down next to me on the edge of his hospital bed. "So what do you want to talk about?"

"Where are you going when you leave here?"

He gives me a strange look. "Well, home, of course."

"Is Melissa coming?"

Now he's looking at me like I'm crazy. "No. She's got school. God knows she's got enough work to make up." Then he stops and his face falls. "Kimmie, do you not want to come home with me? I mean, if you don't want to, that's okay, but I just thought ... I mean, I didn't ask, but I, well, if you don't—"

"No, no, I do! I just didn't know if you wanted me there or not." I hesitate for a few seconds, then say, "What I did to you was wrong. And I'm sorry. With the therapy, I'm understanding more about why I did it, but I still did it and it hurt you. And I'm so, so sorry for that. I would understand if you never wanted me in your life again."

He reaches over and takes one of my hands. "Listen, we're both at fault here. You jumped to a crazy conclusion that I never gave you reason to reach. And I wasn't very patient. I should've given you more time to calm down and come around, but I was just so hurt that I didn't think I could move back into the relationship."

I feel a tear roll down my cheek. "I'm sorry I hurt you. I really am. I hurt myself in the process."

"And I'm sorry I gave up so easily. That won't happen next time."

With a shake of my head I state plainly, "There won't be a next time."

"Good." He squeezes my hand and my whole world feels right. "So let's just move forward, okay? No more about this. Live and learn and move on."

"Yes. Move on. I agree."

"So you're coming back with me?" Bending down so he can look up into my eyes, he says, "You're coming home?"

"I'm coming home." A peace settles over me, peace that I've missed since that weird day. I'm coming home. What Jaz doesn't understand is that no matter where I went, as long as he was there, I'd be at home. I belong with him. And I won't ever forget that or take it for granted.

We get my car loaded up with Michael and Robyn's help—thank goodness they showed up—and then head to the house. They help unload it while I get him settled, and once they're gone, we're alone for the first time since everything fell apart. I sit down beside him on the sofa and, before I know it, his head is in my lap and I'm combing my fingers through that thick, dark hair. His eyes are bright when he looks up into my face and just says straight out, "Kimmie, I want you. It's been too long."

"It has been too long. But you just got out of the hospital."

"I don't care. I need you." He waits. After a few moments, he sits up, then stands and takes my hand. "Let's go. I'm not waiting anymore."

The authoritative tone in his voice sets me on fire. "Yes, Sir," I gasp and practically skip to the bedroom. Once there, he undresses me slowly, and I note that he doesn't grimace in pain one single time. Either he feels pretty good or he's putting on a damn good front. When I'm undressed, he undresses himself, and I tremble all over at the sight of that utterly stunning maleness in front of me. "You sure you feel all right, Sir?" I ask out of sheer concern.

"No. I'm really tired. So I want to watch you make yourself come, and then I want you to ride me." He wraps both arms around my waist and leans down to kiss me but, just before he does, he mutters quietly into my lips, "Is that something you'd be interested in, submissive?"

I whisper back into his mouth, "Most definitely, Sir."

Straddling his hips, I let myself down slowly on his length and, once seated, I stroke my nub until I'm crying out. His hands trail up my torso and cradle my breasts, his fingers curved upward and teasing my nipples. I can't help it—the tears start and I can't stop them. I'm sobbing when I choke out, "Oh, god, Jaz, I've missed you so much!"

Every ounce of emotion comes through in his voice when he says back, "I've missed you too, baby girl. Every day and every night. I didn't want to live without you."

His hands slide on up my neck and he cradles my face in his hands. "Come for me, baby. I don't want to wait."

The spasms of my orgasm are interrupted when he orders, "Now, ride me, submissive. I want us to come together. You can do it; I know you can."

And that's exactly what we do, with a cry from me and a groan from him. It's glorious, our bodies together in that simple, primitive act, and I slump onto his chest and feel his arms tighten around me. I'm still crying when I whisper into his chest, "I missed your arms. I can't be away from you ever again."

"Sit down right now! I mean it! I'll do it." Shooing him out of the kitchen, I pick up the lunch dishes and carry them to the sink. About the time they're all cleaned up, I hear Jaz's phone ring.

"Yeah. Yes, she is. She's kind of bossy, but I really don't have any complaints." That just makes me snicker. "I'm sure I'm a terrible patient. Uh-huh. No, honey, don't do that. You need to just stay there and make up your work. Kimmie's taking good care of me. I'm fine."

Melissa. She's been working hard to make up her school work from the time she spent here with her dad. As they talk, I hear the baby wail and Candy shows up in the kitchen. "I was an adult film star. Who knew big boobs don't mean a lot of milk?" She picks up one of the bottles I sterilized in the dishwasher earlier that morning and fills it with formula for Petunia; we've all taken to calling her Pet. I'd panicked when I first realized Candy was living here with Jaz, but it didn't take me long to realize that it was simply his way of being kind to her, and she's been a lot of help to me while he's been recuperating.

Once she's wandered back down the hallway with the bottle to feed Pet, I meander back into the living room where Jaz has hung up with Melissa and sits quietly, flipping through a new auto magazine. The smile he gives me is brilliant, and I plop down beside him and take his hand. "So did you talk to them at the office?"

"Yes. They said not to worry about anything. It's all there waiting for me when I'm ready to come back."

I want to scream, *You're not going back!* but I don't. That's my secret. Instead, I say, "You're looking very good today, Mr. Givens."

"And you're looking quite well yourself, Ms. Hendricks." He kisses my cheek and then wraps an arm around me. "So when are we going to do something about that?"

"About what?"

"About that name."

"Whenever you want, Sir. I'm all yours." And I know right then: I've got some phone calls to make. The plan for The Most Important Thing is back on.

It's been six weeks since he came home from the hospital, and the doctor has pretty much turned him loose. There's three feet of snow on the ground, and Christmas is bearing down on us, but I'm looking forward to it for the first time in a long time.

The dinner dishes are done and I plop down on the sofa, closing my eyes and putting my feet up. "Whew! That was a good dinner, but I'm beat."

"Me too. But it's been a great day. I got released to go back to work next week so everything will be back on track, and—"

"Jaz, there's something I need to tell you." He sits bolt upright when I say those words. No doubt he detects the seriousness of my voice.

"Yeah? Please, god, don't let it be bad news. I don't think I can take it. Oh, god, you're not pregnant, are you?"

"What? Hell no! I couldn't be pregnant if I wanted to be. I'm fifty-one, for the love of all that's holy."

"Well, that's a relief. You know, accidents happen."

I roll my eyes. "That wouldn't be an accident. That would be a miracle."

"You know, miracles happen."

"Jaz, please, be serious here."

"Okay. You're scaring me, but okay."

I summon up all my courage before I blurt out, "I have an early Christmas gift for you." He waits until I say, "I sold my house."

His brows drop into the bridge of his nose. "You what? I could've sworn you said you sold your house."

"I sold my house."

"Yeah. So that *is* what you said. Why?"

"Because I needed the money."

His face reddens. "Look, I know things have been tight, what with you having to help me and me not working and Candy and Pet living here, but I'll go back to work next week and—"

"Jaz, would you just shut up for a minute?"

"What?" His eyes go round. "Did you just tell your Dominant to shut up?"

"Yes. I did. And I have a good reason for it too." My

bag is sitting right beside the sofa, and I reach in and pull a folded paper out. "Here."

Jaz takes it in his hands and opens it. I watch as his eyes get bigger and his mouth drops open. "Kimmie?" He doesn't say another word.

"Yes, babe?"

Now his hands are shaking. "Kimmie, is this ... it looks like ..."

"It's a deed. A clear deed."

In nothing more than a whisper, he ponders aloud, "It's the farm. Our farm. Grandma and Grandpa's farm." His head swivels to look at me. "How did you ..."

My eyes close and I bow my head, praying he's not going to be furious with me. "I wanted your dreams to come true. That's all I wanted. It's all I want. Because you deserve that."

The next sound I hear shocks me to my core. Jasper is weeping. Not managing to completely choke down the sobs he's trying so hard to hide, he has the deed clutched to his chest, and he's breathing so hard that he's heaving. I'm just a little scared until I hear him whisper hoarsely, "Kimmie, why? Why would you do this for me? You sold your house! The one thing you owned! Why? Why did you do this?"

I'm still not sure if he's angry or happy, so I just say, "I loved that house. But I love you more."

Without warning, he clutches me to him like he's afraid he'll lose me and cries into my hair. So softly that I can barely hear him he whispers, "All my life. All my life I prayed I'd find someone who'd love me, someone who understood me. It took me so long, but it was worth the wait. *You* were worth the wait." Pressing me back, his tear-filled eyes catch mine, and his voice is weak but clear when he says, "If all of my dreams are going to come true, I'm glad they're coming true with you. You're the woman I've been searching for all these years, and I don't have to look anymore. You're really here."

"I'm really here," I nod through my own tears. "I'm really here and I love you. I want this dream to come true too, baby. It started out to be your dream, but now it's mine too. It's *ours*. The guys are there working on the house right now. Mr. Jennings says it'll be livable in three weeks. Let's do it. Let's go."

The smile he gives me is brilliant. It's the smile of a man who knows his life is exactly where it needs to be, and he nods as the last tear rolls down those perfect cheeks. "Let's go. Tomorrow. Let's just pack up and go, Kimmie. We'll take Candy and Pet with us if they want to go."

I have to chuckle. "Let's wait until we can at least live in it! And that gives us time to get everything together."

"Okay." Then he adds, "And I want to marry you in front of our new home. Please say yes, please?"

My heart is bursting with joy. "Yes. Yes, I'll marry you in front of our new home. Nothing would make me happier."

"Good. Now, let's go down the hall to our bedroom and let me show you how much I love you, future Mrs. Givens."

Yeah. That's all the repayment I need.

CHAPTER SIXTEEN

"What the hell is this about?" Jeffrey's looking at me like I'm insane.

"Private joke."

"But this is very public."

"I wouldn't call this *very* public," I say, looking in the mirror. "I'd call this *somewhat* public."

"Are people other than you and him going to see you and him?"

"Yes."

Jeffrey shakes his head. "Then it's public."

"Oh, get over it. We're just trying to have some fun. And Jaz is going to love this."

He leads me down the stairs and helps me. I'm afraid I'm going to fall and kill myself in those damn peacock blue platform stilettos. But the look on Jaz's face when I step through the front door and glide, er, almost tumble across the porch and down the front steps, is priceless. I can see him shaking with the effort to keep quiet, but when I step off the last step, turn my ankle, and almost go down, he loses the battle and starts to howl with laughter.

I'm laughing too, and everyone is looking at us like we're crazy—well, everyone except Candy. She's laughing too because she gets it.

After Jeffrey passes me off to Jaz, the groom leans in to me and whispers, "Girl, you drive me crazy." He reaches up to straighten the tiara, and I take a look down at the necklace and rearrange it. "You could've killed yourself in those damn blue shoes!"

"It would've been worth it just to see the look on your face!" I whisper back, trying hard not to laugh out loud.

"Tawdry little slut," he snarls under his breath.

"Kinky bastard," I shoot back in a whisper.

"You guys getting this out of your system?" the minister asks us.

"Uh, yeah, reverend. Inside joke," a red-faced Jaz stammers.

"I don't want to know, do I?" We both shake our heads. "Okay, then, ready?"

I nod. "Yup. Let's do this thing."

Three hours later I'm standing, barefoot and exhausted, listening to thunder. "Oh good lord. What a mess." I look around at the house and the porch and wonder how in the world I'll ever get it all cleaned up.

"You don't worry about that. We'll all take care of it. You two just go sit down and relax," Candy says as she shoos me away. "Go on now. Git."

"What she said," Greta echoes. "You shouldn't be messing with this stuff. Hey, Melissa, can you throw me that box of zippered storage bags?" Melissa tosses them toward my daughter-in-law, and Greta catches them with ease. I finally take a deep breath and head back into the living room.

Jeffrey and Jaz are sitting in there, chattering away,

and when I walk in I hear Jaz saying, "... and I'm going to build a little pier out over the water. Of course, we'll stock it, probably with catfish." He looks up when I walk in. "Hey, wifey! Come sit down with us!"

"I like that. Wifey," I say with a smile so big that it hurts my cheeks.

"You guys make me sick, all mushy-mushy," Jeffrey whines, but he's grinning like a jack-o-lantern.

Jaz shrugs. "Get used to it. There'll be a lot of that mushy stuff going on around here."

"I just can't believe you redid the house but put a metal roof back on it." Jeffrey's shaking his head. "I don't know how we'll ever get any sleep with all that racket going on overhead."

Candy picks that moment to pass through the room with Pet. "We like the sound. It's soothing when you get used to it. Right, baby?" She tickles Pet's belly to make the little blond cherub giggle. "She actually sleeps better when it's raining." Candy laughs and gives her a peck on the cheek as she carts her down the hall for a diaper change.

Jeffrey's shaking his head again. "You've even brainwashed the little one. If you'd told me my mom would be a farm wife, I would've called you crazy."

"Crazy mad in love," Jaz corrects.

"Oh good lord." Jeffrey stands and points toward the kitchen. "Want anything? Because I sure as hell need a drink."

"Oh, like you and Greta never acted like that?" I mock.

"Acted like what?" Greta asks as she strolls in.

"All lovey-dovey and silly and goofy," Jaz offers.

Greta grins and pinches Jeffrey on the cheek. "What?

Me and my pookie-wookie here? Oh, no, never." Jeffrey rolls his eyes and makes a face. "We would never ever act like that, now would we, babycakes?"

"No, we would not." I watch with delight as my big son bends down and gives the curvy little blond an enormous, lingering, sloppy, wet kiss on the cheek and she shrieks in disgust. "Never ever. Beer?" he asks as he heads out of the room.

"Me!" Jaz calls back.

"Me too!" I yell.

"Whatever it is, I want one!" Candy shouts back up the hall.

"Beer," I call down to her.

"Yuck! No!" she yells back to our laughter.

Thirty minutes later, Candy and Greta sit at the table while Melissa tells them about her new girlfriend, Rebecca, and they laugh and talk and giggle. Jeffrey, oddly, is entertaining Pet, and I wonder if that's a sign I'm going to eventually have a grandchild. I hear a *pssstttt* and look up to see Jaz standing on the stairs. He motions for me to follow him, and I dart that direction and bound up the risers in record time. At the top, he grabs my hand and leads me through our bedroom and to the door on the far wall.

It opens out onto the balcony, which is really the old roof of the back porch, and the balcony roof is covered with the same metal roofing as the rest of the house. Rain is pouring down and falling in sheets from the edge of the overhang, and when I rest my hands on the railing and gaze out across the property, Jaz steps in behind me and wraps his arms around my waist. "Happy, Mrs. Givens?"

"No." I turn to face him and see the surprised look on his face, but it dissolves into joy when I add, "Beyond happy. There are no words for what I feel right now." I stare into those soft, chocolate eyes and draw a finger down his cheek. "I love you. I have everything I've ever wanted right here with you."

The kiss he gives me unfurls itself like a wide, colorful ribbon and wraps around us in its beauty. I'm lost in it, lost in him, and I don't ever want to be found. He breaks it and stares down at me. "Kimmie, how did this happen? How did you do this? I still don't understand, but I have to tell you, not only am I eternally grateful, but I'm really fucking impressed. You're quite the woman, baby girl."

"But this isn't about me. It's about you. I wanted all your dreams to come true. Have they?"

He just shakes his head at me and snorts. "This isn't about me. This is about *us*. And yes, all my dreams came true about three hours ago right out there in front of this house. Baby, I don't need this farm to be happy, or a new car, or a job, or anything else. I only need you." He takes my hand and runs a finger over that leather bracelet, the one he brought back from Topeka. "And just think—I'm a lot closer to Bixby's now! I can get you another one of these any time you want."

"I don't want another one. I want this one. When it gets too ragged to wear, I'll put it back in the little Bixby's box and put it away. I don't ever want to be without it. It's the first gift you ever gave me, and every time I look at it, I remember everything we've gone through and how hard we've had to fight to be here. When I look at this bracelet ..." I have to stop and swallow hard before I start again. "When I look at this bracelet, I see two scarred, scared hearts trying to find their way to each other. I think about all the fun and all the wrong turns, and all the stupid things we did trying to figure out how to have a relationship that would work. And I see all the sweet nights we spent together back when we were first realizing that if our hearts would just follow our bodies, everything would be fine. Because let me tell you something, Sir," I say, my tone growing serious as I try to stifle a laugh, "I've never wanted any man the way I want you."

"And I feel the same way about you, girl." He kisses the tip of my nose, then nips my earlobe as he says, "You set me on fire."

"Be careful, Farmer Givens," I say with a giggle. "All we have is a volunteer fire department."

"It would take Chicago's finest to put this out, and I don't think even *they* could handle it. It's roaring!"

"Roaring, huh?" I laugh.

"Yeah. RAWRRRRR!!!!" he growls and laughs at the same time, and we both wind up in a fit of giggles. "Kimmie, just promise me one thing."

I nod into his shoulder. "Of course."

"If you're unhappy, tell me. I promise, if I am, I'll tell you."

"Deal. I want everyone in this house to be happy. Giddy with happiness. So happy they shit rainbows and piss glitter." Now he's laughing at me. "I want them to sound like they're on laughing gas all the time, and I want clown suits in every closet. Every. Damn. One. And big shoes. Really big clown shoes."

His grin is mischievous. "How about blue stilettos?"

"Only with big necklaces, dangling earrings, wide bracelets, and tiaras."

He throws his head back and laughs. "And now I know what I'm getting you for your birthday."

EPILOGUE

"Hey!" He wanders into the kitchen smelling of dirt and diesel fumes. His hair's gotten long enough that he's taken to tying it back. I should cut it some evening, but he's just been so busy that I haven't had a chance, not to mention that, for some reason, I actually like it. "Got something for lunch?"

"Sure do. Your sandwich and chips are on the table, and a big bottle of water, Sir."

"Rather have a beer."

"Nope. You'll dehydrate if you don't keep pushing the water. You know what your doctor would say."

"Quack."

"He is not! Mind your manners, Sir."

"Is it finally finished?"

I nod. "Yep. Last room is done, the guest room. Looks nice too. Now all we've got to do is buy some furniture and the renovations will be finished. Oh, and get them to come and pick up the construction dumpster."

"I never thought it could really be put back together after all the years it sat here neglected, but it looks great. I mean, I know we've had to do more work to it than you originally thought, but it's totally worth it." He's thanked me so many times for making this house a home that I finally told him to stop. The giant, old-fashioned gas range in the kitchen is thanks enough. He says it looks so much like his grandma's kitchen in here that he feels like a kid again. Truth is, he sort of acts like one too, and I love it. Especially certain aspects of it.

There's a squeal and a grapefruit-sized ball comes flying into the dining room. "Oooo-weeeeee!" a little voice shrills, followed by the sound of tiny sandals slapping on the floor.

I call to her, "Pet, baby, watch out throwing that thing in the house, you hear? You'll break something."

"Pop-pop, pway baww?"

Jaz laughs. "No, sweetie. Pop-pop doesn't have time to play ball. Nana here will play with you after I leave, okay?"

"Nana?"

I nod at her. "Yes, baby, I will."

"I hab pottickle?"

"No, ma'am. No popsicle for you right now. You've got to eat your lunch first."

Her eyes go round. "Cawwots?"

"Yes. There'll be carrots. And Mommy's bringing you some celery when she comes home." Candy's job at the grocery has meant that I have to watch Pet, but I really don't mind. Life here is so much more relaxed than before.

"Otay. I wub cawwots. Mom-*meee*, Mom-*meee*, Mom-*meee*," she sings as she stomps around and dances to a song neither of us can hear. I don't think I've ever seen a happier child, and Candy has turned out to be an amazing mom.

I turn to watch him eating as I wash the last of the breakfast dishes. "So how's it going?"

He swallows the bite he's got in his mouth and answers, "I've got the first hundred and fifty acres plowed, and the rest will be done by day after tomorrow. Bruce Travelstead is coming with his planter as soon as they get the seed corn here. And the soybeans will be here next week. I'll be glad when I can buy my own equipment, but they've been great about helping out."

"All the neighbors have. By the way, have you seen my garden?" It's a running joke with us, and I watch as his face contorts almost like he's in pain.

"Yeah. Baby, why don't you just quit torturing those poor plants? It's obvious to me that you have a brown thumb." He's trying to keep a straight face, but I can see he's about to crack.

"I want to be the local poster child for how *not* to grow a vegetable garden. I'll talk to Angie. Matter of fact, I suppose I could ask any of the women around here for some pointers. I'm thinking maybe I should try growing some grapevines, maybe do some homemade wine."

He shoots me a huge grin. "Now *that* I could get behind. But keeping the birds away would be a real challenge."

"I'd have to ask around about that too. So how long will it be before the soybeans and corn are self-sustaining crops?"

"Long time. Good thing we've got the cattle. That'll keep us going until we can make some headway with the crops. Actually, that meeting at the extension office last night brought up some things that some of the other farms are doing, and I've got some ideas to talk to you about tonight."

"Sure. I'm open to just about anything."

He grins and moves in behind me at the sink, running his hand down into the front of my shorts. "Just about anything?"

"Yes, Sir. Just about anything."

His breath is warm on my neck as he whispers back, "Sounds good to me."

When his finger finds my clit I hiss out, "Don't start something you can't finish."

"Damn. Okay." His lips press into the side of my neck and I groan. "I'm going out to work. *Somebody* has to work around this place." I slap his arm and scowl. "When does Candy get off today?"

"Six. She'll be home around seven."

A devious smile takes over and his eyes darken in that sexy way I love so well. "Good. We'll have the evening. And I'm going to take advantage of it. See you later, Mrs. Givens." Every time he calls me that, I'm transported back to that day just weeks after his hospital stay when we stood in front of this house, that construction dumpster just a few feet away, and gave our lives to each other in front of our families and closest friends. Just as we'd been pronounced husband and wife, the gray sky had cut loose with a clap of thunder that took us both back to that magical night when we knew our lives were fused together forever. It's a moment sealed in our minds for time and eternity.

"I'll be waiting, Mr. Givens. Sir." I wink at him as he strides out the door, and he stops in the doorway and winks back.

When dinner's done that evening and the dishes are

all taken care of, I hear him tell Candy, "I'm taking Kimmie out for a ride. Don't know what time we'll be back. May be morning."

"Okay. Have fun. Don't get eaten up by skeeters." Candy's determined to be a country girl. It's so cute.

"Won't. Have a good evening, honey." I hear a little smack and I know he just kissed her on the cheek. Ever since we got here, he's treated her like a daughter, and she's flourished under his love and attention. I'm not jealous; I'm proud. I treat her like a daughter too, and she and Melissa get along great. Pet will start preschool next year, and I'm betting Candy tries to get an apartment in town so they can be closer to activities. But for now, they're happy to be here, and we're happy to have them.

Jaz grabs my hand and leads me outside. When we get to the truck, he opens the door. "Get on up in there, girl." As I climb in, he smacks my ass and I giggle, but I won't be giggling for long. I'm pretty sure I know what he's up to. We drive out to the far side of the farm. There, ramshackle but still intact, is the tiny cabin his great-grandparents had built all those years ago. When the road had been moved closer to the other side of the farm, they'd abandoned the little house for another, the one we live in now, but they kept this one up. Jaz's grandparents had actually lived in it for a while after they first married, and he always thought of it as an enchanted place. And it will be tonight.

Once the candles are lit everywhere, my husband strips me and then strips himself. Every ounce he lost after his injuries and surgeries is back, and it's all there in the form of lean, hard muscle. Carrying hay bales, working with the cattle, repairing this and that, they've all hardened him into a strong, healthy specimen of a male, and nowhere is he stronger and harder than that cock pointed right at me. I worship it every night, and every night it makes me glad I've bowed before it. My birthday present this year was a new orthopedic mattress for the big iron bed, thank god. We've spent a lot of nights out here, and the old one was shot. "Present, sub."

Dropping into the most comfortable of the positions I use, I can feel his eyes all over me, his approval of me, my body, and my submission to him. Kneeling there with my back to the bed, I wonder what he's planned for me. When he's finished preparing whatever it is he's doing, his hands wander my body from behind, stroking every curve and making me purr. Nerve endings glowing, I have to struggle to stay still and calm with every cell in my body on high alert. My pussy goes into a frenzy, pulsing and clenching, and I want it filled with him. When he steps in front of me and lifts me, I go with it, wrapping my arms around his neck as he places me on my feet. Hands gripping my wrists, he forces my arms behind me, and I feel the plush pile of the linings in my leather cuffs as it caresses my wrists and ankles. The belt wraps around my waist, and he secures my bound hands to the ring on the back of it. That's the moment my body makes a conscious decision to surrender itself into his hands. Two more cuffs go around my ankles, and he taps my feet until they're far enough apart for the spreader bar. That's when my heart starts to pound. He literally lifts me, turns me around to face the bed, and orders, "Bend over the bed, submissive."

The snap of latex startles me, and then something cold and damp drips down the crack of my ass. This is not something he wants often, but when he does, he takes it, and tonight must be the night. His fingers are insistent as they work the lube into my tight starburst, and then he breaches my forbidden depths with his cock.

"Sssssssss, ahhhhh, Kimmie. God, girl. Yes," he hisses as he presses into me firmly. "Which part of you isn't mine?"

"There's no part of me that's not yours, Master," I gasp.

"That's correct. There's no part of you that's not mine to use as I see fit. And," he adds after slapping my ass hard with both hands, "there's no part of me that's not designed to give you pleasure. I do so like to see you overwhelmed with pleasure. And I plan to overwhelm you tonight." That familiar scent fills the room again, but instead of spreading the lavender oil on my skin, I feel him massage a drop into my clit, and it starts to tingle and grow warm as the circulation to it increases. I can't help but moan and squirm, and he manages to squeeze a battery-operated vibrator between me and the bed and direct it straight onto my hot spot.

"Gahhhh! Oh, god, Master. Please ..."

"No, sub. Wait for me. Wait. Wait." I can feel his pumping grow more insistent, and then he rises on his toes, arches his back, and orders, "Damn, Kimmie, come with me!"

My body shudders as it releases the orgasm, its effects rippling out to my limbs as Jaz buries that fine, hard dick of his in my backdoor. I'm gasping and trembling as he grinds into me and then stills, leaning over and onto my back. He peppers my shoulder blades with kisses that set me on fire, then rises. His hands are warm but demanding as he unfastens my wrist cuffs from the back of the belt, then strips the belt off and places me on the bed. I shudder as he binds me to the headboard, then pulls the spreader bar straight up and secures each ankle cuff to the head of the bed with long straps. Once I'm trussed up, feet straight up in the air, legs spread by the bar, and wrists secured, I'm helpless, completely at his mercy, my every thought focused on how he's going to use me. He smiles down at me and I watch as he cleans us both up, then produces a good-sized butt plug. I guess the breath I suck in lets him know I'm anxious to have it, and he lubes it up and forces it into me as I hiss and groan. His next move is to bury his face in my slit, and he spends his time alternately sucking and flicking his tongue over my clit, and then burying that hot, rough tongue in my cunt. Suck, lick, tongue fuck; suck, lick, tongue fuck. Yeah. And when I come, my arms and legs shaking, he rises up and shoves his strong, bare cock into my hot, wet, aching pussy.

Between the butt plug and his size and shape, I'm zooming along on the jet stream again in just a few strokes. I cry out in bliss as we both come and I once again experience that pleasure I wanted for so long—the heat and wetness of his cum deep inside me, reminding me that I belong solely to him for all eternity. I'm here for his pleasure and, because I am, he's determined to please me.

Restraints removed, we lie here in the candlelight, wrapped in each other's arms, and listen as a lone coyote calls somewhere out in the distance. An owl hoots in a nearby tree, and the crickets sing that familiar song, the one I've become so accustomed to, the one I probably couldn't sleep without anymore.

Three years. This will be our third summer here. I never knew happiness could be this deep and wide. I look at the man who's stolen my heart forever, and he smiles back at me. "Are you happy, baby?" I have to ask.

His gaze soothes my soul. "Mrs. Givens, if you'd told

me, lying in that hospital bed and praying just to see your face one more time, that I'd be here right now with you in my arms and my family's farm around me, I would've laughed. I *still* can't figure out how you did this, but I'm so, so glad you did. There's no man happier than I am."

My heart sings when I whisper to him, "I love you, Jaz. We made it. We're actually here. Every time I look at you and see how happy you are, I'm so glad I found a way to do this and that we found our way back to each other."

"Me too." He kisses the top of my head and breathes into my hair. "And next week, Jeffrey and Greta will be here, and Michael and Robyn. Oh, well, yeah, and Candy and Pet," he grins as I pinch him. "And Melissa and Rebecca will be wife and wife. God, I hope that's the politically correct term."

"Life partners, baby. But wife and wife is good too. I'm so glad she didn't mind moving out here to be in-state at the university."

"It put her within a hundred and fifty miles of us. I think she likes that, not to mention that's where they met. I don't know where she'll go to graduate school, but once they're married, I'm sure they'll make that decision."

"Yeah. I'm glad it's finally legally possible. I'm so happy for them, but I've got to get busy on the stuff for the wedding." Then I go silent.

"I know what you're thinking. I don't like it either, but she's making an effort. I'm sitting down with her while she's here and we're going to talk. I think it'll bring some healing for both of us." I don't really want Meredith here, but she's Melissa's mother, and he's right—she has been making an effort. And I do believe she really was sick. Nothing else can explain what she did to Jaz but, frankly, if he's willing to forgive her, I should at least try, I think.

"I'm okay with it. Your business, not mine."

Jaz shakes his head adamantly. "*Our* business, baby."

"But I *still* don't want you to ever be alone anywhere with her."

He chuckles. "No worries. I'm trying to forgive her, but I sure as hell won't forget."

I nod. "Okay. Good enough." I sigh against his skin. "Then I guess all we'll need is to find someone for Candy."

His eyes fly open wide, and they're filled with mischief. "Oh, did I tell you that I hired a guy today to help out around here?"

"No!" My cheeks hurt from grinning so hard. "Who? What's he like?"

"You know that guy that we met down at the bar?" It's the only bar in town, and there aren't that many guys. Surely he doesn't mean ... "You know, the tall one with the blond hair and blue eyes? And the really, really broad shoulders?"

"Buster Simpson?"

"Yeah! He starts next week. And he just broke up with his girlfriend."

"You don't say! What a shame!" I'm trying hard not to laugh.

"Yep. If I knew a young single woman who might need a boyfriend, I believe I'd introduce them. Mrs. Cox down at the bank says he's a fine, upstanding young man."

I'm laughing now. "Well, we'll have to keep an eye out for a woman like that! Bet we can find one!"

"I bet we can too."

I wait for a second before I ask the question I've been trying to get out for weeks. "Jaz, what am I going to do?

There's no market for leathers and corsets in this town. I feel like I'm not contributing."

"Oh, god, Kimmie, I was just teasing earlier! Not contributing? That's just ridiculous, babe. You do *everything* around here. I couldn't do this without you." He kisses me on the forehead and squeezes me. "And no, I think corsetry and leathers are out. But there's a market for ladies' dresses and kids' clothes and alterations. Why don't you try your hand at that?"

"I might. I love the leather work, but there aren't any Doms here. Just you. You're the only Dom."

"I don't care if I'm the only one, as long as I'm *your* only one!"

I giggle as he digs a finger in my ribcage. "I don't really know if you're the *only* one either, but you're *my* only one. And you're certainly my last one!"

"Your last Dom. I like the sound of that, Mrs. Givens."

"So do I, Mr. Givens," I whisper as I kiss his chest and cuddle into his warmth. "My last Dom. You're the very. Last. One." I pull back and look into his face. "I saved the best for last."

"Thanks for that. Otherwise, I wouldn't have stood a chance." He kisses me, then asks, "You know what we need?"

I'm a little afraid. "What?"

"A dog."

I screw up my face. "A dog? What kind of dog?"

"A big ol' blue tick hound. Or a Treeing Walker Coonhound."

"No. A Maltese."

He stares at me in horror. "NO! No girly dog. I'm a farmer."

I can't help but start to laugh. "Okay, Farmer Givens. How 'bout a beagle?"

"A beagle." I see the gears turning in his head. "And we could name her Daisy."

"Daisy the beagle. I'm good with that." I snuggle again, my hands finding their way around his waist so my finger can trace the scars on his back, the ones that remind me to cherish every day I have with him and never take him for granted. "That's fine with Mrs. Farmer Givens." In my mind, I see us strolling hand in hand along the gravel drive back into the farm, a beagle or two skipping along at our heels. He points and I pop up out of bed, blow out all the candles, and then slip back in beside him. "Goodnight, my-last-Dom-Farmer-Givens."

"G'night, my one and only." Those strong arms hold me close, and I know my forever is right here in this room. There's something else I'm sure of too.

There are no two people in the world who are happier than we are. And that's the only thing that matters—the only thing in the whole wide world. Well, yeah, that and Daisy the beagle.

ABOUT THE AUTHOR

Deanndra Hall is a working author living in the far western end of the beautiful Bluegrass State with her husband of over 35 years and small menagerie of weird little dogs. When she's not writing, she's editing. When she's doing neither of those two things, she's having dinner with friends, spending time with family, kayaking, eating chocolate, drinking beer or moonshine, or looking for something that she put in the wrong place and can't seem to find (which is pretty much everything she owns).

On the Web: www.deanndrahall.com
Email: Deanndra@deanndrahall.com
Facebook: facebook.com/deanndra.hall
Twitter: twitter.com/DeanndraHall
Goodreads: goodreads.com/DeanndraHall
Bookbub: bookbub.com/authors/deanndra-hall

Mailing address:
P.O. Box 3722,
Paducah, KY 42002-3722

Stay in touch. For all the latest news, contests, exclusive content and more sign up for my newsletter:
www.subscribepage.com/deanndrahall

ALSO BY DEANNDRA HALL

~

The Love Under Construction Series

Laying a Foundation with prequel, The Groundbreaking

Tearing Down Walls

Renovating a Heart

Planning an Addition

The Citadel Series

One Simple Mistake

One Broken Promise

One Poor Choice

One Wrong Glance

The Legacy Series

Atonement

Legacy of Freedom

Legacy of Faithfulness

The Witch of Endor Series

Laid Bare

Ripped Open

Torn Apart

The Harper's Cove Series

Karen and Brett at 326 Harper's Cove

Becca and Greg at 314 Harper's Cove

Donna and Connor at 228 Harper's Cove

Savannah and Martin at 219 Harper's Cove

Cheryl and Samuel at 323 Harper's Cove

Tasha and Davis at 333 Harper's Cove

Lily and Brock at 343 Harper's Cove

Siobhán and Gabhain at 241 Harper's Cove

The Me, You, and Us Series

Adventurous Me

Unforgettable You

Incredible Us

The Celtic Fan (independent novel)

Rough Stock (part of the Bad Girls of Romance Series)

The Silent Cove Series

Awakening

Retribution, by Anne L. Parks

Banishing, by Jax Jillian

www.ingramcontent.com/pod-product-compliance
Lightning Source LLC
Chambersburg PA
CBHW051938240626
47153CB00005B/1538